THE CAGE

D. M. SMITH

RHAPSODY

Published 2023 • United States of America

THE CAGE

Published 2023 by Rhapsody Press, Texas, USA

75

The Question

It is night.
A man reclines on a shore.
He sees the rock and the sand and the ocean,
The night sky, ghostly clouds, the night lights.

He knows that he came from the rock and the ocean,
That the stars were always there,
Watching him rise out of sand and water.
And he knows he was once a part of these things,
But is no longer part of them,
Because he can feel the sand and see the stars
And hear the water.

And the question in his mind must be,
What now? Where do I go from here?

There was a coffee maker in its own corner of the big room, and he poured his first cup of the day, brought it to his desk, sat down, and reached for the first stack of paper.

––––––––––––––

Later in the morning, there was a break.

People gathered around an older woman's desk, talking and laughing. Someone appeared with a cake, amid *ooh's* and *aah's,* a few snide remarks about the number of candles, and a strained chorus of an appropriate song.

The woman sighed.

Robert stood up, stretched, and yawned.

At the far end of the room, the door to the glass office opened. The department supervisor emerged. She walked toward the group, trim, well-dressed, probably in her forties, smiling and personable, but not too personable. She congratulated the woman, then, standing with a hand on her shoulder, made a brief speech of appreciation, of team-building, well-practiced, too familiar to remember. But uplifting. The woman mumbled an acknowledgment, trailing off to polite applause, and the cake was cut and served.

Standing around or sitting on desks, people ate cake from little paper plates with little plastic forks. Robert leaned against a wall with a plate, idly listening to snatches of conversation that drifted around him, of boyfriends and card games, shoes and spouses, children and softball–and furtive whisperings about someone, somewhere, who had been fired.

A knot of young men laughed, breaking up. One stopped and asked the birthday girl, "So, Kate, how long have you worked here?"

Robert stopped chewing, the plastic fork hanging motionless over his plate.

Brushing imaginary crumbs from her suit, the supervisor patted Kate's shoulder and walked back to her glass office.

The message was understood. There was a short cleanup of plates and napkins, cups of coffee poured to wash down the cake, and everyone went back to work.

Robert returned to his desk, but sat staring at a far wall.

It seemed such a simple, ordinary question.

How long had he worked here?

He had no idea.

––––––––––––––

At noon, he left the building and walked to a nearby park. The sun was bright, the wind cold, and he wandered the length of the park, hands in his coat pockets, trying to work his way back through time. But the days stretched behind him like the pickets of a long fence, identical, unremarkable, fading into obscurity. Nothing stood out.

Except . . . he could remember going to work under gray skies and icy rain, day after dreary day, not so long ago. That was something. And before that, mounds of dirty snow piled high along the streets, slowly melting, storm sewers gurgling. And before that, cold clear nights of dry powder that sparkled and squeaked underfoot. And before that . . .

Nothing. A blank, returning him abruptly to the present.

He sat down heavily on a park bench.

The old wood was warm with sun, and he slumped back, legs stretched out, forcing himself to take slow, even breaths against the heavy tightness in his chest.

He told himself he was overreacting. Tired. In a bad rut. He should take some time off. His eyes slowly closed, and he listened to the wind, his mind emptying, his breathing growing deeper—until a sharp voice cut across the wind and his eyes snapped open on a young woman standing a few yards away, someone he knew from the office, her face vaguely familiar. But he could not remember her name.

"I said, are you all right?"

He sat up.

"I'm fine."

A group of men passed, boisterous and laughing. The woman watched him a moment, then turned and walked away.

He exhaled and leaned on his knees, the sun warm on his back, and stared vacantly at patterns of cracks in the pavement. But he noticed his watch and rose to his feet.

The low, clipped sounds of his heels striking pavement brought him back to himself, and he walked quickly back to the office.

He got through the afternoon. In the evening, after the sun had set and with a biting chill back in the air, he stepped off the bus and walked to his apartment building. He went up the brick steps, pushed through the heavy front door, climbed the worn balustraded staircase to the second floor, then unlocked the door to his apartment.

Tossing aside his coat, he strode past the spot where he had paused that morning, trying to remember, and into the small kitchen, where he poured an inch or so of straight whiskey into a glass. He took this to the living room and stood by a window, glass in hand, watching outside.

Night fell. Streetlights flickered on. A car drove by in the street below, refractions of headlights sweeping the ceiling of his darkened room.

His forehead rested against the cold pane.

It was no use. No matter what he tried, no matter what he thought about, beyond a certain point there was nothing. It was not that his past was unremarkable. It just wasn't there.

The empty glass slipped from his fingers and thumped on the carpet.

"Damn."

3

In the morning, Robert arrived at the department as usual. He walked to his desk, as usual, glancing at the light, but stopped, his coat half off, because the light was still red.

He looked around. It was the right desk. He reached down, but the forgotten coat half on and half off caught his arm, and he yanked the coat off, then rapped at the light, as though he might knock some sense into it. But the light continued its silent red challenge, mutely insisting he wasn't there.

He threw down the coat and strode the length of the room to the glass office, where he jerked open the door.

Alice Brown had been supervisor as long as anyone could remember. She knew all the ropes, knew who was who, and was rumored to have some mysterious connections in very high places. When Robert barged in, she simply glanced up at him, then went back to what she was doing.

He stood by the door, watching her bent over some papers, checking off figures, circling paragraphs, making notes, not hurriedly, but methodically, deliberately. She reached the bottom of a page, turned it over, and began another.

His voice cracked: *"I have a problem."*

Alice leaned back and considered him, her pen waggling negligently between two fingers, unconcerned, almost smug, secure in some vast knowledge, withheld from him, that told her exactly how this would turn out–while he struggled with an urgent need to walk across the office and slap the look from her face.

Something seemed to shift. His anger evaporated. Hers was the face he expected to see in this office, but she was a stranger, an enigma, wrapped in a veil of familiarity.

"Well?" she prodded.

"Ah . . . it's that damned light. On my desk. It's broken. Again."

"I see."

She picked up the telephone, spoke a few quiet words, and hung up.

"All right, Robert. Someone will take care of it. You've been logged in."

He turned to leave. She stopped him.

"Robert. Please close the door and sit down."

Warily, he complied, taking a chair by the small round conference table.

"Robert, something is troubling you. This isn't like you."

He found himself wondering what would be "like him", but decided not to ask.

"You know, this isn't the first time. You've been difficult to get along with for weeks. It's starting to upset people."

He looked down at the floor, trying to appear contrite. At least long enough to get out of her office.

"Is there anything you want to talk about? . . . No?" She sighed, a little theatrically. "I was afraid of that. Well, if I can't help, then it's up to you. I would hate to lose you. You have been an excellent employee. But it's really up to you."

He nodded, still looking down.

"That's all, Robert. If you change your mind and want to talk about it, my door is always open. Provided, of course, that you *knock* first."

"It won't happen again."

"Then this conversation should not occur again. Please solve your problem."

He got up and walked back across the department. Curious eyes followed. He ignored them, sat at his desk and tried to concentrate on work, but at noon he quickly got up and left.

Outside the building, he hurried down the sidewalk, with no destination, no purpose, other than to get away. And after a block or so, he slowed.

Then he stopped.

Across the broad avenue, buildings rose into the air. Sunlight glinted from windows, columns of them streaming high overhead, although a few had long since been replaced with plywood, disquieting rectangles gray with age and exposure. Higher up still, black specks that were birds . . . He watched them circling aimlessly, across the sky.

He knew he had a problem, and he knew it was serious. But he had said nothing. Why? Because he had no idea what would happen if he did. Possibly nothing. Possibly dismissal. And if he did not have a grip on the past, he understood the present. Dismissal was unthinkable.

He needed information. He needed to know who he was—

That thought took his breath away.

The buildings towered around him, and he searched the faces of glass and steel, opaque, impenetrable, as though guarding some deep secret. Not for his eyes.

The noises of the City came back to him, the normal sounds of a normal day, because he remembered something. Human Resources. Everyone had a file at HR. There might be something there.

He turned, and stopped.

Propped against a lamp post a few yards away, pale hair loose and tossing in the wind, was the woman from the park.

She slouched, arms crossed carelessly, eyes direct, intelligent, and mocking. She was thin under her coat, yet attractive, in a tense way, and when she smiled he felt himself smiling in return. Until she spoke.

"So what did Queen Alice have to say? Did she say you frighten the little girls and boys?"

This grated. Some instinct rebelled, and he closed his mouth.

The woman straightened, her hands dropping to her sides.

"Well, I suppose it's none of my business."

He shook his head.

"She didn't say much. Just threatened to throw me out on the street."

"Really?" The woman smirked. "You must have ruined her morning." She walked up to him, pushing loose hair back over her shoulders. "I'm Agnes. You're Robert. We met a few months ago, when you transferred in." She looked into his face and laughed. "You don't remember, of course."

He stared at her, because she he couldn't possibly mean . . . But the mocking smile seemed innocent, seemed to mock them both. He relaxed a little.

"Pleased to meet you. Again."

"There now, that didn't hurt, did it? You're not so frightening, close up."

"Frightening?"

"No one thinks you're human. But don't worry. Your secret's safe with me. So, where did you work before?"

He answered without thinking, "I don't remember," and hollows darkened under her cheekbones.

"Sorry. I suppose I *was* prying."

"I didn't mean–Look, forget it. Why don't we get a sandwich somewhere? We'll have to head back soon."

"Okay! *Now* you're talking."

They started off, the woman gossiping about the office.

He walked with her and said little. He was thinking about what he had learned.

4

R obert went to see Alice Brown again the following day. This time he knocked.

He informed her he was taking time off to go to Human Resources. She seemed about to say something, and he waited. But she only nodded, her face politely empty.

An elevator brought him to the basement where HR had an office, and he entered a long room, windowless and drab, the walls vaguely green. A yellowed ceiling sagged over a yellowed tile floor and a few small tables and chairs. At the far end was a counter, and behind this sat a hulking figure, reading.

The place was silent, empty, and the figure looked as though it ought to have been covered in dust, a forgotten fixture in a forgotten room.

But the ponderous head rose as he approached.

"My name is Robert Larsen. I'd like to see my employee file."

The low forehead wrinkled.

"Did you make an appointment?"

"No. But you don't look busy."

The man made no move. In fact, nothing seemed to move, but the flesh of his lips and chin.

"It's a big company, friend. It can take time to locate a file. Give me your name and where you work. I'll call you when it's ready."

"Take all the time you need. I'll wait."

This slowly sank in, and the man set aside his book, gravely, then stood up, grunting a little with the effort. He was half a head taller than Robert, and seemed twice as wide.

"Okay, friend. Have it your way." He pulled out a drawer, rummaged through it, and produced a paper form. "Fill this out."

Robert scribbled his name and employee number, then tossed the paper back. Form in hand, the man pushed sideways through a door in the wall behind him.

The metallic sound of thumping followed. Thump, pause, screech. Thump. Longer pause. Screech.

Minutes later he returned, wheezing, face shiny, and placed a thin folder flat on the countertop.

"You must be younger than you look. There isn't much there."

Robert opened it and flipped through a dozen pages. There was a form with his address. A cursory medical report, no health problems noted. A letter stating his new position and salary at the department. Nothing about where he worked before.

"Where's the rest of it?"

The man pulled the folder to him and went through it, one pudgy hand turning each page and sliding it under the fingers of the other flat on the countertop, ample elbows resting on the broad shelf of his stomach.

"Well, this isn't complete. No performance reviews. No pay history. No training certificates. No transfers." The heavy slopes of his shoulders affected a kind of shrug. "Not much of anything."

"I can see that. Where's the rest of it?"

"This is it."

"You mean to tell me you lost half my file?"

"No, it must've been sent to us like this. We have hundreds of these things. We just store them. We can't read them all."

"So what am I supposed to do?"

"Ask your last manager. Where you worked before. They probably have the rest."

He watched the man in silence, but it had no effect. The man just resumed his seat and picked up his book.

"Like I told you, friend. It's a big company." He found his page. "Leave it there when you're done."

Robert pushed the folder away.

On the fourth floor, he strode from the elevator down the short corridor, shoved his way through the door, but stopped short just inside, because the woman, Agnes, was actually sitting on his desk, leaning back on hands spread out behind her, legs crossed under a narrow skirt, one slim foot swinging back and forth, back and forth.

She saw him and jumped lightly to her feet.

"It's about time! You're late."

"Late—for what?"

"Lunch! What else?"

He stood looking at her, his mind still on HR and the thin folder. But he was drawn by the laughter in her eyes. *Of course he was coming,* the laughter seemed to say, and she came over and put an arm through his.

"Come on, my turn to treat. I'm *starving.*"

They left the building, and she led him to a little café on a side street. It was the middle of a busy lunch hour, but they found a small table by a big curtained window, handwritten paper menus propped between the sugar and the napkins, and shortly a dark-haired, dark-eyed young man in a white shirt stood stiffly before them, small pad and pencil poised to take an order.

Agnes was studying her menu, looking languorously over the short list of selections while the young man stared, eyes brazen and suffering. She ignored him, pursed her lips, tapped them with a fingertip, then looked up at him, eyes wide and innocent.

There was a dull *click* as the point of the pencil snapped, and she ordered a sandwich, thanking him with a sweet, perfunctory smile, one hand resting negligently on Robert's arm.

The young man's eyes lingered, becoming cold and black as he turned to Robert.

He shrugged and ordered the same.

The food came and they ate. She talked, legs crossed, back erect, pale blond hair scattered across her thin shoulders, her body at once relaxed and taut, as though held together with sinews not of flesh but intelligence, young and free and cavalier. She told outrageous stories, stories of petty embezzlement, of management blunders, of incompetence overlooked for sex; told them all with undisguised delight, her clear laughter carrying easily over the clatter and din of the restaurant to the young man whose eyes rarely left her, the hunger blatant on his sullen face.

By the time they returned to the department, Robert had made up his mind to stay away from her. He had his own problems.

But the next morning, she was there at the coffee maker, pouring for him, the mocking eyes laughing as though sullen young men were only to be expected. Later, she brought a fresh cup to him just when he needed it, lingering with a slender hip against his desk, grinning mysteriously through wisps of vapor as she raised her own cup to her lips.

He found himself looking forward to lunch breaks with her. Not at the café, but there were other places. And the park. They would bring sandwiches and sit on a bench, or walk from end to end, her arm through his. She would drop the sarcasm and listen intently when he defended the Corporation or explained the reasons behind a policy or the logic of a procedure. When he ran out of conversation, she didn't seem to mind. She would point out a new blossom or a passing butterfly, or just sit with him on a bench, head thrown back, her face offered unguarded to the warm April sun.

One Friday she invited him to dinner.

They took a bus after work to her apartment in a blocky concrete building on the other side of town, and she whipped up something in the kitchen while he wandered about her living room, sipping a drink and looking at drawings tacked to the walls, drawings that seemed like exercises in some new kind of geometry, patterns of lines and angles and intersecting surfaces; some impossibly detailed, with delicate blendings of color and shading; others of massive shapes and sweeping contours. They were each unframed, each unique, but each of the same unmistakable hand.

He stood for a long while before one that looked like a fantastic city.

"That's my favorite."

She was leaning against the doorway to the kitchen, watching him.

"Did you do these?"

She nodded, glancing around the room.

"They're my latest."

"They're amazing."

"Are they? I think it's a substitute for something."

"What do you mean?"

"I don't know. It keeps me from going stir-crazy at night."

They ate in the living room. When they finished, he moved to help clear the dishes, but she stopped him.

"No, you sit. I'll get these. Coffee?"

He slouched back on the sofa, grinning as she gathered dishes.

"Sure."

A minute later she called from the kitchen, "How old are you, Robert?"

"How old do I look?"

Then she was in the doorway, left hand resting in the crook of her right arm, right hand held up and index finger jabbing at him.

"There you go again! Can't you give me a straight answer, just once?"

"Well . . . I don't know, exactly. How old are you?"

"Thirty-one. What do you mean, you don't know?"

"I don't know when I was born. Maybe I'm an orphan."

"Bullshit. *I'm* an orphan . . . Robert, are you hiding something?"

He sat up.

What did he actually know about her? She might be anything. Someone tired of going stir-crazy. Or some kind of informant. There was no way to know.

But there was fear in the room. He could feel it. It was in her face— and it seemed a lifeline thrown to his.

"Agnes, I don't remember. I don't remember anything beyond a few months ago. I don't know how old I am. Christ, I don't know *who* I am. I don't know where I came from."

Her hand covered her mouth.

"Good God . . ."

"I know."

"Have you . . . have you gotten any help?"

"I went to HR, to look at my file. Most of it is missing. I don't know what that means." Her eyes widened, and he started to get up. "I know. I should leave."

But she looked down, crossing her arms. "No . . . don't go."

"Are you–are you sure?"

She was silent a moment, staring at the floor. Then she looked up, and walked to him, holding out her hand and smiling once more. But her eyes were no longer laughing.

"Don't go."

He took her wrist and pulled her down, and she turned, sitting across his lap and kicking off her shoes, slipping her arms around his neck, and he felt her warm breath in his ear, heard her whispering:

"Thank God I don't have to spend another weekend alone."

The smell of coffee woke him.

Robert threw back the covers and sat up, rubbing his head and yawning, looking around for his clothes.

The room was spartan. Early sunlight streamed in through a single window. The walls were bare except for a mirror framed in dark wood above a dresser with a lone hairbrush on it. Next to the dresser, a straight-backed chair, with his clothes, neatly folded.

She came into the room then, a silky wrap floating about her limbs, and tossed him something thick and brown. He held it up. It was a bathrobe, much too large to be hers.

She leaned against the dresser, grinning.

"Sorry, buster. I always keep that around."

He got up, shrugging into it.

"So you like men."

"When I can find one."

Tying the robe, he answered carelessly, "That shouldn't be too hard for you."

The room was suddenly much too quiet, and he looked up.

Dark hollows stood out under her cheekbones, and the voice was icy:

"I'll take that as a compliment."

"Well, I didn't mean–"

"No. Tell me something, Robert. The men we work with. What do *you* think of them?"

"I don't know. Not much, I suppose."

"Well, neither do I."

"I didn't mean it the way it sounded."

"No? Is that an apology?"

He didn't answer. He let his glance slip the length of her body, lithe and tense and not very well hidden under the wrap, then to her face, and the narrow, angry rectangles of her eyes.

"Don't be so sensitive. It doesn't become you."

"No?"

He walked to her, took her hand, raised it easily to the side of his face against the furious stiffness in her arm, and kissed the palm— then bit it, gently.

"No."

———————

He spent the weekend.

They listened to her music, recordings of old classics, Beethoven a favorite. "He makes me smile," she told him. "That makes him worth listening to."

They went to a bookshop, a hole-in-the-wall not far from her apartment, where he wandered about looking at dusty shelves without interest while she haggled with a clerk. When her voice rose clear and insistent from across the shop, he joined her, slipping an arm about her waist.

"What've you got?"

She looked up, surprised, and showed him a book, explaining something about the author. But he wasn't listening. He was looking at the soft pale hair tied up in a loose knot, at the sharp curves of her neck and shoulders, at the small rise of her breasts.

Very slightly, he pressed her to him. It was a gesture of protection. He wondered if she needed it. Or even noticed.

5

Monday morning, he saw the smirks. They were on the faces of young men who had never paid the slightest attention to him before. Even an older man at the coffee bar winked as he walked up, and Robert looked straight at him, silently inviting him to explain what was on his mind. But the man just walked off.

Still, after a week, everyone seemed to have forgotten him again. Everyone but Alice Brown. She beckoned one afternoon, through the windows of her office, and he got up obediently and walked to her door.

"Sit down," she told him. "And close the door."

He did so, relaxed and waiting easily while she tapped on her desk, apparently searching for the right words.

What came out was, "I suppose you know she doesn't have the best reputation."

His mouth tightened.

The tapping continued.

"She has an attitude."

"Well, I suppose I do, too."

"She's not in your class, Robert." The tapping stopped. "You know, you could *be* something."

"What? What are you talking about? Like what?"

"Like anything. Like a vice president."

"Who the hell–who in hell would make *me* a vice president?"

"It's happened before, Robert. And to far less likely people."

"Well, it won't happen to me."

The office was suddenly small, and he was having trouble breathing.

"Don't underestimate yourself."

Whatever she said next was lost in a surge of anger. It came out of nowhere. Hot patches pulled tight across his face. Something dull throbbed in his chest, and the sound of her voice grew distant. He wasn't seeing her, or the office, he was seeing . . . a ghost, a wisp, vanishing before he could grasp it.

The office came back.

"I know you don't want my advice, Robert. But think about it."

Blindly, he got up and left, his hands shaking.

That night, lounging against him on the sofa, one hand moving possessively over his thigh, Agnes asked about the summons.

"Christ, I really don't know."

"Why? What did she say?"

He tried to laugh. "She said you're no good for me."

"Well, maybe she's right."

She pulled away, sitting upright and pushing back some loose hair. "What else?"

"She seems to like you even less than she likes me. Although I can't imagine why."

"Maybe she's jealous."

"Of what?"

"You. Have you thought of that?"

"Don't be ridiculous."

"No? You're a handsome catch, Robert. I'm a nobody. And a supervisor's in a position to get what she wants."

The tightness was growing in his chest again.

"Remember, Robert. Alice knows people."

"What do you mean? What people?"

"People high up."

"Like who?"

"I don't know who. Executives. People like that. Has she ever said anything, you know, suggestive?"

"No. At least I don't think so. But maybe I don't remember."

"Maybe you're lucky to still have your job. Watch out, Robert. Alice could be trouble."

But he forgot about Alice.

From time to time he went back to the dingy HR office in the basement, to check his file. A few more pages turned up, one with his date of birth. Nothing important. At least nothing he could use. And, after a while, he forgot about HR.

He spent most of his evenings with Agnes, at her apartment, never his own. He liked to fall asleep in her bed, her head on his chest, her arm across his belly. His mind empty.

6

The job was paper. Reports, forecasts, estimates, analyses. Boxes of paper arriving and boxes departing, almost daily. A web of paper weaving across two dozen desks and in and out of banks of file cabinets. All under the watchful eye of Alice Brown.

Robert could see patterns, fit pieces together, decipher the meaning behind a column of figures or deduce the reasons for a report. It seemed second nature. But it left him cold. He did his assigned work each day, left in the evening, and forgot about it.

A week after the summons, he was called once more to the glass office, this time for a stack of reports late for the planners at Corporate headquarters. They were on Alice Brown's desk, collected and boxed and ready to go.

It was a menial errand, but a chance to get out of the department and away from his desk for a while, and he lugged the heavy carton from her office, swung it up to hold balanced on one shoulder, then strode to the elevator, where he gallantly punched the button to go down.

A bus carried him across town, the box on the seat beside him.

He watched the City roll by, trucks and cars, streets and buildings. People entered his view, too, shuffling on and off the bus. But they didn't register. Not really. They were anonymous, someone else's problem.

The bus dropped him near a white office tower, and he strode across a broad plaza, holding the box propped on his shoulder, strode past reflecting pools and gardens beginning to flower, then into the building. An elevator brought him smoothly to the twenty-second floor, where a serious young man checked off the reports and signed for them.

Then he was free to go.

He walked back, taking his time, threading his way through the busier streets and intersections, pausing to watch a gleaming car speed by or a work crew climb down an open manhole, or someone cleaning windows ten stories above the pavement. Buildings rose overhead, and the close, hard sounds of people and machines reverberated through tight, shadowed spaces carved out of air by brick and steel and concrete, the distant sun crawling its own way across a slice of sky high overhead, and he felt at home, in a world he understood.

It was a little after noon when he arrived back at the department, the big room empty except for someone reading a book and eating a sandwich by a window, and two people playing cards at a work table.

Agnes was not at her desk.

Two hours later, as he labored over an especially tedious report, he looked up from a pile of cost estimates, his concentration broken by a shrill *creech-creech* as a pair of workmen in overalls pushed a cart though the department.

They stopped by Agnes's desk, her chair still empty, and began unfolding tattered cardboard boxes.

He shoved the estimates aside, got up, and walked over.

"What's going on here?"

A few people looked up, startled by the rough authority in his voice, but he ignored them and repeated the question. One of the workmen, emptying a drawer into a box, drawled with magnificent indifference: "Don't ask us, pal. We just work here."

He looked toward the far end of the room, where Alice Brown stood in her glass office, watching, the phone at her ear. Her eyes met his, but flickered away.

Chuckling over some private joke, the workmen pushed the loaded cart back through the department and out the door. Robert looked again at Alice, but now her back was to him, the phone still at her ear.

That evening, he rode the familiar bus across town to the concrete apartment block. The days were longer now, and it was still light when he walked into the building, climbed the stairs to the second floor, and knocked at her locked door. He knocked again, and listened. But there was nothing.

Outside, he looked up at the face of the building, at the glow of light around closed curtains and blinds. Some of the windows were dark, but he could not tell which were hers.

Strange faces went by. A couple walking a dog nodded to him as they passed.

Reluctantly, he turned and started for the bus stop, glancing back over his shoulder once, as though he might catch sight of her.

The next day he went to see Alice Brown

It was confidential, she told him. A personal matter. A matter for HR. There was nothing more she could say, and she waved it off, dismissing him.

He returned to the concrete building after work.

This time she was standing outside, near the entrance. Relieved, he quickened his step. But then he slowed, at the sight of her standing like that, arms folded, as though waiting to dispose of something unpleasant, and he stopped in front of her, hands hanging awkwardly at his sides.

He whispered: "What happened? What's the matter?"

She looked down, pressing the toe of one plain shoe against the pavement, twisting it.

"It's our VP. Richard Martin."

"What about him?"

Raising her eyes to his, carefully pronouncing each word, she told him.

"Mr. Martin has taken an interest in me. A *personal* interest. I think you know what I mean."

Someone walked around them and into the building, the heavy glass door closing smoothly behind. He looked up at the windows.

"Is he . . . ?"

"*No.*" She shivered. "God, don't look at me like that. There's nothing I can do. You know that."

"I know."

The light was failing. Streetlamps were flickering on. He felt her hand on his arm, heard her low voice: "You know we can't go on. Don't say anything. And for God's sake, don't do anything stupid. Just go home and . . ."

He raised his hand to her hair and stood gazing at the pale strands slipping through his fingers.

She shook her head, and he turned and walked away, into the growing darkness.

He did not go home.

He walked, long after nightfall, without direction, along streets unlit and unfamiliar, past buildings lifeless, dark, and abandoned, like corpses lined up on some forgotten battlefield.

There was nothing he could do. He was helpless, in a way that felt vile, and he concentrated on the act of walking, on the rhythmic shock of pavement striking his heels, on the sweat trickling down his neck. On pushing himself forward. Pushing away the memory of her eyes.

The sounds of his footsteps echoed from unseen walls that drew closer as he moved away from lights and people, away from what he knew, and deeper into the ruin, the sky low and black, propped up by the empty relics of vanquished industry. Something struck his foot, painfully, debris that clattered noisily across the pavement–a momentary relief from the impossibility of what was happening.

It would be worse tomorrow. Tomorrow he would go back to the office as though nothing had happened, go back to work, and lie– mainly to himself, because there was no room in his small world for a truth of this enormity.

When would he forget? In a month? A year? Did convicts survive prison by forgetting the world outside? He shuddered. How could anyone know what was real?

He tripped over something heavy, bulky, and soft, and he staggered, revolted and nauseated, suddenly aware of his derelict surroundings and the sweet, delicate odor of decay.

Then, through a gap between dark, sagging shapes, he caught sight of the distant office towers shooting up out of blight and ruin, and he stopped, gazing across black space at thousands of dots of light rising from the earth, windows looking far out into the night, the unblinking eyes of the City.

It was a sight to stir awe, admiration, even gratitude. But not tonight. Tonight he felt malignance behind those eyes. Malignance and impunity.

The towers were smug, comfortable, powerful. Their inhabitants would be equally smug, secure in their unseen orbits, veiled behind curtains of authority, unconcerned with him. Unaware of him. Disembodied abstractions whose names he might read in a memorandum or report, yet they held the power to light the City. Or change his life.

He knew nothing. His life was a cage, because he knew nothing.

Yet . . . yet, if he could make them notice, give themselves away . . . Expose them, bring them down from their orbits. Then he would know something. And *that* would be real.

One tower stood apart, its lower sides bathed in white floodlight above the unseen plaza and gardens, and he wondered if Richard Martin was there at that very moment, because he thought he knew how to do it, how to reach them, and his body untensed, a strange relief spreading through his limbs like a warm liquid.

7

"You see? You don't have to look up all those costs. Just get the markup from *this* file, here, back it out of the bottom line, and that will give you what you need."

The young man studied the figures, scratched his head, and nodded.

"Sure enough. Don't know why I never saw that before. Thanks. Thanks a lot."

"Don't mention it."

Robert Larsen slapped his back and walked away, and the young man watched, surprised, and a little bewildered. This was not the old spook who had sat by himself in a corner all these past months, silent and remote.

But those months were all Robert had needed.

Arcane systems, convoluted filing, redundant effort, fudged accounting–the department ran on years of accumulated makeshift passing for procedure like so many layers of ancient sediment. No one understood it. No one questioned it. Things were done this way because they had always been done this way. And it kept a room full of trained people fully occupied, five days a week, researching, writing reports, checking, rechecking, and checking again, because the planners at headquarters depended on information, and everything depended on the planners.

It was the kind of problem Robert understood, instinctively. What this said about his past, he had no idea. But he put it to work.

He showed them how to combine two costing forms into one, to save paperwork. Then he showed how the new form could fix one of the filing systems, one that had plagued them for years with lost records. Then, with a little coaching, people were writing many of the reports in half the time, using the new filing system.

Some people resisted at first. No one had done this before. There might be trouble. And there was Alice Brown. She could stop him, or worse, co-opt what he was doing. So he was careful. He would start with a problem that could be solved with a clever bit of ingenuity, something that seemed obvious in hindsight, but that led later to a solution to a more difficult problem, and then another, like pulling on a string to unravel a series of knots. The resistance crumbled, because his ideas worked, because Alice Brown went along, and because he didn't seem to care who took the credit.

Still, there were suspicions. One afternoon, as he tried explaining to an older man how to find the data to compute the marginal return for different uses of gasoline, the man stopped him.

"I don't get it, Larsen. What the hell's in this for you? You bucking for promotion?"

"What if I am?"

"Well, knock yourself out. Just don't expect me to call you 'sir'."

Robert laughed.

It was sudden and a little wild, the first time he had laughed since the night he had seen the eyes of the City.

He controlled himself.

"I'll try to keep that in mind."

And it did come, the first movement from behind the curtains of authority, but sooner than he expected.

Somewhere a decision was made, and on a summer afternoon Robert watched as Alice Brown, dazed and confused, followed two workmen pushing carts loaded with her things out the door, to some other job, elsewhere in the City.

He moved into the glass office.

He did not bring much. No pictures, no mementos. It was an office in a building. But the promotion meant that his plan was working. He had got their attention. And he wasn't through.

He was learning the reasons why departments like this existed, why the planners depended so much on the reports. And he was learning that the department was a mine of information, if you knew how to find it.

Alice had not cared about reasons. She had cared only about doing what was required, when it was required, the way it was required. And it was not just Alice. The Corporation ran on a kind of unspoken understanding, a kind of social contract. You did what you were assigned to do, when you were assigned to do it, the way it was usually done, and this entitled you to a comfortable living. And something more. It entitled you to feel that what you did was important, that it *mattered,* but without ever having to lose sleep over it.

Robert tore up the contract. He rejected *we've always done it that way before,* dismissing it over the stammered protests of people who had never bothered to consider why it was done at all.

But, slowly, they were learning, too.

He did not try to flatter them. He did not ask about their families or socialize with them around the coffee maker. What he did was to explain what they were going to do, how they were going to do it, and why. And when he threw out the old rules, when he handed someone a new responsibility, when he explained why it mattered, he saw the change. Instead of craving reassurance, they were learning respect, *self*-respect. Autonomy.

But there were times, usually at the end of a long day, when a different mood would come over, and the walls of his office seemed to close in, and he would stop what he was doing and stare through the glass, watching the rest of the department, as though watching from a distance, as though they were all going somewhere. But without him.

But then he would remember that night, and the eyes of the City, and why he was doing this.

8

On a crisp morning at the beginning of fall, Robert arrived at the department at his usual time, greeted the usual early arrivals, and walked the length of the room to his office, unlocking the door and stepping over something on the floor inside.

It was an envelope, the word CONFIDENTIAL hand-lettered across its face.

The first mail run would not be for another hour, and he picked up the envelope, locked the door again, and went to his desk. Inside the envelope was a single sheet of paper, 'Employee Transfer' typed across the top. There was a date, today, circled in red, a short list of instructions. And a name.

He dropped the paper and pushed away from his desk.

Outside the glass of his office, people were starting the day, hanging up their coats, pouring cups of coffee, sitting at their desks. They were busy, intent, and he watched blankly for a long time.

Then he folded up the paper and dropped it in a drawer.

That afternoon, long after everyone had returned from lunch, an elevator rose from the lobby and stopped at the fourth floor.

Agnes stepped out, and the door slid shut behind her. She stood with her arms folded and stared down the length of the corridor that led to the old department.

Richard was done with her. He had made that clear. And he wanted her here. The memory of pleading with him, to send her somewhere else, anywhere else, was nauseating. No, that was a lie. What was nauseating was the knowledge of what she would have done, had he asked, not to come back here.

The elevator clunked and began to hum, and she closed her eyes, the air heavy about her. But there was nowhere else to go.

She started walking.

The department loomed, and her steps began to drag, as if a weight were pressing her into the worn carpet. But she reached the door. Then her hand was on it. She hesitated, alone with herself a few seconds longer.

Then she pushed it open.

It was like the painting of a busy office, or the shadows of people burned into pavement she had heard about, after the explosion of a bomb. They were at their desks, at the coffee maker, standing by file cabinets. But no one moved. No one spoke. They just stared at her.

She wanted to laugh. She wanted to feel her old contempt. But she looked into those other eyes–eyes that knew–and could feel contempt only for herself. It was like being sent to a public gallows for some unspeakable crime. She could not move from that doorway.

But the painting came to life. People nodded to her, grinning wryly. Someone came up to her and led her to her new desk. Someone else brought coffee. Others came by with quiet greetings and quiet reassurance.

She smiled a little. What she wanted was to squeeze herself from everyone's sight, but they were busy, and soon enough she was alone again, looking furtively around the room for the one, missing presence.

Then she saw him, in the glass office, at Alice Brown's desk, and she stared helplessly while he glanced up at her, then went back to what he was doing.

9

Agnes awoke late. Her apartment felt unreal, as if she did not quite know where she was or what she was supposed to do.

But she was certain of one thing. She would arrive at work when everyone else did. She would not draw attention to herself, and she quickly showered and dressed, then bolted down cold coffee from the night before.

What surprised her, more than anything else, was how busy the place was. There seemed to be twice as many reports, twice as many boxes of paper coming and going, some from departments she had never heard of. Which was a relief, at first. Because no one paid any attention to her, except to give her clerical tasks, simple ones, information to collate, pages to assemble. The people who gave her these jobs were cordial, but distant. As though she were the new girl who had just transferred in. As though *he* were any other Corporate manager.

That was hard to take.

The next day, an older woman, Kate, handed her specifications for a report. Kate was the sort of person one would ordinarily forget, a woman alone and silent and doing the same job late in life that people half her age did. Now she was delivering, in a flat, brusque voice, a set of instructions and a deadline, while Agnes scribbled notes, trying to follow.

That was hard to take as well. But it might have been worse. It might have been *him*.

The report wasn't complicated, but the new systems were baffling, the new procedures seemed written in a foreign language, and the report took her the rest of the day, and all of the next.

Before she finished it, Kate dropped another on her desk.

"I need *that* tomorrow afternoon."

By Friday her work was piling up, files to cross-reference, forms to complete, specifications for more reports. She skipped lunch and worked steadily through the afternoon, leaving her desk only to pour stale cups of coffee. She had to track down a mistake she had made, probably copying figures from a cost estimate . . .

Surprised by a sudden pang of hunger and the silence around her, she looked up. The department was empty. Except *he* was still in his office—and she shoved her work in a drawer and slammed it shut, to get out of there before he did, before he would see her.

That was Friday.

The next two days she spent alone in her apartment, and three sleepless nights.

The following week was torture. His silent presence in the office at the end of the room, behind a closed door that could open at any moment, was torture.

One day she left early. She just got up and left without saying anything. And no one seemed to notice. At least nothing happened. A few days later, she did it again. It became a habit, two or three days a week. And then there were mornings when she just could not bring herself to go in.

But nothing happened.

Except, she would sometimes hear people grumbling around the coffee maker, about *her*. And there were the dark looks when someone came out of his office with a familiar file in hand, *her* work he must have reassigned, to do over, to meet a deadline. But she couldn't care. All she wanted was to sleep, but at night she would lie awake for hours, dreading the coming morning.

When the confrontation finally came, it was a relief. Had he struck her with his hand, it would have been a relief.

He did not strike her. He closed the door.

"Agnes, sit down."

She remained standing, arms folded, staring at the floor of his office.

"Agnes . . . are you listening? You can't go on like this. This is serious. You *know* that. Do you want to lose your job?"

"Seriously? *Seriously?* Do you think I *care?* I've *lost* everything else!"

"Come on! You can't go on like this."

"Then *fire* me!"

"Oh, for God's sake. Don't be a child!"

"I'm not!"

She flung this at him in righteous anger, and jerked open the door.

But there was only her desk to go back to.

Robert went to HR.

He told himself he had to get through to her, and at HR he filled out forms and provided justification, requesting in bureaucratically precise language a formal probation for Agnes, to be followed by transfer, or termination, should she fail to complete the necessary steps and improvements.

Days later, his manager called. An order had come down denying the request.

Robert put down the phone. His head had been throbbing all day. Now the walls seemed to be moving, the faux wood pattern on his desk seemed to writhe, and he thought he might vomit.

There was a knock, and the door opened a little.

"Say . . . boss? We need you."

10

The door to the glass office was open. Kate stuffed a thick specification for a new report from the morning mail back into its envelope, got up, and walked to his door, knocked without slowing, skirted the small conference table, and tossed the envelope on his desk.

It hit with a slap, and he looked up.

"What's that?"

"Guess, Robert."

He sat back. "Christ, Kate."

"What are you going to do?"

He rubbed his face.

"I don't know. I'll figure out something."

"Really."

She managed not to smirk, but she was enjoying this. It served him right. It was such an old story, the boss tangled up with a pretty

young thing who just also happened to work for him. He ought to
have known better. But they never did.

"How?" she asked.

He picked up the envelope and tossed it atop a pile of others.

"I'll think of something."

"Right. Of course you will."

She went back to her desk. It hadn't escaped her attention that
Agnes was still not at hers, that it was after ten in the morning, and
that yesterday she had not come back from lunch. It hadn't escaped
anyone's attention, she knew that for a fact.

"Right," she muttered.

Alice Brown would never have tolerated this. No real manager
would.

Robert got up and shut the door. He had work to do, and he sat
down and picked up a pile of paper, trying to remember what he was
doing when Kate walked in.

His stomach growled, and he looked at his watch. Two hours before lunch, and he hadn't eaten breakfast.

Christ.

He got up again and left the office. He went to the coffee maker. It
was switched on, but empty, a stinking residue of muck congealed at
the bottom of the glass carafe.

He slammed the counter.

"Fuck!"

They were watching. He could feel it. They were watching and
waiting for him to explode. But he exhaled, snapped off the switch,
and stood waiting for the carafe to cool, trying to remember the assignments he had handed out that day, trying to work out how he was
going to divide up five new reports and still meet deadlines. And trying not to think about Agnes.

But by the end of the week, the new reports went out on time and
as requested, mainly because he wrote three himself, staying late
while Agnes missed two days of work. Although 'work' in her case
was becoming a relative term.

Yet, he said nothing. Not to her. Instead, he blew up at others.
When a cost estimate wasn't completed or a report was late, he would
start summoning people, angrily demanding explanations. Sometimes the explanation was that he hadn't assigned it.

One afternoon, a planner at headquarters called about a missing
quarterly report, an old one the department had sent in like clock-
work for years. Robert slammed down the phone and shouted for the
people responsible.

Two of them arrived in his office, blaming each other. He tried to
follow incoherent explanations of who was supposed to do what, and
when, and how it had gone wrong, and then just screamed, *"Get out
of my sight!"*

They left, and he sat staring at the door, his shirt damp and sour, another headache throbbing, wondering what the hell was happening to him.

That night, when the room outside his office had been dark for hours, he threw down his pen. He could not stand to look at another piece of paper.

But he saw his old desk in its corner of the department. The chair pulled out for some reason, as though waiting for him, and he picked up the pen and went back to work.

11

It was October, early evening, and the department was empty.

Robert sat in his office looking through a list of reports that were incomplete and overdue.

For a month he had worked like this, night after night, and each night had gone home exhausted. And had fallen further behind.

A bead of sweat rolled down his face and dripped from his chin. He sat back. Outside the glass, rows of empty desks were lined up like soldiers awaiting his orders. Taunting him. Seeming to move sinuously in the darkness, their outlines shimmering.

A familiar wave of nausea rolled over, and he clutched the desk and clamped his mouth until it passed and he could slump back and wipe clammy sweat from his face.

Maybe he should eat something. It might help with the headache.

But he got up and started ransacking shelves and drawers, spilling things onto the floor, looking for something to take, anything, because the pain behind his eyes was now pounding insistently.

Then he stopped, because the walls were moving. A loud hum filled his ears.

Lights flashed, splintered, and vanished.

———————

Agnes cracked open the door and peered inside the department. It was dark, everyone had gone for the day, but the light was still on in his office at the far end. She went in and let the door swing shut behind her, bumping softly to a close as she paused in the cavernous room.

They had to talk. If there was no way for her to be transferred, then she had to function here. But she couldn't function if he wouldn't talk to her, and she took a breath and began walking the length of the room, slowing as she approached, and glancing around, because his office looked empty.

She opened the door.

He was sprawled on the floor, shaking, his entire body shaking, like he was being electrocuted.

"Robert!"

She knelt by him, and the shaking stopped. There was a ragged breath. Then his eyes opened.

She leaned closer, saw his eyes trying to focus on hers.

"Robert–can you hear me?" His lips moved slightly. "Are you okay? Can you stand?"

He rolled over, pushed himself to his knees, then struggled to his feet, leaning on her as she helped him to a chair.

Then she was kneeling by him, running a hand through his hair.

"Robert–what happened?"

"Don't . . . know." His voice rasped.

"We'd better get help. Stay right there. Don't move. I'll get Medical Services to send someone over."

She stood up and reached for the phone.

He coughed suddenly, bent over and choking, then recovered and sat back, gasping.

"No. No medics."

"Why not?" Her hand was on the phone, but he leaned over and covered it with his.

"*Wait*. I think–I think I used to know someone. A doctor. Outside the City."

"*Outside* the City?"

He stared at the floor, until his fingers tensed.

"See if you can get a cab. Christ . . . I think I know how to find it."

"Never mind the cab. I have a car. If you're really sure about this."

"You what?"

A car was a luxury, a privilege reserved for executives and a few favored minions, and she quietly explained:

"A going-away present."

He stared at her, and she waited. Then he shook his head and got to his feet.

She drove, following directions that seemed to come to him as they drove through the City, leaving the lights behind, and continuing eastward, into the outskirts. The streets were dark, the headlights sweeping across billows of leaves, green and yellow, as she took each turn.

He touched her shoulder. "See? Up ahead."

She pulled to the curb, the engine idling quietly.

Set back from the road, deep in the twilight, sprawled a dark, angular mass. There were no lights, no signs of life, but under a scattered covering of leaves a walkway led to broad steps and a dark entrance.

She glanced over her shoulder, at the lane disappearing through trees behind them.

"I don't like this, Robert. We don't even know where we are."

But his door slammed, and he was walking towards the entrance.

Swearing under her breath, she cut the engine and got out.

"Robert!"

She caught up with him, but could only clutch his arm as he strode to the door. He fumbled in the dark, until they heard the incongruously cheerful *ding-dong* from within.

Nothing happened. She tugged at his arm to go, then cringed as he pounded the door. A light came on, dimly, somewhere inside.

Then light flooded the entrance.

The door opened.

Framed in the open doorway was the figure of a man, tall, solid-looking, standing quite still. The head was large, the hair white and thinning and scattered across the great rounded forehead. The shoulders were bulky, powerful looking despite a waist beginning to spread. The hand holding the door was large as well, the wrist thick with tendons leading to prominent knuckles and long, capable fingers. The face held her. It was the face of a man accustomed to giving orders, or weighing the lives of others, but disarmed in that moment. Astonished.

He spoke.

"You'd better come inside."

She shook her head, but Robert stepped through the open doorway, and she grabbed his arm and followed.

The door closed, and the two men stood facing each other.

Robert spoke first.

"I should know you. You're a doctor, aren't you?"

The hard eyes widened a little.

"Yes. I am a doctor. But I don't practice anymore, and this is my home, not a clinic."

"I need some advice."

It was a long moment before the doctor nodded. He led them into a broad living room, most of it in shadow.

"Sit down. What seems to be the problem?"

"I passed out a little while ago."

"Oh? What were you doing?"

"Working. I had a headache. I couldn't find anything to take. Then I got dizzy and passed out."

"I see. For how long? Do you know?"

He shrugged, but Agnes found her voice.

"It couldn't have been more than a few minutes. I wanted to talk to him, and I came back after everyone else had left."

The doctor seemed to consider this, his eyes still on Robert.

"Do you have headaches often?"

"From time to time."

"When did you eat last?"

"Yesterday, I think. Dinner."

"Sounds like you've been working hard."

"I have."

"Any trouble sleeping?"

"Sometimes. Sometimes I can't unwind."

"Well, you may have had a conventional migraine. You look tired. Maybe dehydrated. Get a meal and some rest."

"Wait a minute."

She saw them turn, saw the question in their faces, but she had to concentrate on her voice. "What's so conventional about passing out for no reason?"

The doctor glanced at her. "Young lady, it happens." Then he turned to Robert. "Listen to me. If you had gone to a company dispensary, they would have blathered some important sounding mumbo-jumbo, given you some powerful-looking pills, and told you to come back in a few days. But the pills would have done nothing, and the mumbo-jumbo would have meant nothing. At the moment, there is nothing to diagnose."

"That's *it?*" Her voice was rising. "What if something's wrong? It could be serious!"

"Possibly. Life is full of risks. See that you two drive carefully."

"What kind of answer is *that?*" she snapped.

But Robert stood up.

"It's okay. I feel all right now. Just tired."

"Isn't there some kind of test–"

"Young lady." The doctor now turned to face her. "I want you to listen to me. We will watch him. You will help to keep an eye on things. You may call me if anything happens. But you must act like an adult. Don't cry wolf without good reason."

He rose to his feet, adding, "And you, young man. I don't want you to spread this around. I don't practice anymore, and I don't want to see your friends."

"I understand. I won't mention it."

Then they were outside again, walking to the car, their footsteps sharp staccatos mingling in the dark. He reached to open his door, but she stopped him with a hand on his wrist.

"Robert, wait. This is crazy."

"What are you talking about?"

"You need help. You can't sleep, you're having headaches, and now this. You need a doctor, a real one–"

"I don't want a company medic!"

She stepped back. He shook his head, mumbling an apology, then looked towards the house and the entryway that was a slash of light in the hulking shadows. The light went out, and she heard his quiet voice: "I wonder if they expected me to come here."

"Who, Robert? Who?"

"Christ . . . I don't know. Forget it."

"Robert–"

"Forget it!" He yanked open the door, got in the car, and slammed the door shut.

After a moment, she walked around to the driver's side, got in, and pulled the door closed.

Ahead was an unlit streetlamp, a stark reminder that they were parked on some strange road, outside the City, where they had no business being, and she stared at it through the windshield, feeling his presence beside her in the hollow silence.

She sensed him turn, sensed the question, and spoke softly.

"I don't want to be alone tonight."

She wondered if he would answer, unwilling to look at him if he didn't. But she heard his soft exhalation, like a long, low sigh.

"I don't either."

Leaning a little, she rested her head against his shoulder, and for a time there was only the rough feel of his jacket against her face, and the sound of his breathing, soft and even.

Then she lifted her face.

He kissed her, and she tasted him, hungrily, then pulled back, her hand on his thigh, his arm about her shoulders.

Then she started the car.

12

"Where do you want these?"

Robert turned from his desk. Kate stood in the open doorway of his office, holding a stack of envelopes.

There were more on his desk.

But he noticed something different this morning. His breathing hadn't changed. He didn't feel the weight in his chest. And he wondered what it meant.

"Robert?"

"What is it?"

"Well, they want a report on trends in annual heating costs. They want one on seasonal power consumption in agriculture–"

"Oh. That."

"Yes, that. On your desk?"

He could see she was taking a perverse pleasure in this. There was that glint in her eye. But it didn't matter. Not this morning.

"Robert, are you all right?"

"Send them back."

"What?"

"Send them back."

"Are you . . . are you sure? They all have deadlines."

"We can't handle the work we have."

"Well, okay. If you say so. You're the boss."

He gazed past her, through the door, at the department, almost forgetting her presence.

"Robert."

He focused on her.

"Robert, there's a rumor going around . . . about you . . . and Agnes . . ."

He wasn't angry. But he could sense its approach.

"Leave it alone, Kate."

"All right. Is there anything you need?"

"No. Close the door."

She obeyed, and he considered the blank door. This one had been closed politely. Not slammed in his face. Still, it seemed appropriate. Through the glass windows he could see his old desk in its corner of the room.

He could guess how the rumor started. They had arrived together this morning. It would not take any great power of deduction.

But it didn't matter.

What mattered was what had happened here, last night, in this office. Even in the cold light of day, the memory was bizarre and frightening. A conventional migraine? He didn't believe that. But he had no way to know.

There was one thing he was sure of. He had found the doctor's home. *That* was real. Something from his past.

Not far from the office was a bar, and he went there after work and purchased a bottle of single malt scotch whiskey, very old, lovingly preserved, and ridiculously expensive. Then he rode the bus to her apartment, and asked to borrow her car.

At first, she just looked at him as he tried to explain. But then she shook her head and handed him the keys.

"Just be careful. You don't know a thing about him."

There was still light in the sky when he parked on the shoulder by the house in the trees. He studied it a while, a composition of low, interlocking rectangles that seemed to float, weightless, under the trees. He felt as if he had seen it before, but in a dream.

Leaves covered the walkway, and he picked his way to the entrance and rang the bell, whiskey in hand, offering it in token payment.

The old man laughed, and invited him in.

Doctor Paul Stevens lived alone on a country lane in a wooded area just outside the City. Inside the house were rooms of long horizontal lines, sparsely decorated and plainly furnished, the big living room built around a fieldstone hearth and a wall of broad glass panes, floor to ceiling, which looked out on a lawn spreading north to the trees in back. At the end of the glass wall, in a corner of the room, was an old baby grand piano, worn sheets of music propped on the rack, Bach and Haydn visible.

The two men sat in the living room, drinking whiskey and watching leaves sail to the ground under outdoor lights, the yard brown with autumn, and Robert found himself talking about the department, explaining the things he had tried to do, answering shrewd questions that betrayed a more than passing familiarity with Corporate bureaucracy. But he said nothing about his memory.

"Well done," murmured Stevens, leaning over to pour another inch of amber liquid into a pair of heavy glasses, casually asking as he handed one back, "Tell me, how old are you?"

He answered with the information from his file: "Thirty-nine."

"Thirty-nine, you say. Hmm. I was thirty-nine when the last epidemic hit here. The big one. Cargo Flu."

It meant nothing. But he nodded as though it did, adding, "You know, I don't think I ever really understood that name."

Stevens looked at him as if weighing something. "Well, maybe you're too young." He settled back in his chair, swirling his drink, the glass dangling negligently by its rim from long, drooping fingers. "You know, the world was a different place back then. Very different. Crowded. Busy. Some people thought it was *too* crowded, and maybe they were right. There were certainly signs."

"Signs? What sort of signs?"

"Infectious disease, for one. Of course, you could always have an outbreak of some horror like hemorrhagic fever in some godforsaken corner of the world, and hundreds could get sick and die and no one would really notice. There was nothing new in that. But when new diseases, and new forms of old ones, started showing up in places that had not experienced a real epidemic in generations . . . well, that was a warning."

"And this was due to population?"

"Population and the way we lived. Goods and people traveled everywhere, day and night, all over the world. Ships and trucks and airplanes. It was perfect for spreading pests and disease. And we knew it long before Cargo Flu. Long before. Agricultural blights, parasites, invasive species, we had it all. We *knew.*"

"So . . . how did they deal with that?"

"Not very well. There were almost no precautions."

"Oh, come on. They must have done something."

"Not as much as you might think. And this one took everyone by surprise. You see, Cargo Flu is a virus. An unusual one. It adheres to the cellulose in cardboard and paper, and those trucks and airplanes were carrying millions of packages every day. Billions. All over the world. That's how the thing first spread."

"Maybe this is hindsight, but it's hard to believe no one could anticipate something like that."

Stevens laughed, the sound of it harsh and brittle.

"Well, you have to understand! The world was run by *politicians.* What they called 'democracy'. And a politician is someone who keeps his job by telling people what they want to hear. No one wanted to hear they couldn't send a package or step aboard an airplane, anytime, anywhere. Not until it was too late."

"But did it really spread that fast? It had to start somewhere, right? Why wasn't anything done to stop it before it got out of hand?"

"Because it wasn't that simple. You see, at first the thing was just a nuisance. It's a bacteriophage. It infects bacteria living naturally in the human gut. When it first appeared, it might give you a case of the runs for a few days, but you got over it. So there wasn't any real urgency about it. No one was about to disrupt big, expensive transportation systems, or anything else for that matter, just to contain a little abdominal distress. You see? The authorities simply went around telling people to wash their hands.

"But viruses are funny things. They change. They mutate."

The old man gazed outside. The room was silent, but for the slow tick of a clock. Then he smiled, but in a way that did not reach his eyes, and picked up his drink.

"Well, this one changed. And in a very clever way. It caused the host bacterium to release a substance that acted like a kind of chemical messenger. A signal. After a few days, when enough bacteria had become hosts, the concentration of that chemical reached a threshold that somehow triggered the entire viral population to burst free. It filled the gut and entered the bloodstream, and from there infiltrated the airways and sinuses. And lungs.

"At this stage, the symptoms were similar to an allergy. Bouts of coughing and sneezing. Nothing too alarming. The fever and chills didn't start until later, sometimes days later, and in the meantime the victim went about his business spreading the virus everywhere. They weren't too careful in those days, and it spread like wildfire."

"Christ! And this was a mutation?"

"Something like that. At first we thought it might be a completely new illness, but we saw a pattern. It kept popping up randomly in one place after another, but always in places that had experienced the original. It spread out from there. So somehow it acquired a new trait from something common to its environment. Maybe us humans. It had already taken root in thousands of locations, and the new form was showing up everywhere. So now we had a much more virulent contagion on our hands, and no way to contain it."

"*How* virulent? Not just a nuisance, I take it."

"Hardly. It moved too quickly. The lungs were especially susceptible, for some reason, and the natural response was inflammation. A very aggressive form of pneumonia. Left untreated, the lungs would fill with fluid. There were the usual symptoms. Labored breathing, progressive weakness, followed by acute respiratory distress, ending with suffocation and multiple organ failure."

Robert was silent a moment, his limbs heavy with whiskey, trying to imagine a world in which millions were drowning in their own fluids.

"You said 'left untreated'. Was there a way to treat it?"

"Well, we improvised. We could purge some of the fluid with physical therapy. We could give oxygen. We had antiviral medications. The idea was to give the body time to mount its own defense."

"So, did that work?"

"In some cases. If we caught it early. But the drugs were expensive and hard to get. We needed trained people, and the supply of trained people got shorter every week. When the epidemic started, a hospital might have the resources to treat fifty cases a day, but a hundred would come through the door. A week later, after a few doctors and nurses had come down sick or just disappeared, two hundred would come through. A week after that, we stopped counting." The old man shook his head. "It was a losing battle. Many patients took their own lives, if they had the strength. And many doctors helped them."

"Helped them . . . how?"

"Well, morphine was palliative. It took away the panic, the sense of suffocation, and it was one thing we could get plenty of. We could put a patient on an IV, and show him how to control it. When he was ready, he could slip away on his own, painlessly. Or just wait for the end."

"Christ."

Stevens swallowed a mouthful of whiskey, then leaned forward, elbows on knees spread apart, his voice a thick growl.

"It went on like that for months. The authorities were helpless. Everything broke down. They went to martial law, of course, but that was a disaster. Troop movements just spread the virus, until whatever was left of them deserted. We had more trauma patients than we knew what to do with, let alone cases of Flu. When we triaged in my ER, the ones we expected to die were put on morphine right away. It was euthanasia, pure and simple. As humane as we could make it, but euthanasia nonetheless. We needed every square foot of space to deal with the ones we could save."

"And you went along with this?"

"Went along with it? Those were my orders. But it was the only possible decision. And I have no doubt every other facility did the same. God help them if they didn't."

"I suppose . . . I suppose I can't criticize. It must have been chaos."

"It was worse than chaos. We were overwhelmed. We were on our own, completely. Governments everywhere were useless, self-serving, incompetent. It was a crime, an absolute crime. The politicians had already sold off or contracted out everything that mattered. To private business, you understand. Smart operators with the right connections. Shrewd, maybe, but most folded up and disappeared when things got serious. Most, but not all."

"And that's where the Corporation came from?"

"Right. Probably in other cities as well. It was the perfect opportunity for the right person, in the right place at the right time, to build an empire. Someone as ambitious and driven as James Dornan.

"But I'll tell you this much. In the end, that's what saved us. Not the politicians. Not the do-gooders. Not the lawyers or the big money on the golf course. Not religion. Just raw ambition and *competence.* The City was burning. The streets were ruled by looters and gangs. D'you know, there were even people who said it was all 'God's plan'? They tried to sabotage us . . ." He sat back, staring in wonder at the memory of it. "It was insane. Absolute insanity." He lifted his glass, looked at it, and drained what was left. "I was running an ER here when the Corporation took control. It was hard, desperate work. But we stopped it. Stopped the Flu. We turned the City around. Of course, a lot of it is sealed to this day. And there are areas outside where the bug is still lurking in the debris. So we keep a lid on things. But we saved ourselves. So did others. We saved civilization."

"So it's still out there? It's not over?"

Raising his arms over his head, Stevens yawned hugely.

"Well, one day we'll figure out how to neutralize it. Right now there are more pressing problems."

"But what if it mutates again? Or whatever it did."

The old man chuckled.

"I suppose I talk too much. Don't let it scare you. We haven't seen a case of Flu in fifteen years. Longer."

"Well . . . I suppose you're right. There *are* more pressing problems."

13

Doctor Paul Stevens liked to say that the only thing wrong with government by the people was the people. And if anyone objected, which wasn't often, he would laugh and point out that they were the living proof.

Now in his sixties and retired, Stevens had worked for the Corporation for half his adult life. He had no patience with complaints about the way things were run. He had seen the other side.

From a tender age, Stevens had learned to despise the most venerated institutions of society. His parents took him to church, but he discarded religion by the age of ten and refused to go. He mastered his lessons in school without effort, then endured hours as classes dragged and teachers struggled to hold the attention of students who stared vacuously or studiously ignored them. Eventually, he stopped showing up. When he learned that truancy would cause him to fail, despite perfect test scores, he sat in the back of the room and read his own books.

Once a teacher confiscated his book with a prim lecture on 'appropriate classroom behavior' and 'respect for other people'. Later, retreating to a storage room that doubled as faculty lounge for coffee and aspirin, she opened the book, an old hard-bound wrapped in a makeshift paper cover, expecting to find a juvenile thriller, or maybe something erotic.

She found instead pages of mathematics she dimly remembered from college, the margins dark with notes, the handwriting unmistakably that of her student.

She returned the book to him the next day, and never said another word.

In high school, Stevens leaped at the chance to do actual lab work. His lab partners were delighted, because he always did the entire lab himself, didn't care who copied his notes, and always got everything right.

Almost always.

Once he argued that a computer program they were given as part of a physics lab was wrong. He stated his reasons. Receiving a blank look in response, he marched to the backboard, where he proceeded to diagram the problem and its correct solution.

The teacher stopped him.

"Look, son, you're wasting time. The software was approved by the district."

"Fuck the district."

The teacher was unfazed.

"That's what will be on the test."

Stevens refused to use the program. He failed the lab, and the test. His partner suspected that whiz-kid Stevens was right, but it was the test that mattered. The teacher had no idea who was right, but he knew who signed his paychecks.

Stevens didn't fit into any of the categories his classmates understood. He was brilliant, but also athletic, skillful and powerful for his age, a reliable teammate for a pickup soccer game. But he refused to join in organized school sports. He had far more self-assurance than his lack of popularity seemed to justify. His encyclopedic knowledge was legend, but he kept it to himself.

He just didn't fit.

He was an only child, and both his parents worked. In the evenings, while his father played computer games and his mother watched television, Paul ate dinner alone, in his room.

Once his parents were awakened by a call at three o'clock in the morning. It was the local police. Their son was being held.

His mother paced with cigarette after cigarette while his father drove to the station, where he was informed that a girl's parents had discovered his son in their daughter's bed. The boy had told them to mind their own business and shut the door. They had called the police.

When told that he might be charged with rape, young Paul Stevens howled with laughter.

"Rape! We've been sleeping together for a month!"

His father posted bail. Driving home two hours later, he tried to explain to his son that it was against the law to have sex with a fifteen-year-old girl.

"We're almost the same age," the boy objected. "Besides, when I met her she was sleeping with some dumb jock."

A few miles later, he added, "The law makes no sense. I nearly got in trouble for having sex with an undercover cop. I thought she was a hooker."

"*What?* Where? What happened?"

The boy shrugged. "I paid her double, and she left me alone." Then he laughed. "Maybe she was a hooker after all. I never thought of that."

The charges were dropped after a dean at the high school arranged to give Stevens tests to graduate early, Stevens agreed to move away to attend college, and his father handed the girl's father a substantial check–after dropping the name of a certain young male athlete.

In college, Stevens struggled to get through his first-year required courses. Two things saved him. First, no one bothered him too much for cutting a few classes, so long as he did the work and aced the tests. The second thing that saved him was a biology class.

Paul Stevens discovered biology, then chemistry, anatomy, physiology—and never looked back.

He entered medical school at the age of twenty-one. He was twenty-eight when he completed his residency, with a pile of student loans, a ten-year-old car, and an abrasive impatience. He found a job in an emergency room and threw himself into it, rising quickly into administration, and for a number of years he lived in a world of his own. One he understood.

But the world changed.

When the Corporation took control, Doctor Paul Stevens barely noticed. The City was in the throes of Cargo Flu. Half of it was in flames, and it seemed the other half was in his ER. Many people came in with Flu, but many more with gunshot or knife wounds, or other trauma, or severe burns. Diseases out of the pages of history appeared. Cholera. Typhoid.

Stevens worked thirty-six-hour shifts, triaging and treating. Only when he could no longer stop his hands shaking or his knees buckling would he retreat to his office to sleep a few hours, then catch up on death certificates and other reports, then phone all over the city in search of supplies that were not to be had. Then he would stride again into the thick of the ER and relieve a couple of doctors who were stumbling with fatigue, too demoralized to know what they were doing.

"Go. Get some sleep. I'm good for hours."

Surrounded by death and suffering, Paul Stevens moved impatiently, audaciously, decisively, fueled by a wild exhilaration. Every movement, every decision, every syllable he uttered *meant* something. As fast as the world fell to pieces, his brain and his voice and his hands put the pieces together again.

But once in a while he escaped, to the roof of the building. From there the City lay at his feet in agony, but a muted agony, fifteen stories below, and he could stand and watch a sunrise, his throat taut, feeling nothing but how glad he was to be alive.

On the roof one afternoon, he sat on the edge of a skylight, exhausted, sipping hot tea and gazing across the City, trying to imagine what it would be like when the Flu was beaten and they could start to rebuild.

Tea spilled and his head jerked at the sound of gravel scattering and a small shriek. A few yards away stood a tall, dark-haired woman in scrubs, one hand over her mouth, brown eyes sparkling with laughter.

"My *God*. You frightened me."

He stood up, chuckling.

"I haven't frightened anyone in years."

She walked to him and extended her hand, introducing herself.

He held it a moment.

"Paul Stevens. Pleased to meet you. Why don't you sit down? No one will miss us for a few minutes."

They sat on the skylight and talked, about anything but what was happening in the streets below. A half hour slipped by, and his tea remained untouched beside him.

They had been quiet awhile when he asked, "So, how are you holding up?"

"Fine. And you?"

Weeks of brutal fatigue must have left him careless, left his guard down, because he spoke the truth without thinking.

"I'm having the time of my life."

Even as the sound of his own voice died away, he thought, *You idiot! Now you've put your foot in it.*

He picked up his tea. And she regarded him with a strange look. But not the look of fear or loathing he had expected.

A slow smile formed at the corners of her mouth.

"So'm I."

Within a week, Stevens knew he had found the love of his life.

After six months, any remaining shred of public government in the City had ceased to function, its operations ceded to the Corporation, which had beaten or acquired all of its competitors. And no one had any time to spare for the few lone voices crying bribery, kickbacks, and darker things.

Using whatever means necessary, even starving parts of the City to force people out, the Corporation beat back the chaos and replaced it with order. A new kind of order, for a new age. A smaller age. One of rigid rules and rigorous planning.

Within a year, Stevens was running emergency medicine across the City. He was married. He had challenging work. And he was in awe of James Dornan, chief executive of the Corporation.

It was not the world he had expected, or imagined, at the beginning of his life. But it was a world he could live with.

14

The scotch had been a good investment.

Robert had learned a great deal without raising eyebrows at work, and now he was thinking again about his next step.

The City was an island, fifty thousand souls living together and working together, employed by, and watched over by, the Corporation. They had survived the plague, and they continued to survive, protected by policies and by planning, and by an ocean of wilderness surrounding.

He knew from the office that other places had survived, hundreds of miles distant, and sometimes there was trade. But trade was slow, a risky business of sketchy bargaining, quarantines, and unpredictable losses. So the City had to be self-sufficient. This was the job of planners, hundreds of them in the building that was headquarters. And the planners left nothing to chance.

Orders were sent to the big farming areas north of the City, for instance, instructing how much wheat to plant, and how much corn. The planners then set prices for flour and bread, and for everything else, making sure that nothing went to waste and that no one went without, using the power of money to manage this small world where there was so little room for error.

But for this the planners needed data, a lot of data, and Robert's department was one link in the chain that supplied it. He was learning to understand the system that had kept them alive for the last twenty-odd years. And he was learning to see where it was going wrong.

If the cost of running a tractor longer, to plow more fields, looked cheaper in the dry pages of a financial report than the investment needed to resurrect a second tractor from the scrap heap, the second would be left to rust while the first was run into the ground. And the mechanics and technicians who had to watch it rust had long ago given up arguing with faceless bookkeepers compiling numbers at Corporate headquarters. Tools, machinery, even buildings, that were not being used up or worn out, were rotting with neglect, and Robert decided his new mission was to show this to the planners, and through them their invisible bosses.

But the bookkeepers and planners were not so easy to impress.

He tried to talk about it with Agnes, but she wasn't impressed either.

"Look Robert, it's a job. Okay? You do your job, then go home and forget it. That's how it's done. That's what everyone does."

"This is *more* than a job. That's what I'm trying to explain. I'm *building* something."

"What?"

"A team. An organization."

"What for? Do you expect some kind of reward?"

"Oh, for God's sake! I've just explained it."

"Honey, no one cares."

He couldn't answer. Because she was right. It was what he heard, in different ways and different words, whenever he tried to send a warning, unsolicited, up the chain.

No one cares.

"Okay?" she prompted.

"No. It's not okay."

"Look, you can't change it. And you're just making yourself miserable. Over nothing at all." She smiled, trying to lighten the mood. "And you're lousy company when you're miserable. You know?"

They had sat down to dinner at her apartment, only he had not touched his meal.

Now he stood up.

"You're right. I should go."

He walked past her to the door.

"Robert! Oh for God's sake–*Robert!* You can't keep *doing* this!"

He let himself out, closing the door on the sound of her rising fury: *"Damn you!"*

Outside the building, he stood under a lead-gray sky and buttoned his coat, turning up the collar against the cold mist of a Sunday evening in November. The sidewalk was deserted, streetlamps beginning to buzz and flicker on, and he hesitated, looking at the lights glinting on wet pavement, thinking he should take the bus. But he had nothing to do, and he jogged down the steps and started walking.

A few days later, he called Agnes to his office. When she arrived, he held up her latest report.

"Agnes, how many times do I have to explain it? You *know* how to do this."

"But it's too complicated! What's wrong with the old way? We did it that way for years."

"Not anymore. You know that. I can't accept this."

"Well, I thought it had to go out today. If I do it over, it'll be late. But you're the boss. Tell me what to do."

He ended up sending it out the way it was.

But when she turned in another report done the 'old way', he made her fix it.

The third time, he stood by her desk, balled up the report, and flung it across the room.

"Do it over!"

She got up and stalked out, telling him, "Fuck you. Do it yourself."

He did it himself, that night. But he couldn't do everything, and when someone else followed her example – "What's wrong with the old way?" – he exploded, then apologized, then spent a half hour explaining why the old way was not good enough.

When others began repeating her irrefutable "No one cares", he called his manager.

"I can't have her working for me. It's disrupting the whole department. There must be somewhere else she can work."

The reply was exasperated. "Deal with it. It's out of my hands."

"Who made the decision? Let me talk to them."

"Forget it. It's closed. Just do the best you can."

But his best was not very good. The disease was spreading.

He spent days tracking down a series of inexplicable errors before narrowing it down to a single employee, an older man he summoned to his office.

The man shrugged.

"Sorry about that, Larsen. Mistakes happen."

"Mistakes! It's a mistake when it happens *once.* This is negligence. You *know* better."

"Yeah, I'll see what I can do."

A week later, he summoned the man again, throwing a file at him when he walked in.

"Did you just make that up?"

"Well, maybe I was a short on time."

"The hell you say! I could *fire* you for that."

"Yeah? Like your girlfriend?" The man smirked and walked out.

That night he locked up the office hours after everyone had left and took the last bus home to his apartment, watching dark streets pass by and thinking he should quit, wondering if that were possible, wondering how long would it take to starve.

But he did not quit. And he would not go back to his desk in the corner, to his cage of ignorance. Not willingly.

And there was something in her presence, in her stubborn, mocking intelligence. An answer of some kind. Not a solution, but a reason. And there was the house in the clearing outside the City, the evenings when they would drive out together to see Stevens, go for walks, talk for hours, exist in a different world, a world of their own, just the three of them. They would spend a weekend together, and he would return to the office feeling himself again.

It never lasted. More and more, he spent his nights in his own apartment, his stomach in knots, standing by a window with a drink in hand, waiting for the alcoholic haze that would let him sleep.

15

Agnes sat at her desk, reading a book.

Robert was working, his office a small pool of light, the rest of the department in shadow. It was a Friday evening in December, and they were expected at the doctor's for dinner. But he had wanted to finish something first.

Through the glass, she could see him massaging his temples, then pouring a tumbler of water, then bent over the desk again, writing furiously.

She tossed down her book and yawned.

Why in God's name does he do it?

Watching like this, from a distance, she wanted to comfort him, to bring him something to eat or to drink, to sit with him and talk quietly. About nothing. About everything.

But she leaned back and closed her eyes.

What's the point?

It could not go on. It had already gone on too long. And she knew she would have to be the one to end it. Maybe tonight. Maybe . . . if he worked a little longer . . . she might find the words that would free them both . . .

The muffled sound of a crash brought her upright, looking around. But there was nothing out of place.

Except Robert.

She ran to his door.

He was lying in a puddle of water, and she stepped around broken glass and knelt by him, calling his name, shaking his shoulder. Then she noticed his eyes. The lids were parted, but there were no pupils in the open slits, only whites.

Then she was at the phone, punching the number to reach Stevens, her voice steady—which frightened her, she was shaking so badly.

She hung up and backed away from him, arms folded across her body, watching his face that looked gray as death. But, once in a while, his chest seemed to rise.

Footsteps echoed through the department.

Stevens crossed the office and crouched by Robert, feeling his neck, lifting each eyelid. He produced a small syringe and deftly injected its contents into an inert shoulder, then propped Robert up in a sitting position. Pulling one limp arm about his own burly shoulders, he hefted the man to his feet and half-carried him out of the office, urging him to walk.

She stayed behind, wishing she had the strength to leave and never come back.

Some minutes later, the two men returned, Robert's eyes dark and sunken, but open, and he was walking under his own power. Stevens made him sit at the small conference table, found another glass, and filled it with water.

"Drink that. Slowly."

Watching from where she stood with her back against a wall, she asked, "What was in the shot? What did you give him?"

"Epinephrine."

"But—why? What happened?"

Stevens seemed to recite to himself.

"In cases like these, you must restore blood pressure quickly. It's a gamble. The risk of stroke . . ."

She stared at him as it sank in. "And exactly what kind of case *is* this? You *know*, don't you!"

He glanced at her, a silent warning in his eyes, but Robert pushed himself upright.

"Well?"

Stevens faced him.

"Listen to me. I want you to stay with me tonight. I want to make sure you're stable. In the morning, we can talk."

Robert gave a slight nod, barely perceptible, and the doctor turned to her.

"And I'd like your help."

She looked down. She could not let them see her face.

"All right."

They took the doctor's car. Robert sprawled in the back. Stevens drove, and she sat beside him in the front, watching streetlights sweep by in the early winter darkness.

They reached the house. They took a light meal. Before sending him to bed, Stevens took vital signs and warned Robert that he would wake him hourly.

"You seem fine now. But we're going to make sure."

She wandered into the living room.

When the doctor came out, she was seated at the piano, looking over sheets of music.

He sat down nearby.

"Do you play?"

Without answering, she chose some pages from a Haydn sonata, smoothed them out on the rack, raised her hands over the keyboard, and began playing, tentatively, stopping and starting as she lost her place in the music . . . until her fingers seemed to find the keys, and the bright melodies filled the room, the notes laughing as they echoed from the walls, and she played, eyes closed, lips parted, her shoulders swaying with the music and the movement of her hands.

She reached the end and smiled in the sudden quiet.

"I haven't played since I was a child."

"You must have been quite accomplished!"

Her hands folded in her lap.

"I had to quit when our house burned. Everything was gone. My piano. My music. And my parents."

"I see. Well, you're welcome to play here, of course."

"Thank you." She ran her fingers along the polished wood. "You've taken good care of it. The tuning's almost perfect."

"Agnes, I want to ask you some questions."

" . . . all right."

"I take it Robert has been . . . difficult, let's say. Irritable. Angry. Possibly fearful at times."

It was an effort to control her voice.

"Yes."

"For how long?"

"Weeks. Longer . . . Paul, I *love* him. But I can't *take* it any longer!"

She looked away, wiping her cheeks with the heels of her hands.

"I just can't take it."

"I understand. Get some sleep. We'll talk in the morning."

16

A wan December sun was lifting over the pale yellow horizon, casting long shadows of naked trees across the straw-colored back yard, and irregular bands of light across the floor inside the doctor's living room, where Robert Larsen stood with a mug of coffee.

A cardinal dove for the ground, a streak of red brilliant against the dull brown of the trees; it foraged a moment, then flashed out of sight.

The house was silent. Yet it was imbued with life. Smooth wood beams and grooved planks stained gray slanted overhead, glowing softly, welcoming the early morning light into the broad room, so that the sun and the trees seemed a part of the house, and the house a world of its own. His eye was drawn along bold lines of heavy beams, along planes and set-backs and patterns of angles, across the flat expanse of dark hardwood around the fieldstone hearth—endless variations on themes of horizontal repose and vertical thrust, themes drawn from the earth outside the glass, the architect's proportions and rhythms sculpting a space within at once surprising and yet inevitable, and serene, so that it was no longer possible to imagine this particular place on earth without this particular house. It was not just geometry, not just the physics of structure, but the thought of a human mind made visible, a mind that had known how to make a world. He sipped the hot, biting liquid from his mug and gazed outside, grateful to exist in this world, wondering at the mind that had made it, whether it had perished in the madness so long ago.

Agnes entered the room.

He recognized her step and turned, an involuntary smile forming. Then he saw her face.

She stood at the edge of the room as if surprised to find him, unwilling to come closer, but afraid to turn away. He watched her, thinking how she belonged here, how the house was really built for her, a setting in wood and stone for her peculiar grace and tension.

Then he walked to her and took her hand. Her eyes closed, but her hand did not clasp his.

"I'm sorry," he said. "I know it's been hell for you. It's been hell for us both. If you want to leave, I understand. You don't need this. You don't have to explain. We can end it here and now."

She did not look at him. But her fingers tightened on his, and then her weight was against him, and he was holding her, gently stroking her hair.

They went outside. They wandered the yard, coatless, her arms wrapped about his arm, her head on his shoulder, and for a time they were alone and alive, and only the sun and the trees and the frozen earth were real, and Robert forgot to wonder at the mind that had made this.

"Well, you two! Aren't you cold?" Stevens called from the sliding glass door.

She did not look back, only held his arm tighter, and he kissed her temple, lingering.

Then he led her back to the house.

"Come in, come in, come in," murmured the doctor. "I think it's time we had a little talk."

"Young man, you are a remarkable case."

Robert listened, sprawled in a comfortable chair, one leg thrown over its arm, feeling a sense of ownership, over this room, over the sunlit world outside.

Stevens leaned against the piano, sipping coffee.

"You must have crossed some powerful people at some point. But you don't remember any of that, do you."

Agnes looked up from where she was lounging on the sofa. They had never talked about this. Not here. Not in front of him.

Robert shook his head.

"No. I have no memory of it."

"None at all?"

"I can remember as far back as last winter. That's all."

"Nothing before?"

"Nothing before."

Stevens nodded. "Someone knew his job."

"His job? What do you mean? Who?"

"Someone of extraordinary skill, to be sure. But not acting on his own. In the vernacular, Robert, about a year ago you were 'gelded'."

"Just what the hell are you talking about?"

"You'll have to excuse the metaphor. An informal term used by the medical profession. The technical name is 'Complete Electrochemical Retrograde Amnesia'. CERA. A combination of certain drugs and electroconvulsive shock. When done properly, nearly all memory of persons and events is eradicated. Motor skills, speech, and so on, are unaffected, or nearly so. The faculty of memory itself is not harmed. The subject retains other information, and once the drugs wear off resumes his normal accumulation of memories."

A clock ticked from somewhere in the room.

"You did say *medical* profession."

"Like everyone else, Robert, the profession serves the Corporation. Usually this means treating illness. In rare cases, it might mean rendering someone harmless. Or making an example of him." He looked away, his voice growing harsh. "I'm not here to debate it. These are the facts. You're going to have to face them."

"But–*why?*" Agnes blurted.

"An excellent question. Was Robert a danger? Did he commit some intolerable offense? The irony of the punishment is that the victim no longer remembers his crime."

Robert got up and walked to the glass wall. These were the answers he had wanted. Some of them. But he looked out at the bright yard where they had walked just a short time ago, and felt nothing.

No. That wasn't right. He felt numb.

"All right. All right. There's nothing else to explain it. But tell me, what do you know about this . . . this punishment, if that's what it is. Is it reversible?"

"No. Your memories were not suppressed. They were destroyed."

He stood very still. This had never occurred to him. That his past wasn't hidden. It was lost. Forever. As though it had never existed.

He swallowed.

"What about these attacks? I've had two of them now."
"A side effect. Probably residual damage from the electroshock."
Electroshock. Damage.
He stared outside.
"Is there a way to prevent them?"
"You mean medically? With a drug? I'm afraid not. We have no drugs for this."
"There's *nothing* you can do?"
Stevens walked to a chair and sat down, leaning forward on knees spread apart, bulky shoulders hunched, the long fingers drooping and the hard eyes looking up from the under the great, rounded forehead.
"Listen to me. What you call an 'attack' develops over time. Most people get over daily irritations and get on with living, but the after-effects of CERA are like a short circuit. You react in a way that sets the stage for more frustration, more anger. A vicious cycle that feeds on itself until there's a breakdown. A seizure. This is considered useful in some circles. Incapacitation. But I believe you can learn to control it. I believe you can train yourself to break the cycle."
"And if I can't?"
"The seizures are dangerous. We don't know why, but there is an acute drop in blood pressure. I'm going to prepare a kit with a few syringes of epinephrine. I'll show Agnes how to do the injection. But you have to remember, this is a last resort. The injection itself could kill you."
"Robert . . . *my God!* How can you *listen* to this?"
He had forgotten her. Her face was pale, her eyes terrified, and he tried to answer gently: "Because it seems to be the truth."
To Stevens: "Why? Do you have any idea why?"
"If I did, Robert, would you really want to know?"
"Yes. I would. Even if the truth is worse than I want to think."
"I wish I could help you, Robert. Believe me."

————————————

An hour later, Agnes left the doctor's house and took the silent country lane on foot, her body swallowed in a huge coat Robert insisted she wear.
Her mind was a bruise.
A pale sun followed, but soon disappeared behind a heavy wall of darkening cloud, the air cold and lifeless. Not a bird fluttered. She was far from the City, far from anything she knew, but she kept walking, until the ache in her legs and freezing numbness in her hands and feet forced a halt.
She could not see ahead. The road wound through dense, naked trees, revealing nothing. Small flakes drifted around her, and she stood listening to silence, then to quiet sounds that came to her. A dog barking faintly in the distance. Snow falling on dry leaves. The sound of her own breathing.

Robert was waiting when she arrived back at the house, tried to speak as he took her coat, but she shook her head and walked past him to her room.

In the evening, as the three sat to dinner together, snow fell thickly through cones of light slanting from electric fixtures outside.

She ate little. The soft flakes drifting to earth were like a soothing hand to her brow, and her thoughts drifted back to a night like this when she was a child, ten years old, before the fire. It had snowed all that day, and her father had stayed in town. Her mother had sent the maid and cook home early, and it was just the two of them drinking hot cocoa together in the living room after a simple meal, and she had played the big grand piano for her mother, surprising her with a difficult new piece she had learned, and her mother had listened, rapt, eyes shining . . .

She felt the unfamiliar sting in her own eyes, and came to herself as snow swept across the yard in a sudden gust of wind.

Robert was talking.

"How long have you lived here, Paul?"

"Let's see. A little over fifteen years, I think. We claimed the property and found the architect shortly after we were married, but we had to wait before we could build."

"Why was that?"

"Well, it was a big step, building our own home. Not something people did every day. But we fell in love with the plans and the property, and it was what we both wanted. So we waited. When the time was right, and we could afford it, we had it built. It was a stretch, but we both worked."

"You picked a good location."

"I know. It was away from the City without being off in the wilds. Things were still unsettled back then. The epidemics were still quite recent. But Mary felt safe here."

Agnes winced.

"Was she your wife?"

"That's right. When we got the land . . . well, it was supposed to be the place where we would settle, raise a family, and grow old together. I suppose that's a luxury. That I should be grateful for the time we had. And I am."

"What happened?" It was a whisper. She was almost afraid to ask.

He watched outside a moment. "The last epidemic flared up. I tried to help her. But I couldn't get the drugs I needed. I just couldn't get them . . ."

"I'm sorry."

"No. No need. It was a long time ago."

"And you never remarried."

"Never wanted to. I had plenty to keep me busy, and I wasn't interested in anyone else." He smiled. "I hope you're not feeling sorry for me."

"Well, no . . ." She tried to smile back. "But it *is* sad."

"No. It's just life."

She fell silent, watching snow fly, wondering whether she would ever know that kind of acceptance. Or wanted to.

———————————

It snowed into the following day, but tapered off in the afternoon, and Robert and the doctor split firewood on a stump behind the house at the edge of the yard, the air heavy and cold under a dull gray sky, earth and trees muffled in a thick white blanket, and as Stevens took a turn, Robert offered that it must have been devastating to lose his wife so soon after building their home.

The axe careened off the edge of a log.

"Yes. It was." The doctor swung again, and the log split cleanly in two.

"The last epidemic. Cargo Flu. It was treatable, wasn't it? Isn't that what you told me?"

"Yes." The doctor swung. The axe arced over his head. *Thunk.* A log split.

"And the treatment wasn't difficult."

"Not particularly."

Thunk. Thunk.

"But the drugs were impossible to get? Even in a hospital?"

Thwack.

This log had a knot. It had split part way and held, and Stevens had swung with such force that he was unable to dislodge the axe.

Robert tried as well. "We'll need a wedge."

They walked to the tool shed, where the doctor dug out wedges and a short-handled sledge. As they carried these back, he explained.

"There was very little left, you understand. Just a reserve. So getting the drugs was a matter of who you were. And I wasn't anybody."

"Weren't you running Emergency Medicine?"

"I still wasn't anybody."

"So what did you do?"

The doctor propped up the log with the axe handle, placed a wedge in the open split, and tapped at the wedge with the hammer until the axe came loose.

"I tried to steal them."

He swung harder. The hammer hit with a dull *clang,* and the wedge bit deeper, the log creaking with the strain.

"I bribed a dispensary pharmacist for the combination to his drug locker. He took the money and turned me in."

One more swing and the log gave way with a *crack,* and the doctor was able to part it with his hands.

He stood up.

"It was a stupid thing to do. I was held for days. The Chief of Medicine put in a word with someone, and they let me go with a warning. But by then it was too late. Mary had died. Alone. In quarantine."

He tossed the pieces onto the pile.

"If you don't mind, it's a painful subject."

"Of course, Paul. I'm sorry."
But Stevens was looking past him, and Robert turned.
A lone figure had appeared by one corner of the house.
Stevens waved, and the figure walked toward them, a young man with a lean, wiry build, hair unkempt, clothing threadbare, shoes laced with frayed cord, and alert gray eyes in a boyish face.
"Max," greeted the doctor. "This is Robert Larsen. Robert—Maximillian Wyse."
A bare hand emerged from a coat pocket. Robert took off his gloves and shook it.
"Pleased to meet you, Mr. Wyse."
"Max. Sorry, Doc. Didn't mean to interrupt. I'll come back another time."
"Nonsense. Join us for coffee. I'm cold."
The young man glanced at Robert, hesitating.
"Well, okay. Coffee would sure hit the spot."
They put away the tools and went inside to the smell of a freshly brewing pot.
"Now that's a neat trick, Doc!" The young man laughed, stamping snow from his shoes. "All you have to do is think about it, and the coffee boils itself? Or have you found a–"
At that moment Agnes appeared, her figure lost in a man's shirt much too large for her, pale hair tied up loose, eyes clear, intelligent, questioning.
"Holy sh–" The young man stammered. "I'm sorry! I almost embarrassed myself."
Stevens pushed past him, chuckling.
"Oh, I'm sure you'll find other opportunities."
The four sat by a window in the kitchen and drank coffee from steaming mugs, and the young man talked about life as an exile outside the City, trying too obviously not to stare at Agnes, while Robert studied him, wondering how he managed to survive.

That night, in his own apartment, long after midnight, Robert concentrated on breathing. On taking slow, even breaths. On the position of his body. On the sliver of light high on a wall from a streetlamp outside.
On not thinking.
Eventually, he fell asleep.

17

Max Wyse sat comfortably with a glass of whiskey, watching the frozen yard fall into darkness.

He had always liked the doctor's home. The houses he knew were shelter, wooden boxes with windows cut out like portholes in walls erected as barriers against the world outside, rooms wedged unceremoniously together, and the whole wrapped up in clapboard, or sometimes crumbling brick. He had never particularly liked them, had never really thought about liking a building, until he had seen the way the outdoors could flow into and complete something that became more than shelter, more than a home. Something that made him feel more than an exile.

He had first met Stevens a year ago.

It was autumn. He had been sent to question a farmer who claimed a horse had been stolen and was hiking a familiar trail through a back wood. It was an easy trail, and he had strolled along captivated by clouds of glowing yellows and fiery reds, leaves blazing against a clear afternoon sky and the gold and green of fields and pastures.

Then he was on the ground, writhing in pain.

An older man ran up. Carefully setting down a rifle, the man squatted by him, pulling away his hands clutched at his side, peeling back the torn shirt. Sure fingers probed until Max yelled out as a sharper pain hit his side.

The man sat back, wiping his hands on a handkerchief.

"Well, there's a fractured rib. But I don't think there's anything more serious."

"*Shit!* You must be from the *City!* Can't you tell a man from a deer?"

A brief smile flickered.

"Young man, if I had thought you were a deer, we wouldn't be having this conversation. You came through the trees at exactly the wrong instant." He got to his feet. "But consider yourself lucky. You were shot by a doctor. Here, can you stand? You'd better come with me. I need to take care of this."

"Like hell."

He stood up holding his side, but the sight of his bloodied hands and blood-soaked shirt changed his mind. The only 'doctors' he knew were a pair of women whose practice was mainly delivering calves and colts.

They walked to a car parked by a paved road, then drove to the house in the trees, where the doctor cleaned and dressed the wound, and gave him something for the pain.

He fell asleep, and woke after sundown.

Everyone Max knew kept the City at a wary distance–even if a few seemed always to have a little smuggling going on. Rarely did anyone ever actually go there. They didn't feel welcome. And City people always seemed to be looking over their shoulders.

But when he sat down to dinner with Stevens that evening, it was like waking from a troubling dream, to find reassurance again in familiar surroundings. He could not explain it. But he felt at home.

He stayed the night, sleeping soundly, and woke early, his mind clear and calm despite the ache in his side. The doctor made breakfast, and he had walked home, inventing a story to cover where he'd been, should anyone ask.

From time to time he came back, slipping away when he was sure no one noticed. Until today, he had always found the doctor alone. And he had always been welcome.

Stevens returned from driving Robert and Agnes to the City, and the two had a cold meal, smoked cigars, drank whiskey, and played chess.

The doctor mentioned, apparently in passing, that Robert and Agnes might have to go into exile.

"Exile!" Max sat back, astonished. "Why, on earth?"

Stevens was studying the chessboard.

"Well, Agnes may be a little too independent to suit the tastes of her employer, but I suspect her only real crime is being involved with Robert."

"So what's *his* crime?"

"I would venture to say he was once a man of responsibility, but no longer trusted. It must have been a serious business. His memory was destroyed." Stevens fingered a bishop. "Possibly as a warning to others. All very legal, I'm sure, with a trial, and evidence. But he has no memory of it."

"Jesus! That's a pretty grisly way to deal with someone you don't trust. Why not just kill him?"

The old man sat back, laughing.

"Sometimes you astound me! Just *kill* him, you say?"

"Hell, what's the difference? Someone gets out of line, you fire him and he starves. You don't trust someone, you wipe out his mind. Christ, why not just shoot people? Wouldn't that be easier?"

"Young man, just how long do you think we'd last if we started killing people who dissatisfy us? With all due respect, I don't think you understand much about organization."

"Well, we manage to keep our *own* community pretty well organized!"

"Hmpf. You have, what, a few hundred people tending their farms and minding their own business. If that many. We have thousands who have to be fed, sheltered, and kept safe. And they live pretty damned well. They're busy, productive, and we haven't seen a case of Flu in years. Have you thought about the kind of organization that takes?"

"Look, Paul, I'm not stupid. But I'd like to know what the difference is between killing someone you don't like, and taking his mind from him."

"We don't do either arbitrarily. We don't punish people just because we don't like them."

"No?"

"Apart from occasional abuses that occur under any system– yours as well, if half of what you say about Jack Ryan is true—we punish according to rules. And to ensure that everyone understands the rules are to be taken seriously. If you like the word, we act according to law."

"According to *your* law."

"Well, of course. Whose law should we use?"

"Look, I'll admit Jack can be a horse's ass. But he still has to face everyone. Maybe that's our strength. Maybe that's more important than organization."

"Oh, don't be ludicrous! You might be too young to remember, but civilization once hung by a thread. Organization is what saved us. *All* of us, you included. It was not a job for the faint-hearted. And maybe there was a better way. But if there was, no one came forward with it. We did what we had to. As, I'm sure, you do."

It was not the first time they had argued about this. He resented the doctor's idea of organization, and resented not being able to explain why.

"Yeah, well, talk about your friends."

"Do you think you can you help?"

He shrugged.

"What can I tell Jack? Or anyone else? Why was Robert Larsen punished like that? And if this girl's in trouble just for sleeping with him, what's going to happen to anyone who *hides* him?"

"Why should anyone know?"

"Come on, Doc."

"Well, I suppose I was hoping you could think of something."

"Yeah, well, you haven't given me much to go on."

The doctor leaned over the board again. "There isn't much I can say."

Max considered the old man.

"What about you?"

"What about me?"

"What's your interest in Robert Larsen? I gather you haven't known him long."

"He's a friend," Stevens muttered, moving his bishop. "I don't know what else to tell you."

"You know, it feels like you're lying. And that's not a nice way to treat this friend."

"It's for your own good."

"Yeah, I was afraid of something like that. Look, I'd like to help. They seemed decent enough. But I have a responsibility to people who trust my word. Not to mention what Jack could do to me."

"I suppose you're right."

They played on in silence, until Max tipped his king – "I'm done" – and sat back, covering his glass when Stevens offered the bottle.

"Say, Doc. Here's something you might be interested in. Something I got from Jack."

"Oh?"

"Yeah. Believe it or not, he was approached by the Corporation. Someone high up. With a business proposition."

"That *is* a little unusual." The doctor stretched and yawned.

"This one sure is. They want him to sell a drug."

"A *what?*" Stevens snapped.

"Well, a drug. That's what he said. And apparently illegal, according to *your* law. They want him to sell it to their own workers."

"No! Who was the contact?"

"Ah, that I don't know."

"What did he say about the drug?"

"Well, not much, really. He was so proud of himself he couldn't resist letting on. But either they didn't tell him much, or else they put a scare into him. Why? Any idea what it is?"

"The damned fool! He's playing with fire."

"Why, Doc? What's going on?"

But Stevens seemed to forget him, staring at something only he could see.

"Hey, come on, Doc! This is *Jack* we're talking about. I need to know."

The old man looked at him. "I want something from you first. I want the name of Ryan's contact."

"How in hell am I supposed to get that? How do we even know he gave the right name?"

"Max, you're going to have much bigger challenges ahead. I hope you're up to it. Find out something, the contact's position, the name of the drug. Anything."

"Look, Doc, Jack isn't going to—"

"Forget that! What I know came at a high price. I want this from you."

18

When Max was a boy, fifteen years before, he had stumbled into the settlement south of the City, where scattered exiles were just learning to live off the land. They had taken him in. And this had probably saved his life.

Survival was a struggle in those days, even with a farm, and the settlers kept mostly to themselves. But not completely. Everyone seemed to know the old eccentric living off by himself in a small shack hidden away in the trees by a long grassy field. Gray-haired and close-mouthed, he went by the name of Aubrey, and any other name he might have had had long since been forgotten.

But that didn't matter. Because Aubrey was famous.

Aubrey owned an airplane. It was a small red biplane, polished and fast, with a clear bubble canopy that held just him. No one knew where he found the gasoline to run it, and he was forever working on it. But he kept it immaculate, and it ran like a top.

What mattered was aerobatics.

This was a serious business. And Aubrey was a serious man. Not one to blast off and do whatever popped into his head. He would work out a routine up high, practicing methodically, sometimes for weeks, until he was absolutely certain of what he was doing.

Then, on a Sunday afternoon, people would gather around his field and watch him put on a show down close to the ground, a breathtaking display of speed and precision, and Max would never forget the convulsion in his chest as that red projectile thundered past just yards away, wheels in the air, Aubrey's head a few feet from the ground, or the hollow rumble as the plane rolled under the pines surrounding his makeshift hangar, or the pungent fumes drifting through sudden quiet after the engine sputtered to a stop. People would crowd around, clapping and shaking their heads at this crazy old man who climbed down from the cockpit grinning like he was sixteen, and children would swarm to lay hands on that marvelous machine that had touched the sky.

Years later, Max could still feel the skin slick and warm under his own fingers.

One sweltering summer's day toward the end of his boyhood, as a young Max Wyse walked patrol with Jack Ryan, the familiar drone of the airplane followed them from high over the fields. Aubrey had been working on a new maneuver, where he would put the plane into a vertical climb, straight up, holding it until it ran out of speed and fell back, tail-first. As it fell, it would flip around and point nose down, plummeting until he pulled it out of the dive.

The distant engine snarled, and they stopped to watch Aubrey round out the bottom of a big, lazy loop, then rocket straight up. There was something about that red airplane rising effortlessly through a clear summer sky, sunlight glinting from its wings. It was a symbol, a metaphor for something Max could not name, but that mattered to him almost desperately, and he stood straight, in admiration and in gratitude. He wanted to salute the man.

Even Jack Ryan watched in silence.

The plane slowed, reaching the top of its climb, then paused, seeming to float, twisting slowly. Then it slid back and flipped around. But something didn't look quite right. It was dropping at an odd, sloppy angle, the wheels pointing a bit up, the canopy a bit down, and Aubrey first pulled the nose down through the vertical, then continued pulling up as the plane dove faster, leveling out near the ground and disappearing behind a distant rise in the fields, the engine screaming.

Then a low *crump,* and in the distance a thick black column billowed upward.

Time stopped. Max stood rooted in place, watching the rising black cloud, his eyes refusing to accept what he had just seen ripped from his life.

Ryan spat.

"Well, that's that. I knew he'd get it sooner or later. Let's go see what's left."

He choked suddenly with a murderous fury. He was sick, sick to death of Jack Ryan and his gutter mind and his carnal piggishness. But he could only grit his teeth against the ache deep in his throat.

He started walking.

It was hot, slow work, trudging through soft furrows of ploughed earth, and Ryan, who had grown considerably overweight over the years, lagged farther and farther behind.

At the edge of a big pasture, Max waited while Ryan caught up.

Oily black smoke swirled from the crumpled airplane burning maybe fifty yards away. And there was something else. The field was brown with dry grass, but a large black circle extended outward from the wreckage. He realized what he was seeing. The grass was afire, the edge of the circle a low ring of orange flame nearly invisible in the sun.

He sprinted across the field, tearing off his shirt and beating at the flames. But the fire was spreading. There were farmhouses nearby, and everything was bone dry.

Ryan just stood and watched, but Max ran until his feet bled, shouting and hammering on doors. The fire eventually burned out on its own, but not before it caught and damaged the roof of a barn. This was a serious loss, even if no one was hurt, and he complained about it later, loudly and bitterly, not least of all because of Ryan's infuriating uselessness. Although he was careful to say nothing about that.

"We were lucky this time! It could've killed someone!"

Ryan was unimpressed.

"It was a freak accident. What can you do about it?"

"What about storing water on a cart or something, to put out fires? We could do that if we had better roads. What about telephones?"

Ryan erupted with a howl of laughter, stinging Max into silence.

"Yeah? And who's gonna to do it? Who's gonna grade roads? These rugged individualists? You think they'll leave their precious fields to work on roads? And how're we supposed to get telephones?" Ryan spat, loudly and contemptuously. "Shit, Max. Grow up."

The next summer, lightning struck and burned another barn, this time to the ground, trapping and killing a few animals inside while the family fought to keep the flames from the house. For weeks afterward, Max roved on his own until he found a large plastic tank abandoned in a warehouse near the City. Then he persuaded a farmer to donate a rusty trailer that could be pulled by horse.

They kept the tank on the trailer, filled with as much water as one horse could pull, and when the next fire broke out—in someone's kitchen—they got the trailer there with enough people to form a bucket brigade and save the house.

Ryan was nothing if not shrewd, and took credit for it, managing at the same time to avoid doing anything more. But he was in charge. Max was just the youngest member of his gang.

At least they had accomplished something. And it wasn't a bad life. The exiles paid for security, Ryan and his boys patrolled and visited and poked their noses everywhere around the community, and that was usually all that was needed to prevent anyone who might be tempted from helping himself to someone else's tools, food, or daughters. Ryan kept his gang small, and they were able to live comfortably, very comfortably, on the fees they collected.

Ryan called it 'taxes'. Some people, with darker memories, called it 'protection money'.

What was known around the exile community as the 'main road' was an old farm path of dirt and ruts and grassy mounds, often barely passable by foot, much less a hay-cart, after a hard rain. But it cut a convenient east-west line across the entire settlement. South of it stretched gently rolling hills and decent farmland. To the north, dense woods alternated for miles with meadows and brushy marshland, eventually running up against acres of low, abandoned buildings, the sprawling wrecks of industry just outside the City.

The community's eastern boundary was generally held to be a vacant two-story frame house situated on the south side of the road, vacant because the land around it was too rocky to farm. Sometimes used when people had need to meet, the house was well-constructed, the windows intact and the roofline straight, but the yard was a thicket of brambles, and in spring a riot of wildflowers.

Some miles farther east, the road eventually disappeared, giving way to broad stands of young pine and old hardwood, followed by many more miles of flat, open country, and eventually the sea.

West of the house, trails branched off the road north and south, leading through trees and fields to farms and ranches. In a wooded area about five miles west of the house was a big clearing by the road, where stood the 'pub'. This was a long, low structure, bare of paint, that might once have been a feed store. It had a big room used as a dining area, with a bar built out at one end, small rooms added in the back for living space, and a stable in the clearing behind.

The owner of the pub was a middle-aged man, burly and quiet, who had lost his wife to an early outbreak of Flu. But he had a son, and together they had escaped the madness and ended up here. Two strong backs and a mastery of the art of brewing beer had been the start of a business, a foothold on survival. They had built on that foothold with a kitchen run on a wood-fired grill, then branched out into wine-making, and by the end of their first year, as the settlers were becoming a community, the pub was becoming an institution.

About a mile or so west of the pub was an actual paved road. Northward, it led to the City, and exiles called it the North Road. But turning left, the blacktop led south and west through wild country. No one went there. Rumor had it that a few days' journey on horseback would lead to a built-up town, or maybe a whole city, with not a soul left living. Emptied long ago, it was said, by Cargo Flu.

Sitting around a table at the pub, a few nights after his talk with Stevens, drinking warm beer with Jack Ryan and the gang, Max screwed up his nerve.

"Jack, a couple weeks ago you said you were talking with the Corporation. With some big shot. About a business deal."

Ryan took a long pull at his beer, wiping his mouth with the back of his hand.

"Yeah, what about it?"

"I don't like it."

"Well who the hell asked you?"

"You can't trust them, Jack. You know that."

"Yeah? When did you get to be such an expert on the Corporation?"

"I'm not. But neither are you."

"Butt out. It's none of your business."

"Come on! When you expose us like that?"

Ryan's upper lip curled in a characteristic sneer.

"*You're* not in any danger."

"If you're dealing with them, they're learning about us. You don't think that's dangerous?"

"You think I spill my guts? You think I'm stupid?"

"How do *we* know what you're telling them? You've been keeping the whole thing a big secret!"

By the looks on most of the other faces, this was true.

"What about it?" Ryan turned on them. "What about it? Anyone *else* here scared?" No one answered, and he thumped the table. "*Well?*"

"Come on, Jack," Max pressed. "It's one thing to do a little business with a few nobodies in the City. Lots of people do. But if we found anyone else making secret deals with Corporate honchos, you can bet we'd put a stop to it. *You'd* put a stop to it. Damn, Jack, don't you think you owe us an explanation?"

No one spoke. They might not be too eager to challenge Jack Ryan, but the Corporation was nothing to fool around with, either.

"All right, big man." Ryan lounged back, watching him through hooded eyes. "I'll tell you what's going on. *Nothing.* A big, fat, nothing."

"After all the big talk? That's hard to believe."

"Well, believe it. You think I'm stupid? I had a meeting with some vice president. He said he has a drug he wants the peons to use. Makes 'em real horny when they take it, but the next day they're nice and calm and do what they're told. I told him we could use some of that around here." He smirked, and a couple of the boys sniggered. "But you get messed up. Absentminded. A little stupid. Keeps the peons from plotting conspiracies."

"So what does he want with us?"

"This guy's pretty sharp. He wants them to use it, but he doesn't want them to know that. So it's going to be illegal. He wants someone from outside to sell it, so they have to smuggle it in. He thinks that'll make it irresistible. And you know what? He's probably right."

One of the brighter lads spoke up.

"Yeah, well, if it's illegal, how do we sell it and not get caught? Are the cops gonna be in on it?"

"Nah. They don't know about this." He picked up his beer, leering at Max. "I'm a little smarter'n you give me credit for, big man. I asked him that very question. I told him I wanted assurances."

"Okay, okay. Maybe you handled it all right. But you can't just leave us in the dark like that."

"Fuck off."

For days afterward, Max walked his patrols and stayed away from the doctor's. But one frozen evening, about a week later, he was waiting in the shadows by the house when Stevens returned from the City.

"Max! Where have you been?"

"Not so loud, Doc." He shivered, glancing at the empty lane. "Let's just get inside."

Stevens unlocked the door and led the way to the kitchen, switched on a light, opened a cupboard, and pulled down a bottle.

"Drink?"

Without waiting for a reply, he put a little ice into two glasses and poured.

"Well, I managed to get some information. But I'm really on Jack's shit-list now."

Stevens handed him a glass. "Sorry to hear it."

They walked into the dark living room and stood by the glass wall, watching the line of trees across the yard fade into night.

A clock ticked from somewhere, the sound disquieting. A sense of aloneness had been growing in him, since the confrontation with Jack. Aloneness, and uncertainty.

The doctor seemed to sense it.

"Times are changing, my boy," he murmured.

"Changing how?"

"Young executives. A new generation. Ambitious, gunning for the top. It's almost certainly happening in other cities as well."

"And we're going to get caught in the middle."

"Possibly . . . You know, Max, it's human nature to seek the light. But it's also human nature to give in to darkness. That's why the world needs leaders."

"I'm sure as hell no leader, Paul. If that's what you're thinking."

"Time will tell. What have you found out?"

He hesitated. The world outside was gone now, just a velvet hint of indigo above black treetops. Dim, homely light from some hallway crept into the corners of the room, and the night outside the glass seemed flat, unreal. Even the City seemed unreal.

But the clock continued its steady tick . . . tick . . . tick . . .

"According to Jack, the drug is an aphrodisiac. But it also affects you mentally. You're not as sharp, or you can't remember things, something like that. It's supposed to keep people in line. He says the Corporation wants it smuggled in, so no one knows where it's really coming from. I couldn't get any names."

Stevens was quiet, absently swirling his glass.

Max watched him. "Does it mean anything?"

The old man slowly nodded.

"It fits. If it's what I think it is. A drug called *rope*. And the scheme would be the brainchild of someone I know quite well. A certain Mr. Richard Martin. One of the ambitious young executives."

"And you think this guy met with Jack? Maybe Jack didn't make such a good impression. It hasn't gone anywhere."

"Maybe not." Stevens lifted his glass, considered it a moment, then finished it off. "I hope you don't have an early day tomorrow. There are things you need to know. But I'm hungry. Let's eat first. Then we'll talk."

19

The City was a sea of buildings. Many were deserted, long abandoned to slow decay. But some were well maintained, clean, and busy.

In what was once the financial district, huge office towers crowded the main avenue, with one exception. Behind a broad plaza and reflecting pool stood a solitary edifice of concrete and glass. Not the tallest, but the most prominent, this building was floodlit at night while much of the City remained dark, without power, and it gleamed from afar across black wilderness like a beacon marking an oasis of civilization.

This was the Corporation's headquarters.

High along its western face was a boardroom, with a long mahogany table, its edges worn smooth by years of meetings, its lustrous expanse kept polished by two silent custodians with starched uniforms and meticulously clean hands, who never shared the room with company executives.

About two years before, as the sky outside this room turned a sullen red and the rest of the building emptied for the day, Doctor Paul Stevens stood by these windows, looking out over the City.

Boardroom meetings went with the job, and Stevens had stood here many times since reaching the position of Vice President, then Senior Vice President, for Medical Services. He never tired of the view.

Other executives were gathering as well, and waiters in white jackets served coffee and tea, the buzz of conversation growing a little noisier with each new arrival. Stevens turned from the windows when the conversation suddenly quieted.

The last arrival was a stocky man, completely bald, in pressed slacks and a tailored shirt open at the collar, one thick wrist wrapped with a heavy gold watch.

Two women followed. One, blue-eyed and steel-haired, dismissed the waiters and sat down in a leather chair by the head of the table. The other, middle-aged and silent, sat across from her with a pad of paper.

James Dornan, founder, chief executive, and soul of the Corporation, took his seat between the two women.

The rest sat down.

Dornan joked quietly with a few people nearest him. Then, in a familiar ritual, he leaned back and surveyed the length of the room. The others waited. No one spoke. There was no more frivolity. Each person accepted the absolute seriousness of the business at hand. Whatever it was.

Dornan slapped the old wood.

"Okay. Let's get on with it."

The silent woman began writing.

Robert Larsen, Vice President for Security, got to his feet.

"As you all know, I requested this meeting. Certain of my people believe they've identified a threat. I want you all to hear this, but bear in mind that it's preliminary. It's not our official view, as yet. Personally, I'm not convinced."

"If you're not convinced," grumbled Richard Martin, Vice President for Logistics, "then why don't you have your people finish the job before wasting *our* time with it?"

"Because to finish the job we are going to tread some dangerous ground, and I want everyone in this room to be fully informed."

Steven approved. It showed a healthy respect for the risks. He knew there were some in this room, like Martin, who would view it as a sign of weakness, but Robert Larsen was a little different from the others, serious, diligent, loyal to the Corporation, dedicated to the City, and Stevens took an interest in him. He did not think it far-fetched the man might one day make a credible chief executive, after Dornan stepped down.

"Some of you may know Dan Carter, my director of intelligence. I've asked him here to explain."

Larsen resumed his seat.

The small man beside him stood up and walked to the end of the table, opposite Dornan. He stood with fingertips pressed against the smooth wood, and with a hint of a smile.

"Mr. Martin. If you saw a gold bar lying on the ground, would you cross the street to pick it up?"

"Don't waste my time. Get to the point."

"The point, ladies and gentlemen, is that the world has not seen war in many years. The world is not prepared for war. Or so it seems."

The room was quiet. This was not a word anyone had expected to hear. It was not a word anyone had heard in a very long time.

Martin chuckled unpleasantly.

"Are you serious?"

"I am. Think of it this way. Suppose everyone kept his money in a certain bank. Suppose further that it became known this bank was unlocked and unguarded. It stands to reason that, sooner or later, someone would help himself to all that money. So if *your* money were in that bank, Mr. Martin, what would *you* do?"

Elizabeth White, Martin's boss, interrupted.

"Well, I for one would take care of my own money. Where are you going with this, Mr. Carter?"

Carter scanned the faces before him with a smug assurance that was irritating, offensive, and impossible to ignore.

"You've all heard the old saying that a good offense is often the best defense. This continent, what we know of it, is now ruled by a few intelligent, ambitious men and women. If they weren't a little more intelligent than the people around them, they wouldn't hold the positions they do. That bank would be a tempting prize. If it were taken, the victor would emerge that much stronger, and his rivals that much weaker."

"Well, Mr. Carter, I'm still confused. What's your point?"

"The point is this. Someone could decide to strike first, while the rest of us are defenseless, and so strike with impunity. Intelligent leaders will realize this, and the stronger, more successful ones will make it an absolute priority not to be second."

Dornan gazed down the length of the table.

"Is that so, Mr. Carter. Then you expect us to believe that war is inevitable."

"I do."

"Do you have any evidence?"

"Not directly."

"Yes or no?"

"We have detected patterns of activity suggesting military intent."

"Patterns of activity!" Martin threw up his hands. "Unbelievable. Larsen, you and your director of so-called intelligence are chasing shadows."

"We can't ignore this—"

Larsen had started to come to his feet, but stopped at a look from Dornan.

"Mr. Larsen. I appreciate that your technical people wanted to raise a flag. Noted. But the world is not run by technical people. And unless you have some pretty compelling evidence to the contrary, I don't believe any successful businessman would gamble his assets on a reckless military adventure." He shrugged. "The unsuccessful ones, I don't worry about."

Carter smiled faintly, looking like a patient teacher.

"All it takes is one who is not quite as successful as he thinks he ought to be. Or might be."

"I agree with Richard. You're wasting our time." Dornan began picking at his nails, usually a reliable sign a meeting was over.

But Stevens spoke up.

"I'm not so sure. I have a fair grasp of history, and I'm inclined to agree with Mr. Carter. If not with his manner of delivery."

Dornan looked up.

"Come off it, Doctor. Business is business. War is not good for business."

"War has made many a fortune, Jim."

"It's destroyed far more."

"That may be true, but beside the point. If just one firm thinks war will improve its situation, then it will do well to take advantage of everyone's lack of preparation. It therefore behooves us to prepare."

"Do you realize what you're saying?"

"I'm afraid I do. What could be a more effective defense than a preemptive strike against a neighbor who might harbor ambitions? And we have to consider who might come to that conclusion regarding us."

"Evidence?" Martin snapped his fingers. "This is pure speculation."

White replied, "Maybe so, Richard. But I think I'd like to know more before I dismiss it out of hand."

Stevens was convinced that Elizabeth White's rise to senior vice-president was due in no small part to her uncanny grasp of the mind of James Dornan. Some years before, after her husband had passed, rumors concerning these two had made the rounds. But White was a force in her own right, and Stevens was careful not to underestimate her.

Now Dornan shifted in his chair, looking annoyed.

"I think you're all missing the point. What you're really saying, Doctor, is that we have no choice but to go out and conquer as much as we can, as fast as we can, because someone else may be thinking along the same lines, and we have to stop them before they can stop us."

"That's entirely possible. But there are other possibilities as well."

"Such as?"

"Such as treaties and alliances."

"And how can you trust your allies?"

"It isn't easy. But it has been done."

Darkness had descended outside. Strings of lights glittered far below.

Larsen spoke.

"This is the point of the meeting. Right now, it *is* speculation, but too dangerous to ignore. So I've tasked my people with a military assessment of every habitable city that we know of. It will have to be done covertly, of course. We'll infiltrate exile communities near other cities and cultivate terminated employees. We'll infiltrate our local exiles, identify any foreign agents, and feed them misinformation, or possibly capture and interrogate them."

White's intake of breath was audible.

"That sounds like a dangerous business. Won't you tip our hand if one of your agents is caught?"

"We've considered that, and I think Pharmacology might have an answer."

Dornan glanced sideways at Stevens. "I might have known." He cleared his throat. "All right, Mr. Larsen. Is your assistant finished?

"Unless you have further questions for him."

"No. I've heard enough. You may go, Mr. Carter."

Curtly, Carter nodded, then left the room.

The door closed.

Dornan leaned back, fingers laced behind his head, gazing at the ceiling while the rest waited.

"I don't like what I'm hearing." He sat up, looking at White. "It's no way to run a business."

White turned to Larsen. "As I understand it, Robert, you in Security think war is inevitable because everyone is defenseless. Do I have that right?"

"Remember Dan's analogy. If you leave a bar of gold lying around, eventually someone will think about picking it up."

"I take it, Richard, you don't agree."

"Why take the risk of stealing someone's gold if you're coining your own? And why worry about anyone who isn't?"

"William? Thoughts?"

William Baird was Vice President for Commerce.

"In the long run, we'll make more 'gold' by trading than we could possibly acquire by looting. Bear in mind we trade what we're good at for what other firms are good at. The law of comparative advantage. We're better off having them to trade with. And they us."

"Robert?"

"You all know," Larsen began slowly, "that a certain amount of trade goes on with exiles. Unauthorized, of course. A black market. What you may not know is that Security is involved."

"Are you saying Security is in the black market? Would you care to explain that?"

Stevens had explained it to her before, several times. But she seemed to enjoy ignoring him.

"Because it's impossible to eradicate! And we need monitor it, for obvious reasons of public health."

"That much is true," Larsen agreed. "But it's also a source of intelligence. And we've learned recently that someone is buying up small arms. Any quantity they can get."

Martin shrugged. "A group of exiles."

"Unlikely. Exiles are generally armed already. And this buyer, whoever he is, seems to command unlimited funds."

White looked at Dornan, and Stevens caught his slight nod before she turned back to Larsen.

"Which brings us to your plan to infiltrate. Is that the right word?"

"It is."

"Tell me how you can be so sure your agents won't fall into unfriendly hands."

"I can't. But Pharmacology has several behavior-modifying drugs in development, and we think one could eliminate the risk that any of our people would break under interrogation."

"The word 'interrogation' might cover a lot of ground. I would imagine it includes torture."

"I'd be more concerned with other drugs. But Dr. Stevens assures me our technology is unique."

"That isn't what I meant. Do your agents understand what they are getting into? What they are risking, personally?"

"They will. When we select them."

Her mouth closed. She seemed to draw back a little, as though discovering a truck driver seated at her dinner party.

Dornan prodded. "So, Doctor?"

"So, in my view, we should use whatever advantage we have. Pharmacology is one area in which we are very much ahead. Consider that we manufacture our own antibiotics, our own analgesics. We even barter them. There is no sign yet that anyone else has developed this ability, or recovered it."

He paused, looking around the table.

"You will understand that what I'm about to tell you is confidential. Not to be repeated outside this room.

"Elizabeth, you are aware of a substance we refer to as *rope*. Mr. Martin has introduced it into parts of his organization."

"I am aware of it. I'm not so sure what I think of having my people turned into junkies."

"Well, if you keep firing them at the rate you have been, we'll end up with a hostile army in our own backyard. But let that go. I don't want to debate the merits of *rope*. I merely want to point out what we know how to do already.

"We have another program, which we call *wire*. It is related to *rope* in that both have the effect of rendering the user more tractable. Easier to manage. But *wire* is different. It concentrates attention, increases aggression, reduces sensitivity to pain. In small doses, it has demonstrated the ability to make a user extremely intent on his objective and unusually tolerant of discomfort. In higher doses, once we learn to control it, we expect the result to be a fanatical soldier who will not stop fighting until he is killed."

White blew out her cheeks and looked at Dornan.

"Are you aware of all this?"

"He sends me reports."

"I'll say this much." Martin chuckled. "*Rope* works like a charm. We tried it out on one of our delivery fleets. The drivers go to work, drive until we tell them to stop, then go home and–"

"Yes," Stevens interrupted. "It isn't finished, but I'm pleased with it so far."

"What's not finished about it?" asked Dornan.

"The memory component."

"Ah, right. You want to fuzz up their memories."

"It was Elizabeth's idea."

"You exaggerate, Doctor," she declared coldly.

"Only a little. Elizabeth asked if we could help with these dangerous attempts among workers to organize. As you know, we've had some success with memory. It's a promising approach. Assuming they take it after work, we want it to impair their memory of what happened during the day, but wear off enough by morning to let them be useful again."

Dornan tapped a neatly manicured finger on the dark wood.

"Better watch where you leave that stuff, Doctor. If I forget where I put my keys, I will be fanatically intent on having your balls cut off."

Obsequious laughter rippled around the conference table.

Stevens just shook his head.

"So. Mr. Larsen plans to hook his agents on this *wire* and hope they die before they talk."

"What I hope is that it doesn't come to that. But if it does, I don't think they'll talk."

"All right." Dornan pushed his chair back and stood up. "Security will plan this operation. But nothing goes forward without final authorization from me. Pharmacology will continue development, but I want to personally approve any use of these drugs beforehand, and I want a report on every study. When will your plans be ready, Mr. Larsen?"

"In about a month, I think."

"You have two weeks. Dorothy, I want a full review in two weeks."

The steel-haired woman inclined her head.

Dornan paused, tapping the table. "Any questions?"

Stevens suspected there were many, but no one asked.

———

They were in the living room, sitting in comfortable chairs in a circle of light, the rest of the room in shadow. Stevens paused to refill their glasses, and Max slowly picked up his drink.

"Jesus, Doc. You sure I should know all this?"

"You said it yourself. You're going to get caught in the middle. You should know what's going on."

"Yeah, but . . . what am I supposed to do about it?"

"I don't know. Just listen. I'm not finished." He settled in his chair and went on. "Eventually we succeeded with the memory component for *rope*. It was not an easy thing to accomplish, but in the end it worked better than we anticipated. It interfered mildly with the brain's ability to process the events of the day, because it was taken at night for the sexual enhancement and was in the bloodstream during sleep. We used it in a few situations where labor problems threatened to get out of hand. It worked quite well. But it was hard to make. Large batches were inconsistent, and we weren't able to deploy it widely."

"Christ. Couldn't you find a better way to deal with labor problems?"

"Do you have any idea what's at stake? Have you ever tried to reason with someone who has no rational basis for his demands?"

"Yeah, Doc, okay. Okay."

"Well, *wire* was another story. It worked, as far as increasing concentration and aggression went. But our test subjects would sleep just an hour a day, sometimes less. Their comprehension became erratic. After a few days of it, they were borderline psychotic."

"So, after all that, your drugs didn't work?"

"Technology never happens on schedule, Max. But it happens. Just listen.

"Robert's plans weren't ready in two months, let alone two weeks. He had only sketchy information on exiles, mainly your community, and it wasn't much to go on. So he decided to start small by placing a few agents nearby, without *wire,* to learn enough to place others farther out, close to other cities.

"It was a reasonable plan. But Jim didn't have Robert's patience. And you could see Carter's theory growing on him. It's not at all hard to imagine what might tempt another firm. We have very productive agricultural areas north of the City. We have the hydroelectric plant. We have industrial shops and machine tools, fleets of trucks and cars, and enough fuel in storage to last many years.

"So, when results didn't happen quickly enough, he reorganized. He put Elizabeth in charge of Medical Services, and I was sent back to the lab to personally direct the work on *rope* and *wire.*"

"Elizabeth White? What did she know about medicine?"

"Not a damned thing."

"Then why put her in charge?"

"Because I'm one of those 'technical people' who can not be trusted to run the world. You see, people like Jim Dornan take one thing in life seriously. *Power.* Of course, they deny it. They don't like the word."

Max laughed, feeling oddly relieved.

"Of course not! That would give away the game!"

"Listen to me, Max. This is important, and you'd better understand it. Someone like James Dornan spends his entire career in one large organization or another. For him, the taste of power is the taste of freedom. Of autonomy. Of control over his own destiny. And that's what matters."

"Oh, come on! There must be other ways to control your destiny."

"Not really. In this world there is only one way to make life bearable, let alone enjoyable. *Organization.* It's how we build specialized knowledge and specialized skills. It's how we get economies of scale. It's why I have electric power, running water, fresh food, and can drive to the City whenever I like."

"And we don't even have a decent road. Yeah, okay, I think I get it."

"Well, when you work in an organization, either you are making the decisions, or someone is making them for you. It's really that simple."

"So one guy has freedom, and everyone else is his slave?"

"Everyone else gets to make a few decisions within the limits of their authority, then jockeys for more power, more autonomy. Unless they don't care. And a great many don't, which is fortunate, because every organization needs workers. Technical people. We can't all be in charge."

"Maybe that's your labor problem, Doc. You don't think they care about freedom."

Stevens chuckled.

"Very clever. Maybe you'll be a leader after all."

"Don't bet on it."

"Well, Bill Baird was put in charge of Security. But Bill was too cautious. He didn't realize the wind had changed. He held Robert back, and that was exactly the wrong thing to do. So Jim moved Security under Richard Martin, and that was the beginning of the end, for Robert. You can't imagine what it was like for him, working for Martin."

"Sounds like Martin was after Dornan's job. I suppose Robert was competition."

"Right. But the competition was over. Martin had won that battle. But winning wasn't enough. He wanted Robert beaten, humiliated, destroyed somehow. It was like a sex urge. I could never understand it, but he was relentless about it. Of course, Robert was no fan of Martin's, but he did his damnedest to stay professional and do his job. But I suppose it was just a matter of time."

"Why? What happened?"

"I wish I knew. I was out of touch with everything but *rope* and *wire*. Robert would drop by from time to time. He told me what he could. He said Martin had changed his tune about Carter's theory of war, and was now supporting it.

"Martin is a shrewd operator. Very shrewd. People underestimate him. He's managed to work himself into every plan for defense. Logistics and Security have become our *de facto* War Department. They've even cleared tracts of land outside the City for military training. Maybe you've seen it. They don't try to hide it. I know it sounds crazy, but I really think Martin is advertising, provoking, trying to ensure the threat is real, trying to justify his new empire. Where a prudent man like Bill Baird might see a foolish risk, Martin sees opportunity. No matter what happens in the end, victory or standoff, it'll be good for Richard Martin. Probably land him the top job when the time comes. People like that never expect to be hurt by the forces they unleash. And the smart ones are usually right.

"Well, *wire* was still not ready, and we didn't know when it would be. So they went ahead without it. Agents were inserted. Analysts collected data. They mapped communities, like yours, documented leadership structures, opened files on key people. They probably know more about Jack Ryan than you do.

"They turned out a monthly report and distributed it to senior management. I let Robert read my copy. He told me some of the findings were being altered. He thought Martin and his staff were massaging the intelligence for their own ends. But there was nothing he could do."

Stevens paused, and lowered his voice.

"Looking back on it, I'm convinced Robert was planning an escape. I don't have a shred of evidence, mind you. He never said anything. Not to me. But I could tell there was something on his mind. And by this time he knew a lot about exiles. I wouldn't be at all surprised if he had made contacts of his own, outside.

"Well, one day he just disappeared. Vanished. I called, left messages, stopped by his office. I was worried, because I didn't think he'd actually go without letting me know. I asked Elizabeth if she had seen him, and she told me he'd been arrested. Told me to keep my nose out of it."

"Arrested! Holy Christ! What'd you do?"

Stevens got up. He walked to the glass wall. A pair of eyes glowed from somewhere in the trees.

"Nothing."

"*Nothing?*"

"I tried to see Jim. But I couldn't get in. I asked my staff what they knew. The question terrified them, but I don't think they actually knew anything. Eventually, though, I learned the truth. Robert was tried and convicted for espionage. Then his memory was destroyed."

He turned to face Max, his back against the glass.

"At first I thought it was like losing Mary. I tried to think that. But I had fought the disease that took her, and I was helping the people who destroyed him. So . . . I retired."

"That's *it*? You *retired?*"

"That's it."

"I don't believe it."

"No? Then tell me, what would *you* have done?"

"How in Christ would I know? I wasn't there!"

"You know all you need to. You know as much as I do."

"Come on! The Corporation was your life, wasn't it? If anyone would know what to do, *you* would."

"You know everything that matters. You just don't accept it."

"No, Paul. I do not accept it."

"You know, that's a luxury not many of us can afford. So, tell me. What would you have done?"

"All right, for starters, how about a nice fatal accident for that evil bastard, Richard Martin? I'll bet you could arrange that."

"Tell me what that would accomplish."

"Well, it would rid the world of *one* nasty piece of work!"

"Right. But there are more where he came from. It would be revenge, nothing more. You don't know any more than I do about the events leading up to Robert's arrest. Robert was a Corporate executive, not a boy scout."

"Then I'd find out! Blow the lid off! Shake things up!"

"No. You wouldn't. Look, this is what I keep trying to tell you. In this world, people can not survive as isolated individuals acting on impulse. For the sake of all of us, we must have a system of rules and enforcement. You don't like to hear this, but we enjoy freedoms today that would be inconceivable without the Corporation. We have plentiful food, comfortable shelter, safe streets. And we take it all for granted, where twenty years ago we didn't know if any of us would be around much longer.

"I've had a lot of time to think about this. There are things I might have done against them. But it would have been pointless. Just reckless self-indulgence. Accomplishing nothing."

"Paul . . . we may need rules. But that doesn't excuse the things you've just told me."

"On the contrary! There may be better ways to run a business—or a society—but you won't find them by mindlessly tearing down what you have. And until you learn to understand this, you'll be of no use to anyone.

"I am retired. I do some consulting in the City, but I'm not involved in any of this. I suppose I'm not trusted enough. So I couldn't keep tabs on them. The drugs just seemed to disappear, and I used to think they couldn't get the bugs worked out.

"But I've been doing some snooping, and it seems *rope* has been successful. They've solved the problems. They can manufacture it. And we have to conclude that *wire* is not far behind. And the possibility of war not far behind that.

"I don't like this any more than you do, Max. But it isn't going to do us any good to focus too much on Richard Martin. There are other corporations out there, and other Martins. Dan Carter may very well be right. He's a smart man. Maybe war *is* inevitable. It's a bloody stupid thing, and it could mean the end of all of us. I don't know what can be done. But I do know this. None of us will accomplish anything alone."

"What about Robert? What have you told him?"

"Nothing. Not about this."

"Why? Don't you think he should know?"

"No, I don't."

"Why not?"

"Because there's nothing he can do, Max. Just leave it. Let sleeping dogs lie."

———————

Long after Max had retired for the night, Stevens remained in the living room, sitting in semidarkness and nursing a drink, and thinking he had just betrayed the trust of nearly everyone he knew.

He swirled the drink. Melting ice clinked softly in the silence, a silence that seemed to end in the reflection of the lamp beside his chair, on the other side of the glass wall.

20

Everywhere there were signs the countryside was nearing the end of winter. Bare trees shed ice that slipped from wet limbs and flashed in the sun, tumbling to earth. Snow receded day by day, revealing rotted leaves and pungent earth, and green shoots, and streams beginning to gurgle and roar with meltwater.

Max repeated nothing of the doctor's story. But he did ask Jack Ryan if he thought there might be spies around from the City.

"Spies!" howled Ryan, his big belly shaking with laughter. "What'n hell would *spies* want around here?"

"I don't know."

"*Spies!* Oh, shit! Where'd you get *that* idea?"

He did not explain.

Each day he walked his patrols, slogging along muddy trails, the smells of wet bark and wet earth drifting through the cold damp air, and there was reassurance in familiar sights and familiar sounds. Cows pushed and jostled around farmers forking out dwindling rations of winter hay. Brush was cleared and burned, piles of embers smoking in the sun. The ground thawed, and a rusty horse-drawn plow made the rounds from farm to farm. The Corporation seemed a long way off.

But the idea of war was haunting.

He had always kept to himself, not having much to say to the farmers and ranchers he passed each day on patrol. Not unfriendly, really. Just preferring to wave from a distance. But now he was uneasy, troubled by the idea of Richard Martin, sensing the man's ambition, the force of his personality, imagining people around him working feverishly to win his approval or avoid his anger. Martin felt real. The doctor's story felt real. But it was not the sort of thing a Corporate executive would talk about with a country exile, and he kept it to himself.

Instead, he found himself stopping to make small talk. And people surprised him. They were only too willing to take a few minutes out of a long day's work, and more than a few minutes. They needed the talk as well, if only about the weather. There was a hunger for new faces, for conversation with someone from outside daily farm life, someone they did not see every single day and night.

And he found on people's minds more than the weather. He learned things. Like how many wanted better roads. How many wanted to do business with the City.

"That could be dangerous," he would point out.

"But they have things we need."

"What would they want from us?"

Apples. Beer. Cheese. Horses. Hunting guides. Everyone seemed to have something to sell. The community was self-sufficient, as far as essentials went, but self-sufficiency is hard, especially without mechanical power. Such tools and machines as people were able to put to use were hand-operated, falling apart or nursed along, patched up where possible. Running water and electric power were to dream of, stories to tell bored grandchildren. There was an underground trade with the City, a black market, but it was illegal on the Corporate side, and Ryan tried to put a stop to it whenever he found anyone doing it outside his gang, on grounds of security. Although no one was really afraid of Jack Ryan anymore.

One afternoon, Max was talking with a rancher about being able to pick up a telephone instead of having to ride five miles to see if the vet could come over, but noticed the shadows lengthening, and broke off.

"Sorry, Dan. Gotta go. Got a patrol to finish."

When he finally joined up with the gang at the pub, he was hours late, and the conversation faded as he walked up to their table, Ryan watching in silence when he pulled out a chair and sat down.

"Where the hell've you been?"

"Oh, just got to talking with Dan Walsh."

"Talking? You? What about?"

"I dunno. Nothing special."

"Like what?"

"Just BS. What's the big deal?"

"Since when did *you* start BS'ing?"

"Come on. Lay off. I'm tired."

"Cut the bullshit. You're not one of them. Remember that."

"Yeah, I know, I know. But . . . listen, Jack. We need to *do* something. Something besides stand guard and collect taxes–"

"Taxes is what buys your meals, boy! And everything else you have. We do enough. Remember that."

"Okay. Okay."

He tried to keep his visits shorter, tried to finish his patrols earlier. But the serious exchange of ideas with people he had always looked up to was irresistible, and he did not want to go back to waving from a distance.

Ryan cornered him a few nights later, beer sour on his breath.

"Maybe you didn't hear me right the first time." Ryan shoved a thick finger at him and thumped his chest in time with the words. "So let's get this straight, right now. I hear the talk. If they want to build a new road, or a whole new city, I don't give a crap. We're not paying for it. It's none of our business. It's none of *your* business. You got that?"

"Yeah, Jack. Okay."

"I don't want you giving these farmers ideas."

"Okay, Jack. Okay."

The next day, picking his way around the worst of the spring mud near Dan Walsh's place, he heard the familiar voice call, "Hey, stranger! Got time for a cup o' joe?"

Walsh's lean, somewhat balding figure was propped against a rail fence, and Max worked his way over and kicked at a post, knocking layers of mud from his shoes.

Walsh grinned.

"In a hurry today?"

"Hey, Dan. Yeah, I dunno. I think maybe I'd better pass. Jack's been riding me pretty hard."

With theatrical contempt, Walsh turned and spat.

"I don't know why you put up with him."

"Hell, Dan, I get paid. Why d'ya think?"

"So you're going to be one of Ryan's goons the rest of your life? I don't see it."

"Yeah, neither do I. But what else can I do? I don't know a thing about farming."

Walsh chewed his lip, looking off to one side as though addressing someone else.

"You ever talk to John Anderson?"

"Nope. Don't patrol that way."

"Well, maybe you should. He says a lot of the same things you do."

"Yeah? Like what?"

"You're a big boy now. Go find out for yourself."

21

Halfway up a long hill, legs aching from trudging over miles of muddy trails, Max sat down on an old stone wall to rest.

It was a brilliant, blustery day in March, the unpaved road lined with trees full of bare, willowy branches clicking together in the wind. Small striped furry things dashed in and out of the wall, rustling through layers of last year's leaves. A jay landed in the crook of a tree above, cocked its head to inspect him, then flew on.

He was miles south of the main road, and had not been this way in years. At the top of the hill was a man he had met but once or twice before. Wily and shrewd, John Anderson had lived here as long as anyone could remember. He raised cows and sheep, grew apples and hay, and was notorious for having the only actual working tractor within miles, run on gasoline he smuggled from someone in the City.

The stone was rough and damp and cold, and when the cold had crept under his coat, he got to his feet and resumed the climb. The wind began to buffet, and at the top of the hill he bent into a gale, forcing his way toward a white house and gray barn.

Anderson appeared from behind the barn and braced himself against the wind, wiped his hands on a rag, then tramped toward the house. But he saw Max and stopped, frowning, until Max was close enough to hear over the wind.

"Well, well, well! Young Maximillian Wyse! What brings you way out here?"

"Hello, John! Am I interrupting anything?"

"Just the usual chores. What can I do for you?"

Anderson was shorter than Max, but tough and stocky, hair thick and white, eyes a startling blue in a brown, weathered face. He stood leaning against the wind with his thumbs hooked in his belt, as though anything Max had to say could be disposed of right there, in the front yard.

"John, I need some help."

"What sort of help?"

"I . . . Well, I want to do something about Jack Ryan."

"*Ryan?* Like what? You two have a falling out?"

"Not exactly. But we don't see eye to eye."

"Well, I don't see where that involves me."

Max shoved his hands in his pockets, hunching his shoulders against the wind.

"Look, John. I love this town. We have some good land and some good people. But we need things. Electricity. Telephones. Better roads. What would you do if you needed help in a hurry?" Something flickered in the old man's face. "What if you had a fire?"

Anderson turned his head from the wind and spat.

"I can put out a fire."

"Sure you can. If it's small enough. If you're here."

"So what're you talkin' about? You want to saddle us all with a bunch of taxes and guv'mint? I'll take Ryan."

"You pay taxes now. Do you have any idea how much he collects, or where it all goes?"

The old man gazed past him, scowling as though with a bad taste in his mouth.

"Don't know that I want to know."

"We'll never get anywhere like this, John. Not with Jack and his gang running the town."

"They don't run the town."

"Oh, don't they! It took me the whole morning to hike out here through all this mud, but no one can afford to fix the roads because you're all paying for his gang to drink beer and watch other people work!"

Anderson threw back his head and roared laughter into the wind.

"Look who's talkin'! Man, that's rich."

"Yeah, John. I should know. Do you think you're getting your money's worth?" The laughter stopped. "*I* sure as hell don't."

"You still haven't said what you want."

He hesitated. He knew this was crossing a line.

"We need to get rid of them."

A thoughtful scowl creased John Anderson's face.

"Damn! You want an old man to do your fightin' for you! Is that it?"

"No, John. I want to put them out of business. Without tearing us all apart. And I don't know how to do that."

"Put 'em out of business?" Anderson seemed startled. "Put 'em out of business . . . Hmm . . . I can see where that might be a puzzle . . ."

The old man rocked on his feet, back and forth, thumbs hooked in his belt, while the wind whistled around them and flattened patches of bedraggled grass scattered across the yard.

"Tell you what you do, son. You let me think a while."

"Okay, John."

"No promises, boy." The older man chuckled unpleasantly. "So you're through with Jack Ryan, are you? Gonna have a tiger by the tail. You know that?"

"Yeah, John, I know."

"Son, you only think you know."

The wind died down that evening, and John and May Anderson sat on their porch and listened to the relentless quiet as a blanket of shadow crept across the earth beyond the hill, until the sun finally dipped below the horizon and the yard sank into dusk. May got up, patted his shoulder, and went inside, letting the old screen door slap softly shut, and presently dim yellow light from a lamp in the kitchen glimmered on the railing.

Anderson remained where he was, watching the stars appear and thinking about this afternoon.

The Wyse boy showing up today seemed a sign. Or maybe a warning.

Where do we go from here?

It was not the first time he had pondered this. He knew trade was on everyone's mind, for manufactured goods and for Corporate money. A telephone was outlandish, of course, but everyone agreed the roads were a problem. And there were other things to think about, less tangible but no less important. Property deeds. Marriages. Inheritance. Contracts. Disputes used to be rare, especially in the early days when it was a struggle just to find enough to eat, but that was changing. And God knew farming wasn't for everyone. More young people were getting restless. And did young Wyse hit the nail on the head! An awful lot of good money was going to pay a handful of grown men watch other people work.

Anderson knew the next step would involve organization. It was a thought he had once found so repugnant he would simply spit and forget it. But he did not spit now.

He was not a man to ignore reality. Each year, the ranch seemed a little bit bigger, the work a little bit harder. May shuffled painfully around the house trying to keep up with the work of a woman half her age. The roof had been patched in so many places it was more patchwork than roof. Even the tractor was worn out. He doubted it would last through the summer.

Each morning, before his wife awoke, Anderson would drag himself out of bed and into the bathroom, to stare shivering into a cracked mirror at his aging body and withering limbs. And each morning he would remind himself that growing old was not for cowards. He would pour cold water into a pot, wash and shave and dress, and force himself to become John Anderson again. He gave silent thanks that he was still able, though he believed in nothing and had no one to thank.

Now he rose to his feet and leaned against the railing, peering into twilight.

It's now or never.

22

Son, you only think you know.

It had been a stupid thing to do, going behind Jack. Really, really stupid. Anderson's words only confirmed it.

But maybe the old man would forget.

Max walked his patrols, clutching that hope. Maybe Anderson would forget, and things could stay as they were. It wasn't such a bad life, all things considered.

But a week later, he found a note in his room at the farmhouse where he boarded. There was to be a meeting that night, at the vacant frame house on the main road east.

Be there, the note said.

He decided he'd better. He had no idea what Anderson had in mind, but if Jack was going, it would be best to know just how pissed off he was going to be, and how much groveling he would end up having to do.

It was shortly after sundown when he approached the old house. Yellow light glimmered in a few of the ground floor windows, from the 'meeting room', a large room with windows on adjacent walls that had probably once been someone's formal dining room, in the old days, before the plague.

Inside, a handful of people were talking quietly around a long table where a tall oil lamp had been lit. Anderson waved a lackadaisical greeting as he came in, and Max found a chair in a corner and sat down.

A half-hour later, Jack Ryan strolled in, glanced around the room, then parked himself in a big chair by the table, looking impassively at Anderson.

The old man nodded.

"Glad you could make it."

Ryan said nothing.

"Look, Jack. You've done well by us. Everyone here knows that. No one can complain about the service you and your crew have rendered over the years."

Max resisted an urge to roll his eyes. Ryan said nothing.

"All the same," Anderson went on, "it's time we made some changes. We can't stay like this forever. We're a community now, and we need to put our heads together. You probably know Max here has been talking about a telephone system." Ryan slid a hooded glance toward him as he slouched lower in his corner. "I don't know how he's going to make that work, but maybe he's right about some things. Maybe you have some ideas. Maybe somebody else does. We can't afford to ignore good ideas, Jack."

Ryan leaned back, folding heavy arms over a huge belly that strained the buttons of his shirt, and that seemed more menace than weakness.

Anderson's china-blue eyes held his.

"So what we need now is an election. And we're going to start having one every year."

Ryan's mouth opened a little. Then his lip curled. He turned to look at the others.

"Well, hell. If everyone here wants to get involved with running an election, *I'm* game."

"It's time, Jack," Anderson replied gently. "We're not just a bunch of refugees anymore. We've all been pretty successful. And we need to take the next step."

"The next step?"

"Laws. Government."

"Government? *You?*"

"I want us to be able to pool resources. Privately, so we can get things done together that we can't get done alone, so we can write contracts and deeds and record them. And publicly, so we can get things done for all of us. Like improve the roads. Like talk to the City about trade."

"I don't get it."

"No? Okay, think about it. We all pay taxes, right? But we all want more out of it than just a few patrols. Hell, Jack, you going to sit there and tell us you haven't seen this coming?"

"I still don't get it. How's this involve me? We have an agreement. I do my part. Where's the problem?"

"The problem is you're *private*. You don't answer to us. We need security, and maybe you're the man for the job. But taxes have got to go to government, and government has got to answer to *us*."

Ryan looked around the table. The others weren't watching Anderson. They were watching *him*.

"So we have some work to do," the old man went on. "We'll have to ratify the town charter. Then we can hold our election."

"What? You've already written a *charter?*"

"No, Jack, not yet. Don't worry, you'll be included. I figured the people in this room would be the charter committee. Any objections?"

Flushing red, Ryan opened his mouth, then seemed to think better of it.

Anderson slapped the table.

"Okay! We'll start here tomorrow, same time. That all right with everyone?"

Without a word, Ryan got up and left.

The others grunted assent and slowly made their way out. Max waited until the room was empty, then followed.

Anderson was loitering outside, and Max looked around, but there was no sign of Ryan.

"Think this'll do the trick, boy?"

"Jesus, John. I don't know. You really think Jack'll go along with it?"

"Times have changed. Personally, I don't think the man has much choice. But you watch your back, son. Just watch your back."

23

Most of the members of Anderson's charter committee were old enough to remember the time before Cargo Flu, and old enough to be suspicious of anything smelling of *guv'mint*. But they were ready for that next step. Usable roads. Trade with the City, that wasn't just smuggling. Maybe even telephones. Some kind of progress, something for all that tax money. At least a government of their own they could control, keep from getting out of hand, and by the third meeting of reminiscing, dozing off, and arguing, they were ready to get on with it.

They agreed to a short list of town officers. They agreed to elect a Town Committee, responsible for making laws, approving a budget, and setting taxes. And after another meeting of debating, crossing out paragraphs, and correcting spelling, they agreed to a brief document that was carefully copied out onto clean sheets of paper.

This was brought around from farm to farm. Anderson must have prepared the ground well, because it was not two weeks before it seemed everyone in the community had read it and discussed it and voted for it. And at the end of April, he held a small ceremony to mark the occasion. Per the new Town Charter, he also announced the election, for the first of June.

There was no rush of candidates for office. Except that Max and Jack Ryan each declared for President.

It had dawned on Max that he was out of a job.

Also per the Charter, Anderson's group was the first Town Committee, and they set out to draw up a budget and set salaries and taxes, making it clear that town revenue was public money, held in trust. What was past was past.

This was nothing short of revolution, the demise of Jack Ryan's private business, and it made Max nervous. The big bastard's lifestyle was about to get seriously crimped, yet Ryan gave no sign. The farmers had gotten ideas, Max was in the thick of it, and Ryan acted as though he hadn't a care in the world.

Which made Max *very* nervous.

For two weeks the Committee met every evening and grappled with how to pay for a small police force, road crew, and firefighters, without raising taxes. But higher taxes were beginning to look inevitable.

Barbara Hutchins, owner of a small dairy farm north of the main road, proposed they should charge 'dues' instead of 'taxes'.

"No one likes to pay taxes," she explained.

"Hell, no one wants to pay *anything*," retorted a tired and testy Anderson.

"But you only pay dues when you're a member of something, something that's partly yours. Taxes are like protection money. You pay because someone wants your money and is stronger than you."

"I don't see what difference it makes. If you live here, you pay."

Ryan broke in.

"Look, she's right, but there's a better way. We do what they used to. We write a report every year that shows where all the money goes, down to the penny. Keep it where anyone can come and read it. Call it the Town Public Report. Then it's not protection money, it's *their* money. See?"

For a long moment, Anderson stared at him.

Then he burst out laughing.

"You've got some gall, boy! A real politician! I'll hand you that."

Ryan shrugged.

"You want them to trust us, right? Hell, John, it's common sense."

"I suppose it is, boy," Anderson chuckled. "I suppose it is."

Max just listened, keeping his mouth shut, wondering what the fat bastard had up his sleeve.

The voting began at dawn on the first of June. Anderson and his Committee opened the door to the meeting room and remained to witness the signing and collecting of ballots as people came and went throughout the day. At sundown, they declared the election over, and shortly announced the results to a small crowd of Committee Members, candidates, and casual spectators.

For the office of Town President, Jack Ryan had won handily. Max had come in a distant second, and was declared Vice President. The other officers were declared. Anderson read them out. Chief of Police. Town Secretary. Fire Chief. Director of Roadwork.

Afterward, Max saw them gathered in a corner of the room, talking and laughing with Ryan and Anderson–and he left, walking home in the dark.

He had a pretty good idea where he fit in.

24

The pub was empty. As was the glass in front of him.

Max leaned on his elbows, pondering the glass, wondering why in hell he had ever gone to see John Anderson in the first place. Certainly not for this, weeks of doing nothing but watch Jack Ryan run the town.

Jack Ryan. *Christ.*

The day after the votes were counted, Ryan started organizing. He called meetings, hashed out goals, set dates, and the freshly-minted town officers found themselves hustling, to recruit a fire crew, to find

and train police deputies, to hire willing laborers for the back-break-
ing work of digging and filling the main road. Ryan supervised, ca-
joled, bullied, and hounded.

This was not the shiftless, beer-swilling Jack Ryan everyone
thought they knew. This one had plans.

But those plans did not include Max Wyse.

His eyelids drooped, and he yawned and rubbed his face.

"You done?"

He looked up. The owner of the pub stood there in a grimy apron,
sleeves rolled up, face shiny with sweat.

"How about one more, Bill. Then I'd better–"

Bill walked off, poured a glass, clunked it on the bar, and disappeared.

Christ.

He got up, fetched the beer, and brought it back to his table.

A half hour later, the pub was still empty, and he got up again, a
bit less steady, and drifted toward the bar.

"Hey . . . Bill?"

No answer.

He left some money on the bar and went out the front door.

The sun was low and sinking into the trees, but it was bright
enough to make his head hurt. He got on the road and started walking
homeward, thinking he probably should have left an hour ago. People
might talk. They might think he was a waste of town money.

He laughed at that, staggering a little.

Max decided to visit Barbara Hutchins. He remembered her smiling at him, during those long meetings before the election, as though
especially glad to see him, and after breakfast the next morning he
hiked out to her place.

He found her working in the barn behind her house.

"I know you're not on patrol, Max. We have deputies now. So what
can I do for you?"

"Uh . . . well, what do you know about telephones?"

"I know I haven't used one since I was a little girl. Why?"

"Wouldn't it be great to have one?"

"Sure. Do you know how to do it?"

"I'm trying to find out."

"Sorry, Max. Can't help you."

"Yeah, well, didn't think it would hurt to ask."

She went back to what she was doing, scraping bark with a hammer and chisel from a straight length of ashwood, the rusty head of
an axe lying on the ground near her feet.

He watched her, not wanting to leave.

"What is this, Max? You really have nothing to do, is that it?"

"Well, maybe I could help out around here–"

"Max! For God's sake, we're paying you to do a *job*. You'd better
work that out with Jack. I'm busy."

He mumbled something and retreated.

Two days later, while taking an early dinner at the pub, he heard some news. That Jack Ryan had bought a piece of property. That there was a run-down house on it, and he was paying his old gang to fix it up. That he was going to rent it out. The Town President was going to be a landlord as well.

Several beers later, he stumbled out of the pub and stood in the middle of the road, echoes of the noise and laughter inside slowly fading from the haze of his brain, leaving behind the news about Jack.

He swore bitterly and staggered off, but the road seemed to turn beneath his feet and he veered into the trees, where he was violently ill. For a long minute he leaned over, gagging and spitting the foul taste from his mouth, until his stomach settled and his head began to clear, and he could get back on the road.

It was two miles to the farmhouse where he boarded. When he reached it, he went directly to the bathroom. There was cold water waiting in a pan, and he rinsed out his mouth, washed his face and neck, looked around for a towel–and stopped.

In the mirror was a stranger. Pale skin. Puffy eyes. Dirty black stubble. He hadn't changed his clothes in days. Or bathed; he could smell himself.

A cold weight seemed to settle in his belly.

This was the town drunk.

He stumbled to his room, pulling off his foul clothes.

That night, he lay awake, sweating. Every distant trill of an owl, every creak of the house, came to him clear and unmuffled.

No one needed him. No one listened to him.

No one wanted him.

––––––––––––

He snapped awake. The room was still dark, but the window was turning gray. And it came to him that he knew someone who just might listen.

He had contacts of his own, people he knew who smuggled with the City, and after an early breakfast he found one and paid to have a message delivered. Then he hiked out to the Hutchins place once more, this time to arrange with Barbara to rent a horse.

25

Sunday morning, Max collected the horse.

He rode back along the main road, past the pub, and turned onto the paved North Road, and after a couple of miles he found a well-worn trail beginning at the western edge of the pavement.

The trail led him through miles of backcountry, stunted trees and grassy meadows, then into a long pine wood, tall and quiet. It was midday when he emerged from the pine and came out onto another blacktop. To his right, the asphalt descended for a few hundred yards toward the shore of a lake, where it passed a white clapboard structure.

According to Bill, the pub-owner, this was a restaurant. It was supposed to be popular with hunters and anglers from the City. Also with smugglers. A place where people tended to mind their own business.

He rode toward the building. The pavement shimmered with heat, and sweat trickled down his neck. The lake spread broad and cobalt under a blazing summer sky, stretching east to the horizon and the distant shapes of the City.

Extending out over the water was a long wooden deck with a few tables shaded with umbrellas. He dismounted and tied the horse in a bit of shade near some parked cars, and tucked a small flat box under his arm. The deck entrance was next to the restaurant, and he stepped onto hot gray planks. They were old and worn, but planking and rails gleamed in the sun and smelled of paint, making him conscious of his tattered clothes as he walked the length of the deck, dragonflies swirling as he passed faded umbrellas, the deck shuddering a little with each step.

"Robert Larsen, I presume?"

Sitting in the shade of an umbrella, Robert raised an eyebrow.

"We know each other."

Max lowered his voice. "Right. But nobody here knows that." He placed the box in the middle of the table and sat down, grateful for the ancient canvas blocking the sun.

"I see." Robert dropped his voice as well.

"Did you bring any money?"

"Was I supposed to?"

"It's supposed to look like a business deal. Like we're smuggling."

Robert took out some bills and tossed them across the table.

Max pushed the box toward him.

"Those are good cigars, Robert. Try to look interested in them."

"Let's get to the point." Robert glanced at the road. He looked nervous. "Tell me why I'm here."

Max knew this was dangerous, and probably in ways he could not imagine. He was sitting with a man who had once run Corporate Security, if he believed the story Stevens had told. It was not too late to change his mind, have something cold to drink, and go back home.

But he remembered the other night, and the long, empty weeks preceding.

"How much do you know about your past?"

Robert seemed to stiffen. The deck started shaking rhythmically as a heavy-set waiter walked up.

Max asked for a lemonade, and the waiter strolled back to the building.

"Just what the hell is my past to you?"

"I think we can help each other."

"I can't imagine how."

"I know quite a bit about your past. And I'm willing to tell you what I know. On one condition." He paused, but Robert just waited. "Okay, the condition is simple. Just give me your word never to tell anyone where you heard it."

"And just what makes you think my word is worth anything?"

"I'm willing to take that chance."

"Really. Sounds like you might need me more than I need you."

"I haven't said yet what I can do for you. So you might want to reserve judgment."

The deck began shaking again. The waiter returned and set a tall glass down in front of Max.

Clear cubes of ice in a dripping glass filled to the rim with a cold, translucent liquid–it was a thing of beauty, and as the waiter walked away, he sipped, cautiously, then drank, his brow knitted with pleasure, until he put the glass down with a heavy sigh, thinking it might be worth moving to the City just to have ice in the summer.

"Okay, here's what I'll do. I'll tell you what I know. Then you make up your mind. If you want to give me your word, I'll tell you what I can do for you. And what I want in return."

He began the story he had heard from Stevens, but without mentioning the doctor. Robert leaned back, his legs stretched out, fingers laced behind his head, gazing out at the water as though nothing of consequence were happening. But something changed at the name of Richard Martin, and by the time Max finished, the man didn't seem to be breathing. A good twenty seconds passed with only the quiet rattle of a dragonfly's wings.

Then Robert nodded, as if to himself.

"Well, well, well. Where in the world did you hear all of this, Mr. Wyse?"

"Max. Here and there."

"Here and there."

Robert got to his feet, picking up the box.

"Thank you for the cigars, Mr. Wyse."

He walked off.

Max sat and watched him, wondering what the hell he had just done.

26

Monday it rained.

It began at dawn and grew steadily darker and noisier, until wind and rain rattled his window, and shots of thunder boomed overhead.

After breakfast with the family he boarded with, Max returned to his room and tried to read, picking through the motley collection of books he had acquired over the years, from people he knew with no interest in books, his small room crowded with them–although he had long ago learned to keep this to himself, to avoid the taunts of Ryan and his gang.

But nothing held his interest. The walls seemed to close in, and he paced the room, peering out the window and cursing himself for an idiot, trying to imagine what it would be like to work for a living, wondering what anyone would pay him to do.

Tuesday dawned bright and clear, and he was out of the house early to take breakfast at the pub. Then he walked five miles to the vacant frame house, now outfitted as the Town Office.

He was in a mood to stir up trouble. With Jack Ryan, if possible.

But there was only the town secretary, carefully copying something from papers neatly arranged on the desk in front of her.

"Hi, Martha."

"Hello, stranger."

"Jack around?"

" 'Fraid not."

"Mm . . . too bad." He watched her, absently, trying to think of something he could do, somewhere he could go, that would keep him away from the pub.

"Max, do you want something?"

"Uh . . . " He glanced around. "Yeah. Where're the minutes?"

"What?"

"The minutes. You know, minutes of meetings."

"Oh. We aren't keeping any."

"You aren't? Aren't there officers' meetings?"

"Yes, but . . . Jack said not to bother."

"Jack said–" He stopped, remembering who he was talking about. "You're Town Secretary. Don't you know what your job is?"

"Well, of course I have work to do. But Jack hasn't decided everything."

"Look, Martha. You report to the Town Committee. Right?"

"Well, I don't know. I don't think Jack–"

"*Jack* has nothing to do with this! You don't work for him. You're a town officer. The *people* elected you. You work for *them.*"

"Well, sure, that's easy for you to say. You don't have to deal with him."

"Christ. Look, I was here when they decided this. I know what they wanted. I'll come to the next meeting, and if Jack has a problem, I'll back you up."

"Well, Max, you haven't been *invited* to the next meeting. So what about that?"

It was easy to let anger seep into his voice.

"All right, Martha. This is what you're going to do. You make sure I know about each meeting. You make sure *every* officer knows. You have an agenda, and you write up the minutes. And if Jack doesn't like it–or anyone else!–I'll take it straight to John Anderson, and I can guarantee you John'll straighten things out."

Martha was young, twenty or so. Her father had died when she was seventeen, apparently of food poisoning. Shortly after that, her mother had disappeared, and there had been rumors. But as an only child now living on a farm by herself, Martha had stated in no uncertain terms that she had no interest in the farm, in marriage, or in children, and had sold the place to a neighbor and moved into a small house on the main road, where she kept to herself. It was John Anderson who had persuaded her to stand for secretary, and it was Anderson's name that got her attention.

"Well, there's going to be trouble. That's all I can say."

"Then it's time we had it out. This isn't a private business. That's why we changed everything. Remember?"

He left the office, whistling.

Wednesday, he awoke to broad daylight and pulled the covers over his head. But he was wide awake, and hungry, and he rolled out of bed and pulled on the clothes he had worn the day before.

The family he boarded with would feed him, but they were too close, separated by a door and a few feet of space, and he tried not to see too much of them. Good fences make good neighbors, he remembered reading somewhere, and it seemed like sound advice.

It was only when he was about to leave that he noticed a small white envelope on the floor, by his door.

Inside the envelope was a handwritten note.

Sunday. Same time, place. Bring something different.

It was the same as before. Hot sun. Dragonflies. And Robert Larsen sitting alone in the shade of an umbrella.

Max pulled out a chair and sat down, pushing a small volume wrapped in plain brown paper across the table.

Robert glanced at it. "What's that?"

"Exactly what it looks like." A book of pornographic stories was all he had been able to come up with on short notice. "Pretty hot stuff, too. But I have some special connections." It was an effort to keep a straight face.

Flicking it aside with the back of his hand, Robert muttered, "I didn't come here for fuck books."

"No?"

"Look." Robert glanced around. There was no one visible, but he leaned closer. "I was a little abrupt last week. But I was playing your game. We were spending too much time whispering for anyone to think I was just buying a few contraband cigars."

"Well, okay. So now what?"

"So now I want to hear your proposition. You have my word. I won't reveal you."

"Um, all right. Let's start with what I can do for you. If this works out, I can make a place for you. You and Agnes. Away from the City."

Robert's face didn't change. He didn't move.

"What do you want from me?"

"You know what *rope* is? The Corporation's looking for someone to sell it. They want someone from outside the City to sell it to smugglers inside, who'll sell it to workers."

"Why the subterfuge?"

"They want it to be illegal, so no one knows where it's coming from."

"I see. And you know this how?"

"Someone I know heard about it."

"Heard about it from whom?"

"From Richard Martin."

Seconds ticked by. A bead of perspiration crawled down Robert's face.

"What do you want?"

"I want to take them up on it."

"Why?"

"For the money."

"Is that all?"

"What else?"

"Are you going to manufacture it?"

"No, not me. Too complicated. They're already making it. I want to take it in bulk and deliver small parcels. It's safer, and it accomplishes what they want. And I'll have something to hold over Martin's head later, if I need it."

Robert stared.

Then, abruptly, he laughed. He slumped back and laughed for a long time.

"Well, well . . . I suppose that could work, for a while. Sooner or later it'll blow up, of course. And you're crazy if you think you can hold anything over Richard Martin. But I suppose it could work, for a little while."

"Why should it blow up?"

"Why? Because if I were Martin, I'd have Security running real investigations and catching real smugglers. You say they want it to be illegal. I suppose that makes sense, but it's not illegal if no one's ever caught. They'll find your operation, trust me. Maybe sooner than you think, if you're expendable. Don't underestimate these people. They aren't stupid."

His scalp prickled, and he felt hot. But he could not stop now, not while he had Robert's attention.

"Okay, so it'll work for a while. But I can't approach Martin on my own. I mean, I have some contacts, but nothing like that. That's why I need you."

"To do what?"

"Arrange a meeting. Keep an eye on Martin. Act as my broker."

"And in return?"

"As I said, I'll make a place for you. Away from the City."

"Just for helping you make a deal, is that it? And exactly how will you deliver your end, if you don't mind my asking?"

"My town has a president. Right now it's a guy named Jack Ryan. I'm vice president. Which means I don't do anything. I want *his* job, and when I'm elected, I'll be able to set you up where the Corporation won't find you."

"Really."

Robert looked abstracted for a moment, like a man doing a sum in his head, not too difficult.

"You haven't thought this out very well, have you? Whether or not the Corporation finds me depends on whether they decide to look." He winked. "Unless, of course, your idea of hiding us is to hide the bodies. And whether you get elected, assuming you people are holding elections, depends on things that are outside my control, and probably yours as well. So I don't see how any of this helps."

He hadn't thought it out at all. But an idea occurred.

"Ryan will be the middleman. When it blows up, it'll be Ryan who gets caught in the explosion."

This sounded hare-brained even as he said it, but Robert looked impressed. Or at least entertained.

"Now, I suppose that could work, *if* you can handle Ryan and he doesn't take you down with him. A big very *if*. Now, let's see. All I need is something I can hold over you."

"Over me? Why? What've you got to lose?"

"Come off it. What better way to make me disappear, and rid yourself of a dangerous problem, than to leave me buried in the woods?"

"Well, I suppose you're right, logically speaking. But that isn't what I had in mind."

"So you say. But even if I were to give you the benefit of the doubt, the idea would have to occur to you, sooner or later."

"And there's nothing I can say that would change your mind."

"You're planning to turn your partner over to the Corporation so you can take his place. What would you think if you were in my shoes?"

"He's not my partner. But I suppose I see your point."

Robert stood up, chuckling.

"Well Max, it was interesting. I'll give it some thought. Maybe next week, eh?"

As he walked off, something hit the water with a *ker-plunk*.

27

In the evening, a few days later, he walked to the doctor's. He was worried Robert might have said something. But they drank whiskey and played chess, and Robert did not come up.

There was something else on the doctor's mind.

"Tell me what your friend Jack Ryan has been doing."

"Jack? Oh, the usual. Holding meetings. Pissing people off."

"He doesn't seem the sort of man to content himself with a few meetings."

"Well, he's renting out that house, of course."

"That can't take up much of his time."

"I dunno, Doc. Why?"

"Has he mentioned anything more about selling drugs?"

Max swallowed.

"I don't think so. Not to me, anyway."

"Well, I don't suppose he would."

"What do you mean?"

"You're a troublemaker, as far as he's concerned. But we know he has contacts. Do you know if he's using them?"

"No clue."

"Well, keep an eye on him. See what you can find out."

Stevens topped off his own drink, then paused with the bottle, glancing at Max's glass almost untouched.

"I'm good, Doc, thanks."

"Feeling all right?"

"Yeah, I'm okay. Just trying to watch myself."

The doctor swallowed a little whiskey and nodded.

"Very admirable. So, what about you? What have you been up to? You haven't said much, and I haven't seen you in a couple of weeks."

"Nothing much going on, really."

"No? You have a government now. Aren't you part of it?"

"Yeah, but Jack's in charge. I don't have a say in anything."

The old man studied him, swirling his drink until a bit splashed over the rim.

"You mean he's shutting you out."

"Yeah. That's about the size of it."

"What are you doing about it?"

"What *can* I do? The son of a bitch runs everything! Still."

"Max, there could be something serious going on. He seems to have a lot of time on his hands. And don't forget you have knowledge that not many people do."

"I keep telling you, Doc, I'm no politician."

"And I keep telling you that attitude is a luxury you may not be able to afford."

"So what am I supposed to do? I can't just take over."

"Think of something! Take some responsibility. You do have an idea what's at stake, don't you?"

"C'mon on, Doc. You're in the same boat I am. What can *you* do about anything?"

"D'you think this is a *game*? Do you think *Ryan* thinks it's a game?" The old man shook his head. "I've got to hand it to him, though. The man's a survivor."

Max didn't argue. He left a short while later.

The outline of the main road, when he reached it, was barely visible in the dim luminescence of a quarter moon rising behind him. But it was familiar, and he started homeward, the night sultry and soft.

There was bright moonlight in the yard outside his window when he awoke, eyes wide, the echoes of a gasp mingling with the wisps of a terrifying dream.

He got up and dressed, shut and latched the window, and left the farmhouse, silently closing the front door. For a while he lingered in the yard, listening to the whisper of a night breeze in the branches above.

When the sky grew light, he was on an old patrol trail that ran by Dan Walsh's house. Smoke was rising from the chimney, and Walsh was in the yard, gathering firewood.

He did not want to see Dan Walsh. He did not want to see anyone, and he turned around and hiked back the way he had come.

28

It was hot.

The heat was a cocoon, enervating coils that wound tighter and tighter, leaving people limp and dazed and gasping for breath. Farmers got up before dawn to begin chores in the dark, and by midday were sheltering indoors to escape waves of heat radiating from every sunlit surface. The afternoons were long, hazy, and still, the fields empty and baking in dusty silence. With sundown came small relief, and the nights were claustrophobic, restless, sleep coming in fits long after midnight.

Saturday evening, the town officers drifted lethargically into the meeting room. Martha had notified everyone, and Max slumped wearily into a chair. It was growing dark outside the open windows, but the room was stifling, lit dimly by a low flame rising in the glass chimney of a single lamp.

Martha placed a few limp sheets of paper on the table in front of her.

Ryan noticed.

"What do you think *you're* doing?"

"Taking notes, Jack. To start a book of minutes."

Ryan stared at her, blankly, as if confronted with an inanimate object moving unexpectedly on its own. Martha seemed to shrink, but then sat up, her hands flat on the table.

"Jack, I'm town secretary. They made the job for a reason, didn't they? It's not right for us to go on without good records. After all, what if something happened to you?"

"Huh?"

"How would Max take over, without good records?"

Ryan's eyes widened. Then he slammed the table.

"*Fuck!* Is that what this is? Fuck *you!* You don't have enough to do? You and your fucking–"

"Jack! Jack! You don't have to yell!"

But Ryan's voice pitched higher.

"Fuck that! You don't *listen!* What the fuck've I told you? Who the fuck put *you* in charge?"

"Jack, I'll take care of everything! *Please!*"

Ryan shot to his feet, eyes wild, rivulets threading down his face now scarlet and patchy yellow.

"*Jack!*" Max shouted. "It has nothing to do with me! John Anderson wants this!"

Sweat dripped from Ryan's face. Suddenly, like a switch flipping, he sat down again. He coughed loudly, spat on the floor, and looked around the table.

The others watched him, speechless.

Ryan glared.

"Well?"

They made their reports. There were complaints from the firemen. A deputy had quit after taking a swing at the chief of police. The improvements to the main road were not going fast enough, and people were complaining. They were complaining about other roads and trails needing work, too.

Ryan pursued it all, each report, relentlessly, making decisions and giving orders, and Martha covered pages with rapid scribbling. But the heat was a fog, and at some point the pencil slipped from her fingers and she was dozing, her chin cupped in her hand. Until the table thumped under Ryan's fist, and she jerked upright.

"I'm sorry!"

"Okay! You with us now? I've got something else, but it needs to be off the record. No one talks about this. You can put a note about that in your minutes. Whatever. I don't give a . . . hoot."

She looked at Max. Wearily, he rubbed his face and nodded.

"Let's hear what he has to say."

Ryan leaned back, grinning and cocksure despite dark, damp patches staining his shirt.

"Nobody pays any attention to anything outside this pissant town. But there are other cities out there, and other corporations. And they're not just sitting on their asses."

Stifling a yawn, Martha mumbled, "What are they doing, Jack?"

"Going to war."

Max stared, wondering if he had heard what he thought he heard. "*What the hell!*"

Heads swiveled to him. He was on his feet, but dropped helplessly back in his chair.

Ryan smirked.

"There's going to be war. The Corporation wants our help. And they'll help us in return."

"But–" Martha stammered. "Why should we get involved in someone else's fight?"

"It'll be our fight, too. Think about it. We're right in their back yard."

"Holy shit," someone muttered. "What're we supposed to do?"

"Defend ourselves! What else?"

"*How?*"

"With the Corporation's help, that's how. They'll give us weapons and training."

"My God," Martha whispered, staring at Ryan as though the words were only now reaching her. "My God, are you *serious?* Do you seriously think there's going to be *war?*"

Ryan shrugged, looking as if she had asked whether it might rain next week.

"But what should we do?"

"Like I said, defend ourselves."

"But we can't fight an army!"

"No, but we can sign up as allies. That's all they want, to start with."

Max could not imagine who Jack was talking to, but he was certain of one thing. It had to be stopped.

"We don't know enough! And the Committee has to be involved."

"Where does it say that?"

"Oh, for chrissake! They'll vote a resolution or something, as soon as they hear about this."

Martha looked relieved.

"That's right! The Charter says we carry out policy and enforce the law. We can't commit the town on our own. That's the Committee's job."

Ryan wiped sweat from his face with a tattered rag, then balled it up.

"Whatever. But I'll tell you this much. If we don't make up our own minds first, nothing'll happen. They'll argue and fuck around until it's too late to matter."

"We don't know enough!"

"So what do you want to know, big man? It's simple! Do we defend ourselves, or not?"

"No, it's *not* simple. We don't know if this is real. We don't know what other corporations are doing. Christ, how do we even know there *are* any others? There's a *lot* we don't know."

"So what do you want to do? Go ask them?" Ryan cracked up laughing, drops of sweat scattering from his hair. "You may not like the Corporation, boy, but they have a lot more information than *you* do."

"All right then! Get 'em in here!"

"What?"

"Get your corporate pals over here, so they can tell us what they know and what they want."

"Why the fuck should they?"

"Because they need us. They need *something,* or they wouldn't be sniffing around here."

Others were nodding now. "Makes sense."

Ryan spat.

"We're wasting time."

"Then don't waste any more! Get 'em *in* here!"

Abruptly, Ryan stood up and strode from the room, his face red and tight.

A minute went by and nothing happened. The others looked around the tabled and shrugged. Apparently the meeting was over.

They stood up and filed out.

Grateful to be outside, Max stood at the side of the road, breathing the night air, waiting for his nerves to settle. Someone struck a match near the house. Shadowy figures untied horses in the flickering light, and mounted up. The match went out, and quiet scrapes and thuds of hooves went by him in the darkness, and faded away.

"What your fucking problem?"

He jumped. The words hissed from the dark, and the hulking gray outline of Jack Ryan became visible.

Shit!

He took a long breath.

"I don't like it, Jack. I don't think they're telling you everything."

"Yeah? And what do *you* know about it?"

"Not enough. That's my problem."

Ryan's voice was like a snarl, like something baring its teeth:

"Don't fuck with me."

Then he was gone. There was a creak, then the tromp of one last horse passing by.

"Max?"

He turned. "Martha?"

"It's me. Do you mind if I walk with you?"

"Uh, yeah, sure. I'm right here."

He waited until she touched his shoulder. Then they started off, following the road by feel, stumbling occasionally in the dark.

She wanted to talk.

"Do you think he's right? Jack, I mean. It's so crazy."

"I don't know. Maybe. I just don't trust him, and I sure as hell don't trust the Corporation."

"Oh, I hate this! *Politics.* I was so excited about working for the town. But I never thought about *war.* And God, this *bickering.*" She stumbled and clutched his arm. "I never knew you and Jack were such enemies."

"So you heard that. Well, don't let it bother you."

"Don't you patronize me, Max! I'm not a child."

"Look, it's nothing, okay? We just don't get along."

"Well, when did that start? I always thought–"

"Just drop it, Martha."

They walked on in silence, until she sensed her house near.

He waited while she made her way to the door, unlocked it, and fumbled a moment, until the warm glow of a lamp framed her young face in the open doorway.

"Well, Max Wyse. You're not much of a conversationalist. But thank you just the same."

"Sure. 'Night, Martha."

29

Sunday, Max rode out to the lake again. He had nothing better to do, and Robert had mentioned he might be there.

The deck was deserted. The lake smelled of something rotten. He picked out a table and settled in a chair, waving away flies, sipping lemonade, and shifting the flimsy bit of chair whenever the sun emerged from behind the umbrella.

When the last sliver of shade had retreated from his table and the dregs of his third lemonade stood glittering in the sun, he got to his feet and walked irritably across the blistering deck to the restaurant.

It was dark inside, but cooler, and as his eyes adjusted he could see a dozen tables spread out in a large room, and a handful of customers nursing an assortment of drinks, fanning themselves and talking in murmurs.

The thought of his room at the farmhouse was claustrophobic. If only he could stay here awhile, lose himself in the anonymity. But the ride home was a long one, and he settled his tab.

Outside, he used the facility, then mounted up, angrily, and kicked the horse into motion.

Tall pines lined the road like two walls of a green canyon, passing slowly as hooves clopped lazily on hot pavement. He found the opening to the trail, stopping to look back at the restaurant, a white rectangle standing out painfully bright against the dark blue of the lake.

Then he rode into the pine.

Gauzy layers of branches crisscrossed high above. Below, it was dim and airy and cool and private, hoof-falls muted on the forest floor. It should have been a pleasant ride, but he rode in a dark funk, chewing over his idea of making a deal with the Corporation.

Sure, it might be dangerous, smuggling drugs, doing business with the City. But if he could make some money, and if it got rid of Jack . . . He ducked under a low branch, reveling in the thought of Jack Ryan in a City jail. Finally out of business. Out of his life.

Until something rolled down his throat. The old weight lodging in his belly. The cold weight of reality.

Jesus.

Jack would never fall for this. Not in a million years. He was a survivor, as the Doc liked to say, his Corporate pals were survivors, and he could hear the old man laughing, pointing out in how many ways they would skin him alive.

Even Robert had laughed.

The trail came out of the pine and snaked around stands of thick brush and stunted trees, the air close and stifling. His shirt stuck to his ribs, sweat ran down his face, and he wondered if they had given the horse any water, back at the lake. He should have checked, and he swore, watching the animal's long neck bobbing as it walked

"Can't even take care of a stupid horse."

He was back where he started, with his do-nothing job as vice president, and no prospects. And there was so much they *could* be doing. If only someone would listen! If only *Jack* had listened, over the years–and memories of arguments with Jack Ryan grew more numerous and more eloquent as he rode–if only they had done something with all that money they had collected, something besides drink beer and . . . and . . .

Well, son of a bitch!

No wonder the old bastard was so comfortable. He must have hidden a nice pile of cash somewhere and kept it to himself.

He swore bitterly, cursing life, cursing the fat son of a bitch for coming out on top once more–until the horse crashed into the brush and jerked to a halt, head low, ears flattened, and Max came to himself with a start, realizing he had been jerking the reins.

Heart pounding, he coaxed the animal back to the trail, then halted.

Sunlight filtered through the crowded trees, making bright patches on silky tufts of yellow grass. Insects circled through the fuzzy light, and he watched, slumping on the horse, searching for an idea, for something he could do, somewhere he could go.

What he wanted . . .

He sat up.

What he wanted was the presence of a mind that understood the world, and needed nothing from Max Wyse.

He kicked the horse.

The sun was deep in the trees when he arrived at the doctor's and climbed down. Stamping life back in his legs, he led the horse around the house to the back yard.

Everything hit him at once. The sizzle and smoke of steaks cooking. Three faces staring up at him. Doc Stevens at a grill, some utensil forgotten in his hand. Agnes on a recliner. And Robert Larsen, sitting atop the picnic table.

He stopped. His face was hot. He knew he should get back on the horse and leave, but he had nowhere to go, just his room at the farmhouse, and he led the horse to the far edge of the yard, tied it up, gave it a bucket of water, then walked past Stevens toward the house.

"Going to clean up a little, if you don't mind."

"By all means."

He went in through the back door. In a bathroom, he hung his head under cold running water and toweled dry. He paused at the mirror. Sun-burnt, sweat-stained, rat's nest for hair, he looked like a castaway–or a drunk. No wonder they stared.

Outside, Robert and Agnes were setting out plates. Stevens was turning the steaks.

The sight of Agnes in the fading light, pale hair and smooth, tanned shoulders, slender waist and long flowing skirt–the sight of her in the shadows of evening was bewitching. He could not take his eyes from her, until she caught his stare and he looked away, his face hot again.

Steaks and roasted ears of corn were served.

He ate in silence, suddenly famished. The evening was quiet, just an occasional thumping hoof-fall from the edge of the yard and the sigh of a warm breeze through unseen branches above. He became conscious of an ache deep inside, to feel at peace, with the world, with these people.

"Well, Max." The doctor's voice came to him. "You're very quiet tonight."

He could feel Agnes watching, and he groped for something to say, something that would justify his presence.

"Doc–is the Corporation trying to arm *all* the exiles?"

He looked up. Robert's face had darkened, and he realized too late that by saying this in front of Agnes, he might be placing her in actual danger.

The thought made him angry.

"Something's going on, Doc. I need to know what it is. Who're the spies in my town?"

The old man's voice had a low warning:

"I don't know who they are, Max."

"But you could find out."

"*I do.*"

He turned in surprise. To Robert.

"I know who they are. Some of them."

"You!" Agnes demanded. "How do *you* know?"

"Someone left me a message. A package. Reports. Memos. Things of that sort."

Stevens peered at him.

"I'll be damned! You mean, you left yourself a time capsule?"

Robert's mouth tightened. But he answered.

"I suppose you call it that. I found it a few days ago, in my apartment. I must have known what was coming."

Agnes shivered and looked away. Max leaned forward.

"Robert, are you sure this is real?"

"What do you mean?"

"I mean it could have been planted."

"I suppose that's possible. But there's also a letter. From Robert Larsen number one, to number two. I think it's real."

"Why? What does it say?"

"I'd rather not discuss it."

"Well, be careful, Robert. Don't put anything past them."

"I don't. But I suppose you'd like to know who they are. Your spies."

"Yeah. I would. And anything else you can tell me."

"I can't help you with your business proposition. It's too dangerous."

He shrugged. "Yeah, I know it. It was a stupid idea. Forget it."

"What's this?" Stevens broke in. "What business proposition?"

"It doesn't matter," answered Robert. "But I'm willing to trade information."

Maybe information he could use. "Okay. What've you got?"

"Names, dates. Who they are, when they were recruited. What their assignments are."

"What else?"

"That should be enough."

"Robert, I need anything you have that can help me decide what to do."

"Damn it, Max! What's this all about?"

"I'm not sure, Doc. But I think you were right. Jack's been talking to someone. Maybe Richard Martin. They're feeding him stories about war. He says they're looking for allies, that they want to give us weapons and some kind of training."

Agnes stood up. She walked away and stood at the edge of the lawn, her arms folded, staring into the night.

Robert watched her. He seemed about to get up, then stayed where he was.

Later, she confronted him, alone, in the kitchen.

"Max, I have to ask you something."

Maybe it was the brittleness in her voice, maybe her rigid bearing, but he felt again that he was an intruder, an unwelcome guest without the sense to leave.

"Sure, Agnes. Anything."

"Can you–can you really do it? Give us a place to go?"

He swallowed, the cold weight in his belly–it was only a brief hesitation, but it was enough. The hollows darkened under her cheekbones.

"Agnes, I'll do whatever I can, believe me. I just don't know much about the Corporation, about what they can do. It would help if I knew more," he tried to hint.

But the hollows only deepened, and she turned and left.

He heard her voice in another room. Then Robert's. And a minute later, the car.

Max stayed the night.

In the morning, as the two men ate breakfast, Stevens was unusually terse. They finished eating, cleaned and dried the dishes. Then Stevens poured the last of the coffee, unplugged the electric maker, and sat down again.

"Max, you are on very dangerous ground. Do you understand this?"

He sat across from Stevens.

"Well, maybe so, but what else am I supposed to do?"

"Do you understand that you, personally, are crossing a line? If Robert is discovered passing information, they may come for whoever received it. That would be you. Have you considered that?"

"Uh . . . no."

"Well, I've been thinking about this proposal to arm you. I have to assume that anyone living as you do is already armed, so they must be planning on equipping you with something more than hunting rifles."

"Yeah, I suppose that makes sense."

"One part of the Corporation may think it's a smart idea to let you slow down an enemy, should one appear. But other parts will see a heavily-armed group of exiles as a risk in itself."

"So?"

"So, have you given any thought to what they might do to mitigate that risk?"

"What do you mean?"

"I mean, while one group is supplying you with machine guns and hand grenades, another might be planning to make you a little less independent."

"What do you mean? How?"

"They might take over your town. They might set up a puppet to run it. They might start a little war as pretext."

He looked down at his mug.

"I didn't think of that."

"Well, now you have something new to think about. I hope you're ready for this."

"All right, Doc, I'll think about it. But I'd better get back."

He got up, rinsed his mug, and went out the back door.

Stevens followed.

As they stepped outside, Max stopped short.

"Oh, *shit.*"

Still tied at the edge of the yard, and straining at the rope, the horse had torn up a swath of lawn and left behind piles of dark manure.

"Damn it all, Max! Can't you find someone to show you how to take care of that thing?"

"Ah . . . Christ! I should've fed him something. I'm sorry, Doc. I'll take care of it." He shook his head, thinking, *What a farmer I'd make.* "You know, Doc, life used to be a whole lot simpler. Sometimes I wish–"

"*Oh, for the love of God! Will you ever grow up?*"

He didn't answer. He went quickly to the tool shed.

Stevens watched, the anger already fading.

He was tired. Tired in a way he dreaded. In a way that felt empty, and final. But he felt the earth beneath his feet, felt the house behind him, and the mood passed.

To hell with that. This is my *world.*

30

The summer heat was broken by an afternoon of thunder, wild wind, and torrential rain, and evening fell cool and clear, the sky luminous long after sunset, wet fields glowing softly in pellucid light that only gradually faded into twilight.

The walk to the doctor's house was a pleasure. The town was making progress, grading and improving drainage, and most of the main road was even and firm despite the rain. Max was sorry to leave it behind as he turned onto the familiar trail and picked his way around muddy hollows, protruding tree-roots, and dripping branches.

He came out of the trees, crossed a small field, and stopped in the City lane. Stars burned in the deepening velvet overhead, and he stood listening to silence, watching night fall, held by a piercing regret, one that came over him at times, with no object, no reason. Just a nameless regret.

The gray shape of an owl went gliding across the lane and disappeared into shadows, and he looked up once more, lost for a moment in the stars.

Then, reluctantly, he turned to go in.

Loose gravel scraped under his foot and scattered noisily across the pavement. Something bolted from the side of the house, a dark shape that ran up the road toward the City.

Max froze, trying to make it out. Then he sprinted.

For a short distance he kept up, but the apparition pulled away, and he broke off, stumbling and gasping for breath. Then he loped back to the house and joined the doctor and Robert inside, relating what happened.

"So he took the road?" asked Stevens. "Toward the City?"

"That's right. And, Jesus, he was fast."

"I wonder how long he was there?"

"You mean, how *often* has he been there." Robert exhaled, shaking his head. "If he's from the Corporation and heard us the other night, I'm dead."

Max could think of other explanations.

"I don't know, Robert. Is that the best the City can do? Send someone out to peek into windows? This guy probably had nothing more on his mind than a little burglary."

"Maybe so. You know, Paul, you're pretty isolated out here. You could be an easy target."

"I'm not as easy as I look."

"You had no idea he was there. He could have clubbed you from behind."

"So? There isn't much I can do about that."

"Get a dog."

"What?"

"Get a dog. You can take care of yourself if you're not taken by surprise. Get a dog so you won't be."

"What am I supposed to do with a dog? I don't know the first thing about them."

"Smaller than a horse!" Max laughed. "And a lot cheaper to feed."

"Get your own dog."

It was just the three of them, sitting around the kitchen table under a shaded lamp, lighting cigars and pouring whiskey, the rest of the house in darkness. A large brown envelope lay in front of Robert, and this he pushed toward Max.

"That's for you. A few reports, and the list of spies. Most are minor players. They'll probably be sent on to other places, if they haven't already. I don't think they'll do you any harm. But there *is* one name you need to know about. Someone who could cause real trouble."

But Max had already emptied the envelope and was scanning the list.

He passed it to the doctor.

"I don't believe it."

Stevens nodded. "This seems too easy."

"Yeah, doesn't it. Where's your evidence?"

Robert reached over and tapped the envelope.

"Read the reports. And there's something else you should know."

Max shuffled through the papers. "This is all you have?"

"What else do you want?"

"Whatever I can lay my hands on! This guy's *not* going to be easy to take down. If it's even true."

Stevens tossed the list back to him. "Are you surprised?"

"Well, yeah. I mean, he sticks out. Draws attention. Why would anyone want *him* as a spy? And how long has he been doing it?"

"About a year, I think," answered Robert. "But he's not just a spy. The others are being trained to blend in. Ryan's being exploited for his position."

"Jack Ryan," mused Stevens. "I should have seen it. But you said there was something else Max should know?"

Robert blew a long jet of smoke at the ceiling.

"Yep. Ryan is selling *rope*."

"*What?*"

Even as he blurted this out, Max knew it had to be true.

The doctor snorted.

"Makes perfect sense. You mean, though, he's selling covertly. To workers, or smugglers."

"That's right," said Robert.

"And he's selling what the Corporation supplies him."

"Right again."

"And the workers risk arrest if Security discovers them."

Robert blew another jet. "Probably."

"How long?"

"Going by the dates, I'd say eight or nine months."

Max slammed the papers.

"The son of a bitch *lied* to me! When he said he had been *approached,* he was already working for them? Christ! Christ almighty!"

The doctor tapped ash from his cigar.

"Sometimes I really don't understand you. What did you expect? As far as he's concerned, you're a troublemaker."

"It's all in the reports, Max. They wanted a local asset, and they set Ryan up selling *rope* as a test. It's a shrewd plan. They could recruit an ambitious, unscrupulous individual, have him do something they wanted done anyway, and if he didn't work out, an anonymous tip to Security would safely dispose of him. And if he *did* work out, then they had something to hold over his head later, if he caused trouble. These people aren't stupid."

"Nasty, dangerous people," the doctor sniffed.

Robert laughed.

"I thought you were the worldly one! Realpolitik, isn't that the word? Don't tell me you're offended by it."

"Of course I'm offended. Just not surprised."

"Well, Max, this should be enough to hang him. Don't you think? Isn't this what you wanted?"

But he just stared at the list.

Jack Ryan was dangerous all by himself. Now he had Corporate friends. Now he was an 'asset'. And the Corporation would surely want to protect its assets. Particularly this one.

31

They brought the doctor a dog, a young golden retriever with big clumsy feet, a wet tongue, and an insatiable appetite for attention. It bounded from the car when Robert and Agnes arrived the following Saturday, and immediately jumped at Stevens, who irritably shoved it away. But they had planned it well. Agnes was all smiles and gaiety and winsome laughter as the dog chased around the yard, and around Stevens, and as the day wore on there were signs of a thaw, the old man grudgingly patting the animal.

After dinner, they talked in the living room over glasses of whiskey and wine, the retriever stretched out at the doctor's feet.

"So, Paul," began Robert in a pause. "What are you going to call him? You can't keep calling him 'Hey, you'."

"Why not?"

Agnes grinned. "Don't be such a grouch."

She knew they had won, and she reached over to ruffle the retriever's ears. The shaggy tail moved across the floor, but the dog stayed where it was. "Look how much he likes you, Paul. He doesn't want to leave you."

"I was thinking I'd call him Bob."

Robert rolled his eyes.

"Well, whatever you like," she replied lightly. "He's your dog."

A clocked ticked from somewhere in the room. Stevens grinned into his glass.

"What about Jack?"

The dog pricked up its ears.

"Jack?" echoed Robert. "As in, Jack Ryan?"

"Who's Jack Ryan?" she asked.

Stevens chuckled. "Oh, someone Max knows."

"You mean an exile?"

"Not just an exile. A real scoundrel."

"You're not going to name this gorgeous animal after a common criminal, are you? You have no taste!"

"As you just pointed out, he's my dog. Right, Jack?" Stevens stroked the dog with his foot, and Jack put his head down between two paws, closed his eyes, and sighed.

Agnes sighed and shook her head.

"Men."

She was dressed and wrapping sandwiches when the doctor shuffled into the kitchen the following morning.

"What's all this?" he mumbled, rubbing sleep from his face and reaching for the coffee maker.

"The weather's so nice! Might be the last of summer. I thought we could all hike someplace for a picnic. What do you think? Know any good spots?"

"What I think is it sounds like a good outing for you and your boyfriend. Have fun."

"Oh, come on, Paul." She put an arm through his and leaned against him. "No fun without you. My boyfriend's not much of an out-doorsman, and it would do you good. Come with us!"

"Well . . . there's a small lake a ways east of here. It has some interesting rock formations."

"Okay!" She laughed. "Rock formations it is." She kissed his cheek and went back to wrapping.

Later, they piled backpacks into the car and set out, the doctor driving east, away from the City.

The road led through young pine and old hardwood, crossed streams and brooks, and curled around hills. She watched a huge sycamore approach, enormous open limbs majestic against a royal blue sky. It towered overhead and swept by; then the road descended, the trees thinned, and the countryside turned flat, empty, and straw-colored.

The sun was high and bright, and she lowered her window to let the wind in her hair. Miles of open country went by. The yellow grass turned marshy, and in the distance strange white birds skimmed low over streaks of shimmering blue. A little ways off the road, one ancient tree still stood its ground, heavy limbs gnarled and rotting, scattered leaves casting no shade, already falling.

The lake came into view. Slabs of concrete went by, piles of brick and broken glass, tangles of rusted metal. She thought they looked like bleached bones, the remains of something long dead.

The car turned, and they passed a long boat ramp, then parked above a sandy shore dotted as far as the eye could see with huge boulders and rocky outcroppings, some with easy slopes and natural steps. They got out of the car and hiked a ways, chose an easy outcrop, and climbed to the top, dropping their packs and looking out over the water.

The lake stretched two or three miles across, blue and sparkling, yellow cliffs rising on a far shore. The water looked cool, inviting, and she wondered aloud whether it was safe to wade.

Stevens shrugged.

"I've never set a foot in it."

"Come on," offered Robert. "Let's have a look."

The two clambered down. Robert took off his shoes and walked to the water's edge, scooped up a handful, sniffed at it–then tasted it, frowning.

"Well?" She kicked off her shoes.

"Well . . . come on!"

They raced and splashed, waded hand in hand, and stopped to skip stones. The sun and the solitude were intoxicating, and she stood for long minutes with her head thrown back, luxuriating in the sun on her face.

"This is so wonderful!"

A while later, they climbed up with bare feet to rejoin the doctor and Jack waiting on a flat area worn into the outcrop.

Robert tossed his shoes aside.

"Lunch ready?"

"You have the wrong rock," Stevens grumbled. "Yours is over there."

Tying back her hair, Agnes grinned. "May I help, Paul?"

"You may."

Robert remained standing, looking over the water.

"I thought this was a lake, Paul."

"Looks like one to me."

"But a lake would be fresh. This is salty. Are we that close to the ocean?"

"Well, we're miles from the coast, but I understand a lot of inland water is brackish now. Some kind of sea inundation. Started years ago. I didn't know it had reached this far."

"Well, it has." Robert turned and shaded his eyes, looking back at the broken remains they had passed earlier. "You know, I don't think I ever really thought before how much has changed."

She looked up at him. "What do you mean?"

He pointed toward the far slabs of concrete, sunlight glinting on the hairs of his arm outstretched against the sky.

"Well, who built those buildings? What were they for? Was the lake fresh then? Did people live here?"

Gazing into that same distance, she murmured, "And what happened to them?"

"They died," said Stevens.

Slowly, she came to her feet.

What had happened to the world twenty years ago–it had never seemed quite real to her. Not like the fire. Not like her parents. Rather an abstraction, something one might read about in a book and try, not too successfully, to imagine. Now a shadow seemed to pass over, and she stared at the distant ruins, breathless with a sudden, appalling connection: the thought of innumerable, muted souls.

The doctor's voice reached her.

"Come on, folks. Let's eat. Life is for the living."

"Amen," answered Robert.

They ate. Her mood lifted. They bantered and laughed. But in the lulls of conversation, more than once, she found herself drawn to the ruins.

Afterward, they relaxed in the sun and the silence, Robert lying on his back and watching fat cumulus clouds drift overhead.

"I wonder," he mused, "if there's any property for sale in Max's town."

The doctor sat up.

"What are you talking about?"

"I'm thinking of buying some property."

"Am I missing something?"

Robert propped himself on an elbow.

"Well, what's to stop me? I have money. If someone wants to sell, they can sell. Or not. I can't force them."

"Just what do you think you're doing?"

"What do you mean?"

"Damn it! Don't insult my intelligence."

Robert glanced at her, then replied, "I'm getting out, Paul."

This was new. He had not mentioned it to her. "Robert?"

"I have to do something!" His face darkened. "I'm not about to spend the rest of my life as Richard Martin's trained monkey!" His eyes flashed at Stevens. "Or would *trophy* be a better word?"

"How would we live?" she asked quietly.

"I have some ideas." His voice was raw, and she could sense him trying to control himself. But there was a tremor in his free hand. "And we can hire help. I have enough money stashed."

"And you think you can just *buy* your way out?" demanded Stevens.

"I think I can resign and go live wherever I choose."

"And you don't think they'll have anything to say about that?"

"Why should they? They know there's no information I could take with me." He laughed, a little wildly. "That was the *intent,* wasn't it?"

"If they ever get a hint of the documents you have . . ."

"They won't."

"For all you know, they planted them!"

"I don't believe that. I have good reason not to."

"The letter to yourself?" she asked, but no one seemed to hear.

"And if you're wrong," growled Stevens, "just where does that leave *me*? When you two disappear and Security starts asking questions? Have you considered that?"

Robert shut his mouth. The muscles of his jaw knotted. But he looked away.

Stevens got up and began picking up the remains of the picnic.

She moved to help.

Part II

Childhood Ends

32

The meeting room was in shadow. A single lamp stood on the big table, its flame turned low to conserve oil. Face blood-red in its yellow rays, knuckles gleaming white, Jack Ryan clutched the edge of the table as though some force in the darkened room threatened to tear it from his grasp.

Sun-browned ovals that were faces hovered in the gloom, dumbfounded.

"What's the big deal, Jack? Why can't we have a simple meeting with them?"

Ryan's arms started shaking.

"*Because,* you stupid sons of bitches! I already *told* you what you need to know!"

At the far end of the table from Ryan, Max sneered.

"Don't tell *us* what we need to know. Set it up! Like you were supposed to."

Ryan surged to his feet, his chair tumbling over and banging against the wall behind him.

"*I don't take orders from you, boy!*"

"Fellas, fellas, listen!" The fire chief quickly held up his hands as if holding the two apart. "We can't settle this here. Let's take it to the Committee. Let's see what *they* want to do."

Ryan leaned over, planted both hands flat on the table, and twisted his head to look the fire chief in the face.

"Yeah. You go hide behind your *fucking* Committee. But don't come whining to me when they fuck it up."

He straightened. He kicked the fallen chair out of his way and strode from the room.

The heavy front door slammed. The old windows rattled.

The fire chief shook his head, muttering, "I guess that's that."

The officers got up and filed out, the lamp flickering a little as each passed, until only two remained. Martha, her face in her hands. And Max, slouched in his chair.

She wiped her eyes.

"Do you *have* to do that?"

"What?"

"*Push* him like that."

"Seriously? You were here last week. You heard what he said. He was going to set up a meet. And now he changes his mind?"

"Well, maybe he's right. He knows the Corporation better than we do. Better than *you* do."

"But that's just it! We don't *know* anything. The *Committee* doesn't know anything. Christ, do you really want to get involved in a war, on *Jack's* say-so?"

"Oh, I don't know who's right! But I *do* know you keep making it worse. Always arguing with him. Always criticizing, setting him off."

"Yeah, sorry, but he's got a job to do."

"Max, he's *doing* it! He's working too hard!"

"You're kidding, right? Jack?"

"Yes, *Jack!*" Suddenly, she was livid. "What's the matter with you? Don't you ever notice anything? The road? The crews? The deputies? Maybe if you spent some *time* around here, helping out, instead of disappearing off into the woods whenever you get the chance!"

"Oh, come on. I notice things. But someone besides Jack Ryan is digging ditches, aren't they?"

"Of course! *Lots* of someones! That's just it! Jack has done a tremendous job organizing. You have no idea how many problems he's solved. And the Committee's no help. They just argue about everything until you want to pull your hair out. But you wouldn't know, would you? You're never here."

He looked down at his hands. This did not seem to be a good time to point out there was nothing for him to do.

"Don't take this the wrong way, Max, but exactly why do you want to be vice president? No one thinks you're very interested in it. And after tonight . . . why, there's already talk of asking you to resign. Did you know that?"

He stood up.

"Yeah, okay, Martha. Let's get out of here. I'll walk you home."

Outside, a bright moon hung overhead, the road a pale gash that cut across the dark countryside. They started off, walking apart, Max thinking that maybe he should beat them to it and just quit. It was tempting. Until he pictured himself wandering from farm to farm, begging odd jobs.

The problem was Jack. The idea of taking him down with some papers from Robert was ridiculous. There were powerful people behind those papers. Dangerous people. People like Richard Martin. The papers were still taped under a drawer in his room. Maybe he should burn them.

After all, would Anderson even listen? Would he care? Because Martha was right. Things were getting done. And that was all that really mattered, wasn't it? They didn't need Max Wyse.

He shoved his hands in his pockets and hunched his shoulders against the thought that had been haunting him for weeks: They didn't need him.

Martha's house stood out clearly in the silver light. When they reached it, she let herself in, the door closed, the lock snicked, and shortly the curtains were suffused with warm, yellow light.

He shivered, turned away, and looked down the road that stretched onward through a heaving sea of dark fields.

Jack and the gang had once been a kind of family, the only family he could remember. It had been a stupid thing to do, making an enemy of him. Truly, truly stupid.

But maybe he could fix it. Maybe, if he groveled enough, if he stopped sniping and tried to get along, things with Jack could go back to the way they were.

It was the only idea that made any sense.

He started walking.

Tomorrow. Tomorrow he would do it. He would find Jack. They had to talk. There had to be a way.

The lone gray figure grew closer on the moonlit road ahead, and he bore down with silent, loping strides. Then he accelerated.

Then he sprinted.

The figure began to turn, but too late.

His fist hooked and buried itself in something soft. His target doubled over, and he was on him, kicking and punching, throwing his weight into it, sweeping away pathetic attempts to block his attack, until the figure collapsed in the road. He went on kicking, solid kicks thudding into torso and limbs. Then he backed away, panting for breath, watching the crumpled shape in the moonlight.

The shape did not move.

A final kick for luck, and he jogged back down the road, the way he had come.

Max came to his senses. His sides were on fire. The moon must have set, it was dark and he was cold, but it hurt too much to move, even to roll his face out of the dirt. So he lay shivering, wondering who they were, had they meant to kill him, would they come back. But it didn't matter. He could not make himself move.

When he awoke again, there was warmth on his back.

One eye opened.

He could see that the warmth came from the sun. That the dry roughness under his face was dirt. That he was still in the road.

He could move, and he pushed himself to hands and knees, gasping with pain that knifed his back and squeezed his ribs like an iron band. From the damp, stale odor that reached his nostrils, he had urinated on himself sometime during the night.

Holding his breath, he pushed to his feet, and the brightly lit road began to turn. His stomach revolted, and he leaned over, vomiting, clutching his sides in agony.

Then it was over.

He straightened, wiped his mouth, looked around. When he had his bearings, he began limping in the direction of home.

33

The sight of a man hanging dead from a tree, during his years with Ryan's gang, had always unsettled him, but now he thought he understood, and after two days of sleeping and pissing blood, Max left the farmhouse. He wanted to find the Chief of Police.

It was a long way to go, taking shallow breaths as he shuffled along the main road. But he finally reached the town office, where he found Martha working as usual, although what she did all day he wasn't entirely clear on.

He mumbled hello and looked around for something to sit on.

She continued working.

"I said, *hello.*"

"Well, I'm busy."

"Too busy to say hello?"

"Max Wyse, I don't think I want to talk to you."

"Why? What have *I* done?"

"What've you done?" She laughed shrilly. "What have you *done? Where have you been?* How could you cause so much trouble and then not even show up?"

"Show up where?"

She looked up at him then–and jumped to her feet.

"Max! My God! What happened?"

"Bandits, I guess."

She led him to her chair and made him sit, then stood over him, gently turning his jaw this way and that, examining the bruises.

Some of the dull pain seemed to ebb away.

"Are you all right? Where did this happen?" Then she was angry again. "I'll bet you were sneaking around the woods!"

"No, it happened right after–" He had been about to say, *right after I walked you home,* but stopped, for some reason. "It was right on the main road."

"Why didn't you send word? Don't you board with someone? Couldn't they let us know?"

"I guess I don't see that much of them."

"Why am I not surprised?"

"Come on. Where's Bert? I want to tell him. Christ, Jack never let this kind of thing happen when *he* was running security."

The front door opened.

In walked a tall, sun-burnt man, who nodded to Max and smiled at Martha, a long, slow smile under smug, knowing eyes.

"Hi, babe."

Max recognized him, one of Ryan's boys, the last to join the gang before everything changed.

"Sleep all right?"

Martha hadn't answered. She was looking at the floor, blushing furiously, and he watched in amazement, not too sure what he was feeling, only that it wasn't very pleasant.

The tall man chuckled, "Tonight?"

Softly, she answered, "All right."

"Okay. See you then."

It was a long moment, after the door closed, before she could look up again.

"That was Greg."

"Yeah. I know."

"He's really very nice."

"Uh-huh."

"Max, I'm sorry. I've been mean to you."

"Forget it." He wanted to get out, and managed to stand up again. "You were right. I've thought it over, and I'm going to resign."

"Oh, no, Max! Don't quit!"

"No, it's better this way. Saves everyone a lot of trouble. I'm not cut out for it, and no one really wants me around."

"But what will you do?"

"Guess I'll work for someone. It's probably time I learned something useful. Just do me a favor, if you see him, and tell Bert what happened."

"I will, Max. Just be careful."

He promised to keep in touch, limped out door, and shuffled home.

In the morning, he went to the pub for breakfast, and to think over his future.

There wasn't much to think about.

Why had he quit? He had no idea. He hadn't planned it. But staring blankly at his second cup of coffee, it occurred to him that he'd better resign to someone besides the town secretary.

Someone like John Anderson.

Ah, Christ.

It would be a long hike out to Anderson's place. He really needed a better way to get around. Especially if he was going to look for work.

Bill, the owner of the pub, kept a couple of horses stabled out back, and after a long talk about care and feeding, and buying and selling, they struck a deal for board.

Then he limped and shuffled to Barbara Hutchins' place.

She was working in her barn. This time she greeted him.

"Hey, stranger! Looking to rent that bay again?"

"I was thinking I might buy him."

"No! Really?"

"That's what I was thinking."

"Well, let's see." She thought a moment, then named a price.

"Yeah? That much? Huh. Guess it wasn't such a great idea after all. Well, thanks just the same."

"Wait a minute! Haven't you ever heard of bargaining?"

"Well . . . " He countered, and eventually they settled on a price, after she agreed to let him try horse and tack for a week and bring it all back if it didn't work out.

He counted out most of his savings. Beads of sweat prickled his forehead, and he rode away thinking he'd better find another way to make a living, and pretty damned soon.

———————

After breakfast the following day, he rode out to Anderson's place. The days were noticeably shorter, hay was drying in the fields, and he told himself he'd better get this over with and get on with finding work. Winter was not far off.

He rode up the long hill. The pale dust coating trees and the clop of hooves on dry, caked ground reminded him how much had changed, since he had hiked up this hill last spring.

At the top, he climbed down from the horse and shouted.

"Hey, John! Anybody home?"

Anderson emerged from the barn and walked over.

"What brings you out this way? Nice animal. Yours?"

"I'm trying him out."

Anderson stroked the long face. "What's his name?"

"Ah . . . his name?"

The old man laughed.

"You got to give him a name, boy! You can't just call him 'no-name'."

"Yeah. I'll have to think of one."

"Well, I don't suppose you came all the way out here just to show him off, did you?"

"Uh, no. Not exactly."

"Well?"

He looked down. It was as if what he had come to say were stamped on his forehead, and it made him feel small. Small, and a coward.

"By the way," the old man rambled. "Where'n hell were you the other night? The way I heard it, you and Ryan almost had it out over this meeting. Why'n helln't you show up?"

He coughed.

Anderson spat.

"Don't shit me, boy. You got a girl, she'll keep. You got a job to do. Remember that."

"Look, John, I got the tar kicked out of me. Right on the main road. I was home. Never even heard about a meeting."

Anderson peered at him.

"You sure did, didn't you. Ryan?"

"What? No. Couldn't be."

"Why not?"

"He's not that good."

"Got a whalin', did you?"

"Yeah. Never had a chance."

"Did you report it?"

"Uh, not yet."

"We have a police force, you know. They should hear about this."

"Yeah, I've been trying to find Bert."

"Well, you still haven't said what you want."

He looked past Anderson toward the barn. The paint had peeled off long ago and the gray boards had shrunk, leaving an irregular pattern of chinks in between.

"Tell me about the meeting."

"Go read the minutes. I don't have time to be your secretary."

"I don't trust the minutes."

"Don't trust Martha's note-taking? Well, I guess she hasn't exactly had her mind on her work lately. That's the trouble with you young people, you know."

"Come on, John."

"Well, let's see. Seems your City friends are worried about an invasion."

"*My* City friends?"

"Word is you've been hobnobbing with Corporate types."

"I have some contacts, if that's what you mean."

"I don't know that it is."

"So? What *do* you mean?"

"Well, never mind. Maybe just loose talk. Your contacts say anything about this?"

He hesitated, feeling the old man's eyes on him.

"Just some wild rumors. Crazy stuff. About war."

"Maybe not so wild. Looks like they want us out front. Which means they're scared."

"Maybe."

Anderson frowned. "I suppose they could have something else up their sleeve. But I don't know what that would be."

"That's just the point, John. We don't *know* anything. And I don't trust them."

"Yup. Neither do I. Neither do I."

"So what did Jack say?"

"Not a helluva lot. I take it he has contacts, too, and he isn't saying who they are, either."

"They can't be people he's just run into. What's he hiding?"

"Good question, boy. Why don't you go get us some answers?"

"That's what I'm trying to do."

"Well, you won't find any around here."

"Not so fast. What did Jack say he was going to do?"

"Well, we had a little disagreement about that. Seems Jackie-boy was all set to run off and sign a treaty or somethin'. We put the brakes on. Told him we wanted to meet with these mysterious Corporate types, hear what they have to say."

"Good. And?"

"Well, he was pissed. Plenty pissed. For some goddamned reason. Makes a man wonder. But he said he'd do it."

"Think he will?"

"He'd better. Or he'll be out on his ear."

"Yeah? How?"

"We'll pass a resolution or something."

"Yeah?"

"We'll do something, don't you worry about it. We're the Committee. The president's not in business for himself."

"No, but I don't trust him either. All right, John. I'll get out of your hair. Unless you have something else to pass on."

"Can't think of it."

Anderson seemed to hesitate. He stood looking across the top of the hill.

"You know, son, I thought you had a decent chance to win that election. I really did. Jack surprised us. In more ways than one, I guess. But I'm not sayin' I'm all that happy about it."

Max climbed on his horse, thinking he had one more reason for John Anderson to be unhappy, taped safely under a drawer in his room.

"Well, maybe next year."

"Let's hope we make it that far. You keep an eye on our boy, hear?"

"Right. If you'll look me up once in a while when you're in town, instead of making me ride all the way out here just to pry a little information out of you."

Anderson cackled, slapping the animal's flank.

"Well, hell! What's the use of having a horse?"

He walked back to his barn.

––––––––––––

The sun was setting when Max swung down from the saddle, reveling in the creak of leather, and tied up the horse, pausing to stroke the long neck and admire the sheen of its brown coat and black mane.

Then he went inside the town office.

The rest of the officers were gathering for the weekly meeting, and greeted them, at ease for once, safe in the knowledge that John Anderson was 'not all that happy' with President Jack Ryan.

Ryan was late. He strode into the meeting room, looking around as though he owned it, then swept two people aside, a hand on each, pulling them in for a close, heated discussion. From his side of the room, Max tried to pick out what was being said–until he saw Ryan's hands, and his mouth went dry.

The knuckles of one were scraped raw. The other was bound up with a dirty cloth, and evidently giving him pain.

He stared. It wasn't possible. It just wasn't possible. Maybe it was a coincidence, a fight with someone else. Or maybe Ryan had had help–although why anyone in the old gang would hold a grudge against Max Wyse, he could not fathom. But he fingered the handle of a big hunting knife he had dug out and cleaned up and honed, and started wearing on his hip.

Ryan called the meeting to order.

Martha took notes.

The agenda was mundane, as usual, and Ryan tackled each item with his usual ferocity.

Max stayed quiet.

When the last item had been disposed of, the windows had long since gone black and people were yawning, ready to wrap it up and go home and to bed. Martha stacked her notes, and Ryan slapped the table, ready to adjourn.

Max cut him off.

"All right, Jack. Let's set a date to invite your Corporate pals."

The room went silent. Nothing moved, except a black wedge of shadow that shifted across Jack Ryan's shirt. Max felt a tingling sensation, hairs standing up on the back of his neck.

"*What?* It's simple! We set a *date.* You relay it to your *contacts.* We all get together! How hard can it be?"

"I told you," Ryan's voice grated across the room. "I don't take orders–"

"*Do your damned job!*"

Ryan shot up, balancing on the balls of his feet as though he might fly across the table, Max a half second behind him, the handle of the knife jutting out from his hip.

No one breathed, until Ryan broke the silence.

"I'll take care of it."

The words seemed to exude through Ryan's clenched teeth, and the black eyes said, *I'll take care of you, too.* They didn't change when he looked around at the others, shoved his chair aside, and walked from the room.

The front door slammed.

There was a sound like a wet gasp, and Martha ran from the room, one hand over her mouth. One by one, the others got up and left, shaking their heads.

All but the Chief of Police.

Sitting comfortably with his chair tilted back, fingers laced over his round belly, the Chief drawled placidly, "Put your foot in it, didn't you?"

"Lay off, Bert."

Bert Morrow was unmoved.

"Why didn't you give him a chance to explain himself?"

"There's nothing to explain."

"Maybe. Maybe not. You and Jack been mixing it up?"

"What?"

"Fighting. You both been fighting. What I want to know is, you been fighting each other?"

"No."

"Just a coincidence, hm?"

The Chief nodded to himself, his chair banged to the floor, and he got to his feet and ambled out.

Martha returned, scooped up her notes, and headed for the door.

"Martha."

She stopped, her back to him.

"What?"

"How are you getting home?"

"Greg is waiting."

"Oh."

"Is that all?"

"Yes. Good night."

She left.

He stood by himself, watching the lamp's steady flame, thinking he had been right the first time. He should have resigned.

34

Stevens had been right.

It was a vicious cycle, of anger and mental fog, feeding on itself, that led to an attack, a seizure, and Robert had learned to control it, to hold it at bay, to stand guard behind a barricade of indifference, a wall of steady breathing. The department did its work, at least what was needed to get by, and for months he had avoided another attack. All he had to do was show up, watch over the same routine Alice Brown had, and not think.

That last was especially important: To not think.

It was a truce, an uneasy sort of peace, but one he might have lived with throughout his remaining years–if he could endure years in which nothing he did would ever matter. But the peace was shattered on a hot summer day by a bulky envelope he discovered in the back of a closet, by the letter it contained, addressed to him, and by the name in that letter.

A few short, blunt paragraphs, rectangles of black print on a white page, informed him that Richard Martin had framed him, had railroaded him, had then taken his memory from him. He read the letter three times before he noticed the signature at the bottom.

His own.

He sank blindly into a chair, trying to recall the face of the man who had done this, the man who had beaten him, who had taken her . . . He closed his eyes against a rush of images, unspeakable and unbearable–until he came to himself in the middle of the room with a stab of pain in his shin and the hollow *pop* of a light bulb bursting as a lamp crashed to the floor.

"Shit!"

He kicked the lamp aside. The letter was still clutched in his hand, and he stared at it, then balled it up and flung it across the room.

After a long minute, he exhaled. He looked around.

Papers were scattered across the floor, and he gathered them up, then read them, leaning over a table, lifting each page and turning it over to read the next. Memos. Reports. Names of spies.

He retrieved the letter, smoothed it out, and read it again

It was clear that the last thing he had done, as Martin closed in, was to make sure he would not forget. And, looking at a thick wad of cash with instructions on where to find more, something else was clear. He had planned an escape.

That thought was paralyzing. Escape to where?

But with that thought came the germ of an idea, and through the weeks of summer the idea took root. It became a plan. A way to start over. A way for his life to amount to something, outside the City.

35

"**M**ax, I want to buy some property in your town."

It was early on a Sunday morning, the first weekend in September. Robert and Max sat atop the picnic table in the yard behind the doctor's house, the rest of the house still asleep.

The young man yawned.

"What for?"

Robert rattled a few stones in one hand, and threw one across the yard still gray with dew, watching it disappear into the trees.

"I'm getting out. Leaving the City. And I think if I move quickly enough, they won't know what to do about it until it's too late."

"Christ, Robert. What makes you think they won't come looking for you?"

"Why bother?"

He drew his arm back, feeling the tension gather around the weight in his hand, then hurled it forward, and the rocked sailed across the yard and into the trees, where it bounced from an unseen limb with a loud *thunk*.

"As far as *they* know, there's nothing I can tell. Right?"

"What if they find the time capsule?"

"I don't see how they would. But I suppose it's a chance I'll have to take."

"Is it a chance Agnes has to take? Does she know about this?"

"That's none of your business, my friend."

"The hell it isn't. Don't confuse me with one of your employees."

He sent another rock spinning into the trees.

"Well, she knows. She doesn't like it, but she's going to have to make up her own mind. And she will."

"All right, then. Go buy your property. Just keep her out of harm's way."

"Why, Max, she'd be flattered."

"No, she wouldn't. She doesn't think I'm worth spit. But I like her, and I don't want to see anything happen to her."

Robert chuckled, tossing the rocks aside.

"You're right about that."

There was the sound of tapping on glass. Behind them, in a kitchen window, Stevens held up a coffee mug. Robert waved and turned back to Max.

"Listen, I need some help. It could take weeks to find what I want. Maybe months. And I can't just walk away without a place to go. That's what I meant by moving quickly. I have to stay at my job and keep up the front until I'm ready. So I need an agent. That would be you. What do you say?"

"Hell, Robert, I don't know about that."

"It will be a business deal. I'll pay you." He looked pointedly at the young man's frayed clothes. "Don't tell me a little extra cash would hurt."

"Well, maybe. But if you really want to do this, I think we'd better pay a visit to John Anderson first."

"Who's John Anderson?"

"Someone who knows just about everything there is to know about our town. And everyone knows him. They say he was the first to settle here. We need to talk to him. Some people might not go for the idea of someone like you moving in from the City. But if John's okay with it, you probably won't have trouble with anyone else."

"All right. If you say so."

"What about the Doc?"

"What about him?"

"Does he know?"

"He knows. But I'd rather you didn't bring it up with him."

"Yeah, okay. Listen, it's a pretty long hike out to the Anderson place. You should rent a horse."

Across the yard, Max's horse was tied to a tree.

"You mean . . . like that?"

Max laughed.

"Something like it. But don't worry. It's not hard. And you're going to have to learn, sooner or later. So how about it? You going to be around next weekend? I think I can get one for you then."

The brown beast turned its head, seeming to look his way, and equally skeptical.

Robert sighed.

"Well, okay. I suppose you're right."

--- --- ---

Robert was waiting outside the doctor's house very early the next Saturday morning.

The sky was sapphire and clear, the trees across the lane a gray wall seeming to defend this place, an outpost of civilization, against whatever wilderness lay beyond. But here and there the gray barrier was relieved by autumn patches of pale yellow and dull red, then pierced with glints of orange sunlight revealing movement behind the wall, Max Wyse coming through the trees atop his bay gelding, a spotted gray mare following on a rope behind.

Max came across the road, climbed down, untied the lead rope, and led the mare to Robert.

"You ready for this?"

"Uh . . ." The mare stood quietly. "Does it have a name?"

"Don't worry about that. Look, she's really gentle. And the best way to learn is by doing. Just remember to mount and dismount from her *left* side. Otherwise you might spook her. You won't need to do much else. You'll really be along for the ride. Okay? Here."

He accepted the reins. For a moment, he considered the great head and neck. Then he grabbed the horn of the saddle, stepped into the stirrup, and swung himself up.

The mare sidestepped once, then stood placidly.

"You're right. I think I'll manage. He seems gentle enough."

"She."

"Right. She."

Max mounted up. For a moment he studied Robert, looking up and down as though for anything out of place.

"Okay. Just give her a nudge with your feet when you want to go. Pull back, gently, when you want to stop. Watch what I do. But she'll pretty much follow on her own."

Then they were moving, crossing the road, Max leading the way and the mare dutifully following onto a trail that wound through the trees, and for a time Robert had little to do but duck under branches.

Eventually, they came through the trees and onto a wide dirt road. Max turned right, the mare followed, and soon they were surrounded by rolling fields and dry brush and brown grass, the road wide and even.

Feeling a little more confident, Robert nudged the horse forward, to ride abreast of Max.

"How far is it?"

"Oh, maybe an hour. Maybe two. Depends."

"Christ, do you do this a lot? My backside hurts already."

"Yeah, you'll sleep tonight. But you'll get used to it."

"Where does this road go?"

"All the way through town."

"How far is it to town?"

"You're in it. Look. See that house? Way ahead?"

"Okay. I see it."

"That's the town office. That's where we hold our meetings. We call this the main road. Doesn't have a real name. When you see a side road or a trail that leads off from this, it'll go to someone's farm. You can't pull a cart over all of them. Not yet, anyway. We're working on it. But you can ride or walk."

The terrain passed by. Slowly. Yard by yard. Open fields and distant trees. There was a regular thud of hoof-falls, but no other sound, no other movement, and he supposed that this was what he had expected. But what he felt was a kind of waiting. Everything seemed to be waiting, the whole countryside, but it would always be the same. Nothing would change. Here was a different world, one that measured time by the drift of the sun from horizon to horizon, by the changing leaves, the cycle of crops, and the long pendulum of generations rising and falling. It was a world without reason. It existed; that was all. You might take refuge here. You might survive here. But it was hard to imagine living here.

He rode alongside Max in silence.

They left the road and crossed acres of farmland, riding single file over a trail that traced the angular borders of crop-fields and pastures, until they reached another unpaved road lined with willowy trees and a stone wall. Beyond the stone wall were brown fields and a few grazing cows.

Something prompted him to ask, "Anderson's?"

"I think so. A lot of it."

They followed the road up a long hill. At the top of the hill stood a gray barn and tall house, the paint peeling, the yard bare but for scattered patches of stubborn grass. They rode up to the shaded porch and halted, the horses warm and glistening in the sun.

Pale blue eyes glittered from the shadows. A brown weathered face became visible, belonging to an old man slouched in a chair.

"Hello, John."

The old man nodded. "Max. What've we here?"

"John, this is Robert Larsen. Robert is thinking about moving into town."

The pale eyes seemed to widen.

"Is he. No law against that, I suppose."

"John–"

Robert climbed down. He stood by the steps to the porch and looked up at the man in the shadows.

"Mr. Anderson. I live in the City. For reasons of my own, I have decided to leave. I have the means to purchase property, or clear unclaimed land and build what I want. I understand the name John Anderson carries some weight around town, so I came here to introduce myself and ask your advice. If this is not a convenient time, I can come back another day."

"Well, well . . ." Anderson shifted in his chair. "Maybe we'd better talk about this. Why don't you two come on up here, where it's cooler?"

Robert went up the steps, and Anderson rose and shook hands.

"I imagine you two could use something to drink."

"We'd appreciate that."

Anderson went in through a screen door. Max led the horses to a gray wooden trough, tied them, and was coming up the steps as Anderson reappeared with three glasses on a tray.

"We don't have ice, I'm sorry to say. But the well is cool." He sat down, mopping his forehead with a tattered handkerchief. "There's an ice house a ways down the road, but the ice never lasts very long. You'll have to give up a few things if you really plan on leaving the City, Mr. Larsen."

He accepted a glass and sat down.

"I know it's a bit rustic out here. But to tell the truth, I'm counting on that."

"Counting on it? How so?"

"Business opportunities."

"You don't say! What do you have in mind?"

"I'm still working on it."

Anderson eyed him. "Well, I'd like to hear more, when you're ready. So tell me, how long have you and Max known each other?"

"Oh, just a few months. Max gets his hands on some interesting items from time to time. If you know what I mean. In the City, we call it the black market, but I assume there's no problem with it out here."

"What sorts of items?"

"He managed some very agreeable cigars recently."

"Well, well! Does Mr. Larsen have an exclusive?"

"Well . . . no." The young man coughed. "But I don't really get that much stuff, and . . . and . . ."

"And what you get goes to your friends in the City. I suppose that makes some sense. So, Mr. Larsen. People don't generally leave the City. Not in my experience. Not voluntarily."

"Are you asking why?"

"I suppose I am."

"It's a long story."

"Well, I have time, if you do."

He drank a little water, stalling for time. This would be a step he could not undo. But he remembered the eyes of the City, its impunity, the letter, and he began talking, about his amnesia, about his discovery that it had been deliberately inflicted. He talked about what he had tried to do with the department. He mentioned the time capsule. But he did not mention Stevens. Or the letter.

"So there you have it, Mr. Anderson. It seems I have some money. And I intend to use it to start a new life, away from the City."

Anderson scratched his jaw.

"Well, well. That *is* quite a story. You wouldn't think civilized people could behave like that, would you? Well, well . . . so tell me. What else do you know? Heard anything unusual lately?"

"Unusual? Some rumors. That they're preparing for a war of some kind. Presumably against another corporation. But that's just an assumption."

The old man looked startled.

"It *is* an assumption, isn't it?"

"I take it the rumors have reached here as well."

"Right from the horse's mouth, you might say. Seems they want our help. Want to talk about it, anyway."

"No discussions yet?"

"Nope." Anderson chuckled. "We've been having a little trouble in that department. You can ask Max about it."

"Well, Mr. Anderson. Now you know something about me. If you don't mind, I'd like to learn a little more about your fine town."

"And I suppose I'm the man to tell you. Although . . ." Anderson paused. "You may have left out a few things. Through no fault of your own, of course."

Robert shrugged.

Anderson settled back in his chair.

"Well . . . let's see. We were pretty much the first ones out here, the wife and I. At least there wasn't any welcoming committee. Twenty years ago, that was. Done pretty well, too. Might not look like much, Mr. Larsen, but we didn't start with much. Hell, I didn't know first thing about farming, not back then, at the beginning. And I don't think anyone else around here did either. We all had to learn. And there was no one to show us."

"No one? Everyone had died?"

"No. Gone. Left. No idea where or why. But we never found any bodies. And no one came back."

Max stirred.

"So how did you get here, John? You're not from the City, right?"

"Well, son, that's a bit of a story."

"Well, we have time." The young man grinned.

"All right. All right. It was quite a ways from here, where we started. A couple hundred miles. In a place that was coming apart. We had a sorry excuse for a government to begin with, which I suppose goes without saying, and when the shit really hit the fan with the plague and all, the bigwigs started bailing. City councilors, landlords, rich lawyers. Anyone with means. A few officials, the bureaucrats, tried to hold things together, and we stuck it out as long as we could. But when the water stopped, it was time to go.

"We took a truck and got about halfway to the coast. Ran out of gas. We had some food with us and a couple of guns. I didn't like the look of things, so we kept moving. Ran low on food pretty quick, and I shot what I could. Thank God it wasn't winter, though. I don't think we would've made it.

"Anyway, we found this place. Stumbled on it by dumb luck. No people around that we could see. And, like I said, no bodies. So we thought it might be safe. There were farm animals, some grain stored, some vegetables still in the ground. I worried about the City for a time, but they held together. You know, Mr. Larsen, sometimes your Corporation scares hell out of me, and I don't mind saying it. But they got the job done. The City looked like it was going to make it, so we took a chance on this place."

"What about everyone else?" asked Max.

"Other people found their way here too—Something on your mind, Mr. Larsen?"

"I'm surprised you weren't overrun. There must have been thousands of refugees, all looking for a place to go."

"Well, yes and no. Living like this ain't easy, and it sure wasn't back then. We took a chance. We were completely on our own. Most people don't really want that, and most headed for the City, once word got around that the City had jobs, places to live, and food."

"But you stayed here."

"That's right. Look, I'm not saying it was an easy decision. We talked about it—a lot. But we thought we could make a go of it." He winked at Max. "I'll tell you something, son. I owned a construction business where we came from. That's why I don't like guv'mint so much. As soon as you get enough people together, you got to organize 'em, and then people find ways to game it. Graft, kickbacks, bribes. Like rats and cockroaches, anywhere there's people. But out here . . . well, you check around. Most had their own businesses too, one sort or another. They feel the way I do. They don't like being told what to do, and not by some punk with a fancy title and his hand under the table."

Max laughed. "And now we have our own *guv'mint,* thanks to you!"

"And we're going to keep a real close eye on that, let me tell you."

"Sounds like there's more to the story, Mr. Anderson. When did you start your government? What changed your mind?"

"You know anything about Jack Ryan?"

"I've heard the name."

"Jack's been with us a long time. I guess you could say he's a businessman, too, in his own way. Just a different line of work."

"Well, there's something else that goes with people, and that's thieving. It got to be real problem back then, after a bunch of us settled here. At first it was random, like food stolen, or a horse, or a gun. One fellow passing through got caught at it, and people kicked shit out of him, then gave him some food and sent him on his way.

"But it didn't stop. It changed. It wasn't random anymore. More stuff was being taken. There were break-ins, but never any witnesses. It was like somebody figured us all out, when we were out planting or picking, or doing fence work, when people were at home, when they were off visiting. Kinda got ugly for a while, with some of us accusing others of it. Or their kids. But most of us figured it had to be from outside."

"Why was that?"

"Well, we couldn't see it. At least I couldn't. Too risky. If you've already got something good going, and everybody knows everybody . . . I mean, where the hell would you hide a fella's horse? And you'd have to have a pretty good idea how you'll get run out of town if you're caught.

"Well, we figured it was outsiders, probably somebody who'd set up nearby and been watching us. And we figured we were going to have to do something about it. Like make up a posse. We talked about it, anyway. Had some meetings. But it's a lot easier to talk. We all had work to do, more than we could handle, and not many people were volunteering to go off riding through the woods, maybe for weeks, maybe come up empty or get killed."

"Is this where Jack Ryan comes in?"

"That son of a bitch rode right into town! Out of the blue. Had a couple of his boys with him. Said he knew about the bandits, had been watching them, and wanted to make us an offer. He'd get rid of them, he said, but he wanted us to hire him and his boys. Private security. Like some kind of sheriff."

"I see. Does sound a bit suspicious."

"Well, not only that, his idea of payment was a little rich. Ten percent of what we all produced. Imagine that!"

Max whistled. "He never thinks small, does he?"

"Nope. And it nearly cost him, too. If we hadn't all been so scattered, he might've had a real mob on his hands, a pretty ugly one. But maybe he'd that worked out too.

"Anyway, we had more meetings. More arguments. Some people thought it was a good opportunity to set a trap and get rid of one problem. But most of us thought it would be better to put him to work. After all, even if he was the culprit, someone else would come along later. It would never end. We needed protection for the long haul, and it was going to cost us one way or another. At least Ryan was volunteering. And he'd have his own stake in making sure we all had a chance to be successful.

"But of course no one was going to pay ten percent! That was sheer robbery, all by itself."

"So what happened?"

"What happened? We negotiated, that's what happened. We got him down to five percent. And we had to work to get some of our own to swallow that. Wasn't easy. A few had to be convinced he wasn't the original thief, or they weren't going to go along. So Ryan agreed to deliver the bandits before he'd get paid anything."

The old man shook his head.

"Well, he delivered, all right. And put on a helluva show doin' it. Came up with a real raggedy pair of so-called bandits, and announced they would hang. In public. Everyone was invited.

"Mr. Larsen, we're not a bloodthirsty bunch. We didn't like it. And we didn't like him making a spectacle of it. But we couldn't change his mind. He said he had to send a message to anyone else around.

"Well, we were in it now. Frontier justice, some people said. The hangings went ahead. And I think the message came through loud and clear to everyone else."

"Christ."

"And they weren't the last," Max added. "Not by a long shot."

"Nope. But Ryan kept good. He started patrols. His boys walked and rode all over town, every day, poking their noses everywhere. Got to be a bit of a nuisance sometimes, but I think that's what did the trick. The constant presence. Who knows? Maybe some of that thieving *was* our own, after all.

"So now we had our protection, and we were *growing*, believe it or not. New people showed up, honest people, willing to work. New farms were started. And every once in a while Ryan recruited someone else for his gang.

"But I'll tell you about someone else who showed up, back then. Young boy, just a scarecrow, wandering down the road. Lost and starving. Sure was filthy. Didn't know where he belonged, or where his home was. Didn't even know who his parents were. Just seemed sure of his name. Ryan, of all people, took him in. Cleaned the boy up, fed him, gave him a place to sleep. Made him into a kind of mascot. And he's sitting there right next to you."

Max was studying his hands.

"Okay, it's true, as far as it goes. What do you want me to say?"

"Just checking, boy." Anderson grinned. "That was, what, fifteen years ago? Fifteen good years. And we've all done pretty well. Enough to trade with the City. Even use Corporate money.

"But times change. Ryan was in business for himself. Nothing wrong with that, I suppose, but too much money was going to him, and nothing was going to move us ahead. I'll give Max some credit. He put his finger on it. We had to make some changes. And we did. So now we have our own government. A real one, with elections. We still have Ryan, but he works for *us*, not the other way around."

Robert sat back and gazed over the railing, past the horses by the trough, past the old barn. There was a horizon beyond the rim of this hill, hazy and bright, that he had not noticed before. Maybe there was an answer out here after all.

"So that's our story, Mr. Larsen. Still interested?"

He got to his feet.

"I am. Very much so. Thank you for your time."

The old man stood up as well.

"When do you plan on moving out here?"

"As soon as I can."

"Got any property picked out?"

"Not yet."

"Well, I'll ask around. Pretty much everything cleared is being worked, but you never know. Sometimes money talks."

They went down the steps and walked to the horses.

Anderson invited him back, adding, "You, too, Max."

"You sure, John?"

"As long as you behave yourself."

"You know, sometimes I just don't know quite how to take you."

The old man winked.

"Well, it's my personal conviction it pays to keep young people guessing."

Robert grabbed his saddle, took a breath, and swung up. And after a moment, remembered to pick up the reins.

Max mounted. His horse began walking toward the road, and the mare followed. They started down the hill.

"Max, do you think it would possible to rent a room out here somewhere? Isn't that what you do?"

"Maybe. Bill might take on a boarder at the pub. I think he has a spare room. Would that work?"

"I don't see why not."

"I'll talk to him. But what about your property?"

"I want to spend some time out here while we're looking. I have a few ideas I want to start on. Would Bill take on a horse as well?"

"I can ask. Are you thinking about buying? I can find out about that mare, if you're interested."

"Sure, why . . . "

Something caught his eye, and he reined in, carefully.

Miles away in the sunlit haze to the north, a tall column of smoke, blue and gray, rose straight up, until it reached an altitude where the wind blew westward, and a flat gray trail stretched away as far as the eye could see.

"Max, look. What do you suppose that is?"

"Jesus. I don't know. It doesn't look like a natural fire. It's been burning a good while, but it hasn't moved from that one spot."

"How far would you say it is?"

"Ten, fifteen miles. Hard to judge. But a good ways from anything in town."

"The Corporation. Maybe clearing land."

Max nodded, shading his eyes.

"Or advertising."

36

For a change that Monday, Max was busy, persuading Bill to take on a tenant and another horse, negotiating with Barbara over the mare, invoking John Anderson's name whenever awkward questions were asked. He was doing something useful, and the heady feeling lasted throughout the day, right up until dinner.

He walked into the pub that evening and waved to the owner's son, Mike, wiping glasses behind the bar. Mike beckoned to him, drying his hands on a towel as Max walked up.

"Hey, Mike. What's up?"

"Yeah, hi, Max. Say–you in trouble?"

"What're you talking about?"

"Mr. Ryan was in here today. Asking questions. About you."

"Yeah? What sort of questions?"

"Like where were you. Who you been seeing. Had you been anywhere out of town."

"What did you tell him?"

"Not a damn thing."

"Why not?"

"Didn't like the way he asked. Made me want to punch his lights out."

Max laughed. "Yeah, I know the feeling!"

"Still and all, Max, he *is* your boss. You in trouble with him?"

"Look, Mike. The sonovabitch is *not* my boss. He doesn't pay me, and he can't fire me. And where I've been is none of his damned business."

Mike spoke quietly. "Is anything going on? Maybe it's none of *my* business, but you sure been acting strange lately. Hanging around City people, from what I hear."

"Look Mike, Jack doesn't like me, and he'd like to get rid of me. But I haven't done anything wrong. Okay?"

"Okay, Max. Whatever you say."

The rest of the week he waited, restlessly, and on Saturday was up and dressed and walking to the pub while it was still dark, and after breakfast, helped Mike saddle the two horses.

At the doctor's, the front door opened as he reined in and dismounted, and Robert came down the walkway with a noticeable spring in his step. Agnes's car was out front, and he opened the trunk and hauled out a heavy duffel bag. Then he hefted the duffel onto the back of the mare.

Max held one end while Robert strapped it down.

"What's all this?"

"Books."

"Yeah, I can tell that. What kind of books?"

"Engineering, mostly."

"Why? Is it a secret? Or do you like making me work for it?"

Robert chuckled, cinching the straps.

"I'll tell you about it later."

He lifted another duffel from the car, heaved it onto the horse, and strapped it down. Then he slammed the trunk.

"Ready?"

"Yeah. Sure. Let's go."

They rode to the pub.

Robert stowed the duffels in his new room, then paid three months' rent plus board for the horse.

"By the way," he asked Bill. "Is there a way to lock my door?"

"Lock your door?"

"I'm not ready to move in just yet, and I expect not everyone is as honest as you and Mike."

"Well, I suppose there's always a bad apple or two."

"All it takes is one. I'll be working on some business ideas, and I don't want to lose trade secrets to competitors."

"Competitors? You expect *competitors* around here?" Bill snorted. "Well, your door won't lock, but there's always someone tending front until we close up at night. Keep your windows locked."

"All right. I suppose that will have to do, for now."

Bill walked off, muttering something about *City people*.

When they were outside, Max asked, "You really think someone's going to steal your ideas? Out here?"

"Maybe not. But don't forget the spies."

"Oh. Yeah. Christ."

"So, Max. Any plans for today?"

"Not really. Why? What do you have in mind?"

"I want to explore."

"Explore what? Farmland?"

"No. I want to look for junk. Anything that might be salvaged. Whatever we can find."

"Junk? Well, that shouldn't be too hard."

They were odd things Robert was interested in. Wire drooping from old poles. Rusted hulks of cars and trucks, which he poked and prodded, tugging at springs and tubing. The roofless wreck of a house, where he noted pipes and wire in the skeletal walls. He sketched everything in a small notebook.

Later, as the sun lowered behind the trees, Max decided it was time to call it a day.

"We'd better head back. It's a long way to the doctor's."

"All right." Robert peered down the trail they had been following. "Doesn't look like there's anything that way, anyway."

At the main road, they turned the horses and rode eastward, the sun sinking behind them.

Max was tired, hungry, and irritated over the lunch he had missed.

"Okay, Robert. What's with all the secrecy? What're you after?"

"Whatever I can find. Pipes, tanks, wire. Anything."

"Why? What the hell for?"

"First I want to map it. Then I want to buy a few acres out here, so I can work on small-scale experiments over winter. Next spring, after the ground dries out, we can haul back what I need to build something bigger."

"You still haven't said what for. What kind of experiments? What are you trying to do?"

"I don't know yet."

"Well, hell, what're we doing?"

"I can explain what I'm thinking. But I'm still working on it."

"Well, I promise not to tell any competitors."

"Okay, wise guy. Think about this. Conditions outside the City are pretty backward, technologically speaking. We have cars and buses; you ride horses. We have electricity and telephones, and you don't even have a postal service. We have refrigeration. You pack ice in the winter, and it runs out before summer. We have running water, hot and cold. And so on."

"Yeah, well, we do the best we can with what we have. You've had a lot more to work with."

"Exactly! That's my point. We have these things because the Corporation salvaged what was left from the ruins. Oh, we do some light manufacturing, but most of what we use is beyond our ability to make. *Way* beyond it. Gasoline, for instance. We have years' worth in big storage tanks, but we don't know how to make more. We get power from the hydroelectric plant, but only one generator works. The rest are being used for parts. And when the last copy of some critical part wears out, the power will stop. A lot of this comes right through my department, and I can see it happening all over. Wherever you look, it's the same story. We're using up something we don't know how to replace. And I'll bet it's the same in other cities, as well. We're living on borrowed time. All of us. And it's going to run out."

As Robert talked, he found himself wondering if anyone, even John Anderson, had ever stopped to consider what might happen to their community if tens of thousands of people living just a few miles to the north suddenly ran out of gasoline, or electric power.

"Now, the exile communities, like yours, are basically self-sufficient. You've lasted this long living off the land, so you'd have to be. Barring some kind of catastrophe, I suppose you could go on indefinitely.

"But not everyone wants to go back to this. It's hard work, living as you do. And it's precarious. Don't be offended, Max, but you have to admit, it wouldn't take much for you people to end up in pretty serious trouble. Like a long drought. Or a crop blight. Or hoof and mouth disease."

"I'm not offended."

"Good. And that's not the only thing. It's not hard to understand why men like John Anderson, who escaped the plague with their lives and not much else, might be content with what they have. They have a right to be. They've accomplished a lot. But there must be plenty of young men and women around here who are getting restless. They want something more. I happen to think you're one of them, by the way."

"I won't argue. But I don't see where this is going. What are we supposed to do?"

"Bear with me. I've spent a lot of time thinking about this. Let's just take an example. I've heard you talk about a telephone system. That would be an excellent thing to have. But unless you build it out of salvage, there's a lot more you're going to have to figure out. For instance, you'll need wire. A lot of it. That means you'll need copper, and a way to heat the copper and draw it into wire, and a way to insulate it. And you'll need to refine the copper from ore, so you'll have to identify the ore and mine it. And so on."

"I'll take a telephone any way I can get it. What's wrong with salvage?"

"Nothing, I suppose. Except the Corporation has a long head start on you. Salvage is a wasting asset. Every year it's rusting, rotting, or being hauled away."

"Well, that's just the problem, isn't it? What're we supposed to do? Fight over it?"

"No. Not fight over it. *Build* it. The way it was done originally. Not with scrap, but with your own industry. Then it's yours, and it's growing with you. You see?"

"But how do you start? You can't make wire without machines, can you? And you probably can't make those machines without other machines. Everything depends on everything else! Where the hell would you start?"

"That's an excellent question. It shows you've been listening. And here's the answer. You find a suitable beginning. You go back far enough in industrial history to a point where simple engineering can stand on its own. That's what I'm working on. Industrial history.

"Take coal and iron. Coal extraction ties in nicely with iron smelting. The engineering is relatively easy. And the products! Think about ammonia, just plain ammonia. Ammonia can be derived from roasting coal for smelting, and you can use it for all kinds of things. Ammonium nitrate can blast stumps and boulders out of a field. Easier to plough, plant, and harvest. It can add nitrogen to the soil to give you a bigger harvest, or maybe more pasturage for more animals. Ammonia can even be used to make simple refrigerators, and if you can cool or freeze some of what you produce, you can produce more without it going to waste. You see?"

"Yeah."

What he was seeing were machines . . . buildings . . . airplanes, taking shape in the steel-blue vault above, like a stairway for him to climb . . . Until he looked again at the empty fields and the shadows of plodding horses stretched ahead on an empty dirt road now red with the setting sun, and he shook his head, trying to keep bitterness out of his voice.

"Sounds interesting, Robert. But I don't see how you build all that industry out here. Not with a bag of books and a map of junk. I mean, I'm trying not to laugh."

"Laugh all you want. I don't plan on doing it all myself. That's the beauty of it. I don't have to. I just want to get in on the ground floor. The way I see it, once someone starts the ball rolling, other people–you know, those restless young people–will find opportunities of their own, to make money, to do something exciting, to get away from following a plough around Daddy's farm all day."

"But it can't be that easy, can it? Or someone'd be doing it already."

"Of course it's not easy. But imagine what it would mean! And I think it's within our reach."

"Wait a minute. What do you mean, *our* reach? *Whose* reach?"

"Oh, don't worry. I mean the town in general. I don't expect you politicians to get your hands dirty."

Maybe it was because he was tired, maybe because he hadn't eaten since breakfast, but he snapped.

"Now you hold on a minute! You have no idea what it was like out here, not that long ago. How can you have any kind of industry without a road good enough to pull a stupid cart over? How would you even set up a smelter, or anything else, if pieces of it are carried off every night by bandits and smugglers–who are probably the same people supposed to be protecting you from bandits! What's changed around here is that we elected a few people to *organize* things, like police, like road work, like fire-fighting. And the people we elect answer to *us*. That's what *you* call politicians! You wouldn't be so interested in this place without them."

"Okay, okay! Truce. You're right. It was a cheap crack. I didn't mean anything by it."

It was dark when they reached the doctor's.

Robert dismounted and staggered a little.

"Christ, I think I hurt in places I've never felt before."

A stab of light from the entry lit up the walkway, and the door opened. Two silhouettes appeared, one coming down the walkway.

Agnes turned and went back inside, and Robert swore and went after her.

Stevens walked up to Max.

"So, he's going through with it."

"Yeah, I think so. Give me minute, will you? I need to tie these two up."

The old man shook his head.

"Maybe you'd better not. I'm afraid Miss Agnes is in a pretty ugly mood tonight. I don't envy Robert. Why don't you come back tomorrow? If you like."

"Yeah, Doc, okay. Sure."

Stevens walked back to the house.

The light went out.

Max finished tying the lead rope by feel, then mounted up and rode back.

He returned Sunday evening.

The doctor was alone, and they sat with whiskeys in the living room, played chess, and talked about Robert's ideas.

"What do you think, Doc? He makes it sound good, but I don't see how he can do it. It's almost like building a new world."

"I certainly think he's underestimating it. Are you two partners?"

"No, we're not partners. I don't know a thing about engineering, and I don't see how you can learn it all in a few months with a bag of books."

"Well, at least he has money. He won't starve."

"You know, one thing bothers me. This idea that the Corporation is living on borrowed time. That it's going to run out. What do you make of that?"

"I think he seriously underestimates the Corporation."

"Well, what about the idea that it depends too much on salvage?"

"We use everything we can. Salvage is part of it, but it's not the whole story. I'm not an engineer, but I happen know we've been casting iron for years."

"Yeah? Do you get the iron from ore or from scrap?"

"Couldn't tell you. Not my field."

"What about drugs, then?"

"What about them?"

"How are they produced?"

"Making pharmaceuticals is a bit more complex than casting pieces of metal. What are you driving at?"

"I'm trying to understand these things. Help me out."

"We make drugs in a laboratory. It's time-consuming, labor-intensive, and they're expensive."

"So . . . what happens if you run out of something? Like, say, gasoline."

"This isn't the old days, Max. We have hundreds of people who do nothing but plan. We're not going to just run out."

"But you only have so much, right? It *has* to run out, sooner or later."

"We'll be ready when that happens."

"How?"

"Again, not my field. But the planners keep tabs on everything. Robert should know this. There are departments like his all over the City, and the reason they exist is to supply information. As long as the planners do their jobs, we'll be ready."

"As long as they do their jobs."

"Of course, Max. That's what organization is all about."

37

That week, Robert went to work as usual, went to the office in the morning and unlocked his door, locked it again in the evening and went home again, as usual. Nothing changed. It was an ordinary week.

Yet, he felt . . . lighter. And he knew that Agnes had noticed. Although she said nothing.

Friday evening, they drove to the doctor's.

Saturday morning, when it was light enough, he set out.

Alone. On foot.

The trail through the woods was easy to find, but it turned and twisted under tangled trees that obscured the sky, and he was quickly disoriented. Still, he kept on, telling himself that he had to get used to this, finding his own way outside the City. He started checking his watch, mentally setting a time when he would stop and turn around and try to find his way back.

Twenty minutes later, he was out on the main road.

Walking, he found, is an excruciating way to travel. Excruciatingly slow, and excruciatingly tiring. After an hour of seeing only grass and brush, he was becoming convinced he had somehow gotten onto the wrong road. But no, that couldn't be right. He had passed the town office a while back. At least it had looked like the town office.

After another half hour, trees were crowding the road again. Presently, he made out the familiar gray structure ahead.

The pub was not exactly bustling, just a handful of people he didn't know and Mike behind the bar with a look of surprise on his face as Robert walked in.

The small buzz of conversation died.

He felt the stares, heard the quiet whispers. But it was what he had expected. Even his clothes screamed *City,* and he had already decided how he would handle it.

"Mornin', Mike! Sit anywhere?"

"Ahh . . . yeah, Robert. Anywhere you like."

He glanced around the big room, nodded to a couple of people, and picked out a table.

Mike came over with coffee, took his order, and returned a few minutes later with a steaming plate of eggs, toast, and a slab of ham.

"Thanks, Mike. How's Bill?"

Mike topped up his coffee.

"Oh, he's good. We had a cook who quit, so he's in back."

"Tell him I said hello."

"Okay. I will."

Around the room, conversation resumed, if a little quieter than before, and punctuated occasionally with suppressed laughter.

He ignored it and ate.

His feet hurt. His legs ached. Dust ground between his teeth. But the food was good, Mike kept his coffee hot, and a couple of people nodded to him as they got up to leave.

Fortified, he paid his tab and went out to retrieve his horse.

He was careful to stay on trails that were easy to follow, used the sun to keep track of direction, and rode as far as he dared, mapping and sketching. He found another wrecked car, some oblong metal tanks, but little more, and by mid-afternoon he was back on the road. He arrived back at the pub with plenty of daylight left.

Max was waiting.

"Glad you're back! Mike said you went exploring. Any luck?"

"Not much. I suppose there really isn't much around here. I should look farther north, closer to the City. There ought to be some industrial buildings. Maybe old factories."

"There are."

"Do you know the area?"

"Yeah, I do. And some of it is pretty dangerous. There are places that were closed off during the plague that you should stay away from. There used to be signs posted, but nowadays you really have to know. And there might be bandits. Which can be anyone who doesn't belong, but some of those guys used to kill for a horse. You shouldn't go alone. I'll come with you."

"I'll hire you. You can be my guide."

"Oh, don't worry about that. Happy to help."

"Max, I expect to make money at this. We have a business deal, remember? It's only fair."

"Well, okay. You're the boss."

38

South of the City were many acres of sprawling warehouses, rows of abandoned trucks and trailers, rust-streaked machinery enclosed behind chain-link fence, an industrial graveyard crisscrossed with concrete streets, cracked and dusty. Over most of this the Corporation exerted its control. It was an important source of salvage, and wandering prospectors were hunted down as thieves. But there were also areas the City stayed away from, probably suspecting a residue of Cargo Flu. No one but a few exiles went there.

One street of smaller, mostly empty warehouses was familiar to Max from his younger days traveling with Jack Ryan to meet up with smugglers, or just venture into the City. To get there, Ryan used a broad grassy path that must have been a back road at one time, branching east from the North Road and looping up toward the City. Max avoided it, mainly because Ryan used it, preferring instead an obscure trail he had found, which led to the same warehouses but in a more roundabout way.

After breakfast, he and Robert left the pub and rode up the North Road.

He rode along the shoulder and reined in when he found what he was looking for, a familiar gap in the undergrowth marking the trailhead. But there was something else. Twigs and small branches, green leaves still attached, were scattered in grass recently trampled.

Leaning on the pommel of his saddle, he peered into the trees. It seemed he heard voices, and after a minute he was sure of it. Faint, but unmistakable.

He beckoned to Robert, and they rode farther up the road, then tied the horses out of sight. Cinching his knife more tightly on his belt, Max led the way into the undergrowth, angling south and east from the road, toward the voices.

The brush was thick, and it was slow going, until they broke through and crossed over a long meadow yellow with autumn, then into a fragrant stand of old fir. Beyond this lay another meadow, and under the bright climbing sun a large shack stood out maybe fifty yards away, the door ajar. Horses idled nearby.

They crouched in shadow at the edge of the trees and watched.

Robert whispered, "What do you think?"

At that moment the door flew open, banging against the wall of the shack, and someone stumbled out, then backed away from the door.

Out of the shack strode Jack Ryan, followed by three others, Ryan bearing down on the lone figure while the others fanned out as though cutting off escape.

A voice floated across the meadow.

"Jack! Jack! I'm sorry! I forgot!"

"You forgot!" Ryan's voice was like tearing cloth. "You stupid fuck! You're *always* forgetting! And you know why? 'Cause you're a fucking *rope*-head!"

One of the others laughed.

"Yeah, but I'll bet Martha likes his rope!"

"Fuck Martha! And fuck *you*, you stupid shit!"

A good ten feet separated them, but Ryan covered it in two strides, grabbed the figure's shirt, and yanked him around so violently the shirt ripped and the man stumbled, and Ryan was on him, white fists flashing in the sun.

The man fell to his knees, blood dripping from his face.

One of the boys stepped between them.

"Jack! Enough! Enough!"

This was a mistake. Ryan's arm shot out. The heel of his hand struck chest or sternum with a thud Max heard from across the meadow, and the man went down like a sack of flour.

Hauling his first victim to his feet, Ryan propped him with one hand and hammered with the other, the man's head snapping like a doll's, until he slipped from Ryan's grasp and collapsed. The remaining two were already on their horses, and disappeared down the trail, but Ryan continued his mad dance, stomping and kicking, until he finally staggered away and leaned on his knees, gasping for air.

The man who had tried to intervene climbed to his feet, coughing and spitting, then crouched by the still figure.

"Well?" panted Ryan.

Max leaned forward, straining to hear.

"I think he's dead."

Ryan straightened up. *"Fuck."*

"You didn't need to kill him."

"I warned him, didn't I? Told him to stay away from that shit. Fucker never did listen."

"You still didn't need to kill him."

"Yeah, didn't plan on it."

"Now what?"

"Now the fucking shipment's late! Just like last time. Someone's gonna be pissed. But . . . there's nothing we can do about it. So, fuck 'em all."

The other jerked his thumb at the body. "No. I mean *him.*"

"What about him?" Ryan rubbed his face. *"His* problems are over."

Whatever was said next was lost as they mounted up and rode into the trees, one riderless horse towed behind.

The meadow was silent. Dragonflies hovered and danced, iridescent blue and green in the sun.

Max stood up and jogged to the body splayed out in brown grass. He stood over it, his throat raw, remembering Martha's furious blushing.

Robert caught up and stopped beside him.

"Did you know him?"

He closed his eyes. A crow cawed in the distance.

"Yeah. Greg. One of Ryan's old gang. Not the worst . . . ah, *shit.*"

"What now?"

"Jesus, I don't know. But we can't leave him here. Animals will get to him."

"Then we'd better get the horses."

Slowly, he nodded, and turned away.

They took the trail back to the road, stepping warily onto the pavement. Then they started walking.

"So that's Jack Ryan," Robert mused.

"That's him."

"Has he always been like that?"

"What do you mean?"

"The man was insane! I don't think a normal person could fight like that."

He thought of the night he had been left for dead in the road.

"Ryan may be using *wire*," Robert went on. "You know about *wire*, don't you?"

"I know about it."

"Can you imagine an army like that? But trained. Disciplined. And equipped."

"No. I can't imagine it."

They retrieved the horses, rode back, and dismounted near where they had left the body.

He looked around stupidly. "What the hell . . . ?"

Robert pointed.

"There."

Greg was now in the withered grass by the shack. They ran to him, Max glancing around, fingering his knife and wishing it were a gun. But there was no sign of Ryan.

"He must have crawled here." Robert crouched down and felt the neck. "I think he's still alive."

"Christ! Can we get him to Paul?"

There was no easy way to do this. They had to sling the unconscious man over Robert's saddle, and Robert rode behind Max while he towed the mare, dividing his attention between keeping the mare to one side of his bay, Greg across the saddle, and the horses on the trail.

It was a long ride.

There was no one home when they arrived at the doctor's. But when they lifted Greg down, they knew it no longer mattered.

They laid the body out in some shade, and Max moved away and slumped to the ground, sitting with his back against the house. He kept seeing Martha's face. He felt like he was waiting, but could not understand why.

A clop of hooves on pavement startled him, and he looked up.

Bert Morrow and two wide-eyed young deputies rode across the lane into the yard and stopped before the body.

Bert swore.

"What the hell happened here?"

Max groaned, and the Chief raised his voice. "I asked you a question!"

"Fuck off."

"Don't push me, Max."

"What're you going to do, Bert? Arrest us? You don't even have a jail."

"I can arrange something, if I have to. Do I?"

"Get lost. We were trying to help."

"And how were you going to help? What happened here?"

"Nothing happened here! Greg got the shit kicked out of him near the North Road."

"Is that so? And you dragged him all the way out here?"

"Listen to me, Bert. The man who lives here is a doctor. A real one. With medicine. If we had gotten here sooner . . . Well, what would *you* have done? *Pray* over him?"

"Who did it?"

"Jack. Jack and his *goddamn* fucking goons! Why don't you go talk to him?"

"I will. Where did this happen?"

"Near the North Road! Chrissake, *listen.*"

"And what were you doing there?"

"Looking for salvage."

"Is that so."

"Look, what do you want? Jack beat him up because some kind of deal went wrong. That's all we know."

"What kind of deal?"

"How should I know?"

"Something to do with drugs?"

He stared up at the Chief, forgetting to close his mouth.

"You know, Max, you're right. I don't have a jail. I don't have a court. I don't even have much in the way of laws. But I'm guessing that makes me judge and jury, for now. Until someone tells me different."

Max shrugged and looked away, trying to dismiss him. Trying to dismiss a gnawing sense of complicity.

"You'd better wise up, Max. And you better start telling the truth."

"Oh, for fuck–"

"You lied about fighting with Ryan! That was a mistake! Lying about something's not even a crime! And you're still not telling me everything you know about *this*. That's another mistake."

The Chief glanced at Robert. Then, abruptly, he wheeled his horse and galloped across the road, into the trees, the two deputies racing to catch up.

Robert watched them go. "Who was that?"

"An actual Chief of Police, if you can believe it."

"Oh? Seems to know his job."

"You think so?"

"It didn't take him long to find us, did it?"

"Yeah, you're right . . . . I wonder how in hell he knew about this place."

"I don't know. But someone has to do something about a burial, and soon. Is there a cemetery in town? A church?"

"There's some kind of church off in the woods. I don't know if they have a cemetery, but I doubt Greg spent any time attending. They probably won't want anything to do him."

"So how do people get buried around here?"

"Christ, Robert. People are buried on their farms. A family plot. But Greg didn't have any family. Not around here."

"Well, I don't suppose your friend Jack Ryan plans to do anything about it. Or your actual Chief of Police. And we can't just leave him here. We'll have to do it ourselves. Unless you have a better idea."

But Max stared across the lane, struck with a new thought. Someone had to tell Martha.

He closed his eyes.

Bert has got to do something! That fat bastard can't just walk away from this! Like everything else he does.

"Max?"

Wearily, he got to his feet.

They found tools in the doctor's shed, and buried the body at the edge of a quiet meadow, away from any trails. It was a long afternoon's work, and the sun was setting when they finished piling heavy stones over freshly turned earth.

They stood awhile in silence, lingering in the deepening shadow before the grave, and Max again felt the sense of waiting.

He looked up, at trees arching overhead, their tops splashed crimson fading to gray as he watched.

He rode through the twilight to Martha's, but the news had already reached her, and she opened the door with eyes red and swollen.

"What do *you* want?"

"I–I just wanted to say I'm sorry."

"Why? *You* didn't like him. *No one* liked him. Why are *you* sorry?"

"Did you like him?"

Her eyes widened.

"You–you–I was in *love* with him!"

"I know. I'm sorry. If it seemed like I didn't like him, well, maybe I was a bit jealous. But I really had nothing against him. We tried to help."

"Oh, you threw him on a horse and took him to one of your damned *City* friends! That's what you told Bert! That's your idea of help! But you were there . . . you watched Greg beaten . . . Why? Why did you let it happen, Max? Why?"

He swallowed.

"Martha, it was over before we could do anything. We tried to get help. At least we were able to bury him decently. I can take you–"

She wailed, ran inside, and slammed the door.

For days afterward, he stayed away from the office, hid at the pub, holed up in his room.

It wasn't fair. What else could they have done? Wasn't this what the police were for? What the hell was Bert waiting for?

But he forgot the questions. Ryan sent word to the Committee. The Corporation was ready to meet.

39

Tall white clouds drifted through a clear October sky. A taste of summer lingered, in the warm air and straw-colored fields, in the dry and dusty road, in the kind of day that brought back memories of a gleaming red airplane.

Max arrived at the town office and tied up his horse. He started for the front door, but stopped, looking up at the billowing clouds, shading his eyes as though the plane might suddenly appear, snarling up high. But there were only black specks that were birds, circling aimlessly high above.

He went inside.

In the meeting room, John Anderson reclined in a chair tilted back, his feet propped on the table, snoring. Max dragged a chair to an open window and sat down to wait.

Musty smells drifted to him from the brown thicket outside that must once have been someone's garden, and he found himself wondering who might have sat by this window, so many years ago . . . what had they seen . . . had they ever flown in an airplane . . .

He leaned against the sill, sick with his nameless regret.

A while later came a shout, "They're coming!" Anderson's feet slid off the table, his chair hit the floor with a hollow *bang,* and he got to his feet muttering, "About goddamn time."

Max followed him outside in time to see a cloud of yellow dust drift down the road as a white automobile turned in and parked in front of the office.

The engine whirred quietly. Bright sunlight glinted from the windshield. The windows were rolled up tight, yet the people inside were talking with no sign of discomfort.

Air conditioning!

A handful of children materialized, thrilled by this glamorous machine, daring each other to touch it, but Bert Morrow was there to shoo them away.

The engine stopped. The doors swung open. Three men climbed out, two strangers with Jack Ryan, Ryan cocksure as ever.

One of the City men, short and pale, squinted in the sun, and was already beginning to sweat. Yet there was a trace of smugness, too, hard to pin down, but impossible to ignore. Not an actual smirk, but a hint of one.

The other was tanned, athletic, hair steel gray and close-cropped, eyes flat and expressionless. When he moved, it was with the fluid precision of a jungle cat, yet he stood easily, with just a hint of animal tension coiled and ready.

He spoke in a bored monotone.

"You the people we're meeting?"

"That's right," replied Anderson. "And you are . . . ?"

"Frank. This is Don. Don Cooper."

"Pleased to meet you, Frank. Don. I'm John Anderson. And this is Max Wyse."

The flat eyes turned on him, and there was a flicker, as though this was not the first time they had heard the name.

Frank nodded.

"Let's get started."

Inside, Max sat down with Anderson on one side of the meeting table, while Ryan joined Frank and Don on the other. Bert stayed outside, guarding against eavesdroppers.

That Ryan was sitting here, in the town office, with the Chief of Police standing guard outside, grated on his nerves, but there was nothing Max could do, and he stayed silent. Ryan glanced at him once, black eyes hooded, but looked calmly away.

Anderson frowned. "Well, gentlemen. What can we do for you?"

Frank nodded to Cooper.

"Your show."

The pale man cleared his throat.

"Mr. Anderson. If you saw a gold bar lying on the ground, would you cross the street to pick it up?"

"A what?"

"A gold bar, Mr. Anderson. Would you cross the street to pick up a gold bar?"

"Well, son, I don't know."

His face growing hot, Max snapped, *"I would."*

Cooper smiled.

"And you're not alone. Think about this, gentlemen. The world has not seen war in twenty years. The world is not prepared for war. Or so it seems. Think about that."

"Seems to me," Anderson replied slowly, "the world has better things to think about."

"You may be right. But consider. This continent, what we know of it, is ruled by a few intelligent, ambitious men and women. Maybe the world *does* have better things to think about. But ambition plays by its own rules. Mr. Anderson, suppose one of these ambitious individuals decided to strike militarily against his neighbor?"

Cooper paused, one eyebrow raised.

"Well, I don't know. Suppose he did."

"If his neighbor was defenseless, and if this individual made the right preparations, then his conquest could be swift and decisive."

"Maybe. But what would he do with it?"

"Whatever he wanted! Strip the productive assets. Impose a tribute. Enslave the population. Whatever he wanted."

"Sounds to me like more trouble than it's worth."

"That depends. Now, suppose one of these individuals began to suspect his neighbor of making preparations against *him.*" Cooper leaned forward. "Do you see? He would have to arm himself–thus confirming the suspicions of his neighbors! Do you see the point? It is a foregone conclusion the corporations—or whatever passes for government out there—will arm. Whether out of fear or out of greed doesn't matter. And it is inevitable that, once armed, one will eventually strike another, if only in perceived self-defense."

Anderson eased back in his chair, his face creased with an ugly grin.

"Is that what your employer is doing?"

"I'm not at liberty to say."

"Well, son, *I'm* at liberty!" The old man fairly spat the words. "I *know* about your training camps outside the City! I *know* about the mock-up streets where you practice house-to-house combat! You haven't hidden it, it's right out in the open! It's practically an advertisement!"

Stunned, Max stared at him—then glanced at Frank, but the bored expression hadn't changed.

"Is that what it is, *Mister* Cooper? Advertising?"

"I prefer to think of it as flexing our muscle. It shows we aren't defenseless. Who knows, Mr. Anderson? One of our good corporate neighbors might have attacked long before now, if those camps weren't there."

"Maybe they'd be better neighbors if you weren't so busy flexing your muscle!"

"It's what they're all doing, believe me. We have the evidence."

Frank's bored monotone cut across Anderson's reply.

"He's told you the way it is. You have to deal with it."

The old man flushed a painful red. But he answered evenly.

"So exactly what do you want?"

"We want to help!" chirruped Cooper. "Mr. Anderson, we want to extend an invitation to you and your town. Right now you're defenseless. We can change that."

"What for?"

"It's in everyone's interest, that's what for! It's in our interest, because it's one more obstacle in the path of a potential assault. It's in your interest for the same reason."

"I've heard this argument. One of your good corporate neighbors can take the North Road right into the City, for all I care. It doesn't concern us."

"Oh, but it does! Even if an assault were only planned along what you call the North Road, an enemy would still have to secure his flanks and rear. That would mean occupying your town, turning it into a staging area, a defensive position. Your people would be unfortunate collateral." Cooper paused a moment, inviting objection, but Anderson remained quiet. "As Frank says, that's the way it is. You have to deal with it."

The smirk on Ryan's face was now more than he could stand, and Max interrupted.

"I'd like to hear what Jack has to say about this."

Ryan glanced at Frank. It looked like a reflex, and Max sneered.

"What's that, Mr. President? You need permission?"

The upper lip curled.

"You heard what you need to know."

"Is that so? And what exactly is it you *don't* think we need to know?"

Frank looked down at his hands. "I don't know what Jack thinks he's talking about. You two know the situation. You can work out the angles for yourselves. Personally, I don't see how you can avoid it. But it's your call."

Face still burning, Anderson was struggling to control himself.

"Well, Mr. . . . ah, Frank. Why don't you explain just what it is we're deciding."

"You're deciding whether to stand up for yourselves. With our help, of course."

"And what if we decide to stand up for ourselves, without any help from you?"

"Fine. Whatever you think best. Personally, I'll just write this town off and forget it."

"Now why do you say that? Just what is it you're offering? Besides scare stories."

"Small arms and training. Lots of training."

"Training in what?"

"How to handle weapons. How to build defensive positions. How to manage a battlefield. How to skirmish, how to retreat. Military tactics suitable to a militia. Or an insurgency. If you people don't know what to do when the time comes, it'll be carnage. You need months of training."

"I don't know that I like what I'm hearing."

"Doesn't matter what you like. All that matters is what you're faced with."

The flat eyes gazed at him indifferently, the fingers of one hand drumming idly on the table.

Ryan was laughing, but soundlessly, and Max noticed him then, *really* noticed him, noticed the unnatural brightness in his eyes, the unfamiliar gauntness in his face, the tremor in his hands. He noticed, and realized with a shock that Ryan had looked like this for weeks.

Maybe months.

Christ, he's falling apart. He's using wire, *and he's falling apart.*

He glanced at Frank. *Watch out, Jack.*

Anderson was speechless. Max answered for him.

"We'll need some time."

Cooper smiled brightly.

"Well, you can give us your answer later. Jack's going to show us the local public house."

"I had in mind a week or two. We'll have to discuss this with the rest of the Committee."

Frank got to his feet.

"Fine. Talk it up."

"One more question, Frank. Have you recruited anyone else?"

"You'll learn the answer to that when you join us. If not, it's none of your business."

Frank walked out without looking at anyone else, and the rest got up and followed.

Frank, Cooper, and Ryan climbed into the car, Frank in the driver's seat. Doors slammed. Gravel crunched as the car backed into the road, then scattered as it turned and accelerated towards the pub, a thick plume of yellow dust churning behind like the tail of a land-bound comet.

Thumbs hooked in his belt, his face still red, Anderson kicked at the dirt.

"Ain't that somethin'."

"John—how did you know about all that? About what they're doing?"

"I have my ways, boy. You're not the only one who has contacts, you know."

Then Max shut his mouth.

Today was Saturday. The men from the Corporation were on their way to the pub. Which was where Robert might be. Robert, whom they would probably recognize, and who could have no idea who *they* were.

He sprinted for his horse, stumbling around Bert.

"Going somewhere?"

Max ignored him, swung onto the horse, and bolted, galloping toward the pub. He could not overtake an automobile, but he might head off Robert before they saw him, if he was off exploring or in his room with his books.

He pushed the horse hard, forcing it to gallop for long stretches, but it was a good twenty minutes before he trotted the panting animal past Frank's car parked out front, tied it up, and sprinted for the back door, where he let himself in and immediately collided with Bill, who stopped him with a meaty hand on his chest.

"Just a minute, now, son. This is *my* house, you know."

"Sorry! I've got to find Robert. Any idea where he is?"

"Yup."

"*Where*, damn it?"

"You tell me what's going on."

"Look, you have a couple of strangers here with Ryan?"

"Who are they?"

"They're from the City. I don't want them to see Robert."

"Well, you're too late. They're all drinking beer together."

"*Oh, shit.*"

"Who is he, Max? What's going on here?"

"Later. I'll explain later."

He went back out, sprinted around the building, then sauntered in the front door and casually walked over to Frank's table.

"Well, well, well. Frank. Don. How do you like our little pub?"

Frank leaned back.

"Oh, it's you. Pull up a chair."

He sat down. "Hello, Robert. How're things?"

"You two know each other?"

"We do a little business now and then," Max answered.

"Frank was just explaining to me how unusual it is for a Corporate employee to willingly leave the City. Isn't that what you said, Frank? Unusual?"

"That's what I said."

"Well, you may be right. There are things I don't remember. So, Max. Anything interesting for me?"

"Not this week."

"Too bad. I'm almost out of cigars." Robert took a pull at his beer.

Frank was watching him.

"I'm curious about something. How did you get here? Do you have a car?"

"The car's at the edge of town. Why?"

"I didn't see another car when we came in."

"A horse is more practical out here. Besides, the car's not mine, and I don't think the owner would appreciate my driving it around dirt roads."

"Who's the owner?"

"A woman."

"Why doesn't she come with you?"

"She prefers the City."

"And you don't."

"I like a break from it."

Frank seemed to consider this. Then he got to his feet.

"Well, bud, watch your step."

He walked off, athletic, cat-like, Cooper and Ryan hurrying to follow.

When they were out the door, Max blew out his cheeks.

"Jesus! What'd I miss?"

"Not much."

"Do you think they recognized you?"

"I think so. Cooper couldn't take his eyes off me."

"Christ. Any idea who they are?"

Robert shrugged. "Friends of Jack Ryan, I supposed."

Then it dawned.

"Robert! You know who Don Cooper is?"

Robert nodded, picking up his beer.

"I wondered about that."

40

The following morning, long before daybreak, Max and Robert set out from the pub on horseback, heading south on a trail Max had learned about from Bill. The was air still, not a breath of movement, but with a chill bite of autumn, and they rode through a pungence of damp grass and damp earth, around dark clusters of tangled trees and bushes, stars still burning white and blue overhead, muted hoof-falls the only sound.

A broad field opened around them, the eastern horizon a silvery band to their left, and Max, wide awake despite the early hour, inhaled deeply, drawing the sharp cold air through his nostrils, acutely conscious of the smells and the stars and the glowing horizon. Of how glad he was to be alive.

The trail led through a long wooded area, gray and dense, and finally to another clearing hard by a river thirty yards across, the sky now steel-blue, one bright star still visible above the trees south of the clearing. Here they stopped and unpacked tackle borrowed from Bill, and by the time they threw their first hooks into the water, ghostly streaks of orange arced overhead.

They stood apart in grass heavy with dew and worked their lines, the black water moving sluggishly, gurgling among rocks near the shore. Max felt an extra quality to existence, an extra clarity, like a film cleaned from a window and revealing things he had forgotten. Like how he had felt on his first patrols, so long ago.

They had not exchanged twenty words.

In an hour they caught a dozen fish, shimmering gray with dark vertical bands, which they brought back to the pub as the sun rose. Bill and Mike fried them with potatoes, and the four ate together, talking little, until Mike cleared away the dishes and they sat lingering over cups of strong, black coffee.

Max felt alive, ready to start the day. But there was nothing to do.

He looked at Robert.

"Going exploring today?"

"No. I'd better head out. Agnes is waiting, and it's a long walk back to Paul's house."

"Well, suppose I ride with you and bring your horse back here. You won't have to walk."

"Sure. Thanks."

Robert seemed in no great hurry, despite Agnes waiting, and they rode at an easy walk, but in silence. As the town office went by, the older man shook his head, as though trying to shake off something nagging.

"Sorry to be such a wet blanket."

"Anything wrong?"

Robert chuckled.

"No, not really. Today's my birthday."

"Oh?"

"I turn forty today. If you believe the file Human Resources has on me."

"Well, do you feel any older?"

"I suppose not."

"So what's the problem?"

"What's the problem? I'm forty years old! I'm a nobody trapped in a pointless job working for people I despise."

"Yeah. I think I know the feeling."

Robert laughed. "I'm glad you're not trying to cheer me up! Really. Agnes tried. Her idea is that no one's job really matters, that everyone gets over it sooner or later, and the sooner *I* get over it, the better. Now *that's* depressing." He stared ahead. "We had a nasty fight over it."

"I guess I can see why you're not in a hurry."

"So, Max, how old are you?"

"Me? Oh, might be twenty-nine. Might be thirty. Don't know for sure."

"Now you'll have to explain that. Why aren't you sure?"

"Well, you heard the story of how I got here."

"When we visited Anderson? I take it you lived with Jack Ryan. Is that right? Although it's a little hard to picture, if you don't mind my saying."

"Yeah, well, I didn't have any records. No file at Human Resources."

"But I can't imagine a young boy not knowing how old he is."

"I don't remember, Robert. I don't remember my parents or anything else. I just remember walking along this road until somebody found me."

"Christ, I didn't realize we had that much in common."

"Well, I don't think about it much. Why worry about the past?"

"Agnes said something like that."

"Maybe she's right." Robert said nothing, and after a minute, Max asked, "How is she?"

"Fine. She just doesn't want to leave the City."

"But you do."

"I have to. I have to get out and start something new."

"Like a new industry."

"Like anything that will be a living and be my own."

"Yeah. I can relate to that."

"Well, what about you? What are *your* plans? You don't seem too thrilled with being Jack Ryan's vice-president, and I can't say I blame you."

"Somebody's got to keep an eye on him."

"Doesn't sound like much of a career to me."

"Come off it, Robert. Nobody talks about careers around here."

"Why not? You're young. You should think about your future."

"Yeah, one of these days. Listen, I keep thinking about Frank and his sidekick, Don, Dan, whatever his goddamned name is."

"What about them?"

"I wish they hadn't seen you."

"Forget it. I don't think it matters."

When they arrived at the doctor's, Agnes was waiting, was not too happy about it, and stalked to the car without saying a word. Robert followed her. Moments later, the car turned around in the City lane and sped away.

Stevens stood watching. "I don't envy him."

Max knotted a rope to the mare's halter ring and climbed into the saddle, lead rope in hand.

"Guess I'll see you later, Doc."

At the main road, he urged the horses to a trot. The movement, and the need to concentrate on the lead, were a relief, and he kept it up as the town office passed.

But he slowed as Martha's house neared.

Then he stopped.

He dismounted and walked to the door. He knocked. There was no answer, and he went on knocking, until the door swung open and she stood there, face swollen under a nest of dank hair, eyes gleaming with a malignant light.

"What d'*you* want?"

A cloud of alcohol assaulted him, and he stepped back.

"My God . . ."

"*Fuck* you!"

That expletive from her was a greater shock than her appearance.

"Don't do this, Martha. For God's sake—look, come with me. Let me buy you a meal. When was the last time you ate?"

"*Fuck* you. I don't *need* your help. I mean, look what happened the *last* time you helped!"

"Come on! That's not fair."

"Well, *life's* not fair! *Is* it?"

She stepped close, pushing her face into his. The alcohol was asphyxiating.

"Some people are honest and work hard, and they get screwed! And some people don't do a *damn* thing, and lie about it, and what happens to *them,* Max? What happens to *them?*"

She shoved him away, stumbled inside, and slammed the door.

He stared at it, unable to turn away.

It was as though some demon from hell had ripped away his clothes, even his skin, and left his soul naked, exposed to all. With nowhere to hide.

Agnes pulled to the curb.

The street looked quiet, lined with old brownstone buildings and fat gnarled trees dripping yellow leaves. It was a street that seemed to suit him. And she had never seen it before.

He sat without moving, staring through the windshield.

"Robert?"

He seemed to fumble a moment. His door opened. But he stopped, the door ajar and the wind whistling.

He pulled it shut again.

"Robert?"

"I saw a man out there killed. Beaten to death."

It was a moment before she could whisper, "When?"

"A week ago."

"Why didn't you—"

"And yesterday there were two men from the Corporation. I think they're involved with Security. And I think one of them used to work for me."

"My God! What were they doing?"

"I don't know."

"Who was the man who was killed?"

"I don't know."

"Robert . . . have you made up your mind? What are you going to do?"

He shook his head, opened the door, and got out.

"Wait–Robert–"

But the door slammed, and he walked up the steps and into the building.

41

Robert went to work on Monday, carried along by habit. He handed out assignments, reviewed reports, made telephone calls. There was nothing different. But it felt unreal, part of another person's life. Someone he didn't know very well.

Tuesday, it stormed.

It began at noon, sheets of water cascading down the windows and shots of thunder that rattled coffee cups; then a steady downpour into the afternoon, and he had to splash though cold puddles to get to the bus after work.

In the morning, he stood atop the steps outside his apartment building looking down at sidewalks layered in wet leaves, the trees now bare and exposing the distant towers, obelisks that shone silver under the gray and white overcast.

He stood watching them, wondering how a man could be beaten to death and forgotten, and his killer sit down to a beer in a pub as though nothing had happened. Looking at this street, the genteel brownstones and the distant skyscrapers, it seemed a mad, deranged dream. But a dream should fade in the light of day, not linger, haunting, at the edge of awareness.

A bus turned the corner, and he went down the steps.

Later, reviewing a stack of completed reports, he heard the door to his office open.

Agnes stepped in, closed it, and sat down by the small conference table.

He knew why she was here.

She asked, "Have you decided?"

He did not want to think of that, of leaving the City. Only of how lovely she looked. Of how exquisitely the house in the clearing outside the City–and the world that house implied–fit her. That was the world she needed. That *he* needed.

"Robert, you have to make up your mind."

"I know."

They sat looking at each other, the silence more intimate than a touch, until she rose, opened the door again, and left.

In the afternoon, two people he had never seen before entered his office. One shut the door.

"Robert Larsen?"

"That's right."

"My name is Jane Smith. This is Stephen Miller. We have some questions."

"Then make an appointment. I'm busy."

"That's not how this works. May we sit?" Without waiting for a reply, she pulled out a chair and sat at the conference table, where Agnes had sat a few hours before.

"Who the hell are you?"

"I believe I've answered that."

"What gives you the right to barge in here?"

"Calm yourself." She smiled, faintly. "We all work for the same company, and this is an office in a company building."

"What do you want?"

"We are conducting an investigation. You are acquainted with Dr. Paul Stevens. Is that correct?"

He shut his mouth. The old tightness was in his chest.

Miller drawled, "You don't want to do this the hard way, fella. Trust me."

He felt his hands shaking.

"Get out."

The woman laughed. "I beg your pardon?"

He got up, walked past them, opened the door, and stood holding it.

"Get out."

She stood, stepping closer to him and speaking quietly.

"I will give you some time. Speak with your manager. But think about this very carefully. Because in the end, Mr. Larsen, you will answer my questions. Like any other employee."

She walked out.

Miller followed, grinning.

42

A week went by. Max waited, but nothing happened. There were no meetings. There was never anyone at the town office. He hadn't been paid.

And a man was dead.

On a cold, cloudy day, he rode out to the Anderson place.

Anderson was struggling with potatoes, filling sacks from piles drying in the yard, lugging the sacks through a bulkhead in the side of the house, down into the cellar. As Max tied his horse, the old man finished filling a sack and hefted it up, but the tattered fabric ripped, and a load of potatoes spilled on the ground.

Anderson flung the sack aside, spitting curses with abandon.

"You picked a bad time to come out here and socialize, boy!"

"Let me help, John."

They worked together for an hour, carrying sack after sack of potatoes down the concrete steps. They ran out of sacks and used their coats to carry, piling loose potatoes in the cellar atop layers of stuffed sacks, off the damp floor.

When it was done, they closed up the bulkhead and sat on the big porch, the old man slumped and kneading his thigh muscles.

"I appreciate the help, son. But I know you didn't come out here to lug potatoes."

"John, what the hell is going on?"

"What?"

"Have you been to the office lately?"

"No. Why?"

"Well, neither has anyone else. There hasn't been an officers' meeting in a month."

"Well, you ask Jack about that. That's *his* department. He's president."

"I think he's gone back into business for himself. Do you know that he killed a man a little while ago?"

"What? Who?"

"Greg . . . O'Brien, I think his name was."

"Didn't know him. Bert know about this?"

"Yep."

"Well, that's why we have officers. I can't do their jobs for them. And *you're* an officer, too, don't forget. You're the one who should be coming up with answers."

"Jesus, John . . . All right, what about the Corporation? What are we going to do about that?"

"I don't know! Haven't talked with the rest of the Committee yet."

"Come on, don't you think this is important?"

The china-blue eyes flashed.

"Well, we've all been a bit busy! In case you hadn't noticed."

"Yeah, okay, I get that. But I don't think this can wait. Do you?"

Anderson exhaled, easing back in his chair.

"All right, maybe so. Maybe so. I'll get the rest together."

"When?"

"Soon."

"Let me know when. I want to be there."

"All right." Stretching his legs out, the old man closed his eyes and nodded. "Maybe that's a good idea, son."

———————

Saturday afternoon, the Members of the Town Committee straggled into the town office, two of them an hour late, and an irate John

Anderson stood up and brought the meeting to order with an angry smack on the table.

He told them about the men from the City, about their story of coming war, about the Corporation's offer. And he gave his considered opinion of it.

"The sons of bitches can't be trusted."

"Neither can our own damned guv'mint, from what you're sayin' 'bout Ryan," someone complained. A voice cursed Jack Ryan. Someone else cursed *guv'mint* on principle.

He was sitting to one side, but Max could see the town dissolving in the indifferent shrugs, the empty faces. And his job with it.

He got up.

"I have something to say."

Anderson waved him on and sat down.

He drew a nervous breath.

"Look everyone, we made a good start a while back. We got things organized. We had our election. But now we have a problem."

He looked around, saw they were listening, and his voice steadied.

"Our president . . . our president's gone back into business for himself. No one's in charge. Our secretary's in no condition to work. Our chief of police isn't talking to anyone. We don't know what the road crews are doing. Or the fire crew. We don't even know if any of them are still on the job."

There was a bark of a laugh from a man he knew raised sheep and goats.

"Sounds like *you* don't know much of anything!"

"I know our leadership's gone! There's no organization left."

"So? Maybe we don't need a bunch've leaders. What've they done, anyway? Besides bring the damned Corporation around here."

"You put this government together, right? And now you're ready to give up on it? After just a few months?" He looked at Anderson. "Do you think that's going to keep us from getting pulled into a war?"

"So what are you sayin', son?"

"Here's what I'm saying. If we don't do something about this, and do it pretty damned soon, we may not be around to talk about it next year. Not as a town, anyway. A collection of refugees, maybe."

"Son, I'm *not* dealing with the damned Corporation. If that's what you're driving at. I don't trust that man Frank, and I don't know that I believe all this talk about war. Personally, I don't see it."

"I don't trust him either. And I don't like his punk sidekick. But none of that matters. We may *have* to deal with them. But the first order of business is to get our government back to work."

A beefy fellow snorted. He was sitting comfortably with his back against the wall, short legs splayed out.

"No shit! What government? All they ever done was dig some ditches. Anyone coulda done that."

Max rounded on him.

"*That's right,* goddamn it! Anyone could have done it! But no one ever did! Because it took that sonofabitch Jack Ryan to *organize* you bums and make it happen!"

Then the man was on his feet, heavy face dark and scowling, and Anderson was on his feet as well, moving quickly between them.

"Back off, Max! There's no call for this!"

He stepped back and shook his head, rubbed his face.

"Sorry. Guess I . . . "

The beefy man sat down slowly.

Anderson watched them both a moment.

"All right, all right. Maybe Max here is a bit strung out, and maybe he has reason. But he's right about one thing. We got a little work to do. So maybe it's time we had him take over as acting president, until we can find Jack and decide what to do with him."

This was confirmed with a show of hands. Then they instructed him, in no uncertain terms, that he was not to deal with the Corporation on his own.

Anderson made him repeat it.

He walked out of the room, a little dazed, slowly realizing it was now his job to track down the other officers and convince them to come back to work. The chief of police. The fire chief. The road boss.

The town secretary.

He rode up to her house the following morning.

She opened the door, pale, but no longer disheveled, and stepped aside, wordlessly inviting him in.

They sat at her breakfast table, clean and bright with sunlight streaming in through a small window, and drank coffee together in silence. Like survivors of a shipwreck, they had no need for words. The things that mattered were too simple, too obvious.

Then she broke the spell.

"Max, I'm sorry about the things I said."

"Forget it. You weren't yourself."

"I don't know what I'm going to do. I'm in trouble."

He looked at her, not comprehending, and she sighed.

"God, Max. I'm going to have a child. Greg's child."

He put down his coffee and swallowed, hard.

"Have you . . . have you eaten?"

She laughed then, brushing away sudden tears.

"Is that all you think about?"

"You've got to eat, Martha. When was the last time you had a real meal? Why don't we go to the pub and have breakfast?"

"I'm a mess. I can't go there like this."

"Look, we'll take my horse. You'll end up dusty from the ride, so there's no reason to clean up now. Bill's a pretty fair cook, and you won't have to lift a finger."

When she hesitated, he got to his feet, urging, "Come on! You'll feel better after you eat. Then I'll bring you back here and leave you alone."

"Well . . . all right. I *am* starving."

Over breakfast, he told her about Frank and Don and the report to the Committee. She listened for a while. But shortly she stopped him.

"Max, I have to resign. I don't think I can sit across the table from anyone anymore. Certainly not Jack. And maybe not you, either."

"Well, look, you don't have to decide anything right away. Take some time. Get back to being yourself."

She shook her head, smiling gravely, in a way that left him cold and bleak inside.

"There's no going back, Max. Not for me."

43

Monday Max spent tracking down the other officers. He started out with a grim determination, after rehearsing his arguments. That the Committee had made him acting president for reasons of their own. That they would soon enough get around to appointing a real president, if they were through with Jack Ryan. But the others surprised him. When they learned the Committee was still involved, and actually meeting, they were only too ready to pitch in. No argument needed.

Although the Chief of Police had his own warning.

"Just don't think you're above the law. Whatever it is."

At the end of the day, Max rode to the pub for an early dinner, basking in a new feeling of accomplishment, waving to Mike as he walked in.

Mike waved back, but his hand turned mid-wave to point toward a dark corner of the room, where a familiar figure sat hunched over a glass of beer.

Astonished, Max walked quickly to the table.

"Robert!"

There was no response.

"Robert–are you okay? What're you doing here?"

Slowly, Robert looked up. His eyes did not seem to focus.

"Why . . . hullo to you, too."

He jerked out a chair and sat down. *"What's going on?"*

"Had a bad day Friday."

"You *what?*"

Robert shrugged.

"Guess I couldn't it take any more. Decked some asshole from Security." He looked up, scratching his jaw. "Miller, I think. Came around on his own and thought he could shake me up. I suppose he did. Arrogant prick."

"You . . . *hit* him?"

Robert nodded, deeply. "Then I had an attack. A seizure, as my good friend Doctor Paul Stevens likes to say. Right there, in my office. Like the others." He frowned, staring at his glass. "Someone called

Medical Services . . . But Agnes gave me a shot. Got me out of there. Stayed the weekend with Paul."

"Jesus! What're you going to do?"

He sipped the beer, then carefully set the glass down.

"This is it, I think."

"You're not going back?"

"After the bit with Miller? Prob'ly not." He grinned, then stared down at his glass again, moodily turning it with one hand. "Agnes is frightened. Doesn't want to get caught with a syringe. Don't know if anyone saw it, but . . . can't say I blame her."

"What would they do?"

"Dunno. They'd want to know where she got it, and we don't want them led to Paul."

"So you're ready to leave for good?"

"Well, there's a little money stashed in my room here."

"What about the time capsule?"

"Stashed that, too."

"Damn! What about Agnes?"

He shrugged again, raising his glass, but not before Max saw the pain cross his face.

"Christ, Robert. I'm sorry."

"Forget it. You've got your own problems."

"Yeah. One or two."

"Listen. I can't pay you. I don't have enough here."

"Oh, hell. Don't even think about it."

"I'm going to give you the time capsule instead."

He twitched a little.

"You sure?"

"What am *I* going to do with it? You can put it to better use."

Robert turned in his chair and faced him, his eyes now stone sober.

"I'm counting on it."

"Yeah . . . okay."

"There's just one problem."

"What's that?"

"It's at the lake."

"The time capsule? At the *lake?*"

"I didn't want it in my room."

"But you left money in your room."

"True. But I trust Bill. I don't trust my good friends from the City. In fact, I think someone went through my things, a while back. But they weren't looking for money."

"Jesus! Well, it was probably the right thing to do. But it may not be safe at the lake, either. You've been seen there."

"I know. We've got to get it. Soon."

"Tomorrow?"

Robert pushed his glass away.

"Tomorrow."

———

Well before dawn, they set out.

Leaving the North Road, they took the lake trail through a field of hay-stubble covered in frost sparking with moonlight, then through grassy brush and stunted trees as the sky lightened, then into the tall pine wood, the air cold and damp, branches dripping long after patches of sky overhead turned blue. They rode in silence, listening to the dull thud of hooves on the forest floor and the hiss of a morning breeze high in the pines.

Then they were out of the trees and in the open, descending the blacktop road toward the restaurant a couple hundred yards away, the road still deep in shadow, the whitewashed structure standing out in sunlight against the blue of the lake and dark bands of ripples swept across the water by a cold wind.

Max pulled up short as a figure walked from the distant deck to the building.

"Look! That's Frank."

Robert reined in. "Are you sure?"

"I'd know that walk anywhere."

"That's not good."

"Well, we don't know why he's here. I'm sure Frank's a busy man. Let's just get the hell off the road before he sees us."

They moved behind some brush along the shoulder. Frank emerged from the building, paused and looked around, then disappeared behind it. Moments later, a white car appeared. It backed into the road, then turned and accelerated away, cruising around a bend and into the trees.

"Okay." Robert flicked his reins. "Let's give it a try."

They rode the rest of the way. Inside the restaurant, a party of five men sat around a large table, finishing breakfast, camouflaged hunting jackets draped over the backs of their chairs.

Robert caught the eye of an older man behind the bar, then led the way to a small table in a far corner.

They sat. Coffee was brought. Robert handed the man a large bill. The man took it and walked away, and for a while they sipped coffee and talked about the weather.

The man returned. He placed a few coins on the table, and walked off again.

Robert glanced at the coins.

"Ready?"

"Whatever you say."

As if on cue, the party of five stood up, tossed down some money, and pulled on their jackets. Something heavy clunked against the table.

Four men went out the front door.

The fifth went behind the bar, pushed past the older man, and disappeared into the back.

Robert waited until they were gone, then cautiously led the way to the door. Max followed him outside.

Two of the men stood by the entrance to the deck, blocking it. Out on the deck, two more stood near a table. Behind the table sat a solitary figure, leaning comfortably on one arm like the chairman of the board.

Jack Ryan.

One of the men tossed a small brown package, which landed on the table. Ryan picked up a satchel and handed it over. The man opened it and peered inside.

Ryan leered.

The man stepped back, now holding a gun aimed at Ryan.

"Jack Ryan! You're under arrest! Stand up–slowly."

The others had guns out as well.

The first man grinned. "Come on, Ryan. There's nowhere to go."

Ryan's table exploded, flying upward and smashing into the two men nearest, and he was on his feet, gun in hand, viciously kicking the table out of his way, shooting point blank. The men at the deck entrance shouted and fired, but Ryan had already leaped, crashing to the deck through tables and chairs. He came up shooting and dove again. Furniture tumbled and bounced. One man went down. Then another. The volley of gunfire became sporadic, isolated booms reverberating along the shore.

Then it stopped.

In the sudden quiet, the sparkling tranquility of the lake, and the overturned furniture gleaming innocently in the sun, seemed obscene.

Jack Ryan rose to his feet, leaning against a table, bloodied, but the only one standing.

A cold breeze swept across the water, and Max stared, the old weight in his belly, and a taste like sand in his mouth. There was no other sign of life. Only Jack, swaying a little.

He strode to the deck.

The first man he came to was face down on the planking. A small, nickel-plated revolver lay nearby, and Max crouched down, picked it up, checked the cylinder, then stood up, holding the gun away from his body, keeping it pointed down and plainly visible.

Ryan turned. Blood coated one side of his face. His gun was leveled, looking black and heavy, but his arm was shaking.

Max waved his free hand and walked deliberately to another body.

This one looked nearly cut in two, the waist soaked with blood, the deck spattered with it. Stepping over a fist-sized ball of grayish meat, he waved again.

Ryan seemed to relax. His gun lowered a little.

Max worked his way closer, threading a path around scattered furniture, the revolver still pointed down and away.

He was thirty feet from Ryan, and called, "Did you get the one out back?"

Ryan looked away to his left, where, presumably, the fifth man lay dead.

In mid-stride, Max raised his gun. Ryan looked back. Their eyes locked. Ryan's face tightened and his gun came up, but Max fired, the chunk of metal leaping in his hand, the concussion ripping the morning apart.

He felt rather than heard footsteps pounding the deck, and looked back to see Robert running toward him. Behind Robert, the white car rolled to a stop. A door swung open. He expected to see Frank emerge, and he wondered what Robert had done with the time capsule, but there was an explosion behind his eyes, something struck his head, and he was looking at autumn-blue sky.

Faces appeared against the sky. Robert. Frank. They were talking. Their lips were moving, but there was no sound.

He was icy cold.

Then he was screaming.

44

Early morning. The windows no longer black mirrors, but blue-gray rectangles of dim sky-glow and silhouetted trees. The earth moves through space, inexorably turning, inexorably meeting a new day. The last lamp is switched off, and the close-walled temple of light dissolves into the larger world outside, a world beyond the windows, of other people, and other places.

Paul Stevens walked to a window and peered outside, eyes gritty from a night without sleep. A tremor nagged one arm, but he held himself upright, refusing to bow before the coming day.

Over his long career he had witnessed nearly every physical trauma he could imagine. But none had seared his memory like the horror of last night. Never in his life had he entertained an insane thought, like major surgery without a real anesthetic, without trained helping hands, without x-rays. Now he had done it in a bedroom, his mind still echoing with demonic shrieks as his scalpel separated living tissue, and he had had to stop and put down the knife, to make his hands stop shaking. But once started there was no turning back, and no time to waste, and he had picked up the knife again.

Even with the improvised straps, it would have been impossible without Robert, whose face went bloodless as blood flowed freely, soaking sheets and blankets, and who had needed all his strength to hold immobilized his screaming friend.

And then it was done, the young man thankfully unconscious, only from time to time moaning in his wandering purgatory, the wound sewn tight and even now beginning that mystical process of flesh merging with flesh.

In the bed behind him, Max stirred. Stevens had let the sedative wear off. There was one more task.

The room was hazy, unreal. Strange, with a sense of foreboding. But he remembered a dream . . . and a woman, tall, clad in something flowing and white, who gazed upon him with an indefinable expression. Not a smile, really. More a glow.

He wondered who she was.

From out of the haze a shape swam into view, and a familiar voice asked, "How do you feel?"

He licked dry lips.

"Ahh . . . arm . . . hurts . . ."

"That's to be expected. Here. I want you to drink this."

He felt his head raised and a warm liquid in his mouth. He swallowed. His left arm felt lashed to his side, and a dull ache was beginning to throb with fire.

"Doc . . . d'ya have a pain pill?"

Stevens wiped his chin.

"There was something in the broth. You'll sleep soon."

"Christ. It hurts."

"Max. I'm sorry. I could not save your arm."

He laughed weakly, not getting the joke.

Stevens pulled down the bedcovers, took his wrist, and guided his hand to where his left arm was burning at his side.

He felt his ribs. His hand moved, automatically seeking, until it reached the ball of meat that was his shoulder, and his throat closed up in shock, choking on hot tears, for himself, for the glowing woman of his dreams . . .

Stevens held him down, one large hand planted on his chest, the other stroking his damp hair, until the sedative took him under.

Max opened his eyes.

The ceiling was awash with light.

With one hand, he managed to push himself and sit upright, looking toward the light. There was Stevens, sprawled in a chair, face stubbled with white whiskers, asleep.

His left arm was still burning, and he felt with his right hand, but there was nothing, just his side, and he swallowed, nauseated. And frightened, because there was something else. A kind of insanity, beyond the edge of awareness, beginning to stir like wolves outside the fire-light.

He lay back and tried to focus on the ceiling.

"Doc."

Stevens yawned, sat up, and massaged his neck.

"So. The patient lives. How do you feel?"

"Like it's still there. And it *hurts.*"

"That will take time. The nerves have to heal."

"It's getting bad."

"I can give you a painkiller. Are you hungry?"

"Yeah, actually. Starving."

"Good. I'll bring you a little something. We'll see how you handle it."

He got to his feet, gave Max a pill, helped with a glass of water, and left the room.

Max stared up at the ceiling, wishing the pill would hurry, but grateful in a way for the pain, for its vise-like grip and blazing insistence, like fire keeping something at bay, something lurking in the shadows.

Robert Larsen came into the room then, and sat in the chair by the bed.

"Hey. How are you?"

"Jesus. Robert."

"It's okay now. You're safe."

"Christ. What am I supposed to do?"

"It's okay. You're not alone. You have friends."

For a moment, he could not answer. Not because the words were reassuring. They weren't. They were confirmation.

"What does the Doc know?"

"That you were hit by a stray bullet."

"That's all?"

"Pretty much."

"And . . . Jack?"

"Max, he's dead."

He stared at the ceiling, feeling a hollow emptiness inside, as though something more than his arm had been lost.

"Max, listen to me. Paul has been with you day and night. And you nearly died. Maybe you don't realize this, but I think you're like a son to him."

The door swung open, the doctor returning with a tray.

"Breakfast is served. If it stays down, you can have a real meal later."

"Although God knows why." Robert got up and left.

"What's he talking about?" asked Stevens.

"Dunno, Doc."

He made short work of a slice of toast and cup of broth. Stevens reached for the tray, but Max stopped him, feebly gripping his arm.

"Doc—thanks. Thank you. It's good to still be here."

The old man put a hand over his, then stood up with the tray and left the room.

He lay back, alone.

45

Max stayed at the doctor's, and in the days that came after there were times when he felt strangely alive, and restless, pacing the doctor's living room, thinking about the town, about what might be happening in it now that Jack Ryan was no longer around.

He thought about Robert's ideas, tried to imagine new industry. He wanted to get back, to work on new things, to keep it all alive.

But there were other times.

Getting dressed in the morning. Putting on socks. Trying to shave. Trying to write something down on a piece of paper. Normal things, the simplest things, things no one ever thought about. Now they were humiliation, and loss, and in a sudden rage he would curse Jack Ryan's soul—then feel the weight of the gun in his hand, feel it jump with a life of its own, see the shock in Jack's face—and the anger would drain out, leaving him hollow.

One night, he stood in front of the bathroom mirror staring at the alien thing that was his shoulder, at the raw wound stitched tight, and wanted to disappear, to escape anyone who had ever known him. He wanted to sleep. But with sleep came dreams, of terrible noise, strange faces, and blood.

And he could not escape Stevens. Each morning, the doctor woke him at six, then nagged and bullied until he was up and dressed and eating breakfast, then gave him exercises to do, and nagged and bullied until he did them.

They worked out a way for him to tie shoes, re-laced with a permanent anchor knot at one end and a looped hitch at the other.

He showed Max how to change the bandages.

"Bleach the dressings when you wash them. I'll give you some to take home. Make sure to rinse it out thoroughly and let them dry completely. Use clean water. Boil it . . . are you listening?"

"Yeah. Yeah, I'm listening."

"An infection can kill you, Max."

"Yeah, Doc. Okay."

Stevens cooked their meals, insisting he eat regularly. And it helped. The dreams came less often. They began to fade.

But there were reminders, like a coat that had to be buttoned or it would fall off his shoulder. Like hitting the floor because he tripped and couldn't reach out. Like his meals served with the meat already cut into small pieces. Reminders of life diminished, forever.

Every few days Robert would visit. Once, when Stevens was away on an errand, Robert told him the rest of what had happened at the lake.

As Robert ran toward him, Ryan, slumped across a table but still alive, had fired. It was the last thing Jack Ryan did, before sliding and thudding to the deck. Max went down as well, blood spurting from his shattered arm.

Robert had reached him, had pulled off his own shirt and was ripping it apart, when he felt a hand on his shoulder.

"Are you sure you want to do that?"

It was Frank.

"He's a friend!"

"If he were my friend, I'd let him go. Even if he lives, he'll lose that arm. More likely he'll die of gangrene. Not a nice way to go. Let him bleed. He won't feel a thing."

"*No!* You've got to help me!"

"Why?"

"You need him!" Robert had bellowed, his hands covered with blood.

"*I* need him?"

"*Listen, you son of a bitch!* You want that town to work with you? He's your best bet! *He* knows why it's necessary! Now, help me!"

"Okay, bud. But I hope your pal Stevens can patch him up, because no hospital's gonna touch an exile."

They had tied strips of cloth and wound them as a tourniquet, twisting it until blood stopped spurting, and Max had screamed once, then passed out again.

Then they had loaded him into the back of Frank's car—after Frank covered the seat with a tarp—and raced through the City, then east, to the doctor's.

"Your *pal* Stevens?" repeated Max. "*That's* what he said?"

"I think so."

"Your pal."

"I think that's exactly what he said."

"Damn, Robert. They've been watching you."

Robert shrugged.

"I suppose they watch everybody. It probably doesn't matter."

46

Gray mist and cold drizzle. Another depressing day.

Max turned onto the City lane and started walking.

There was nowhere to go, but Stevens was on his nerves again, and the house was like a prison. He had to get out, at least for a little while.

How long had it been? Two weeks? Maybe three. The rent must be due on his room, and board for the horse. The Committee may have given up on him by now, and found someone to take his place. And maybe that was just as well.

But what the hell am I supposed to do?

The walking added to his anger, because it felt clumsy with just one arm, awkward, like limping. But there was pleasure, too, in the anger. It kept him moving, striding along wet, black pavement, the rain now a steady patter on his face.

Finally, he came to a stop somewhere among dark, bare-limbed trees, his one hand clenched inside the pocket of a dripping jacket much too light for the weather, and he shivered, trying to make out the road ahead through the trees. But he knew there would be nothing. That no matter how far he walked, there was nothing to find. The world was behind him. This was the end of the line.

He enjoyed that thought. The end of the line. Nowhere to go. It felt right. Just where he belonged. But he was cold, the afternoon was growing dark, and he swore under his breath and turned–then stood quite still.

In the middle of the road, maybe ten yards away, some kind of animal stood watching him. Brown fur hung in loose mats dripping dismally in the rain, but the thing stood its ground, silent and intent.

"Jack!"

The dog made so sound.

Max jogged to him.

"Jack! What the hell are you doing?"

He crouched down and put his arm around the animal, feeling it trembling under the wet fur. And, after a minute, feeling a little warmth creep between them.

"Jack, you idiot. You should be home."

The retriever licked his face.

He stood up, took off his jacket, draped it over the dog, then started walking.

"Come on, Jack! Let's get you home. *C'mon!*"

The dog trotted and caught up, and together they walked, shivering, through the steady rain.

Robert joined them for dinner that night, and talked about looking for an old coal mine to reopen. But the doctor was quiet, and when there was a pause in the conversation, changed the subject.

"You're healing well, Max. I'm pleased with it."

"Yeah. Looks like I'll live after all."

"I think you're ready to go home. How do you feel about that?"

His mouth shut as he thought about his tiny room at the farmhouse. About going back to where he had started. With nothing.

But he felt the other two watching him.

"Yeah, Doc. Sure."

"I know it will be a bit of a challenge. But I think you're up to it."

"Sure, Doc."

After dinner, Robert took him aside and handed him a large envelope.

"That's for you."

"The time capsule? How did you get it?"

"It was all arranged. By the time we left the restaurant, it was in my saddle bag. After we brought you here, Frank drove me back so I could get the horses. Little did he know!"

"Jesus, Robert. You took an awful chance."

"I know. Be careful with it."

That night, propped in bed, he read through pages and pages, about agents, assignments, debriefings, and profiles compiled on people he knew. Including an eye-opener. John Anderson had been observed, more than once, hunting and fishing with Doctor Paul Stevens.

That would explain a few things.

Only one item was missing. The letter from Robert to himself.

It was late when he finished. He turned off the bedside lamp, and was quickly asleep.

47

The retriever awoke. His head lifted in the dark. Something was out of place. A sound. Small, but unfamiliar, and he waited, ears pricked. He waited to hear it again.

Nothing happened. He lowered his head. His eyes closed.

Then he was on his feet, quivering, because something *was* wrong–

The silence of the house erupted in an explosion of shattering glass and men shouting, overwhelming the snarls of a half-grown dog swiftly kicked away.

In another room, Max was pinned, a heavy weight crushing the breath from him, a loud voice bellowing, *"Shit! I can't cuff him."*

He was dragged along the floor, into another room, his one arm twisted behind him, everything dark but for stabbing beams of flash-lights–enough to see Stevens on the floor nearby, face bleeding, and silhouettes of men moving about the room, bulky with utility belts and carrying wicked-looking rifles.

A rough cloth dragged over his head. Cord bit his arm and legs. A voice shouted, *"Let's roll!"* and he was lifted and carried out into freezing night air, then dumped onto a cold steel floor. Doors slammed. Machinery roared. The floor bounced and rumbled.

He shouted through the hood.

"Doc! Are you there?"

"I'm here." It was a gasp. "I think I've broken some ribs."

"Who the hell *are* they?"

After some minutes, the floor lurched. Doors screeched. He was dragged out, slung into the back of another truck, and then it was moving, bumping and swaying, something metallic banging at inter-vals, acrid fumes fouling the air. His stump was slammed, his screams muffled inside the hood.

Then he slid and hit a wall, and the vibration stopped.

There was a thick silence, then voices, but the voices faded, leav-ing the sound of his own breathing inside the hood hot and stale like a dry hand covering his face, and he struggled to stay calm against an urgent need to fill his lungs.

Then a loud creak. Something tugged his shirt, and he slid and dropped, hitting frozen pavement with a crack to his head. An engine roared, seemingly on top of him, then shifted, moving away.

He tried to sit up, but this was impossible, his arm trussed to his side, his legs bound together, and he lay shivering, trying not to get sick inside the hood.

Something grabbed shirt and legs, and he was lifted.

Warm air and close, sharp echoes told him he was indoors.

More voices. He was held down on something hard, his good shoulder jabbed with something sharp, and the voices went suddenly quiet.

48

There were bees somewhere nearby. He could hear them, an entire swarm of them, but out of sight, as though hidden in the snow. Was that possible? He kicked at the snow, kicked up great white plumes of the stuff that drifted away, then kicked at the frozen ground underneath, until the swarm resolved into a single dry buzz, and there was something hard against his face.

Max opened his eyes onto a whiteness so bright it hurt, raised his hand to block it, and looked down on a violent assault of orange.

Groaning, he tried to roll over, tried to push himself upright, but his body was stiff, clumsy, and he swung his legs out instead, felt a cold floor beneath his bare feet, and managed to stand.

He was surrounded by three walls of cement block, glossy with gray paint, and a line of thick, gray bars. Outside the bars, more cement block.

Bolted to one gray wall were a steel sink and toilet. He had been lying on a steel shelf bolted to another wall, and was now standing barefoot on dark concrete polished smooth, his body clad in a blinding orange jumpsuit. There was nothing else, no shoes, no other clothing.

Harsh blue-white illumination fell from big industrial fixtures high overhead, out of reach.

The buzz came from the lighting.

He limped to the sink. One faucet gave way with a creak and issued a narrow, tepid stream tasting of rust and mud. The other was dry.

He moved to the bars. Pressing his face against them, he could see a few yards down an empty corridor, and he shouted, his voice hoarse, a raw dryness deep in his throat.

There was a distant scrape. Then a rumble, followed by a dull clang and sharp, echoing footsteps. He backed away as someone approached, a man in a dark green uniform and black boots who stopped in front of the cell, looked him up and down, snorted, and walked away.

Again the rumble and clang, followed by footsteps, fading.

Sometime later, the man returned carrying a metal tray. He slid this under the bars.

"Breakfast."

"Listen, who are you? Where's my friend? What the hell's going on?"

Again the once-over, followed by a laconic, "Save your energy," and the man walked off.

The food might have been scraps for dogs, but he was famished and choked down a hard crust of bread and limp rind of bacon. He shoved the tray back under the bars and drank more of the rust-flavored water.

Then he sat on the steel bed and tried to think.

The lights buzzed. A high-pitched metallic rattle droned, far down the corridor. The sink dripped, *plip plip plip.* There was no movement, even the air felt trapped, and he began to conceive the lights failing and everyone called away, leaving him alone, locked in this cell on an empty corridor.

Buried alive.

He stood up, trying to breathe. He walked around the cell, examining the sink, the toilet, the steel 'bed'. He counted the bars, three times. He shouted again, but the unanswered echoes of his own voice triggered the feeling of being buried, and he hastily shut his mouth, covering it with his hand as though it had acquired a will of its own.

Again he tried to peer down the corridor, squeezing his face against the bars, twisting against them . . . then pounding, shouting . . .

When he came to himself, he was running round and round the cell, gasping for air, bruising his feet, and he stopped, shaking, then staggered as the floor seemed to turn.

His eyes wouldn't focus.

He stumbled to the bed, and fell on it.

There was no way to judge the passage of time, hours or days. He could not recall the world outside. Even with eyes closed, he could see only gray bars and the glare of the overhead lights, unchanging. Timeless.

Panic would come, blind and suffocating, throwing him to scrabble at the bars until his nails ripped and the bars were slick with his own blood.

Then, emptiness, and he would huddle on the floor, propped against a wall, and the seconds would crawl, one by one, by one . . . they seemed to stop, and he could think that he was already dead, only waiting for someone to come and close his eyes . . .

His head lifted, sudden sharp sounds of footsteps piercing like a hot wire pulling him upright.

The green uniform. Something sliding under the bars.

The uniform spoke.

"Lunch."

He slumped back against the wall as footsteps receded down the corridor, along with the quiet sound of laughter.

49

The cell was drifting around him, unreal, as though this were happening to someone else, a madman who had lived here long before him. But he was now that madman.

The drifting slowed, then stopped. He was sitting on the steel bed, leaning against the wall, staring at dried blood streaking one leg of the orange suit. Memories of screams came to him, and he wondered if they had come from his own throat or from somewhere else. But it was quiet now. There was no screaming.

A dull clank jarred the silence. Then a grating rumble and bang.

The cell was being opened.

Two guards. One holding a shotgun and ordering him to stand. The other shackling his ankles and wrist. One shackle dangling against his knees.

The guards laughing. "Let's go, Lefty."

His knees were shaking. He took one step and fell, was kicked hard and dragged to his feet.

He did not fall again.

A long, gray corridor. Then a small room. Inside the room, a steel table bolted to the floor. Metal chairs. No windows. The same glaring light.

He was pushed into a chair. He tried to speak, to ask a question, but something leathery smacked his head.

"Shut it."

The room was quiet, and he waited, the realization slowly dawning that they were drugging him. That it must be in the food.

A door swung open and slammed against the wall. Two people strode in, a man wearing a gray jacket and plain tie, and a woman in a black overcoat. The pungent smell of outdoors clung to them, penetrated his brain, and he wanted suddenly to throw himself at their feet, to beg them to take him away. Please, God, anywhere.

The man grabbed a chair, dragged it noisily to the table, and sat down across from Max, waving a hand in front of his face.

"Anyone home? You listening? All right. We can do this the easy way, or we can do it the hard way. You decide."

Max just looked at him.

The woman paced the room, slowly, hands hidden in the pockets of her overcoat.

"Maybe he likes it the hard way."

"Suits me. What about it, pal? What's it gonna be? And don't fuck with me."

"I don't know what you want."

"Maybe he's brain-damaged," observed the woman, peering through the small, wired window in the metal door.

"You brain-damaged? Or just fucking with me?"

His scalp itched, and he tried to scratch it, but the chain caught and snapped taut, rattling against the table.

"Look at that! The little shit tried to hit me!"

Something struck his head, hard, and he screamed.
"What the do you want?"
The man leaned close.
"Stevens. And you're going to help us get him."
"Don't you *have* him?" It was almost a sob.
"Of course we have him, in *custody.* I want his *ass.* I want big-shot
Doctor Paul Stevens' ass on my wall."
"He means," said the woman, "we want answers."
"Then ask me a question! I can't read your fucking mind!"
Fingers snapped in his face.
"How long did you have the envelope?"
"What–?"
Lights flashed, the floor flew up into his face, and the guards were
hauling him back to the chair, blood dripping from his nose.
After a moment, he answered.
"A day."
"How much did you read?"
"All of it."
"Where did you get it?"
He closed his mouth.
"From Stevens?"
He shook his head, and heard the woman behind him.
"I've wasted enough time on this. See if you people can help with
his memory."
The two left, and presently he was taken back to the cell.
There were more guards waiting, a very large one lounging on the
steel bed. He was pushed. He tripped and hit the floor, the large one
piling onto his back, grabbing his hair, yanking his head back. Fin-
gers jammed down his throat, and he choked, swallowing something
dry and bitter.
The guard gently let his head down, patting his face, and there
was a flash in the corner of his eye and the tug of a knife slicing the
orange suit.
They took turns, pinning him down while one after another raped
him, as though excavating, his face shoved against concrete, rancid
breath and grunts and a hot tongue in his ear.
Then the slam of the bars and a jumble of footsteps receding.
He crawled to the toilet and tried to throw up, kneeling and gagging himself. But his stomach only heaved.
The madman returned.

———————————

The guards came back.
He was sitting on the bed when the bars slid open, unable to
move.
They took their time, and left him on the floor shaking as with
fever.

50

He sat again in the windowless room, staring through a yellow haze at the flat surface below his face. If someone had asked his name, he could not have answered.

But the haze beginning to lift.

Again the man and woman appeared, and again the achingly pungent smell of outdoors penetrated his brain.

The man sat down and studied him, as if wondering whether it was worth the effort.

"Where did you get the envelope?"

Max stared at the half-open mouth.

"*The envelope! The fucking envelope!* Where did you get it? From Stevens?"

He managed to turn his head, right then left.

"Oh, I think you did."

The woman stopped pacing.

"Mr. Wyse, look at me. Are you listening? We have enough on him now. We don't need you."

He squinted up through the glare to see her face.

"Then let me go."

"You want us to let you go? Is that it? Then you'll have to do something for us. We want to tie Dr. Stevens to that envelope. It makes a nice, neat package. No loose ends. I don't like loose ends."

"But . . . he . . . "

"I don't think you're listening. And you're running out of time."

"Why?"

"Because this case goes to trial soon. And after we convict him, I'll have no further interest in you."

Max felt a hand on his jaw, his head was turned, and he was staring at the man's pocked face just inches away.

"And you know what that means, pal. It means you can keep the boys here company," he tilted his head in the direction of the deadpan guards, "until they retire. *Capisce?*"

He nodded.

"Okay." The man stood up. "We'll be back."

Panic rose as the two moved toward a door.

The man grinned.

"Don't worry. You cooperate, you have nothing to worry about. Hear that, boys? Lay off. Clean him up. Give him something to eat. He looks like a fucking refugee."

———————

It might have been the following day when the two returned. There was no way to know. But Max had slept. He had eaten. His brain was functioning. He understood the statement they put in front of him.

He signed.

They left, and the guards took him along the corridor to a different room, where he was handed some old clothes.

He peeled off the orange suit and kicked it away.

They gave him forms to sign, and he signed where they pointed. They directed him to a gray door, and he turned the handle and pushed it open, stepping into blinding light.

He was standing in shirtsleeves on packed snow outside a concrete wall under a brilliant white sky. The door slammed behind him, and he started walking, not looking back, with no thought but to put as much distance as possible between himself and that door. And if that meant freezing to death, he would think about it later, when the time came.

But he heard a voice.

He had heard many voices, but this one was different. It was small, and outside him.

"Get in."

He looked around, searching for the source. There was a white car, its passenger door open. He walked toward it, beginning to shiver.

"*Get in.*"

He leaned over to look inside, at the driver.

It was Frank.

51

Frank drove, and Max watched the City sweep by. Small buildings lined the streets, rising three and four stories, sidewalks white with trampled snow. In the distance, dark skyscrapers seemed to prop up the overcast, slowly passing by, not coming any closer.

He felt at peace.

But he was troubled, too, by unexpected things. By shattered windows, and boarded-up doors. By the unnatural quiet of the streets.

They turned into an alley and parked behind a building, then picked their way around patches of ice to the front, to a stretch of flat gray sidewalk swept clear of snow. Glass doors opened smoothly onto a warm, dry lobby, rows of letterboxes along one wall, two elevators along another.

On the third floor, Frank unlocked a door.

Inside was a small, carpeted living room, a tiny kitchen, a bathroom, and a bedroom, with clean clothes folded on a chair.

Max looked at the bed. He managed to kick off his shoes before his eyes closed and he collapsed and slept without dreaming.

———————

When he awoke, daylight was nearly gone.

He got up, cold and stiff and rubbing his side for warmth. There was a clock on the nightstand, the hands at half-past four. He looked at it a moment, because it felt so natural, looking at a clock like that and knowing right away where you stood in time.

He switched on some lights, almost without thinking.

The apartment was empty. No sign of Frank.

He took a shower, standing for long minutes under steaming water, then shaved off his rough beard, carefully, brushed his teeth, thoroughly, and combed his shaggy hair.

He considered himself in the mirror. The face he saw looked familiar. He leaned a little closer. The features were his, but the face . . . the face belonged to someone else.

He turned away and dressed.

In the living room, he found a scrap of paper taped to the front door, with a single hand-scrawled line.

Stay put.

He went to the kitchenette. There was a kettle, and in the small pantry a jar of instant coffee. He held the jar under his foot so he could loosen the top, then read the directions, boiled water, and carefully poured hot water into a cup with a spoonful of brown powder.

It was dark when he returned to the living room, to stand by a window with his coffee, the bitter cold outside seeping through the glass. A thick snow fell under the streetlamps, now steady, now whipped sideways, a few lonely figures trudging the sidewalks and bending into silent gusts of wind.

He wondered what the date was. His stump seemed fairly healed.

A jagged sound. A key in the lock. Then a voice.

"So. Max Wyse lives."

Frank carried a bag of groceries into the kitchen and returned to the living room.

"That should hold you a few days. I see you're making yourself at home."

"I'm a long way from home."

"You think so? I wonder. You hungry?"

"A little."

Frank indicated a closet. "Grab a coat."

He picked out a warm coat and put it on, his fingers clumsy on the big toggle buttons.

The left sleeve dangled.

Frank noticed.

"Want to pin that up?"

He glanced down at the empty sleeve, and shook his head.

They left the building and walked a block or so to the warm glow of a restaurant. Frank pushed through the door, stamping snow from his feet, and waved to someone behind the bar, a stout man with a round pink face and clean white shirt, who shortly came over.

"Well! How *are* you, Frank?"

"Good, good. George, this is my friend, Max. Max, George."

George stuck out a pudgy hand.

"Pleasure, Max. What'll it be, Frank?"

"Coupla steaks. Steak okay with you, Max? Couple beers."

"Sure thing." George winked. "Carol's been asking about you."

"You didn't say anything, did you?"

"You know me, Frank." George winked again and went back behind the bar.

Frank took a booth in a dark corner and made himself comfortable. Max followed, shrugging out of the coat and sitting down opposite. George returned, placed two beers on the table, and discreetly walked off.

Frank took a long swallow.

"So. How was it? In the cage. Pretty bad?"

He sipped a little beer.

"Bad enough."

"You lasted longer than I expected. But don't blame me. I didn't get you into it. I did get you out, though."

"Uh-huh."

He was waiting for what had to come.

"Robert Larsen told me you're the only one in your town I should deal with. That's why you're here."

"Is it?"

"Look, bud." Frank leaned forward, his arms crossed on the table. "Everyone who goes in there breaks, sooner or later. *Everyone.* Some tough nuts are just harder to crack, that's all. Be glad you're not one of them. They're never the same afterward."

"So you know all about it."

"It's my business to know. Here's what else I know. You owe me. They had good reasons for holding you."

"Reasons? Like what?"

"Loose ends."

"Loose ends! What does that mean?"

"I mean, those people are there to make cases. That's what they do. But some cases are complicated. There are other people involved, important people. There's evidence you'd like to have, but maybe you can't find it or you can't have it. But the more loose ends, the more questions the judges ask. So if you're missing something to make the complicated story, why risk scaring them off? Especially if you have the guy you want. So you make the story simpler. Make it fit the evidence you have. Tie up loose ends."

"The envelope."

"Exactly."

"So I don't get it. It's over. What did they need me for?"

"They made their case, but sometimes a case doesn't stay made. New questions come up. Another piece of evidence turns up. It gets reopened. And when there's a wildcard, like you, who might talk or cause trouble or disappear, they hang onto it, to minimize damage, to make adjustments later."

"So you think they would have held me."

"I know they would. Right alongside a dozen more just like you, rotting away."

"How can they do that?"

"What's to stop them?"

"Don't they . . . the ones rotting away . . . don't they have friends? Doesn't anyone ever ask questions?"

"Would you? Knowing that if you're taken in, you might never come out?"

He could not answer that.

"It's a potent tool. The proof is, it isn't used much. In fact, I'll bet there's less trouble here in the City than in all the little exile communities around us."

A sudden swirl of cold air, and a group came in laughing, stamping snow from their feet. George led them to a table in another corner.

"Is that how you think of us? Little exiles?"

"Not many people think of you at all."

"But you do."

"It's my job."

"So what do you want?"

"I want you to work with me."

"Meaning what? You give the orders, or I go back to the cage?" He tried to sneer, not very successfully.

"Look, it's simple. I need someone I can deal with. Someone who's trusted and has a head on his shoulders. Not some *wired*-up prick like Ryan. I expect you to go back to whatever it was you were doing, which probably wasn't much. But with Ryan gone, you have a vacuum, and someone has to fill it. Of course, if you don't make it, I'll just deal with whoever comes next."

The steaks arrived. One was already cut into small pieces–and he remembered.

"What about Paul?"

Frank sipped his beer. "I don't know."

"Bullshit you don't."

"All right. They've got him on passing information. That's espionage. The usual penalty is CERA."

"What?"

"Complete Electrochemical Retrograde Amnesia. Gelding."

"But–he didn't give me the envelope!"

"That's not what they're after. The envelope's a plant. It's bugged. We took some old reports and some cash, wrapped it up with a forged letter, bugged it, and planted it for Larsen to find. We know exactly who had it and when. What *they're* after is what Stevens has been telling you and your pals. They want that stopped. And they want anyone else who might be tempted to know just how seriously they take it."

"For God's sake, Frank! You can't let this happen!"

"Look. I'll explain this once. Stevens was trusted. He committed a serious breach. And he did it with his eyes open. No one held a gun to his head. He knew what would happen if he was caught."

Frank picked up his glass and smirked.

"Hell, I hear he *invented* it."

When Frank got up to use the restroom, Max put on his coat and walked out.

Snow was coming down thick and fast, and he walked quickly, turning onto different streets at random, to throw off pursuit, to disappear, the sidewalks covered with inches of dry powder hissing like knives and obliterating every footprint.

Cars crawled the streets, tires spinning, snow flying in the beams of headlights. A plow truck rumbled by, piling snow along the curb.

He walked under streetlamps and by bars and restaurants, averting his face from the people he passed, people who talked and laughed and had places to go.

The Corporation was living on borrowed time, Robert had said. But there was no sign of that here.

Spasms of pain stabbed his missing arm. His legs ached. But he kept going.

Stevens had invented it, Frank said. If that was true, if it had been used on his friend Robert . . .

Once, long ago, he had been a boy lost and wandering like this, but down a mud path in the middle of nowhere, wondering where he was and would anyone look after him. Now he had people of his own to look after, people who had little idea what was happening outside their small town, little idea of the scheming and jockeying for power they were being drawn into, slowly but inexorably, like a gathering vortex.

He had to get back, somehow.

. . . It was late. There were few people about. He had no idea what day of the week it was, but they probably had to get up and go to work in the morning. The Corporation wouldn't want them out drinking all night.

. . . The snow had stopped. The streets were empty. There hadn't been a car in a long while, and an icy wind whistled, kicking up swirls of powder. He was shaking badly, aching with cold. Even his face hurt.

He stumbled into the recessed doorway of an old brick building that offered a little shelter from the wind. He knew he should keep walking, keep moving, but he was done, and he grimaced over his earlier thought that there were people who needed him. That his own actions could ever amount to anything, in a world such as this. He crouched in the doorway, huddled in shadow, his arm shoved under his coat, his jaw clenched to stop his teeth chattering, eyes squeezed tight against the racking cold.

Something hissed nearby, and he opened his eyes.

A car had stopped in the street before him, thick white plumes flickering red and whipping in the wind behind it. The passenger door creaked open, and he heard the familiar monotone.

"Get in."

The open door was like a warm, dim cave. He tried to hold still, to blend in with the building. But he was shivering too much.

"Get in."

He stood up and moved out of the shadows.

52

Agnes tossed aside her coat and keys and stood in the middle of her apartment, with no desire to move.

The day had started normally.

Each morning she drove to the office, did her work without an unnecessary word to anyone, then drove home again to the empty apartment. She seldom made dinner. She would lie curled in a chair late into the night, and sometimes awaken in the same chair, the windows brightening with dawn, then get up and wander the apartment switching off useless lights, dreary reminders of how she had spent the evening.

Sometimes she would go to the park and stand under bare trees looking up at frozen limbs black against the gray winter sky. The walkways were kept clear of snow, but rarely did she see anyone, and she could laugh bitterly, and no one would hear.

She had thought about following him. She could find him, Paul would help her. She could stay with him in the wilderness, until one or both of them died in some brutal way. And if Robert died first, what then? She would have to come back here, to the City. If they would have her.

That morning, she had gone to a conference room expecting a routine meeting, but had stepped inside and stopped, shocked out of her lethargy, because the one person in that room was the one person who had no business being there.

Max Wyse.

He had stood up, and she had stared, at first, slowly grasping the horror, then had walked to him and clasped his one hand in both of hers.

"My God, Max. What happened?"

"Oh, someone tried to kill me, and didn't succeed."

She closed her eyes and let his hand go.

"Robert is well, Agnes."

She turned away.

"I'm glad."

"Is there anything you want me to tell him?"

"He made his decision. There's nothing more to say." She walked to the door.

"Come on. You both made decisions. He just couldn't take it here anymore." She stood looking at the door, wondering if he could hear himself. "You know, I really thought you of all people would understand."

Suddenly she was shaking. She whirled around, screaming, "He couldn't *take* it? Couldn't take *what*? The tedium? Boredom? Better to run off with the castaways? *Look at yourself!* You of all people should understand! This is no game!"

53

A piece of glass crunched underfoot.

Max swore. He had swept and shoveled broken glass for half the morning. But he could not get it all. Not working with one arm.

At least the pipes hadn't burst. That was something. The bedroom doors in the doctor's home had been shut, fortunately, and even with smashed windows the plumbing had stayed intact.

Yesterday he had cleared out the snow drifting inside two rooms, then nailed blankets over the broken windows, just something temporary to keep out the wind. That had been a challenge. He had managed it by holding a blanket in his teeth while he pierced a corner with a nail. Then, holding the head of the nail against the side of a hammer's head wrapped in his fist, the blanket still hooked on the nail, he could smack it into the wood to get it started, then hammer it in.

Now he tossed aside the broom and went out the front door—making sure to close it firmly behind.

Outside was a dazzling winter's day, ice glinting on bare branches, long black shadows stark across sparkling white powder that spread into the trees and swallowed all sound, as well as the occasional piece of ice loosed from a limb. When he stood still, he could hear the faint thump of his own heartbeat.

It felt a long way from the City. But not quite as far as before.

He crossed the lane, trudging through shin-deep snow.

Frank had returned him to the apartment the freezing night he had tried to escape. The next day, two Security men had brought him to that awkward meeting with Agnes. He was sure that Frank was behind it, but he could not fathom why.

Then there had been the hearing.

Only a few people were in the courtroom. Three judges. Two prosecutors. The woman interrogator, who ignored him until he was sworn in to testify, then listened intently as he stumbled over his rehearsed answers.

Stevens was not present.

After the hearing, Frank drove him to the pub, and he had worked up the courage to ask where they would take Stevens, when it was over. Frank thought they would send him home after a few days. Or they might put him up in an apartment, where they could keep an eye on him. He wasn't too sure, and he wasn't much interested.

Through Bill, Max hired a part-time woodworker, an older woman who lived a mile from the Anderson place, and the next day she came out with him to board up the broken windows.

He watched while she covered them with old plywood. Once gateways opening onto possibilities, one by one she closed them up, forever.

After she left, he wandered the yard, sat atop the picnic table, watched the light change on the house, and avoided the plywood.

Later, Robert came out to help, and together they worked without speaking, sweeping up glass and debris, straightening up things inside. It was late when they finished and sat in the living room and drank the doctor's whiskey, watching long shadows stretch across the yard.

Max recounted his meeting with Agnes, and Robert got up and walked to the glass wall, staring out at the late afternoon sky.

"I wonder what he's up to? What's his interest in Agnes?"

"He's probably more interested in *you*, Mr. ex-Vice President of Security."

"I suppose you're right."

Watching the house darken without Stevens in it was depressing. He wanted to go home. But there was something else he had to say, and this seemed the right place to say it.

"Robert, the time capsule was a fake. A plant. I think most of the documents are real, but it was planted for you to find, and the letter to yourself was forged. You didn't actually write it. The money was planted, too. There was probably never any more than that."

Robert stood with his back to him. The room was silent.

"Did you hear what I said?"

"I heard. Where did you learn this?"

"Frank."

Robert nodded. He did not feel surprised. He felt nothing. And he found himself thinking, incongruously, that the architect could not have survived, because there was something gone from the room, something important. It was just a room now, just a space with walls, like any other.

Max hiked out to the empty house every few days. He was learning to ride again, but needed the feeling of distance. He wasn't ready for the doctor's house to be too close.

One afternoon, he trudged through snow tinged blue with late shadows, came out of the trees, and stopped, because lights were on inside the house.

There was movement behind a window, and there was Stevens, standing in profile, looking down as if lost in thought, the white hair scattered across the great forehead. He moved out of view.

Max stared at the empty window.

He was not ready for this. He was just not ready, and he turned and worked his way back along the trail. But when he reached the main road, he paused, looking back at the trail winding through the trees.

He knew he would never be ready, and he turned once more.

The sun was setting when he crossed the City lane and stopped at the walkway. Then he took a step, and another, and walked the dozen paces to the entryway and the front door.

He knocked, then knocked again.

The door opened.

In the doorway stood Stevens, separated by a few inches of space, and a lifetime.

"Can I help you?"

Max swallowed.

"My name is Max. Max Wyse. We were friends . . . until . . . I mean, we're still friends." He shrugged, helplessly. "You just don't remember."

The old man considered him a moment.

"I don't seem to remember much of anything."

Then Max realized they weren't alone. At the doctor's side stood the retriever, tail moving slowly from side to side.

"Jack!"

The tail wagged harder, and the dog let out a sharp yelp.

"So his name is Jack?"

Jack barked, again and again, until Stevens reached down to stroke the shaggy neck.

"Well . . . Max, is it? Maybe you'd better come in."

He went to visit Stevens often, a man who had once seemed larger than life, who had created a life for himself on his own terms, and who had built a setting for that life that said something. That meant something. And not just about the man or his life.

Now the house seemed a monument to someone else, and Max wasn't sure whether he went to keep what was left of his friend company, or out of morbid fascination with the wreck of such a life. And he wasn't sure how to live with either answer.

He drifted to the pub again, to fill the empty days, to escape the awful nights. Once in a while he remembered that he might now be town president. But mostly he tried to forget.

Anderson reminded him.

"You've had some time, boy, but you'd better plan on giving us a report pretty soon. We're all getting mighty anxious."

He had winced at the sight of the old man strolling in through the door of the pub, a place where he had not been seen in years.

"Christ, John, I'm really not ready for this. Can't you get someone else?"

Anderson stepped closer, tapping Max on the chest with a thick, brown finger.

"You listen to me. You wanted your chance. Now you got it. And people here are counting on you."

"What if I resign?"

Anderson pulled a crumpled envelope from his pocket, smoothed it out a little, then handed it to him, and his arm seemed to shrink as he reached for his pay.

Anderson held on to it.

"Then I suppose this old man will have to belly up to the bar. But not before I kick your young ass out of town." He let the envelope go.

"Okay, okay, just give me a little time, will you? I'm still recovering."

"Recover later. We're not asking you to turn handsprings. All we need is your brain. Get your friend Larsen to help. We'll appoint him vice president, if that's what you want."

Over a beer that night, Max asked Robert about the job, a job he had once dismissed.

"How much does it pay?"

"You want it?"

"I've got to live. I have a little money left, but it won't last."

"What about your engineering projects?"

"What about them? I don't have the money."

"Damn, Robert, you can't give up on that. It's your–" Something in Robert's face warned him, and he shut his mouth.

The cold weight lodged in the pit of his stomach as he walked home that night. But also a cold determination. He was president. He had a way to live. And no one could take that from him, not until June.

He held an officers' meeting.

Martha had resigned. She had given a letter to Anderson and moved in with a young man on a small farm at the edge of town.

Max read the letter, set it aside, and called the meeting to order.

Afterward, Bert confronted him.

"So you're president."

"That's right."

"Just remember you're not above the law."

Max shrugged into his coat, shoved the dangling sleeve into a pocket, and walked around the Chief, slapping the round man's shoulder.

"Big words, Bert. I hope you're up to it."

He settled into his new job, of problems and complaints. Like the road crew threatening to quit because they didn't think they were paid enough, or maybe because they didn't like going out in the cold. Like disputes over property lines. Like sewage dumped in the river, or arguments over money after someone died. The problems seemed to multiply as people came to expect a civil authority. But he found reassurance in it, reporting weekly to the Committee, briefing Anderson and the others in detail, making sure they understood what their government was doing, and hinting not too subtly at the chaos that might ensue without it.

But he was haunted by the City, by small things, like the jar of instant coffee. Or the stove that started with the turn of a knob. Or the electric clock on the nightstand. He had strange, vivid dreams of a warm apartment on a street that was lighted at night. Of people walking the sidewalks and laughing. Of cars passing by, carrying other people . . . somewhere.

And there was Frank. The Committee had not much interest in talking with the City to begin with, and Anderson's opposition had put an end to it.

But he could not give Frank a final answer.

One cold, clear night he rode back to the pub after a late meeting. There was enough starlight to make out the road, and he let the horse pick its own way while he rode along with eyes half-closed, almost dozing—until the headlights of a parked car switched on, blinding, the horse prancing and snorting and threatening to rear, and he hung on desperately, trying to calm it.

When the animal was under control, the driver's window lowered with a mechanical whine, and Frank looked up at him.

"Well? Did you talk any sense into them?"

Christ.

"It's only *been* a few weeks! It's going to take some time."

"I'm running *out* of time. I thought you could handle them."

"Lay off. Ryan left us a big mess. We've had a lot of work to do. And you don't make it any easier, loitering around in the dark in that damned car of yours."

He spurred the horse.

Behind him, dirt scattered as the car turned. Then the engine roared as Frank accelerated past him, heading toward the North Road and spooking the horse once more.

He watched the taillights recede, his mouth dry.

The next day, he went to see Anderson.

He followed the old man into his barn, trying to reason with him, almost pleading. Anderson let him talk, but his mind was made up.

"Maybe you're right, boy. But if you are, we all might as well give up and go find somewhere else to live."

"Oh, come on! Where will *that* end?"

"I don't know. But dealing with those bastards will be the end of us, right here, just as well as war."

"That's your opinion. You may be wrong."

"You bet! That's why we have the Committee. It's why we have elections."

"John, look, we can't just wait around for the next election. There isn't time. We've got to start talking."

"Says who? Son, you are *not* going to buffalo us! You're playing with fire. You . . . you and . . ."

The old man seemed to choke.

Max watched a moment, then answered, gently, "I know, John. I know. You were friends with him."

Slowly, his jaw dropped, and John Anderson seemed to sag, the lines of his face etched deep. He looked old, truly old.

"Why the secrecy, John? I was his friend, too."

Looking at the floor and shaking his head, Anderson muttered, "You can't take chances with them. He knew it. And so do you."

"Well, he took a chance with *me.*"

The old man raised his head, as though astounded that anyone could be this stupid.

Max felt heat in his face.

"So what are you saying? That I should've stayed away? And maybe I should've left Jack Ryan alone, too! You didn't mind it when I was taking my chances with *him,* did you?"

"Sorry, son. Paul took his own chances. I know that. Had his reasons, I guess. I tried to warn him."

"Meaning?"

"Look, when he saw me, it was a little risky, but it was only on occasion, and I respected his confidence. It got a lot riskier with *you* seeing him practically every week. Then Larsen showed up, a senior executive who was purged. All the makings of a conspiracy."

The shadows in the barn seemed to deepen, and Max hesitated. But there was something here that needed to be understood.

"Okay, John. It was dangerous. Maybe more than we knew. But we can't just ignore them. You know that."

Anderson spat suddenly, jabbing a finger northward.

"You listen to me! I'll be *damned* before I see this town overrun by those *goddamn* sons of bitches who have no respect for anything! I'm *not* going to let it happen! So you just get it out of your head!"

54

A few eyebrows went up at the next Committee meeting when Anderson introduced Robert Larsen, and Robert got up to speak. Clearly, patiently, Robert explained why the Town should undertake a project to settle and publicly record property lines. He argued that titled property was a foundation for law, that the two went hand in hand, that they could not have one without the other. He explained what should be done and how he would go about it.

Somewhat dumbfounded, the Committee found they agreed, and a motion was brought to appoint him to the vacant office of vice president.

One member objected. They couldn't just hire someone to fill an elected office. They didn't have the authority. It wasn't in the Charter. Someone countered that the Charter didn't say much of *anything,* and no one could put everything in a damned piece of paper anyhow. Anderson argued it was the Committee's job to make the law, and the rest went along.

Robert was appointed. And on an afternoon in February, Robert and Max met in the town office to organize the few property records they had been able to gather, mainly from a handful of disputes that had been settled over the years, plus a large farm recently divided among three adult children whose elderly mother could no longer remember who they were. It was a start. Spring was not far off, and

Robert had convinced the Committee they should hire someone to do a survey when the weather warmed.

There was a sound of commotion out front, and one of the young deputies burst inside.

"Mr. Wyse! Mr. Wyse!"

"Hey, hold on!" Max took him by the shoulders, the boy panting, his eyes bulging. "Settle down! Take a breath. What happened?"

"It's old man Anderson," the boy gasped. "And his wife! They're *dead!*"

For one crazy moment, Max wanted to laugh. But the panicked face stopped him.

"The Chief sent me to find you! Says you know of a doctor."

"Bert sent you? Where is he?"

"Up at the house."

He could only stare at the boy, and it was Robert who stated, with quiet finality, "You'd better take us there."

The ride across snow-covered farmland seemed endless.

When they finally reached the top of the frozen hill, the house looked as it always had. Except, there was no smoke from the chimney. And the water trough was a block of ice, the wood split and dripping from one corner.

They dismounted. The deputy led them up the steps and through the porch door. Inside was the kitchen. There was a small table, and two wooden chairs. A few dishes were stacked by a white porcelain sink, some utensils hanging over it. The simple trappings of a hard existence, and Max looked around, humbled.

Bert was crouched by a wood stove.

"What happened?" Robert asked.

Kindling was beginning to crackle, and Bert pushed the door of the stove against the latch, leaving it ajar, and stood up.

"Not sure. What it looks like is the old man had a heart attack. Looks like the wife found him that way and shot herself."

Bert stated this with a steady look at Robert.

"And how do you know this was a heart attack?"

"I don't. Sent for you two to get your doctor friend to look at him."

"Well, our doctor friend can't help."

"No? And why's that?"

"Because his memory is gone. He doesn't even know who he is."

"*What?* How's that?"

Max rubbed his face, trying to rub away the haze of unreality.

"We don't know for sure, Bert. So let's not spread it around."

Bert nodded, his eyes still on Robert.

"You hear that, Jim? Better keep your mouth shut."

"Yessir."

"Well, I suppose you'd better have a look."

They filed behind Bert through a narrow hallway to a small bedroom, Max in back and stopping just inside the door.

John Anderson lay face up on the bed, his features blue-gray, his open eyes clouded white. A woman lay across him, her nightgown and small gray head streaked black with congealed blood.

Bert spoke softly.

"She put the gun in her mouth and pulled the trigger. The fire went out, and everything froze."

Max could only whisper, "He looks . . . surprised."

"Yeah. Like it happened fast."

He could not look away. He had last seen the old man in his barn, defiantly cursing the Corporation, and it came to him then that he had never connected John Anderson with death. Had never acknowledged the man as mortal. In some childish way, he had expected John to be there, always.

Now it was too late.

They filed back to the kitchen. The stove was throwing off heat, and Bert turned down the damper, then sent Jim to get help for a burial.

The boy hurried out, and the Chief slowly buttoned his coat.

"I'm going to run along and get a-holt of someone to watch this place. Don't like leaving it empty."

But he made no move to leave, and the three men stood listening to the old stovepipe creak, until Max spoke.

"Bert, what do you think? Was it really a heart attack?"

"I don't know. I've only seen one other, that I know of, and it didn't look like that."

"What did it look like?"

"Twisted up. Kind of like he went to sleep uncomfortable. You know, here's what *I* think. I think you two know a few things the rest of us don't. Things that have to do with old man Anderson. Things that have to do with the Corporation. And with *your* background" – he was looking at Robert again – "that gives a man something to think about."

"I probably know a lot less than you imagine."

"I'd like to make that judgment for myself. And I shouldn't have to figure out what questions to ask, then figure out whether I believe the answers. That's conspiracy. That's the way *I* see it, until somebody changes my mind."

Bert stood there with his jaw thrust forward, as though waiting for someone to challenge him. When no one did, he turned and let himself out.

Robert watched the door close. He looked at Max, who seemed entranced by the shimmering heat rising from the black stove.

"He's right, you know."

The young man stared at the stove, as though in a dream, but spoke quietly. "Robert, do you really think a woman would kill herself that way?"

"I don't know. I suppose it would have to depend on the woman. I never met her."

"Me neither. But it's hard to imagine." Max pushed the stove door firmly shut, and turned. "This is wrong."

"Meaning?"

"Meaning John's heart attack doesn't look like a heart attack. And I don't think her suicide looks like a suicide. And that makes it murder."

To Robert, it looked exactly like the sort of end to life one could expect out here.

"Easy does it, Max. It could be just what it appears. If it's a little unusual, well, they were an unusual pair. At least he was, and I would imagine she would have to be as well."

"No. Frank is somewhere behind this. And you know it."

"It's possible. Frank may be capable of murder. But how would you prove it?"

"Oh, come on! Do you really think John just had a convenient heart attack? He was the real obstacle to Frank's plans, and Frank told me he was running out of time. That son of a bitch! His corporate masters must have been putting the screws to him."

Robert had a pretty good idea who Frank's corporate master was, and the thought of that here was like a slap to his face.

"It could fit. But what do you want to do? With all due respect, I can't imagine Bert Morrow being much help."

He had left the City because there he had been helpless. And he had left Agnes.

But nothing had changed.

"No!" sputtered Max. "For chrissake, he never laid a finger on Jack Ryan! What's he going to do with someone like Frank?"

It was a dead end here as well. Nothing had changed. Nothing *would* change.

"Nothing," he murmured. "Not a damned thing."

"Exactly! And we've got to stop doing *nothing*. Who's next? You? Me?"

Robert looked at the hallway and the shadows leading to the bedroom. The long arm of the Corporation seemed to reach out, tapping his shoulder, drawing him back to the night Agnes had told him about Richard Martin, the night he had left her and wandered alone, under the eyes of the City, and felt its impunity.

Nothing had changed. Even his trick of steady breathing didn't help anymore.

Steady breathing. My one accomplishment. The summation of my life.

He should have been angry. But what he felt was a growing, luminous clarity.

Except for a slow hiss from the wood stove, the house was silent. But it felt like a pause in battle, a space of time in which to count the dead and regroup before the coming onslaught. He thought of Agnes. He thought of the two people lying in that grotesque tableau down the hall. But what he really thought about was Richard Martin, the man whose face he could not remember.

He spoke slowly and evenly.

"It's time we sent the bastards a message."

"What do you mean? What kind of message?"

"One they'll understand." He had to force the words out. "Frank told you about the time capsule. The letter was forged, you said. But they used real reports. That means we still have the list of spies. We know who they are. And we know what happened to one of them. Ryan. What about the others?"

"One disappeared. Moved out a few months ago. Which leaves three still here."

"You're sure?"

"I've been watching them."

"That's a little unusual, isn't it? For an exile? Moving out?"

"*Very* unusual."

"All *right,* then. We send the bastards a message. One they'll understand." And, as comprehension dawned in the young man's face, Robert added, "Sauce for the gander, Max."

Sauce for the gander.

That phrase stayed with Max long after they left the Anderson place, long after he went home to the farmhouse that night and lay in bed, feeling that a chasm was opening before his feet, still more frightening because he did not understand it.

But he remembered how often people had told him to grow up.

This must be what it felt like.

55

"**M**iss Agnes? Will you please come this way?"

The young woman had stepped in front of her, while the morning stream of humanity broke around them, people arriving for work, heading for the elevators. Her glance automatically followed them, but the young woman's hand was at her elbow, not quite touching but blocking her way as surely as a barricade.

"Please. This won't take long."

"What's this about?" She found herself walking with the woman, although she did not quite remember making the decision to do so. "I don't want to be late."

"You won't be late."

The woman led her into what appeared to be a small conference room.

"Please sit down."

There was a table, and a couple of chairs. Agnes sat, and the woman closed the door, then stood there, arms folded, looking at the floor, her position by the door an unmistakable command.

"What are we waiting for?"

"Just be patient."

Agnes leaned back, sighed, and glanced around the room. It was barren, no evidence of its use.

She crossed her legs, one foot swinging impatiently. She crossed them the other way.

"Can I get a cup of coffee?"

"I'm afraid not."

"What are we waiting for?"

The woman just studied the floor.

Agnes stood up.

"Okay. I have work to do. You can call me when whoever we're waiting for is ready."

"Sit down."

Ten minutes later, the woman stepped back as the door opened and a heavy-set man lumbered into the room, lowered himself into a chair, and placed a thin file folder on the table. Behind him, a workman stepped inside, put a cardboard box on the floor, and left.

The door closed.

The big man opened the folder and pulled out a sheet of paper, which he turned and slid in front of Agnes so she could read it.

She was suddenly very still, holding herself upright as though the paper were radioactive and to move might expose her.

Across the top was typed, *Notice of Termination.*

A pen appeared. She looked up. The man held a small, flat envelope in front of him.

"Please read it and sign. This"–he tapped the envelope–"is your final paycheck. I will give it to you after you sign."

They were watching her, the woman with arms folded, the man with his chubby fingers slowly lifting and tapping the envelope, lifting and tapping . . .

"Why?"

Almost imperceptibly, the man nodded at the paper, his eyes still fixed on hers.

She looked down and read:

> . . . *your services no longer required . . . effective immediately . . . affirm all company property returned . . .*

"But–why?"

There was only the tap, tap, tap of pudgy fingers.

"Don't you know what this *means?*"

She was sobbing, trying to stifle it, but the faces looking at her held a sense of finality. As though everything was done. In the past.

As though she was not really here.

She had work to do, and she wanted to go to her desk. But she watched her hand pick up the pen and the pen move across the paper.

The paper disappeared. The envelope replaced it. The man slapped the folder shut.

"Thank you. Those are your personal items, by the door. Please take them with you."

They waited while she rose and moved around the table, carefully, so as to not to touch anyone. She bent to pick up the box.

The door was somehow open. She went through it.

She was in the lobby, looking toward the elevators. A security guard watched her, relaxed, but alert.

She walked to the big glass doors, and then outside, into a bright world now strange.

She drank herself to sleep that night.

In the morning, when her alarm went off, she got out of bed without thinking, but the gritty feel in her eyes and ragged dryness in her throat reminded her. There was nowhere to go.

She dressed anyway, waited until everyone would be at work, then drove to the building. She went inside, straight to the security desk, and asked to use the phone.

No one answered her calls.

She left messages, for her boss, for co-workers. She came back the next day, and the day after. There were never any answers.

Her savings were meager, but she worked it out. She could stretch her money for two months. Maybe there was someone in HR she could talk to. Maybe she could wait outside the building after work each day, maybe persuade someone to talk to her. Maybe, if she kept calling, someone might answer.

She listed these things on a piece of paper. She wrote out a weekly budget. The list and the numbers, black marks on a clean sheet of paper, were something tangible, an anchor, a temporary relief.

She would give herself a month. If she failed, if she could not get her job back, she would go to Paul. He would help her find Robert.

Then she would beg. It was not beneath her, she could do it, she had begged forbearance from a man she loathed. Now she could plead for help from a man she had loved.

The plan helped. She made a small dinner, listened to some records, and went to sleep.

In the morning, as she worked on her list, writing down names she thought might be sympathetic, or maybe disgruntled, there was a firm knock at her door.

Her pulse quickened. It might mean something.

She went to the door and opened it.

Outside was a man she had never seen before, tall, athletic, his face a startling meld of boredom and suppressed tension.

He said, "I want to talk to you."

56

The news of Anderson's death traveled quickly, and Max expected the town to fall apart again. Only this time he would not have John as an ally. But the Committee surprised him, and maybe themselves, electing Barbara Hutchins chairman in a hastily-convened meeting, and with no debate. No one was more surprised than Barbara, but she accepted the job and had some definite ideas on how things were going to be done.

A week later, Bert's young deputy Jim rushed into the pub as Robert and Max were finishing breakfast.

"What's going on?" Max replied to his stammering. "*Who* wants me?"

"Miz Hutchins, sir!"

"Oh, all right. I'll be along."

"I think Miz Hutchins wants you right away, sir."

"Oh? Well, you tell *Miz Hutchins* I'll be along as soon as I finish my coffee. Okay?"

Jim looked uncomfortable. "Okay, sir. I'll tell her."

The boy hurried away.

Robert groaned. "It's hard to believe anyone could be that wet."

"Oh, lay off. He's just a kid."

Robert got to his feet, shoving his chair in and smiling unpleasantly.

"He calls you *sir,* and you're not much older than he is. How wet is that?"

He walked off.

An hour later, Max arrived at the office and found Barbara at the big table in the meeting room, Martha's minute book open in front of her.

She looked up and pushed the book aside.

"Well, Max, glad you could make it."

"Hello, Barbara. How are you?"

"Busy. Busier than I ever thought I'd be."

"I heard you wanted something."

"As a matter of fact."

She got up and walked to the door, shutting it firmly, then turned to face him.

"Tell me something, Max. How long have you lived with us? Here, in our community."

"Uh . . . as long as I can remember. Why?"

"It must be at least fifteen years now. Isn't that right?"

"I suppose."

"And for most of that time, you either lived with Jack Ryan or you worked for him."

"What are you getting at? Jack's dead."

"So is John Anderson. And his wife."

He stopped himself before he could blurt out: *But I didn't kill John Anderson!*

"So what's your point? What do you want?"

"The truth, Max."

He rubbed his neck. "Anything in particular?"

"Max, you are an officer of this town. I am Chairman of the Town Committee. We are entitled to know anything *you* know that has, or could have, a material effect on the town. And you have a duty to tell us."

He looked away from her.

"Maybe there are some things you really don't want to know."

"I don't think I'm getting through to you! Let me put it to you this way. I have a very strong suspicion that John and May Anderson might be alive today, had you been less secretive. How about it, Max? Am I warm?"

"Hell, *I* don't know . . . I never knew her name."

"Did you know they were married before you were born? Did you know they left home because May was pregnant and there was no water? That she lost the child on the journey here? Do you have any idea how much John blamed himself?"

"He never talked about that."

"No. But May did. So tell me, Max. Is it possible the Andersons might still be alive, if we all knew what *you* know?"

"Christ, for all we know John died of natural causes! That's what it looks like, right? Unless there's something *you* haven't told *me*."

"You're evading the question. Is it possible?"

"Anything's possible! But it's just as likely they'd be dead, and the Committee . . . the Committee . . ."

"What about the Committee?"

"Look, there really isn't much I could've told you. Frank was badgering me about the training thing. He said he was running out of time. But I didn't expect anything to happen to John."

"At least if he had known, he might have been more careful."

"And maybe I should've told him! But you can't seriously expect me to spill my guts about everything to the *Committee*."

"That's *exactly* what I expect!"

"Come on! Can you control them? Can anyone?"

"I beg your pardon!"

"Be serious! There are some things that can't be blabbed everywhere. Some things have *got* to be kept secret."

She stepped back.

"Well, I suppose that might be true. But I don't think it's good policy for *you* to decide what *you're* going to keep secret."

"Got a better idea?"

"I think I do. Max, I'm going to make a deal with you. A pact. Here it is. You keep me fully informed. You tell me what you know and what you do. I'll do the same for you. If you think there's something that needs to be kept secret, then you explain your reasons to me, and I'll decide. And if there's something *I* want kept secret, then I'll explain to you, and you decide."

"That sounds a little screwy."

"Take it or leave it. But if you leave it, I want your resignation. Now. This can't go on."

He agreed, but only to get away from her.

———————

They sent Robert's message.

They picked one of the remaining spies, a loner living near the edge of town, and 'arrested' the man. Then they hanged him, and left him hanging by the North Road, where they knew Frank would find him.

Afterward, he was sick. He was tormented by the man's face, by his terror and his groveling and his struggle as he kicked at the end of a quivering rope and his face turned purple and urine soaked his pants, and then long spasms shuddered through the body, and it was too late to do anything but watch and wait for it to end, and finally what was left hung limp, and silent, a few strands of hair moving in the wind.

Then he knew the chasm was real, that he had stepped over the edge.

Robert just glanced up the road toward the City.

"That's that. Let's go."

The body disappeared a few days later.

He could no longer stand Robert's company. He was revolted by the memory of Robert's preternatural calm watching their victim's agony. As though accepting death. Embracing it. Somehow in love with it.

The days were growing longer. In another time, he would have taken pleasure in the changing season. But it was an effort of will to get through each day, until he could go home, and to sleep.

57

Max awoke in his room, lit a candle, and in the flickering light saw an envelope lying on the floor near his door. He sat on the edge of his bed, too tired to care.

But he got up and dressed. He had gotten into the habit of eating as early as possible, to avoid Robert, and he stuffed the envelope in a pocket and blew out the candle, then walked two miles to the pub through the dark.

Bill unlocked the door and let him in.

The sky outside was growing light when he was finishing breakfast and someone called for Bill. Somewhere a door slammed, and the place went quiet.

Waiting for Bill to return, he got up from his table and lingered at the bar, aimlessly nudging his cup of coffee back and forth. He knew he would have to leave soon. Other people would be arriving, and he did not want to see anyone. He decided he would wait another minute, then just leave some money on the bar.

But he felt a hand on his good shoulder, and looked up at Bill.

"You'd better come with me."

Outside, a gray horse stood in the clearing by the stable, Bill's son Mike and another young man watching, but not approaching.

Then he saw why. There was someone slung over the saddle.

They stopped by Mike.

"Tell Max what happened."

Mike stuck his hands in his pockets.

"There isn't much to tell. The horse just wandered in. I was in the stable when Bob here yelled out."

"Well?" Max asked. "Who is it?"

When Mike hesitated, Bill replied, "Better see for yourself."

He walked to the horse and leaned over, peering at the white, bloodless face, the temple marred by an ugly black hole.

He straightened and walked past Bill.

"Tie up the horse. Don't touch the body."

He was at the back door when Bill called, "What are you going to do?"

"Finish my coffee."

Inside, he carried his cup to a table in a far corner, pulled the envelope from his pocket, tore it open with his teeth, and shook out a folded sheet of paper, his hand trembling as he read the single, typewritten line:

Your move.

He crumpled the paper and shoved it in a pocket. He had to find Barbara before anyone else did.

Outside, he walked past Robert's horse now tied to a rail and oblivious to its burden, and asked Mike, "Is my horse saddled?"

"Yup. Put it on while you were eating."

Mike brought out his horse, and Max swung into the saddle. He kicked the animal, hard, and they surged onto the road, galloping toward the breaking dawn.

Twenty minutes later, he strode through the front door of the office. Barbara was at Martha's old desk, and looked up as he came in.

"Max! What's wrong?"

"We have to talk. In here."

She followed him into the meeting room. He shut the door, waited for her to sit down, and stood for a moment, silently hating himself for the look of concern in her eyes.

"You were right, Barbara. About keeping secrets."

She looked alarmed. But the alarm turned to horror when he told her about Robert, about the list of spies, about what they had done, the words tumbling out until he had said it all and there was nothing more he could say, and he just stood there.

She whispered, "Is there anything else?"

He handed her the wrinkle note. "From Frank, I'm sure."

She dropped it and leaned on the table, holding her head
"Oh, God . . . how *could* you?"

"I don't know. We were convinced that John was murdered. And we couldn't bring it to Bert. We had to send our own message. We thought we had to."

Her face was in her hands, he couldn't see her, couldn't tell what she was thinking.

"Barbara?"

"What do you want?"

"Look, we know how dangerous the Corporation is. But we have to find a way to deal with them, without being corrupted by men like Frank. I thought I could do it alone. But I can't."

There was no answer.

"Barbara, we have to trust each other."

Her hair flew as she looked up at him with an ugly smile on her mouth.

"It's a little late for that, don't you think?"

"Look, I know it's a lot all at once. It hasn't been easy for me, either." She glanced at his shoulder, but he shook his head. "It's not just that. I can't tell you what it was like to see John and his wife . . . to see what we did to Frank's man . . . " He shuddered as he saw it again. "But we have to get past this. You and I. We have bigger problems."

Slowly, she sat upright, placing her hands flat on the table, her face somehow composed despite wet streaks.

"It is no longer your concern."

"What?"

"I am removing you from office. Or the entire Committee can remove you, if you want to force me to explain it to them."

"Barbara, come on! We *need* each other!"

"I want you to leave." The voice was cold, bitter. "*Now.*"

He left.

Outside, he untied his horse and climbed up, but for a long while sat watching the sun lift over the road. Then he wheeled the horse, and kicked, and they flew, pursued by her eyes that had looked into what was left of his soul, and by the sound of loathing in her voice.

He stared at his reflection in the bathroom mirror.

Haunted eyes.

Stump of an arm.

No job. No place to go.

Finished.

He had left the horse with Mike and come directly to the farmhouse. He did not want to see anyone. He did not want anyone to see him, and he spent the day staring at the walls of his room. When it grew dark, he tried to sleep. But sleep would not come.

The house had been silent for hours when he slipped outside.

A waning moon was rising through the trees behind the house, and he leaned against the rough wood, watching spectral fields beyond.

This was the end of the line.

He was a cripple and a fraud. He had ruined every chance that had come his way. In a few weeks his money would run out . . . he closed his eyes, seeing again the body hanging by the road.

Dan Carter and Richard Martin and men like Frank have places in this world. But not me.

He had walked into this town fifteen years before, with no memory of where he had come from. His parents must have died. As millions of others had died.

Millions.

He could not grasp it. Had never grasped it. Millions of people dead, forgotten, as though they had never existed. He did not belong here. He belonged with them. With the dead.

He looked up at silvery light falling through the trees.

Everyone else had died. Yet he had lived.

He must be immune. Immune to the plague, Cargo Flu. The great equalizer. Even the Corporation feared it. Even Frank.

He thought of the stories he had heard, of a town to the west where everyone had died, once a real built-up town with paved streets and running water, but a ghost town now. People stayed away, it was said, because the bug was still there, hiding in the debris, on paper, cardboard, clothing.

He had never seen this town, did not know how far it might be. But if it was as big as rumor had it, he would find it somewhere on the road west.

He could get to Frank. He could find the little apartment, the nearby restaurant, he could find George and find Frank through him.

He had no idea what would come afterward. There was no afterward.

The next day, he bought some supplies, and early the following morning rode to the North Road, and turned left, into unknown country.

58

He followed the road south and west until darkness fell, then camped near the road with a small fire, the night quiet and damp. It was not hard to ration the food he carried. He had little appetite.

In the morning he rode on, the day overcast and cold.

Hour after hour, mile after mile, it was the same. Bare trees and brown grassland and rolling hills. Once in a while, a marshy stream. The only signs of life were birds and small animals, the only signs of human existence a shack in the trees with no roof, or a rusted-out car by the side of the road.

The absence of people, and the steady clop-clop of the horse, had a strange effect. *Calming* was not the word. There didn't seem to be a word. The countryside just seemed to grow more tangible, more real, as though he could feel the texture of each piece of stone, each branch in a tree, even the damp of the pavement, without actually having to reach out and touch it.

In the evening he camped once more, and in the morning continued on.

He had not spoken to anyone since Barbara threw him out. It seemed a long time ago. Long enough that the sound of his own name inside his head was becoming strange.

In the afternoon, he found it.

He found the town, and it was indeed big, bigger than anything he had imagined, miles and miles of streets and buildings and houses. But no people.

It was late in the day, gloomy and cold, when he made camp in a field at the edge of the road, on the outskirts of town. Trees began across a big clearing on the other side of the road, and he collected deadwood and made a fire, and in the failing light pondered gray shapes that had been homes, large two-story dwellings, a whole subdivision of them down the road and past an empty field. It was eerie in the twilight, as though this were a civilized neighborhood, children called in to dinner from their play, and he could not possibly be camping here with a horse and bedroll.

But there were no lights. Nothing moved. Through the growing dusk, he made out broken windows, missing shingles, weeds and brambles where there should have been lawns, and the eeriness passed. It was the houses that were out of place, decaying monuments to a different time, a time that no longer mattered.

Night fell.

He prodded the crackling fire and thought about his plan. He knew what Barbara would think. He could see her eyes fill with disgust. John Anderson would shake his head. So would Paul Stevens.

But John was dead. Paul was gone. The next election would be a farce. It wouldn't matter what Barbara did. Or anyone else.

There was just one comfort. If he did not have a place in this world, before long, neither would Frank.

Morning dawned clear.

Chewing a little hard bread dipped in warmed-up coffee, he watched early rays of sun strike the houses and cast long shadows across brightening, dew-covered yards, as though a normal day were beginning. The houses looked harmless, strangely familiar, and he began to feel curious.

He smothered his fire and walked down the road and into a yard, stepping around scattered bones, some small enough to be from children. The front door opened when he pushed on it.

Inside were dusty floors and moldy furniture, and in one room a skeleton on a bed, lying in a pool of decayed cloth.

He leaned over it, not touching it but examining the skull, trying to imagine a face. Trying to feel something. Grief. Horror. Anything. But there was nothing, just the empty skull looking up at him.

He left and got his horse and rode through neighborhoods, and in the bright climbing sun could imagine them alive and real, as though someone might appear in a bathrobe to fetch the paper.

A school appeared, a sprawling single-story wreck of tile and glass. It stirred something deep inside. He stopped by the playground, suddenly feeling the cool, hard cross-piece of a jungle gym behind his knees as he hung weightless–feeling it as starkly as he felt the saddle and reins–hanging weightless and brushing the ground above with his fingertips while he gazed into the sky below. Until the sky dissolved into something cold and black, and he was alone again.

He spurred the horse and rode around the school, looking in through broken windows at empty classrooms and rotting desks. He tied up the horse and went inside, his footsteps sending echoes through empty corridors and leaving imprints in layers of dust that coated the floors. He passed a wall of lockers and came around a corner. A pile of books blocked his way, dozens of them dumped on the floor, and he stopped, conscious of a sudden, sharp pain. Like a crack in a smooth wall.

He approached, slowly, as if something very fragile were in that pile, or very dangerous. Carefully crouching down, he picked one up.

World Geography.

Pages crumbled as he turned them, and he gazed at faded maps and print streaked and smeared with dripping tears, until the book dropped from his hand with an echoing slap on the floor, and lay still with the others.

He left the school.

The road led into town, and he rode past shops and offices and restaurants, recognized traffic signals, knew which of the dark lenses should be yellow, red, and green–a useless bit of memory that made his throat ache. The sun dimmed and ghostly hands seemed to reach out, tugging his jacket, from cars parked along the streets, some with remains inside, bones and rags.

He spurred the horse and left it behind.

Near his camp, from inside the houses–those with human remains and a roof intact to keep out the rain–he gathered what he wanted. Old clothing. Paper. Cardboard. He made piles of it, then tore off samples to bundle up and take with him. It was hard work, with just his feet and one hand.

That night, as he kept warm by the fire, there was nothing for him to do, but think.

He knew that what he was planning was monstrous. Not only would Frank die, but many others as well. Maybe people he cared about. Maybe people he would care about, if he met them.

His thoughts went back to the lake, and again the gun jumped in his hand as the bullet ripped through Jack, and again he watched Jack's face crumple in pain.

Again he saw the hanged man, saw the face hovering over him, eyes wide and blind, spittle running down its chin . . . and he shivered, in terror of what he could never undo.

He stood up. A cold breeze came out of the darkness and touched his face, and he turned to it, moving away from the fire and into the night.

His feet touched pavement, and he turned to follow.

It was too dark to see, but he could sense the shapes of houses against the sky, see a glint of starlight from a distant window, until the houses fell behind and the road was crowded by brush and trees, the only sound the quiet tread of his shoes and sudden rustlings in the undergrowth as he passed.

The trees fell away. He was out in the open, the breeze in his face, and he followed the road as it wound on for a mile or two, then began to rise. The rise steepened, and the road climbed a long, grassy hill.

He reached the top and stopped under a deep, black dome filled with stars cold and brilliant. And felt no fear. Because he was nothing. If he had had a gun, he would have used it.

And the world can go on without me.

He was a speck, an atom drifting through something immeasurable and vast. If he died, it would be less than if the faintest one of millions of stars overhead winked out. He was days into the wilderness, alone under the infinite and eternal, contemplating the end of his life, and it would matter to no one. Richard Martin was sleeping in a warm bed. Barbara Hutchins would be relieved. Frank would find someone else. He would be a bad memory, quickly forgotten. And the world would go on without him.

As though he had never existed.

His legs folded up and he sank to the pavement, collapsing of his own weight, his one arm wrapped about his knees, and he wept hot, bitter tears that fell from his face unseen in the dark.

After a time, this passed, but he remained where he was, head bowed, as the sounds of night came back to him. A breeze stirred the grass. Something unseen ran across the road. An owl hooted.

He looked up suddenly, astonished, gazing at the black edge of earth where the stars ended—astonished that people who had no concern for his existence, even knowledge of it, had the power to drive him here, to an abandoned road miles from anywhere, looking for an end.

Richard Martin wasn't here. Barbara Hutchins wasn't. John Anderson certainly wasn't.

What gave them this power?

And then Martin and the others vanished like a mist, like an illusion in a shift of perspective, because he saw the answer. He saw his existence as apart from them, apart from everything, as cold and as hard and as real as the pavement beneath him. Nothing else mattered. Only his own mind, and the world he could make for it. And he was conscious of a spark, somewhere deep inside, a hard certainty that *this* was the answer.

The earth pushed against him as he rose to his feet and stood with legs braced apart, his arm held out, palm upturned, the earth flying with him through space, the hill clinging to his feet. The stars were watching, had always been watching, waiting for this moment, and he gazed in wonder at the void where his fingers spread out against them.

His hand dropped to his side. He turned, and for a long while pondered the road he had followed up this hill.

Then he walked back to his camp.

He burned everything he had gathered. It was all quite dry, the fire crackled and roared, and clouds of sparks billowed skyward, toward the waiting stars. The horse stamped and snorted, and he walked to it and soothed the animal until the blaze burned down.

A pool of shimmering embers remained, and he crouched with a stick and stirred them, then held it up, studying its glowing end.

He had to change his manner of consciousness. To see as he saw now, through his own eyes, with his own mind. It would be difficult, he knew, terribly difficult, when he returned to the world and the people in it.

But his life depended on it.

He tossed the stick onto the embers, watched it smoke and burst alight.

The fire was real. *He* was real, and he held on to that.

He pulled the blanket over his shoulders, lay down, and slept.

59

When he awoke the next morning, it was with an ache deep in his belly.

He stood up, shivering and rubbing his side, looking across the field at houses tinted red with breaking day.

There was a little kindling left, and he got a small fire going, drank some warmed-up coffee—and threw up. Then he had to empty his bowel, violently.

Warming himself by the fire, carefully sipping water, he told himself he must have eaten something bad. It happened.

He set about breaking camp. With the bedroll packed and the fire put out, he climbed on the horse and headed east, homeward, slouched low in the saddle, his guts cramping. The day grew overcast, the air still, and darkness came early. When it was time to make camp, he ate nothing, but managed a small fire, wrapped himself in his blanket, and slept as though drugged.

He awoke to rain on his face. It began with a drizzle at first light, then grew cold and steady as he slung the soggy bedroll over his horse, climbed into the wet saddle, and huddled, half-asleep, looking up and down the road to be sure of the way east.

He had to keep moving, and he urged the animal onward through the rain, his eyelids drooping, his brain hazy—but not too hazy to realize that if he began coughing and sneezing he would have to stop. He could not go home.

It rained without letup.

From time to time he stopped to relieve himself and drink a little water. Darkness fell. He had no strength to make camp, and no way to make a fire in any case, and he kept on, shivering under a wet blanket wrapped around his shoulders.

Sometime during the night, the rain stopped. He rode in a stupor, dozing and jerking awake when he threatened to slide out of the saddle.

———

He awoke looking at pavement. There was sunlight on the road, and warmth on his back, and the rough hair of the horse's neck against his face.

But something was wrong.

The pavement wasn't moving.

He kicked the horse, feebly, urging it on.

———

He was still moving somehow, even though there was something cool and clean against his skin, and something soft under his head. But he was drifting through space, and he wasn't ready for that to end.

He felt a pressure on his forehead, soft and warm, and his eyes opened, focusing on brown rafters.

Smiling wryly, Barbara Hutchins took her hand away.

"Glad you're back with us."

Sleep tugged at him, his eyes falling closed again.

"So'm I."

60

There was a window. Outside, bare branches lit with early sun. Wide awake and sharply alive, Max got out of bed and went to the window, looking out at a familiar clearing and stable.

He was in a room at the back of the pub.

Clean clothes were draped over a chair, and he pulled on trousers and opened the door.

"Hey . . . Bill?"

Bill appeared.

"You up? Hungry?"

"I am. But I'd like to wash and shave."

"I'll tell Mike to bring some breakfast. How's your stomach?"

"Fine. Listen, I'm sorry to put you out like this. I'll make it up to you."

Gruffly, stolidly: "Don't worry about it."

He wanted the feel of hot water. Bill brought a pan of it to the washroom, and he steamed his face with a wet towel, carefully shaved in front of a crooked fragment of a mirror, and patted his face dry.

He ate in his room. The food was simple, yet the taste was marvelous. When he finished, he stood by an open window and sipped coffee while morning light and spring air and the smells of earth drifted inside. A feeling of euphoria began to steal over him—and he caught it. Stopped it. Concentrated on the cold air dancing over his body, on the light in the trees, on the smooth mug in his hand. On what he was planning to do.

I'm learning.

There was a crack of sound, and the door opened, and Barbara stepped inside, but stopped with a hand over her mouth.

"Oh, I am *so* sorry! No one told me you were up."

"Come in, Barbara, come in. Sit down. Want some coffee?"

She was staring at his stump.

He glanced at it protruding from his sleeveless undershirt, the angry red scar now muted and healed. The sight of it no longer bothered him. Not too much.

"Hang on. I'll get a shirt."

"No, it's all right. It doesn't bother me, if it doesn't bother you."

"Then sit. What can I do for you?"

There was a chair by the bed, and she sat down in it.

"Well, I wanted to see how you are today. You look one hundred percent better, by the way."

"I feel a thousand percent better."

"That's good to hear."

"You know, I'm grateful for all the trouble Bill has gone to, but I guess I have to thank you as well. That damned horse of yours saved my life."

"Well, Max, he had help."

"What do you mean?"

She took a breath.

"It was that man Frank who found you. Apparently, the horse wandered up the North Road, heading toward the City. Frank found you and drove you here."

"Christ."

"He said it was the second time he'd rescued you."

"He brought me to a doctor when I was shot."

"Oh?"

"Actually, it's the third time. Or maybe the fourth."

"And yet he killed your friend Robert."

She said it quietly, watching his face.

"I think so. Or had him killed. But you know," he mused, looking out the window, "if Frank killed Robert—or John Anderson, for that matter—it wasn't personal. He has a job to do, and he does it."

"You call that a job?"

"Well, I'm not defending him. Wait. If Frank brought me here, what happened to my horse?"

"In the stable. Frank drove me out to where he left him tied up, and I rode him back."

"Thank you for that." When she smiled weakly, he grinned. "Ah, you've met Frank. Interesting man, eh?"

"I don't think that would be my choice of words." She got to her feet. "You know, Max, you might want to put on a shirt after all. You'll have another visitor soon." Her voice changed as she walked to the door. "Shall I send her in?"

"Send her—?"

But she was gone.

Minutes later, there was a knock. He opened the door, and found himself looking at Agnes.

She was smiling, but in a strange way that did not quite reach her eyes, which were studiously avoiding his shoulder.

"Sorry."

He found a shirt and put it on.

"I won't stay long, Max. I heard you were up."

"You heard . . . How did you get here?"

"I'm in the next room. Renting it, for now."

"I don't . . . What am I missing?"

"Max, I was fired. I had to leave."

"Good God. What happened?"

She shrugged, staring at the floor.

"I don't know. One day I had a job, then I was out."

"And you came *here?*"

"Frank brought me. You know him. Frank Gambrell."

"So that's his name. But why? Why here?"

"I don't know, exactly. I suppose he knew I wouldn't make it in the City without a job."

Slow fingers of pity were pulling at him, insidious and sickening. And he did not want to feel pity. Not here. Not for her.

"Agnes, you know about Robert."

"I know."

"I'm sorry."

"Don't be. I expected something like it to happen."

"What are you going to do?"

"I don't know."

"Well, if I can help in any way, let me know."

She smiled again, but in that strange way that made her eyes look dead.

"That's sweet of you, Max."

The door was open, and Bill walked in.

"You planning on going anywhere today? Mike wants to know if he should saddle your horse." Bill did not look at Agnes or acknowledge her presence. She stared at the floor.

"Yeah. Thanks. I have something to do at the office."

Bill grunted and left, and Agnes looked up.

"I should let you finish."

"We can talk later."

"That's good of you, Max."

He let out a long breath after the door closed, picked up his coffee, and took it to the open window. Fleecy white clouds sailed above bare trees, and he thought about his next move. From the moment he awoke this morning, he knew what he was going to do. But it had to be done right.

He pulled the window shut, put on shoes and a jacket, and went out back, striding across the clearing and glancing up at fat green buds in the branches overhead.

Three thoughts clicked together in his mind.

It's spring. I'm glad. I'm ready.

Mike brought out his horse.

He stroked the animal's neck, then took the reins.

"Thanks, Mike. You've done a good job by him."

"I hope you take better care of him. He's a fine animal."

"He is."

Barbara had gone on ahead, and he gave her time, riding at an easy pace, savoring the sights and smells around him, examining the road now slightly crowned, noting the faint, tangled tracks of carts and wagons.

The road crews had done well.

He reached the office, tied up the horse, and went inside.

Barbara was at Martha's old desk, writing something in the minute book. She took the job seriously, and he appreciated that.

"Can you put that down a minute?"

"What? Oh . . . all right. What's on your mind?"

"Let's talk in here." He indicated the meeting room.

She went in, sitting down behind the big table while he closed the door and leaned against it, smiling at her.

She frowned. "What can I do for you, Max?"

"Barbara, I love you dearly. You're a brilliant woman, and I think you're going to make a brilliant chairman. Even better than old John Anderson, rest his soul. But you don't have the authority to remove me from office."

"What? What in God's name are you talking about?"

"I am president of this town. I was elected according to the Charter, and I will remain president until I am voted out of office."

"Yeah? Well, I've got news for *you*, mister. I'm glad you got home safe and all, but I'm warning you. Don't push me. Because I'll lay it all out for the Committee, if I have to. The whole sordid story. *They* can vote on it."

"They can vote till they're blue. They don't have the authority either."

"*Bull!*" She sputtered and laughed. "They're the *Committee!* They *made* this town. They make the laws! What are you thinking? If they say you're out, you're out."

"Nope. And here's why." Slowly, distinctly, as though explaining to a child, he told her: "If it isn't in the Charter, then you can't do it."

"What?"

"You heard me. In fact, I think I'll have that engraved on a plaque and mounted on the wall here. The Committee didn't make this town, they only helped it along. The Charter was voted on by the people who live here. The people who *are* the town. They agreed to it. Think about that very carefully. They *agreed* to it. That made it real. There is nothing in the Charter about the Committee removing a ditch-digger from office, let alone the president. No one consented to give you that authority."

"Oh, Max, nice theory. But it won't fly."

"Want to bet? You want to take this to the Committee? I'll take it to the town! How do you think people will vote on the proposition that you and the Committee can just go and grant yourselves whatever authority you like, whenever you please?"

"You know that isn't fair! You can't spell out everything in a *charter,* for God's sake. We have to be able to improvise. No one knows what the future will bring."

"Good point. But not good enough. You can improvise within the limits of your authority. You don't like those limits? Then ask the town to change them. Change the Charter. In fact, I'll grant you this much. We need a new one. It's been too easy for the Committee to shirk its responsibility. A year has come and gone, and they've done practically nothing. There's a whole framework of law waiting to be written. Hell, we don't even know how to dispose of the Anderson ranch. How do you think that looks? The most productive property in town, and it's still sitting idle."

"I don't think you–"

"Sorry, Barbara. But I'm still president." Red patches rose in her face. "Not only that, but I'm going to run again in June. And I'm going to win."

Her mouth worked.

"Maybe. Maybe not."

He let himself out and rode back to the pub.

Agnes was waiting for him. She flattered him, told him how brave he was, and smiled into his eyes.

But the smile was unnerving, like a veil covering something wounded and corrupt. Maybe it was Robert's death. Maybe it was the shock of losing her job, of ending up in a place she loathed. Whatever it was, he could feel for her. But he could not stand to be around her.

He returned to his rented room at the farmhouse, sitting down to dinner with the family he had once avoided.

61

On one level, the job of town president was the same. Dealing with problems and complaints, meetings and reports. Keeping an eye on things.

But the job was not enough. A week later he rode out to Barbara's to tell her he wanted the Committee to set aside a day for a special meeting.

She laughed in his face.

"Max, how can you have lived here so long and not know the first thing about farming! It's *spring*. We all have *work* to do."

"All right, then. A morning. *Early* morning. In fact, I'll have Bill bring out breakfast. We have the money. Tell them to get here before it's light."

"Why? What's so important?"

"You'll find out."

"At least tell me what you have in mind."

"Nope. Not until we get everyone together."

"You're not keeping secrets again, are you? Do we still have our pact?"

"Yeah, we have our pact . . . "

"But . . . what?"

"Well, there's something else I wanted to talk to you about. About Agnes."

"What about her?" she asked coolly.

"Something's not right."

"Oh, I don't know. Some men go for that sort of thing."

"What? Oh, don't be ridiculous. She doesn't like me. Never has."

"She has a strange way of showing it. From what I hear."

"Yeah, it's strange all right. Something isn't right. Why is she here?"

"Well, think about it. Maybe your little message told Frank more than you intended."

"Like we know who his spies are."

"Like that."

He remembered John Anderson ranting about "dealing with those bastards". But John had been wrong. There was no question about dealing with them.

"Yeah. I was thinking the same thing."

Max went to the pub that evening and found Agnes sitting alone with a glass of wine. He offered to buy dinner. They could talk about her plans. Maybe there was something he could do to help.

She smiled, painfully, and pushed the glass away.

They ate together in a corner. Trying to put her at ease, he talked about the community, about his early days on patrol, about how much had changed. It seemed to work. She began talking about life as a young girl, about the big house in the country, her music, her parents–and he found himself admiring her all over again, the quick intelligence, the confident assurance, even the quiet grace with which she spoke of things lost. He could almost forget why he was here. But her eyes reminded him. There was no laughter in them, but from time to time a deadly emptiness.

Over coffee, the conversation ebbed, and he let it, watching from the corner of his eye as she began to fidget, crossing and uncrossing her legs.

He looked at her and smiled.

She smiled back, patting his arm, her hand lingering. But she could not quite hide the panic in her eyes.

He leaned close.

"Agnes, I know about Frank."

"*Oh–fuck!*"

She collapsed against the back of her chair.

He sipped coffee and gazed across the room.

After a minute, she murmured, "What are you going to do?"

He shrugged.

"What do you think I should do?"

She was staring past him, as though at something behind him.

"You might as well kill me."

"What are you talking about?"

"*You* know." Her eyes closed. "I don't know how long you were in there. I only had to see it. It can be a lot worse for a woman, you know."

At first, he could not answer, the feel of concrete suddenly cold against his face, the reeking, humping weight on his back . . . he reached for his coffee, for the tangible solidity of the cup, while she went on.

"I'd rather be dead."

He raised the cup.

"I don't blame you."

"It doesn't matter what you do . . . I can't stay here, and I can't go back."

"Well, I'm not about to do anything just yet. There's been no harm done, has there?"

"Not to you!" She laughed, bitterly. "But you'll have to do something soon. Or Frank will."

"When did you talk to him last?"

"When he brought me here."

"Not since?"

"No."

"So why do you think you're running out of time?"

"Because he said I have until April. Then he wants a report every month."

"And what do you think he's after?"

Her mouth tightened. "I thought you knew."

"I know several things. But I like to ask questions."

"*Fuck*. Oh, *fuck*."

She huddled in her chair, shaking her head.

He watched for a moment, then stood up.

"Get your coat."

"Why?"

"Because we're going to pay a visit. To an old friend."

He could sense her fear as he led her out back. Mike brought out his horse. He swung into the saddle, and Mike helped her climb up behind him.

"Put your arms around me," he ordered, "and hold on!"

He kicked and the horse leaped, leaning hard into the familiar turn and surging onto the main road.

The night was moonless, the sky like crystal. Stars wheeled and hooves pounded and a cold wind whipped at them as they flew by fields gray with otherworldly mist. He pushed the horse hard, trotting and galloping by turns, her arms holding desperately around his waist.

Then they were winding through the deeper night of trees and damp air and scratching branches, then out into the open again, crossing the lane, jerking to a halt in front of the doctor's house, the horse dancing with agitation, and he dropped to the ground and held the reins short, helping her down.

He pounded the door, Jack yelping inside until the door opened.

"All right! All right! What the hell's the matter?"

"I'm sorry, Paul. I know it's late. But this is important."

Stevens sighed and let them in.

Agnes knelt wordlessly by Jack, ruffling the retriever's neck, hugging him, then looked up and brushed away tears.

"I am *so* sorry to disturb you, Paul! But I'm so very glad to see you, too."

He was looking at her intently.

"Do I know you?"

She came to her feet. "Paul?"

"Paul, this is Agnes. You knew her. She and Robert used to visit together."

"I see, I see. Well, I'm pleased to meet you, again."

She was staring at him in shock so complete that her face seemed wiped of any human meaning.

"I must apologize, young lady. Didn't Max warn you?"

"No . . ." she whispered.

"What's going on here, Max?"

He took a breath.

"Can we sit?"

They sat in the living room, Agnes erect on the sofa, hands clutched in her lap, frightened eyes never leaving Stevens.

"Paul, Frank is playing a new game. Agnes is his pawn. I want her to understand that he can't be trusted, that the Corporation can't be trusted, that whatever they've promised her is a lie."

Stevens looked at him, puzzled. Then his mouth turned down in disgust.

"So you thought you'd show her my head on a post, is that it?" Without waiting for an answer, he turned to her. "I think he's made his point, young lady. Don't you?"

She doubled over.

"Oh God oh God oh God oh God . . What am I going to do?"

"Give up the City," Max told her. "You can't go back. We'll take care of you. But you have to cooperate. I have to know everything you learned from Frank."

She looked up at him, eyes round with terror.

"I *can't*! They'll *find* me!"

"Look, I understand you're frightened–"

"No, you *don't* understand! You idiot, they're *tracking* me! They know I'm here, in this house!" She looked wildly about the room. "I used to wonder if they knew what I was saying, but I suppose if they could do *that* they wouldn't need me . . ."

The two men glanced at each other. She caught it, and leaped to her feet.

"You don't have to scare *me* with what they can do! I know! I *know* about the cage! I *know* about gelding!"

She rounded on Max, both fists shaking.

"You–you–you–idiot! You have no idea! They *track* us. They know *exactly* where we go. There's a transmitter somewhere in my body. And there's probably one in *you*, too. They had you long enough!"

He rose to his feet and faced her, recalling how Frank had driven right up to where he was hiding in a dark doorway on a back street, that cold snowy night in the City. And it was Frank who had so coincidentally found him unconscious along the North Road.

And he remembered her screaming: *This is no game!*

"Maybe so. They've done worse. But I'm still here."

"Yeah?" She laughed wickedly. "And for how long?"

He looked at Stevens, his hand lifted in apology.

"I'm sorry, Paul. I had to try."

Stevens got up and walked them to the door. She hugged the doctor, kissed him, sniffling behind her hand, and he smiled, awkwardly patting her shoulder.

"I wish I could offer you some advice, young lady. But all I can say is, think about who your friends are."

Then they were outside again, on the walkway, and he turned to her, her face invisible in the dark.

"Listen. After they let me out of the cage, I had to stay awhile in the City. I must have lived there once, or someplace just like it, because it felt like home. And I've never felt that anywhere. Not out here. Not like that."

She remained silent, and he looked away, toward the deeper darkness across the street, where the trees began.

"Living out here can be hard. And there's some danger. But there's one thing I have here I could never have in the City."

He wished he could see her face.

"I have freedom."

Still she said nothing, and he untied the horse and climbed into the saddle, reaching down to help her up.

They rode across the street and into the trees, his words echoing hollowly in his own ears, leaving behind wisps of doubt.

But he rode on.

62

Max decided he'd better explain to Barbara and Bert what he had done. He was worried. There was no telling how Frank would react. Or his Corporate masters.

"You think that was such a good idea?"

The three were in the meeting room, sitting around the big table, Bert leaning back, his feet up, his fingers laced across his round belly.

"Christ, Bert, I don't know. I just don't know."

It was Barbara who put it into words.

"Good God, Max. She could be in real trouble."

"You mean," mused Bert, "now that she's useless to them."

"That's *exactly* what I mean."

"You don't think they'll take her back?"

"Who knows? If she's more trouble than she's worth, if she knows more than she should, who knows what they'll do?"

"That's a point." Bert nodded. "That's a point."

A door slammed. From the front office, a voice called.

"In here!" Barbara called back.

Into the room walked Mike, looking distinctly uncomfortable.

Barbara opened her mouth–then shut it, as Agnes walked in and stood beside Mike, dark pockets of sleeplessness under her eyes, and dark hollows under her cheekbones.

But there was an eerie calm in her voice.

"I'm ready. I'll do it."

Slowly, Max stood up. Her eyes met his. They were steady.

"Mike, I take it you brought her here?"

"Did I do the wrong thing?"

"No, you did the right thing. But I'd like you to wait out front. Do you mind?"

"I'll wait."

"Thanks, Mike."

Mike left and closed the door, and Max pointed to a chair.

She sat down, back erect, hands in her lap, looking even more fragile than he remembered. But there was something else. Something more compelling. A kind of purity. A kind of strength. An ultimatum, naked and final, in the steady directness of her eyes.

He took his seat.

"Agnes, I'm going to want you to explain everything to the three of us. Barbara is Chairman of the Town Committee. Bert is Chief of Police."

"I know who they are."

He turned to them.

"We're not going to do this unless we agree to keep what she says to ourselves. It stays between us. Agreed?"

Bert objected. "Before we hear it?"

"Before we hear it, and until we can guarantee her safety. Barbara?"

Staring at Agnes, Barbara nodded wordlessly.

"Bert?"

"Do you expect me to keep a secret if it's something we have to act on?"

"I expect you to cooperate in protecting her safety. Whatever that takes. Including being very selective about what we tell the Committee, if we tell them anything at all.

"Ah–all right."

"Agnes? Are you satisfied?"

"Do I have a choice?"

"Of course you have a choice. You just don't have many good options."

Her hands lifted from her lap in a kind of shrug, then dropped.

"You already know I was fired. No one explained why. They just sent me home. And I suppose you know what that means to someone like me, living in the City. There is only the Corporation to work for. There is no other way to make a living.

"Well, I was convinced there had to be a mistake. I wanted to get to the bottom of it, to get my job back. So I tried to get in to see people. I couldn't get past security, so I used the phone and called. No one answered. I left messages, but never got a reply. I suppose they were afraid to have anything to do with me. I can't really blame them.

"Then Frank Gambrell showed up, at my apartment. He told me he heard what happened. Said he wanted me to answer some questions. Said he'd give me some money for helping him. And . . . well, I agreed.

"He asked me a lot of questions, about Robert, about the department, about Paul. He repeated them in different ways. I don't think I told him anything he didn't already know. I hope not. But I really don't know.

"When he was done, he gave me an envelope. It was a whole month's salary, in cash. I suppose he was making a point. He asked me what I planned to do, and I told him I didn't know yet. He said I should work for him, and I said I wasn't ready for that.

"The next day, two security officers came. They said I had to go with them to answer some questions. I thought it must have to do with why I was fired. It might be a chance to clear things up."

She folded her arms against her body.

"They drove me to a building I'd never seen before. But not to an office. We walked and walked. It was a jail, mostly empty, and they took me to a part of it they call 'the cage'.

"When I saw it I panicked and tried to run. But they grabbed me and dragged me along a row of cells. One was open, and they pushed me inside and locked it."

A shudder ran through her.

"I–I know I'm a coward. I begged, but they just walked away. I screamed and I cried, and when I finally looked around, there was *Frank.* Right there in the cell with me. My God . . . he was laughing . . ."

The room was silent. She rubbed her face and took a breath.

"He said that the cell was mine. Reserved especially for me. And that I could spend the rest of my life in it–or I could work for him. I had to choose. Right then and there. And I agreed, God help me. I didn't know what else to do."

She shivered, staring into her lap.

Max ventured, "Agnes, it's okay. I think we understand. Tell us what happened."

"Well, he explained what he wanted."

"Which was . . . ?"

"To find you, Max. And, well, seduce you. He thought it would be easy. He seems to know a lot about you. He didn't think you'd had a girl in a long while, and he thinks you have an interest in me."

It was only confirmation, nothing more. But it was arresting, hearing her say it. Electric.

"All right. Go on. What was he after?"

"He wants to arm your town. For some reason, it's important to get this started. It's holding up a plan somewhere. He wanted me to find out if anyone was standing in the way."

"Did he ever mention the name John Anderson?"

"Yes. Several times."

"Do you know if he took any action against him?"

"It wasn't my impression, but I can't say for sure. Mr. Anderson was killed, wasn't he?"

"He's dead."

"I don't know, Max. He never mentioned anything like that."

"All right. What else did he want?"

"He wanted me to warn him if you tried to contact any other communities. Exile communities. He wanted me to delay you, if I could."

"Did he say why?"

"Not in so many words, but I gathered he doesn't want exiles organizing on their own."

"I suppose that makes sense. What else?"

"Nothing, really. He didn't want me to have my car, so he drove me out here. You know the rest."

"How are you supposed to report?"

"Through some other agent."

"Who? Have you reported anything?"

"No. I'm supposed to be contacted, but it's too soon."

"All right. Is there anything else?"

"No. That's really all I know. May I go now?"

Her eyes were colorless, the shadows cut across her face, and his mouth went sour with a sudden hatred.

What a waste! What a goddamned waste.

"All right, Agnes."

She stood up. She seemed to waver, then moved toward the door.

Then Barbara was on her feet.

"Wait a minute! Where are you going?"

"To the pub."

"Oh, no, you're not."

Max watched her cross the room to Agnes. "What are you doing?"

"She's coming home with me." She stopped in front of Agnes and put a hand on her shoulder. "Okay, hon? We'll just get your things. There's plenty of room at my place. You'll have privacy, and you won't have to worry about money. And it's safe. Safer than the pub."

Agnes smiled faintly, shaking her head.

"There's something you should know, if Max hasn't already told you. They implant a transmitter in each of us. They track us. They're tracking me now. If they come for me, they'll come to your home."

"That's all right, hon. When I see one of them out here without his fancy car, I might think about getting worried. We're a long way from the City, and you can't just drive up to my place."

"All right . . . " Agnes seemed to sag. She whispered "Thank you", and fell over.

Barbara caught her and half-carried her to a chair, while Bert hurried from the room, returning with a cup of water, Mike one step behind.

They crowded around her as she pushed hair from her face and mumbled, "What happened?"

"Well, you fainted." Bert held out the cup, and she sipped. "How do you feel?"

"A little sick."

"Fear will do that, you know."

"C'mon, hon." Barbara helped her to her feet. "Let's get you home. You need rest."

They left, Mike trailing behind. The outer door slammed.

"*Christ.*" Max dropped into a chair. "Bert, I suppose I should tell you, I think they planted a transmitter on me, too."

"What makes you say that?"

"Well, I didn't know about these things until last night. But think about it. Isn't it a strange coincidence that Frank just happened to find me on the North Road like that?"

"It's a coincidence. Maybe it's nothing more."

"That's not all. When I was in the City, I tried to run away. It was night, and I had a good head start. Maybe an hour. But he drove right up to where I was hiding."

"Hmm. Still might be a coincidence. But something to think about."

"Well, I thought you should know."

"I don't suppose there's much we can do about it."

"No . . . Look, Bert, I've been thinking about something else. Something you said a while back. You said you didn't have much in the way of law. That you were judge and jury, until someone told you otherwise. Remember that?"

"Yeah, maybe I did."

"That needs to change."

"Well, maybe it does. But it's the Committee's job, not mine. Or yours, buddy."

"Exactly. That's why I need your help."

"For what? What can *I* do?"

"Be at the Committee meeting Saturday. First thing. Before light."

"You sure? I don't think they'll like that."

"Never mind about that. Just help me out. *Be* there."

That night he paced his room.

The meeting on Saturday, facing a half-dozen obstinate, unpredictable Committee members, was next. They had to listen. He had to make them listen.

He thought about Stevens. It had been over a week since he had last talked with the doctor, not counting the other night with Agnes, and he already missed the old man.

63

The next day, Max rode out. He reached the house around mid-morning and knocked on Stevens' door.

There was no answer. He was about to knock again, but Jack appeared by a corner of the house, just a dozen yards away.

There was no sound, no movement, just the dog standing there, watching him, and Max quickly crossed the space between them.

Jack led him behind the house.

Under newly-green trees, the remains of Paul Stevens lay in the brown grass, face contorted with *rigor mortis*.

Jack stood near him, crying a little deep in his throat.

Max walked to the doctor. He crouched down, letting out a long breath, and firmly shut the old man's eyes.

The yard was quiet, peaceful, and he sat on the ground next to Stevens under a bower of tangled branches and cold white rays of sun that seemed timeless, his own, the light falling silently to earth like the essence of being . . .

The rays moved across the grass. Birds forgot him, began chirping. A jay called, shrill and impudent, and he stirred, remembering there was a world somewhere.

He covered the body and locked Jack inside. Then he rode to Barbara's, took Agnes aside, and explained as gently as he could.

She nodded, hands hanging straight at her sides. But then her fists clenched and her mouth twisted, and he stepped close and put his arm around her shoulders, and felt her weight against him as her tears dripped, one after another streaking his shirt, and he caressed her shoulder, patiently, waiting for it to end.

Intending a burial under the trees, he returned the following day with two young men he had hired. But Stevens was gone. And the house had been searched, ransacked. Even Jack was missing.

He paid the young men and sent them home.

Inside the house, he picked up and straightened things until they looked the way he remembered, then set out food for Jack, and as the sun went down heard the dog scratching at the back door, and let him in.

Jack wandered from room to room, then came out and lay by the sofa where Max was sitting, head between his paws, eyes wide.

Max reached down and rubbed the shaggy neck.

"Sorry, old boy. He's just not coming back."

He built a fire in the fireplace, drank Stevens' whiskey, and walked slowly about the sprawling room. Night fell outside the glass. Firelight flickered on the heavy gray beams overhead, on the stone hearth, on the piano in its corner, and he watched these things with a sharp, piercing emptiness. One that he could never fill. That he had no desire to fill.

He stood alone in the middle of the room, feeling the space around him, its rhythms drawn from the earth outside now shrouded in darkness, and he felt something slipping away. Something important, but that he could not name. That no one, perhaps, had fully understood.

He stayed the night.

In the morning, as he sat at the kitchen table drinking coffee, Jack waited by his chair, until he reached down and roughed up the long fur.

"Ready to travel?"

The dog looked up at him expectantly.

He got up, rinsed and dried his cup, and carefully set it on its shelf.

"C'mon, Jack. I think you and Bill are going to get along just fine."

64

In the predawn chill of a Saturday morning near the end of March, Bill and Mike lowered a large iron grate onto a circle of rocks surrounding a bed of hot embers. They greased big pans and set them on the grate to heat, started coffee boiling, and when the fat began to smoke, fried bacon and scrambled eggs, and in a short while carried plates heaped with bacon, eggs, and toast, and two pots of black coffee, inside the town office.

While the Committee ate, father and son sat behind the building, by the glowing embers, drinking coffee while the sky above turned a deep, dark blue. A trio of crows soared across the fields, three silhouettes black against the orange glow creeping in from the east, signaling the start of another day.

Bill watched, wondering if he had many left to see.

For the space of a few minutes, he allowed himself the questions he usually shut out. The dangerous ones. Like was there a future for anyone. Would there be something for Mike besides wresting a living from the wilderness until his strength gave out. Would his son ever know what it was to live through his mind.

He knew Mike would have to find his own answers. Mike was a good boy–*a good man,* he corrected himself. He could count on Mike to do the right thing when his old man was no longer around. But Mike could not make a new world, and he sipped coffee and wondered whether the people inside this building could.

When a bright glint pierced the horizon, he tossed what was left of his coffee onto the fire.

"Let's go, son. You put out the fire, and I'll get the dishes. We've got to get along and start the day. We got other customers."

"Okay, Dad."

Mike got up, slapped his father's back, and pulled a shovel from the pile of gear.

The old man was a little moody this morning.

He whistled to himself, throwing earth onto the fire.

Part III

And There Was Light

65

It had stopped raining. It would be hours yet before dawn.

The street was narrow and empty, not much more than an alley between two rows of abandoned buildings. It was silent. Not a rat stirred. Only the lonely wail of a far-off siren and pops of distant gunfire drifted through the rain-mist. Massive black shapes that were skyscrapers loomed above, darkened windows glittering orange, mirrors of flames from somewhere in the City. But here it was dark, and quiet, and the siren soon faded.

Far down the street a single point of light appeared, gleaming on wet pavement. Maybe a window. Maybe a car. But a sign of life, and he waited, motionless. Minutes crept by, the light went out, and then he moved, darting across the street and hugging the shadows on the other side.

He tried a door, gently, ever so gently pressing the handle. Locked. He tried another, and another, until he found one ajar, and he moved it, just enough to slip inside.

From a pocket he produced a small flashlight, its lens covered with black tape pierced with a narrow slit, and he let the dim light play across the walls, across long shelves loaded with murky shapes: Slabs. Boxes. Small cans.

Quickly he moved to the cans. The light revealed labels. Corn. Carrots. Beans. He filled his pockets, a single can in each for silence.

Then he switched off the light and moved to the door, holding his breath, listening, but there was nothing, no sound, and he slipped outside. Instincts honed by months of surviving like this told him that he was alone, and that he must keep moving.

He crossed the street.

Something slammed him, knocked the breath from him, and he was on his knees, the street resounding. Or was that his ears ringing? He tried to look up, but hacked painfully, spattering something black and sticky, and now his ears really were ringing, he was cold, and hit the pavement, shivering, trying to remember where he was. His mouth filled with blood until he was choking, drowning, and night washed over, and only echoes remained.

And Frank Gambrell.

In the days when Cargo Flu first marched through the City, when hospitals overflowed and utilities shut down, when the hollowed-out remnants of inept and officious government finally disintegrated, the City descended into chaos, a war of all against all. Parts of it were in flames, a riot of insanity, while parts were dark with death and the agony of the dying. People cowered behind barricaded doors and the guns of vigilantes, praying the doors would hold and the vigilantes were not just thugs.

But only the gates of Hell seemed to answer.

In those days, Frank Gambrell had walked the streets of the City in a cold fury. He shot dead more looters than he cared to remember, and he shot without compunction.

He joined crews hauling corpses to the morgue, then to a crematorium, then to outdoor incinerators. He joined firemen battling infernos that sprouted day and night, until the water stopped and the fires raged out of control.

He drove water trucks all over the City, delivering the precious stuff to the thirsty. One night he was jumped by three men, filthy and in rags, their eyes feral. They pulled him down from the truck with wiry arms and grasping fingers, pulled him down wordlessly, as though they had lost the faculty of speech, or never learned it, and held him while one locked an arm across his throat.

In a white rage, he threw them off and beat them senseless, then stood over them, shaking like a rag in the wind. When the shaking stopped, he left the truck to whatever mob discovered it, and walked fifteen blocks home.

He found his apartment had been broken into, his few belongings gone. It was four in the morning, and he stood by a window, watching the City, *his* City, in an orgy of self-immolation, and made up his mind to leave, to let it burn.

But James Dornan found him, and found that Frank Gambrell understood instinctively what the Corporation's chief executive needed.

Dornan brought a unity of command and a genius for execution that politicians and bureaucrats had never imagined. He put to work the best people he could find, and brooked no dissent. There was no time for dissent.

In the midst of Armageddon, Dornan grasped that many thousands of people and untold productive assets could and would survive; that the survivors would carry skills that would be lost without organization; that organization had to be imposed swiftly, ruthlessly, and completely. And he understood something else. That no matter what the form, even in the disarming guise of his not-for-profit Corporation, it was still a business.

This was something Frank Gambrell understood. And it became his job, his life, to help Dornan rebuild the City, making it safe for business.

Block by block, street by street, flames were quelled, wreckage cleared, and survivors forced to stay put. Services were restored to parts of the City. Electricity. Water. Police. Other parts were shut down, and everything watched.

At the first hint of a Flu outbreak, an area would be closed off until the outbreak either didn't materialize or else ran its course, any survivors decontaminated, and the area sealed. Dozens of contingency plans were drawn up. If a farming area outside the City had to be quarantined, there would be alternate sources of food.

Gradually, stability crept back into daily life. People were permitted to move about, along carefully prepared routes, for an hour a day. Then two hours. Eventually, the curfews were lifted.

Food was raised and shipped according to plan. Goods were transported by permit. Jobs and homes were assigned. The Corporation opened shops and offices and clinics. Life became recognizable again.

For twenty years, Frank Gambrell had helped maintain order. Twenty years of vigilant, sometimes ruthless discipline. And life had become a peaceful routine. If you lived in the City and worked for the Corporation, and if you stayed in line, your concerns would be small ones. No one had any longer to face the big questions, of life and death. Those had been answered.

Gambrell had served Dornan without hesitation because Dornan was the Corporation, and the Corporation was the City.

But Richard Martin was something else.

Gambrell had watched as Martin rose from warehouse manager to executive. Martin was shrewd, unscrupulous, and with an extraordinary capacity for work, but where Dornan was audacious and determined, Martin was simply ambitious, with no real interest in any job but Dornan's. And too many people stood between him and that job. When Martin realized he could put Dan Carter's theory of war to his own use, he embraced it.

Gambrell said nothing. It was not his job.

He watched Martin take advantage of the caution of other executives, guessing correctly that Dornan, for all his bluster, wasn't so sure Carter was wrong. When Martin was put in charge of Security, it was Gambrell who had to arrange the encampments and maneuvers that would come to the attention of other cities, who would in turn make preparations that would come to the attention of Dornan, by which time Martin had created a *de facto* war department, with enough layers of secrecy that he could control just what information was released, and when, keeping his rivals off balance.

Still, Gambrell said nothing.

In the past year, as Dornan retired from day-to-day business, Gambrell had been left to serve at the pleasure of Richard Martin. It was a job he had come to loathe, no longer able to escape the feeling that it was not to make the City safe for business, but to make it safe for Richard Martin.

And a day in March came when Frank Gambrell put down the telephone and stood in his office without moving.

The voice at the other end had been clear.

"Gambrell, you're being played by your little friend. Time's up. Cancel his ticket." He hadn't answered, and Martin had gone on to taunt, "You can do that much, can't you? Or are you spending too much time with the hicks? Going native?"

"Fuck you," he muttered to the empty room.

But Richard Martin was in charge. A decision had been made. It had to be done. And Frank Gambrell was not a man to shirk what had to be done.

66

Late in the day on a spring afternoon, Agnes stood with a young man in the yard behind the Hutchins house, studying a small mechanical contraption, about two feet long, lying on the ground between them. At one end of it a pair of blades attached to a protruding shaft, looking a bit like a twisted propeller. From the other end several wires emerged.

The young man nudged it with his foot. "What do you think?"

"I don't know," she answered. "It looks better than the last one. I like the way you clamped the blades this time. Maybe that'll hold."

"Should've thought of it before. You going somewhere?"

"What? Why?"

"You keep looking at your watch."

"Oh. Well, Max is coming to dinner–What?"

He was grinning.

"*I* didn't say anything."

"You were thinking it!"

"How do you know what I was thinking?"

"Come on, Steve."

"Well, you have to admit what it looks like."

"Like something it isn't, apparently."

"If you say so."

"I say so. Besides, what's it to you, sonny? We're adults."

"And the talk of the town, let me tell you."

"Seriously? Well, stay for dinner. You can see for yourself."

"And be part of all the gossip? No, thanks. Besides, gotta help the old man tonight. And by the way, he's not so down on this anymore."

"No?"

"Nope. Not since we sold that last generator. He doesn't say much, but I could tell he was impressed."

"Well, don't take this the wrong way, but I'm a lot more interested in paying customers than impressing your father."

"Yep, that's what impresses the old coot. Paying customers." He kicked at the rickety contrivance, gently. "Well, there's got to be a better way. If we're ever going to make any money at this."

A few weeks ago, she had gone back to Robert's old room at the pub, to clear out his things, as a favor to Bill. There were trousers and shirts which she had gathered and folded, sturdy work shoes she had cleaned off, and she had made a neat pile to donate to anyone who could use it.

But there were the books, dozens of them stacked around the room. Structural engineering. Mining. Metallurgy. Electromagnetics.

She had picked up this last, and leafed through a few pages, wondering what he had seen in it. The mathematical notation she recognized from calculus she had studied as a girl, and the first chapters were not hard to follow . . .

She sat down on the bed, the book in her lap.

An hour later, she was staring out the window, the book under her arm, wondering how many junk cars were around.

Then she was stuffing books into an empty duffel bag.

Her first project was to rewind an alternator she salvaged from the rusted carcass of a truck abandoned in the woods. There were electric light bulbs still intact around farmhouses like Barbara's, unused and forgotten, and she wanted to light one. She was convinced it was possible, convinced she could make it work. And after three days of skinned knuckles and bruised fingers, it *had* worked. Barely. A dim flicker.

The next step was to figure out how to regulate the voltage, so it would build up automatically from residual magnetism and run at a steady level. She had solved that problem, and others, spinning the alternator a few seconds at a time with heavy weights and a length of cord.

But then she was stuck. She had no way to drive it.

The answer was Steve Foster. The young man was a mechanical wizard with a pile of metal scrap he had been collecting all his life sheltered behind the family house. Also boxes of tools, and a forge he had built himself.

Dennis Foster had long dismissed his son's tinkerings, until as a boy one day, Steve had showed him a new blade for hoeing he had made with his forge. He made a garden trowel for his mother. He made other things as well. But as a young man, Steve Foster was very clear that he did not intend to spend his life as a blacksmith.

When his father mentioned one night weeks ago something he had heard at a Committee meeting, something about some crazy electrical experiment, Steve had gone to Barbara's to see for himself. And when he saw, knew what had to be done.

He built a water turbine. It was crude, but it worked.

There was a stream behind the barn, where Barbara got her water, and there they built a dam, tested, adjusted blades, raised the dam higher, and tested again. When they could reliably light one bulb, they strung wire to the house, and Barbara had stared in wonder that first night as steady rays of electric light swept away the glow of her oil lamp.

Agnes found another alternator, and they went to work on different windings, on improving the blades, on trying to get more power. When the new one worked, they sold it. The buyer built a dam in a stream according to their instructions, and they installed the assembled alternator and turbine, ran wire to the man's house, and placed two electric lamps in the kitchen. The man and his wife did leatherwork and shoe repair, and the light gave them a few extra hours each day to work, without consuming scarce candles.

Word spread. People were intrigued, and some were willing to spend real money. But then the problems began. The generators broke down. The turbines came apart, or jammed, and had to be rebuilt.

She knew Steve was right. They could not spend all their time fixing something they had already sold. There had to be a better way.

"Okay, Steve. See you tomorrow."

"Right. So long."

———

Frank Gambrell peered through the trees.

The sun was low behind him. Ahead was a clearing and a house that stood out in the raking light. The afternoon shadows crept toward it. He was close enough to hear voices from behind it, but not what was being said.

"Hurry the hell up," he muttered to himself. He was not looking forward to the trip back to the City, on horseback, after dark.

As always, he had gone to the motor pool to pick up his car. The car came with the job, available at any time, day or night, washed and fueled and ready to go. But not this time. This time he had stepped out of the elevator in the basement garage and found no car waiting.

He pushed open the office door.

"Where's my car?"

The clerk behind the counter hardly glanced up.

"Have to punch your card first."

"What card? What're you talking about?"

"Ration card. No gas without a card."

"Fuck that. Get the goddamn car."

"I have to punch–"

"Get the goddamn car!"

"I can't, sir! They'll have my hide!"

The clerk drew back as Gambrell reached over the counter and grabbed the telephone. He punched Richard Martin's number.

A secretary answered. Mr. Martin was in a meeting.

"Get him."

She got him. Martin came on the line.

"What the hell is it?"

"You tell me. I'm at the motor pool."

"You don't need a car for this. Gas is under ration. Take a horse."

"What–"

But the line went dead.

He put down the phone. The clerk was watching, wide-eyed, and he asked, calmly, "What do you know about this?"

"Uh, the gas? They don't tell us much. But I hear we're pumping the last storage tank."

"The last tank? Bullshit. Since when?"

"It's a big secret. But I heard something broke at the plant."

"So?"

"So a whole tank was pumped dry, right into the ground. One of the big ones. The last one isn't even full. It was supposed to be a reserve or something."

The clerk then witnessed something very few people ever had: a crack of uncertainty in the coil of tension that was Frank Gambrell.

"Sweet mother of . . . Where the hell did you hear this?"

"Ah . . . well, you know, rumors."

"Rumors from where?"

"I think a secretary said something. The secretaries know everything."

"And we're down to the last tank? Maybe there's more somewhere else."

"Maybe. But lots of folks are pretty scared, so maybe not. I'm just glad I'm not the fella who was on duty when all that gas went into the ground. Almost a million gallons."

"Jesus H. Christ. Well, he's probably living under a bridge right now, bait for the other spooks. Doesn't get us any more gas, though."

He considered the clerk.

"So. Where do I get a horse?"

Gambrell waited. The sun went down. Twilight descended. Finally, someone appeared from behind the house and rode away.

He knew Barbara Hutchins was at the pub, delayed by a complaining customer who also happened to be one of his agents. So there should be only one person remaining.

He left the trees and walked the rest of the way. He wanted to intimidate her, not frighten her into something desperate or reckless, and decided to simply knock on the door. But a clatter from behind the house changed his mind, and he walked around to the back yard.

She was crouched over a pile of metal parts and wire, hair pulled back, face and hands smudged, and she looked up, one hand braced against the ground, her eyes round with shock.

He stopped a few yards from her and grinned.

"Well, well."

Agnes rose to her feet, her arms limp at her sides, her shoulders sagging. The effect was just right. He could see her will collapsing.

"What do you want?"

"You work for me, sweetheart. Just because I haven't been around, don't think I've forgotten."

Her eyes closed.

"What do you want?"

"I want your report." He wasn't smiling now, and she looked at the ground. "You know, I haven't asked for much. And I could've let those guards have you. But you took my money. You agreed to work for me."

"I don't want your money."

"It's a little late for that." Her eyes were still lowered, and he stepped closer. "Tell you what, sweetheart. I'll make it easy for you. I want just one job out of you. Then I'll leave you alone."

She looked up, and he could see the plea she was unable to hide.

It was that easy. But as he watched her, another thought struck:

He was fifty years old.

Fifty.

Here he was, forcing some stupid woman into helping Richard Martin move one step closer to his goal, of taking Dornan's job. In a few years, if he didn't make any fatal mistakes, he would still be doing it, making the world safe for Richard Martin. When he was too old, he would stop doing it. His life would be over. It was as though he had put a rope around his own neck and handed the end to Martin.

The next realization, the sickening one, was that somewhere in the back of his mind, he had always known this.

"Frank?"

Something had shown in his face. He could see it in hers.

"Shut up. Listen." She looked down again. "I want you to set up a meeting with Max Wyse. I don't want it in a public place. I want it here. You live here now, right? . . . I said, *right?*"

"Yes."

"Okay. Set it up. That's all I want."

The yard was growing dark, and he watched the pale, slender figure, feeling only disgust. This woman would never be free of him. He would own her until he had no further use for her. It was that easy.

"All right," she said. "I'll do it."

Something felt wrong. She seemed to be thinking. And that was not what he expected.

"You don't have a thing for this guy, do you? I didn't think he was your type, crippled and all."

Three things happened in quick succession. She laughed, suddenly and a little wildly.

A voice demanded, "What's going on?"

And the lights came on.

He swung around, momentarily blinded by the light.

There was Max Wyse, sitting on a horse just inside the clearing, his one good hand holding the reins. No weapon in sight.

Gambrell relaxed a little—and looked up, at a line of small, glowing bulbs strung between two trees.

He stared. These were *electric* lights. They had no business being here.

The woman laughed again.

"What do you think, Frank? Like them?"

"What the hell? Where did this come from?"

"Well, we found an electrical engineer!"

"Who? No one's left the City."

"Me."

"*You.* Give me a break."

"I like that, Frank."

She turned and walked under the lights, her arms outstretched as though she might take flight.

"*I* did this. *I* made it." She spun around and faced him. "I know what you think of me! But you know what? You know what? It doesn't matter! *Nothing* matters—except that I made this."

Then she was walking towards him.

"So go ahead, Frank. Kill us. You won't even have to turn out the lights afterward. They're on a timer. I made that too. Too bad for Steve, though. We had the start of a good business."

He looked up and counted the bulbs, estimating the power. Not very much. But still.

"What's your power source?"

"Generator, down in the stream. Steve made the turbine. I rewound an old alternator and made a voltage regulator for it."

"Where did you learn this? I thought you were an accountant."

"I'm good at math. I picked up vector analysis, then electric machines, then circuit theory. It wasn't so hard."

"If you're that good, why didn't you do something in the City?"

"Why?" She laughed. "Why? Because this was *my* problem! And I wanted to solve it."

"Say, Frank, where's your car?"

He looked back at Max Wyse, saw the gun in his hand, and sighed.

"Put it away, Max."

"Come on, Frank."

With a lightning thrust, he grabbed Agnes and whipped her around, twisting her arm to hold her immobilized between himself and the gun.

"You should leave this kind of thing to professionals."

He heard a quiet obscenity. But the gun held steady.

"Where's the car?" Max repeated.

"No car."

He spat suddenly.

"No *gas*. Dumb fuckers *lost* it, for chrissake. They *lost* it."

"No gas? How's the Corporation going to function without gas?"

"Oh, there's more. You're not worried about *us*, are you? I mean, the lights are impressive and all, but you couldn't light one floor of an office building like this." He tried to laugh, but the sound was hollow.

"So what are you going to do when you run out of gas?"

"We won't. We'll fight for it, if we have to."

"Already? The great corporations fighting over gasoline? Savages fighting over a carcass?"

He remembered the night a pack of half-men had tried to kill him over a tank of water, in a city bereft of intelligence. He remembered what he had felt then. He was beginning to feel it again.

No, that was a lie. He had felt it for a long time.

"Not a pretty picture, is it? But there you have it." He shoved the woman, and she stumbled away. "There you have it, when a shit like Richard Martin runs things. So, yeah, we'll fight for it. Because the game is survival."

The gun lowered.

"Listen to yourself, Frank. You're ready to go to war over gasoline, but why don't you stop and ask yourself where it came from?"

"Fuck that. It came from the ground."

"That's where you're wrong. It came from the minds of people like *her*."

Agnes was clutching her arm, obviously in pain, but making no sound, and he looked at her, surprised at a feeling of respect.

"Maybe so. But our so-called engineers don't seem to be able to figure it out. So we don't have much choice."

"*She* never figured out anything, either. Not until she left the City. Think about that."

"So what's your point?"

"The City isn't dying, Frank. You're all killing it. You're planning for war, but win or lose, you'll still be your own worst enemies."

He laughed, this time with a perverse pleasure.

"Well, I can't change that. I don't run things."

But the thought hit like a judgment.

I don't run things.

Agnes was still clutching her arm, and he nodded to her.

"Never mind that meeting, sweetheart. I think I'm through."

He walked past Wyse still atop his horse.

"Watch your step, bud. They may send someone else."

He walked into the darkness, leaving the clearing behind.

"Frank!" Max called. "What are you going to do?"

"What's it to you?"

———————————

When the figure of Frank Gambrell had disappeared from the clearing, Max holstered the gun and swung down from the horse.

Agnes ran to him, briefly clung to him, trembling, and he held her, breathing in the scent of her, the grease and perspiration, the faint odor of soap. Then she pulled away and walked to the lights, the warm glow embracing her, pushing back the night.

He tied the horse and went inside, and a minute later she joined him, turning on a light and looking at him from across the room.

"I think he meant to kill you, Max."

"What changed his mind?"

"I don't know. Something happened when the lights came on. He wasn't ready for that."

67

Max stood at the meeting table the following afternoon, examining a broad sheet of paper spread out and pinned at the corners. It was a hand-drawn survey of the town.

With the fingers of his one hand, he traced the sharp lines of roads and trails and the contours of hills. He smiled over tiny black rectangles that were houses and barns he knew from years on patrol, and frowned over streams and valleys he had never suspected. Much of the map was blank, incomplete. But it was a beginning. A small victory. A step toward an idea that was becoming clearer to him as the weeks of spring went by.

Steve and Agnes were showing what was possible, with their turbines and electric lights. And in his own way, Jack Ryan had been a part of it as well. People would build on what they had, to reach new heights and accomplish new things, and in their pursuit of fortune would bring the town along with them. But their individual reach stood on a foundation of collective action, public action, like roads and police, like management of streams and the river, like laws and property records, and the town survey, and things no one had thought of yet.

He was building something.

At the dawn meeting with the Committee, back in March, he had stood up and asked the Chief of Police, "Bert, what are you supposed to do with the Andersons' effects?"

"Well, I don't know."

"What about the property? The house? The animals?"

"Beyond keeping an eye on them? Don't know. No one's told me. We just feed the animals."

"Don't you think disposing of a large productive property like that is a pretty important affair?"

"Yup."

"Then what are you waiting for?"

Bert glanced at the Committee members, but Max went on.

"Okay, let me ask you this. Who is responsible for dealing with Corporate spies?"

The Chief leaned back.

"I think that would be me."

"Why? Would spies break any of our laws?"

"Don't know that we have any."

"Spies?"

"Laws."

One of the members tried to interrupt, but Max kept going.

"Barbara, who is supposed to settle arguments over property lines? Or sewage dumped in a stream?"

"Oh, come on, Max. This isn't fair."

"Why?"

"Be realistic. These things take time."

"How much time? It's been almost a year."

Now someone did object, and loudly.

"This town's done a helluva lot! Where've *you* been?"

"You mean *Jack Ryan* did a lot. He cracked heads together, to get things organized, to get things done. But Jack couldn't make the law. That's *your* job."

The meeting erupted.

"Don't tell *us* what our job is!" "Who in hell made *you* chairman?"

"All right!" Barbara shouted over the others. "All *right!* Settle down! Max! Does any of this have a point?"

"You bet. Here's my point. People in this town are busy. Busy trying to get ahead. And that's what we want. But if we're all going to get ahead, then we–the people in this room–have got to do our part. And we *have* to get ahead. Or else we're just exiles with nowhere to go if the Corporation sneezes or some natural disaster hits. John Anderson understood this. We've been living on borrowed time. It's going to run out one day."

Barbara sighed, wearily.

"I hate to burst your bubble, Max, but you're talking to the wrong people. We're only farmers, and we've got our hands full as it is."

"Damned straight!" someone blurted. "You don't know what real work is!"

"Look." He held up his hand, to keep their attention. "I know this isn't easy. But people have done it before. And they left behind books about what they did and how they did it. But the books won't do us any good unless we make up our minds to take on the job."

Dennis Foster cleared his throat, his bushy eyebrows and hooked nose converging into an angry scowl over a huge white moustache, ragged and unkempt.

His voice rattled.

"All right, son. You don't have to tell me what John Anderson understood. I knew John. Didn't always agree with him, but I respected him. And John knew better than to start passing laws left and right. You young people are all set to turn everything upside down, but you just don't know. My boy's been tinkering with electricity, God bless 'im, and maybe he's right. Or maybe he just likes bein' around that City gal. But if he's wrong, I can always turn it off, if he don't kill himself first. But it's not so easy to turn off laws."

"So, what's *your* point, Dennis?"

"I know my history, son! In the old days, every politician with a smart idea got a law passed! Most of those ideas weren't as smart as they looked, but we got stuck with 'em anyhow! More rules and regulations and goddamned taxes than anyone knew what to do with. I'd say John Anderson was one shrewd fellow. Smart enough not to start down that road. Smart enough to know that people around here won't stand for it."

"So where does that leave us? What do *you* think we should do?"

"As little as possible! Because you won't know when to stop! One thing will lead to another, until we're all choking on it!"

"Come on, Dennis . . ."

The old man jabbed a tobacco-stained finger at him.

"Son, I was *there*! Before the plague! I ran a business. Or tried to. We had thousands of pages of laws. Everything from where a fellow could smoke to how big his toilet seat had to be. But not one law smart enough to stop Cargo Flu from spreading all over the world and damn near killing us all!"

Other voices chimed in: "Damned straight!" "You tell 'im!"

"Okay, Dennis. I'll give you that. It's a point. But here's another. We have a Chief of Police here who answers to *you*. A year ago, we had

Jack Ryan and his gang lording it over all of us, from the *pub*, for God's sake. I see your hay cart, and yours, and yours, up and down the main road all the time now, where a year ago you wouldn't chance it unless it hadn't rained in a month. No one would. It was hard enough to walk on. Our fire crew has saved at least one home and maybe a few lives. And all of this was paid for with tax money. And taxes are the law.

"That's a beginning. But it isn't enough. We need to do more. You know that, and so does everyone in this room. So you tell me, Dennis, how do we do it and know when to stop?"

"Who says we need more? We *got* the road! Job done!"

"What about property lines?"

"What about 'em?"

"Remember what Robert was saying. We have a growing population. Property is going to change hands. We need to settle property lines, map them, and keep public records."

"I *know* where my property is."

"So, if all your neighbors agree, it should be a snap to record it and be done with it. Right?"

"Come on, Dennis!" Someone laughed. "Don't just argue for the hell of it. Man has a point."

"Yeah, maybe." The old man glared at Max. "But why should I trust *you*? You're just another one of Ryan's good-for-nothings. Why should we trust *you*?"

"Dennis, you don't have to like me. You can even run against me, next election. But for now you have to work with me. Because I'm legally president. That's the law."

Dennis Foster rumbled deep in his chest, "God-damned politicians," and a man beside him grinned and slapped his back.

They argued all morning and into the afternoon. But before they had finished, they voted that the town should start a court, and that a resolution of disputes in the new court would serve as a temporary basis for law, where needed. They voted that the town should hire someone to do a survey. And they voted to start a lending library at the town office.

When it was over, Max had stood up and shook each Member's hand. After they left, he had locked the office and ridden to the pub, his body alive with a quiet excitement.

The feeling came back to him now, as he rolled up the survey and carefully put it away.

He stepped outside the faintly musty building into cool April air and the vernal smells of earth, pausing in the evening hush to watch the sun disappear beyond the road. The fields around the office were an ocean of green, swirling and rippling under a steel-blue sky clear and deep. Soft currents of evening air seemed living, his body tingling to their touch, as though with an electric charge, a kind of attractive tension to the earth, and things of the earth.

He walked to a pair of tall, rustling trees that stood like pillars next to the office, the ground soft and yielding to his step, and under the trees he untied his horse.

He was expected, as he was once or twice a week, joining Barbara and Agnes for dinner and possibly a glass of wine, something that had begun weeks before with an evening of self-conscious awkwardness, alone with two attractive women, each of whom fascinated him in her own way. But there was a bond, too, a reassurance that brought him out of himself, and the dinners had become a welcome break from the routine of town business and his spartan existence at the farmhouse.

He knew there were suspicions around town about Agnes, and he was convinced it had as much to do with her peculiar elegance in this rustic community as it did with any ties she could be harboring with the City. A few young men, and at least one not so young, had tried to break the ice with her at the pub, but her cool reserve usually left them bristling over the insufferable conceit of City people. A lewd rumor spread concerning her living arrangement with Barbara; he just shook his head when he heard it.

He and Barbara had watched her first electrical experiments, a bulb flickering yellow for a few seconds as she directed him to pull on a cord wound around a pulley. Two weeks later, they were dining by electric light, the table awash with a steady glow that drove the night into the corners of the room.

But when Agnes announced that she and Steve had sold a generator to a paying customer, he suddenly grasped that this was not just a clever bit of ingenuity. It might be a rebirth of industry.

He arrived at Barbara's under a velvet sky, tied the horse, and walked across the clearing.

She opened the door and let him in.

"It's just the two of us tonight. Agnes is at the pub." Patting his good shoulder, she turned and walked to the kitchen.

He felt suddenly awkward. Out of place.

"Barbara, maybe I shouldn't even be here. I could be a target."

She glanced back at him, one eyebrow raised.

"Well, change your routine. Don't be so predictable. You surprised Frank, didn't you?"

She turned and entered the kitchen.

He followed her, and she handed him a glass of wine and pushed him toward the living room. "Go. Relax. Dinner isn't ready. I'll call you."

Chuckling, he accepted the glass.

"What's the occasion?"

"That you're still alive. Now git. I'll call you when it's ready."

They ate by candlelight. "I'm not quite used to these electric things," she told him. They talked about town business, about rewriting the Charter, about the election coming up in a few weeks.

Afterward, they sat in the living room by the light of two candles on the coffee table, and she talked about her farm, about her plan to take over a new field, five acres on the other side of a narrow stand of trees, for new pasturage. The wine and the food suffused him with an insistent kind of warmth, exotic, yet familiar, and he rubbed the sweat from his palm, acutely aware of her body close to his, of the narrow concavity in the curve of her back, the lush convexity of her breasts.

She reached across him with the bottle to pour, but he put his hand over the glass.

"I'd better go. It's a long ride after dark."

She started to say something, but he got up and moved to the door.

"Thanks, Barbara. Dinner was good. And it was good to see you."

She stood up, walked to him, and with both hands pulled his head down and kissed him full on the mouth, her tongue darting against his, and before thought or intent could form his arm was around her waist, pulling the length of her body against him, and her hands were under his shirt, moving across the skin of his back.

His face was in her hair, against her neck, and his voice rasped.

"What about Agnes?"

"Staying at the pub."

"What about–"

"Just shut up, and do exactly as I say."

Gently, she bit his ear.

He awoke with the weight of bedcovers on his naked skin and gray light creeping into the room.

Pushing himself to a sitting position, he looked down at the woman sleeping on her side beside him, and he reached over and gently slid down the covers, gazing at the shadowy curves of her neck and back. The movement woke her, and she turned, smiling up at him and lazily brushing hair from her eyes.

His hand moved wonderingly along the smooth skin of her hip and side. When it reached her breast, her eyes closed, her lips parted, and she placed a hand lightly over his.

68

For weeks word of electric light had created a stir around town. Once in a while someone older, with memories reaching back before the plague, would come to gawk at something they had thought gone forever. But Max saw something more, Robert's dream of engineering that could stand on its own coming to life. If not in quite the way Robert had intended.

The three met for dinner again at Barbara's. After they ate, they sat in the living room and talked over small glasses of wine.

He prodded Agnes for news.

"Sold any more generators?"

"No." She grimaced. "We can't. Not yet. We have a problem."

"What kind of problem?"

"A serious one. They keep breaking down, and we spend all our time fixing them."

"Why's that?"

"It's the turbine. Blades break off, or it jams. Then we have to build a whole new one."

"Well, but why?"

"Steve thinks it's vibration. We don't think we're getting the rotor balanced well enough. Our construction's pretty crude–"

Barbara turned her head.

"Was that the door? At this time of night?"

They waited. Another knock came.

Max followed her to the door.

She opened it a few inches, and he heard the familiar voice.

"I'm Frank Gambrell, if you don't remember. Do you mind if I come in?"

With the toe of one foot, Agnes shoved the door wide open.

"Hello, Frank."

She held at shotgun, aimed at his stomach.

Frank just glanced at it.

"You don't need that. I came to talk."

"Can you give me one good reason why I shouldn't pull this trigger?"

"I said I'm here to talk."

"Not good enough."

"I need your help."

"Our help! *Our* help! Are you *insane?*"

Max could see her finger wrapped around the trigger, the knuckle white.

"Agnes, listen, let's hear what he has to say. We can always shoot him later."

"Or we can do it now and save time."

"Listen to me," said Gambrell. "I have to move fast, before Martin gets suspicious. I need your help."

There was something in Gambrell's face, something new, and Max tried to weigh it.

"What sort of help?" he asked.

"Martin is planning a takeover. A coup. I'm not going to let that happen."

"That sounds a little crazy."

"Not so crazy. The City is headed for trouble. When we run out of gas, everything will unravel in a heartbeat. Unless there is strong leadership. And Martin can't supply that."

"And I suppose you can."

"I have the loyalty of Security–"

Agnes laughed, her whole body shaking with it, the end of the shotgun dancing in the air.

"Listen to me!" said Gambrell. "I have the loyalty of Security and a lot of the army, because they trust me to do what needs to be done. For the *City.* Martin isn't trusted. Feared, maybe. But you'd have to be pretty stupid to trust him."

"What happened to Dornan? I thought everyone believed in *him.*" Out of the corner of his eye, Max could see Agnes shaking her head, the shotgun still level.

"He's out of it. For all practical purposes, the man's retired."

"So how does anyone take over? Doesn't the Corporation have rules about that?"

"When a crisis hits, rules go out the window. Martin's planning to manufacture a crisis. I'm going to beat him to it."

It sounded insane. Yet also like the kind of breakdown he had imagined.

Agnes lowered the shotgun a little.

"What will you do with Martin?"

Gambrell smirked.

"I'll let you have him. You'll like that."

"That might be worth letting you live."

Max glanced at her. *What the hell?* Then, to Gambrell, "Even if I believed any of this, I don't see what *we* can do."

"I'll explain it. But not out here. This is a serious business. You can't escape the City, and you know it. You don't have to like me, but you'll like Martin a lot less. Trust me."

There seemed to be no reason to trust him. Yet there was no reason for him to come here, alone and apparently unarmed, to just knock on the door.

"Max?" Barbara ventured. "What do you think?"

He hesitated, drawn again to Gambrell's face.

The old boredom was gone, that was part of it. But there was something more. A kind of finality. A kind of ultimatum.

"What do you get out of this, Frank?"

"Look, I spent twenty years helping Jim Dornan rebuild the City. I'm not going to stand by now and watch Richard Martin piss it all down the drain."

Max reached over and pushed down the barrel of the shotgun.

"I think we'd better listen."

They sat around Barbara's coffee table. They talked in normal tones.

But the air did not feel normal.

"Why haven't you gone to Dornan?" Max asked.

"Why? Because Martin would have me arrested. Probably Dornan as well. And you know what he did to Stevens."

"You told me . . . you told me Paul brought that on himself."

"He did. So did Larsen. But they were in Martin's way. Once he had something on them, he made sure they stayed *out* of the way."

"Sounds like he's already taken over, if he can arrest *Dornan,* for God's sake. What can *you* possibly do?"

"Listen. All of the City's gas is in a big storage facility near the coast. It should've lasted another ten years. But somebody screwed up, and now we're down to a reserve. If anything happens to that reserve, it's all over. So I'm going to use it. I'm going to send a commando team to capture it. Martin will send the army to take it back. But he can't risk a fire-fight near the tank. I'm betting he'll surround the facility and secure the perimeter. Try to starve them out, force a negotiation. It's all he can do. But it's a big area. It'll take a good many men to secure. That will be a major diversion, and give me time and space to maneuver."

He turned to Agnes. "And that's where you come in."

"Me?"

"You'll get a message to Martin. You'll let him know that I'm behind it, that I gave the orders, and that you know where I am. But you want a deal first, for your own protection. I think he'll listen. I think he'll deal with you. With the gas under siege, time will be working against him. He'll either go to you, or someone will take you to him."

"How does that help?"

"You're tagged, remember."

"Tagged?" asked Barbara.

"The transmitter," Agnes reminded her.

"Martin won't be able to find me. Neither of us is tagged. So he'll hear you out, and you'll lead me to him. Once I have him, I'll order both sides to stand down."

"Won't he be suspicious? Doesn't he know I was working for you?"

"I'm counting on it."

"I don't understand. How?"

"Because it gives you a very plausible reason for knowing where I am. And a very good motive for helping him. One he'll think of all by himself."

"And that is?"

"I killed Robert Larsen."

Agnes sank back, her lips turning white.

"On Martin's orders, of course," Gambrell went on. "He had his reasons. But you don't know anything about that."

Only too conscious of the reason, Max could say nothing.

Barbara stood up. "I think we've heard enough."

Gambrell ignored her and leaned toward Agnes.

"Martin has a blind spot. He thinks that what he did to you was humiliation. Nothing more. He doesn't think he really hurt you. He's stupid that way, and it's going to cost him. You'd like to see us both dead, but you'd be happy to see Martin dead first."

Barbara dropped back in her chair.

"Oh . . . my . . . God. It's starting to make sense."

Seeing the horror and compassion in her face, Max could only whisper, "*Jesus.*"

Agnes was watching Gambrell, looking now thoughtful, and Max felt a thrill of fear–and a stab of anger.

He snapped at Gambrell, "And you expect her to risk her life on this . . . this *theory?*"

Gambrell shrugged. "I'll be risking mine."

"Come on! She'll be walking into the lion's den while you're in hiding!"

"I'll do it," stated Agnes.

He wanted to shake her. "Are you crazy?"

She stood up and walked across the room, her back to the others. He followed.

"Agnes, how long are you going to let him run your life? You don't have to do this."

"It's none of your business, Max."

"Agnes, listen. When he came for me, when you thought he was going to kill us both, you told him you didn't care what he thought of you. You showed him what you had made. You told him that was all that mattered. I think you were telling the truth."

Her back was rigid, her cheeks dark.

"You don't understand."

"I understand this. You thought you were going to die, and spoke the truth."

"You don't understand. You *can't* understand."

Gambrell got his feet. His face looked almost gentle.

"Let's go."

In the morning, over breakfast, Max told Barbara he was going to the City.

"What? Why? In the name of God . . . with all the crazy things going on! *Why?*"

"To find Agnes. To bring her back."

"Max, are you insane? How? *How* will you find her? Do you have any idea how big the City is?"

"I have a few contacts. I know someone who can find out where she lives. Maybe she'll come to her senses in a couple of days. Maybe I can bring her back."

"And she's *that* important to you?"

"Listen to me, Barbara. She's a *friend.* Remember? She's *your* friend, too, in case you've forgotten."

"Oh, Max . . . she's made up her mind. She's going to do what she has to do. And you have to let her."

"We need her. The town needs her."

"Are you kidding me or yourself? Someone else can make a generator."

"You think so? I'm not so sure. I think we need everyone like her we can get."

Later that morning, at the town office, he told Bert Morrow.

"I'm going, too," the Chief replied.

"No, Bert. You're needed here. If I don't get back, you and Barbara may have your hands full."

"Buddy, she knows what she's doing. And this is no time to be a martyr."

"Trust me, I'm not."

"Then don't try to be a damned hero."

"Trust me, Bert. I'm not."

69

On a warm afternoon a few days later, a pair of uniformed men leaned against the side of a freshly painted shack built by a broad grassy path, a back-country road that ran through the woods on its way to the City. Gleaming antennae stuck up from the roof, shiny coils and rods, and from time to time the shrieking of jays was interrupted by a burst of static and the flat crackle of a voice from within.

One of the men appeared to doze.

The other dragged on a cigarette. He flicked the butt and watched it arc over the road. Then he nudged his companion.

"Hey."

The other opened his eyes. "Yeah?"

He pointed down the grassy road, long and straight under the trees.

"See? Guy on horseback. Looks like an exile."

"Yeah. Okay, I see him. Go run ID."

"On an exile? What's the point?"

"Just do it, Private. That's why we're here. You run everybody."

He went into the shack. Moments later he later called, "I'll be damned, Sarge! We got a hit."

He emerged again.

"No name, though. Just a code."

"What sort of code?"

"Some kind of security code. Assigned to Frank Gambrell."

"No shit. One of Gambrell's stoolies, then."

"So what do we do?"

"Not a damned thing," drawled the sergeant, looking down the road at the approaching rider.

"We let him go?"

"We let him go."

"Do we let Security know?"

"They already know."

They waited a minute in silence, until the private realized what he was seeing.

"Look at that. Guy's lost an arm."

"No shit, Private."
Presently, the rider reined in, glanced at the shack, and considered the sergeant now standing in the road.
"You boys are new."
"Know where you are, fella?" the sergeant asked.
"That I do."
"Got a name?"
"Max. Max Wyse."
"Know where you're going?"
"More or less."
"Mind if I ask what your business is?"
"Looking for a friend."
"Anyone in particular? Or will any friend do?"
"No one you know."
"Maybe Frank Gambrell?"
The rider smiled, a smirk that turned up the corners of his mouth.
The sergeant stepped aside.
"Okay, fella. I suppose you know your business."
The horse broke into a trot and continued down the road.
"I don't know what that guy's doing for us, but I don't envy him."
"Why's that, Sarge?"
"He's not one of us, but he's working for Gambrell. From what I hear, Gambrell's pets don't last long. And he doesn't like loose ends when he's done with them."

After a mile or so, Max let the horse slow to a walk.
I wonder how in hell they tied me to Frank.
Maybe Agnes was right. Maybe he *was* tagged.
An hour later the sun was setting, and he rode through City streets that were quiet and mostly empty. One couple stood on the steps to an apartment building and stared as he rode by, and he saw fear in their eyes. But it did not seem to be fear of him. It looked like fear of everything. As though it were they who were out of place in their own City. Not he.
When he found her apartment building, night was falling. He tied his horse in an alley. Inside the building were mailboxes, and he found her name, then knocked at her locked door on the second floor.
Nothing. Not a sound.
Outside the building, he looked around. The alley was dark, and the horse blended with the shadows. It was the best he could do, and he settled in to wait, sitting propped against the building with a blanket wrapped around his shoulders, wondering if some kind of policeman would come for him.
But he would not go back to the cage. Not alive. He felt the reassuring weight of the gun on his belt, pulled the blanket around him, and waited.

The gun was useless. He could not reach it.

He tried to run, but something, or someone, was holding him back.

From out of the darkness there was a voice.

"Max."

Where the hell was it coming from?

"Max. Max!"

He tried to answer, but he could not make a sound.

"Max!"

He sat up, the sound of his name echoing in his ears.

"Max–for the love of God!"

It was Agnes.

The blanket had fallen away, and he stumbled to his feet, shivering.

"Jesus."

She glanced around, but the sidewalk was empty.

"Come on. Quickly."

Scooping up the blanket, she led him inside, up the stairs, and into her apartment, where she switched on a single lamp by the sofa, made him sit, and disappeared. Minutes later, she returned with a steaming cup of tea.

"Thanks," he whispered, holding the cup close.

"Max, what in the name of God are you doing here?"

"I came to get you out."

"Are you crazy?"

He sipped the hot liquid. "Maybe."

"Look, you've got to get out of here. Before they find you."

"What about you?"

She moved away, into the shadows of the room, and stood looking out a dark window.

"I'm staying. Here. Where I belong."

He watched her peering outside, as though ignoring him, and he laughed.

She looked back.

"What's so damned funny?"

"Frank won't let you go, will he."

She tried to deny it – "You have no idea what's going on!" – but she couldn't hide the tremor in her voice, and finally her shoulders sagged.

"I have another job to do."

"What job?"

"I have to help him find Dornan."

"What about Martin?"

Her eyes slid away.

"I don't know."

"Bullshit. I think you *do* know."

She nodded. Barely.

"Dead."

"How?"

Her eyes closed.

"Hanged."

The cold weight was in his belly again. He had almost forgotten it.

"Not what you expected. Was it."

No answer. She stood by the window, staring vacantly, the pallor of her skin a spectral contrast to the shadows around her. It made him angry, and he remembered why he was here.

"So what's with Dornan?"

Her back straightened. She pushed loose hair over her shoulders.

"I don't know. Either he's in hiding, or something's happened to him. No one seems to know."

He watched her. *What a damned waste.*

"Sounds like Frank's plan worked. He got what he wanted, didn't he? He's in charge. What does he care about Dornan?"

"I'm not sure. But I don't think he's completely in control, not yet. You know, people always used to gripe about things, about the City and the way it was run. I suppose it's human nature. But everyone still looked up to James Dornan. Now they're frightened. Really frightened. They don't know what's going to happen, and if Dornan reappears somehow, I think they'll follow him. And I think that's what Frank is afraid of."

"Makes sense to me. Sounds like a good time for you and I to make a break for it."

"They'll never let me go. You know that."

She turned back to the window, gazing into the night.

"You'd better leave, Max. Now, while you can. You have a few hours left before daylight. You might make it."

"I'm not leaving without you."

"You're not listening." She didn't move, didn't turn, and her voice seemed to recede into a distance. "You need to go."

Her back was turned. He stood up. He hefted the empty cup in his hand, then hurled it. It smashed against a wall, shattering the heavy silence.

She spun around, her eyes wide, and he started moving toward her, coming around the sofa, knotting the muscles of his jaw.

"Where did you learn to be such a God-damned coward?"

She stumbled against the window.

"Do you know what you are?"

She shook her head, wildly, and her body shifted, as though to run, but her eyes were held by his and she couldn't move.

"Do you know what you are?"

There was nowhere for her to go, and she held her hands palms out, as if to hold him off.

"You're a goddess! You have the power of creation! You see things that aren't there, that no one else sees, and you bring them to life!

He was almost on her.

"If you think I'm going to let you throw that away on some bitter has-been and his rotten schemes—well, I've got news for you, lady! I'll kill you first."

She fell heavily against the window, shrieking laughter, and his breath stopped, but the laughter dissolved in her throat, she slid to the floor . . . and he could breathe again.

Her face was against the wall. For a time her shoulders jerked a little, and he forced himself to stand still and watch.

Then she wiped her eyes, and he reached down and took her hand.

She looked up, her hand grasped his, and he pulled her to her feet.

Then her arms were around him, her head was on his chest, and she was whispering, "Oh, *God,* Max . . . " but he pulled away, roughly, and went to retrieve the blanket.

"Get whatever you need. We've got to go."

"Wait. Max."

She was still by the window, but there was life in her eyes and a smile on her lips that he felt rather than saw.

"Max, would you really have killed me?"

He turned away, rolled up the blanket, and slung it over his shoulder.

"Let's go."

He rode with Agnes behind him, her arms around his waist, the clip-clop of hooves on pavement echoing through streets dark and abandoned. Pops of gunfire echoed from blocks away, and she held on tighter, but they saw no one.

Windows lining the streets were black, and the sight of them brought back the frozen night he had run away from Frank, when the City had been alive. Now it was lifeless, in hiding, and he could imagine its inhabitants cowering behind locked doors in darkened rooms, praying that whatever was happening would overlook them. Cowering, making themselves small, to be overlooked.

There is more to this than fear, he thought, watching dead buildings pass by. After a while, it came to him.

It was shame. The shame of a fantasy shredded like mist in a cold wind. The shame of standing naked before truth. The appalling truth of helplessness.

And with that thought, the unseen people became unreal, ghosts in another dimension that could neither reach nor touch him, and he rode on.

70

"**C**an you drive that?"

Max had stopped the horse in the clearing with the guard shack. There was no sign of the two soldiers he had encountered the day before, but there was a canvas-backed truck parked in the trees.

He scanned the clearing, his eyes gritty from a night without sleep. Tire tracks mingled with boot prints in the dirt.

Early sunlight painted the treetops, and Agnes yawned.

"I don't see why not. If the keys are in it, and there's gas."

He looked back at the road leading to the City.

"Max? What do you want to do?"

He threw a leg over the horse, dropped to the ground, and helped her down.

"Let's take a look."

They walked to the truck. She climbed on the running board and peered inside the cab.

"No keys."

"Okay, let's try in there."

He went inside the shack. Against one wall was a table loaded with equipment he didn't recognize. She came in behind him, startled as something squawked static.

Against another wall was a desk. He pulled out drawers until he found a ring of keys.

"Here. Try these."

They went outside. She climbed into the cab, and shortly the engine cranked, then roared.

"Okay!" He raised his voice over the racket. "You know the way back? Just keep going. In about a mile you'll come out on a paved road. That's the North Road. Turn left. Got that? *Left.* The other way goes back to the City. It's another two miles to the main road. That'll be on your left, too. Remember, it's pretty overgrown out here, so keep your eyes open and don't miss it."

"Why do we need the truck?"

"We don't. I'm going back."

"You what? *Why?*"

"To find Dornan."

He started across the clearing.

The engine stopped. The cab door slammed. Then she was in front of him, blocking his way, her hands against his chest.

"Max! Listen to me!"

He grabbed her arm.

"No, *you* listen. *Just listen.* Whatever is going on must be coming to a head. That's why the guards aren't here. Okay? Maybe there's a chance I can find Dornan and get him out before Frank gets him."

"*Why,* for God's sake?"

"You said it yourself. People will follow him. I believe that. How else could he have built the Corporation? But with Frank running the City, I think it'll come apart. I think Frank understands security and not much else. He's no James Dornan. But if the City falls apart, thousands of starving refugees will take the rest of us down with them. So I'm going to try to find Dornan."

"Max, listen to me! If Frank hasn't found him by now, *you'll* never find him. And you may never get out again! You're tagged, remember? Frank could come for you. And if he thinks you're meddling in his plans, that's *exactly* what he'll do."

He let her arm go, and gently brushed some loose strands of her hair, pushing them back over her shoulder.

His fingers rested there a moment.

"Let's hope you're wrong."

Then he swung onto his horse in a single motion and kicked it to a trot without looking back. A minute later, he heard the truck come to life. It shifted into gear, then faded.

The building that was Corporate headquarters was not visible from the exile community, but Max had seen it from afar, traveling with Jack Ryan years before. Now, as he rode once more into the City, it stood out in the jagged gray skyline like a beacon in the morning sun.

Maybe Frank did not have complete control yet, she had said. People would still follow James Dornan. Which, logically, could mean resistance.

He passed apartment buildings, saw people push aside curtains, watching him furtively. Shops and restaurants went by, then small office buildings, all closed up and abandoned to the crisis.

The streets grew wide and straight, the buildings tall, and he rode onward guided by an occasional glimpse of the white tower caught between buildings.

Eventually, he came to a boulevard broad and black and lined with those monumental shapes like ancient gods, the skyscrapers of the City. A mile or so off, the white tower rose from its plaza in a blaze of sunlight.

He turned onto the boulevard, and rode toward the heart of the Corporation.

On the sidewalks, men in familiar dark uniforms stopped and stared as the horse clopped by. Others ran ahead. He rode on, keeping the horse to a steady walk and concentrating on the reins in his hand, on trying to ignore the uneasiness in his belly and the dryness in his mouth.

Ahead was a barricade, coils of barbed wire stretched across the pavement. To the right of it, on the sidewalk, a group of uniformed men.

He turned toward them.

Several men stepped forward, rifles at their shoulders, black holes converging on him as they sighted down foreshortened barrels, and he reined in as a young officer emerged from the group.

"*Halt!* Put your damned hands up!"

He looked down at these men with guns, and for the space of a few seconds felt himself the clearing again, her hair in his hand, a cool breeze on his face.

"*I said put your hands up!*"

He complied, raising his one arm.

"Get down off that horse."

He swung a leg over and dropped.

One soldier took the reins. Another held a pair of handcuffs, but hesitated, apparently unsure what to do.

Max sighed and lowered his arm.

"I *said* put your hands up!" the officer bellowed.

"Look, I'm not here to cause trouble. I just want to find James Dornan."

From out of the stunned silence, a lone voice muttered, *"Shit! Wouldn't we all!"*

"Shut it!" barked another.

"I have a message for him."

"A message!" The officer was taken aback for a moment, then slowly smiled. "A message? Well mister, that's just about enough to get you a firing squad. *You!* 'Cuff 'im."

He stood unresisting while a soldier handcuffed his wrist to his belt. Another took away his gun. Then they led him across the sidewalk to a blank door.

Inside was a large room, and they brought him to a corner and ordered him to sit, handcuffing his wrist to his chair. Two soldiers stayed behind as the others left, taking chairs nearby.

One of the pair, tall, broad-shouldered, heavy jaw clean-shaven under a bushy brown moustache, looked him over with frank curiosity.

"So what's this about a message, fella?"

"*Knock it off,*" hissed the other. "This guy's dead. We're not supposed to talk to him."

"But this is damned peculiar! Don't you want to know?"

"What I want is to stay out of trouble."

Max forced a grin. "Don't we all."

"Too late for you, though," said the first. "Right? You came looking for it."

"Well, I didn't have much choice."

"So? Why's that?"

He took a breath, and plunged ahead.

"Because I really came to get Dornan out of here."

"You . . . *what?*"

The man erupted in a booming laugh that reverberated through the room, while his companion slunk lower in his chair, shaking his head miserably.

"I came to get James Dornan out of here."

"Then you're a lot dumber'n you look, my friend! What made you think you could just waltz in and waltz out?"

He shrugged. "Didn't know what else to do."

"So? Just who the hell are you?"

"Max Wyse. President of the town south of here."

"How in hell'd you get past Security?"

He remembered the soldiers in the clearing, and the name.

"I used to work with Frank Gambrell."

Dark eyes widened. *"Used* to?"

"Before all this happened. When he was still working for Dornan."

"C'mon, cut it out!" The second man elbowed the first. "You'll get us shot, too."

The big man folded heavy arms and settled back in his chair.

"Yeah, Al. Maybe you're right."

Hours later, a cold meal was brought in. He was uncuffed long enough to eat. The guard was changed, and the waiting continued.

A metallic rattle woke him, someone removing the handcuff from the chair. Nearby stood a soldier with one hand resting on the sidearm at his belt.

Massaging his neck, Max stood up and looked around the shadowy room, but his arm was pulled down and his wrist quickly cuffed to his belt, and he was led out the door.

Outside, it seemed late at night, the street starkly lit and deserted, except for a large truck with a covered back parked halfway up on the sidewalk. A few uniformed men waited by it.

He was led to the truck and prodded to climb in the back. Two men followed and sat on a bench on either side of him. The tailgate creaked and slammed. Gears whined, and the truck bumped over the curb and into the street, then accelerated, the floor rumbling as it drove east, away from the white tower shining through the night.

Over the tailgate, Max watched the City lights recede, the streets growing dark, wondering if he could jump the tailgate and elude these men with his arm cuffed. He shifted his weight, but alert hands grabbed his shirt.

The truck slowed, then swayed roughly as it turned off the road. The headlights went out, and the truck bumped along, springs creaking, the men holding him down.

Finally, they lurched to a halt. The rumbling stopped.

From outside, there was a quiet murmur of voices. The opening over the tailgate was slightly less black than the interior, and he tried again to get his feet under him, but someone grabbed his arm, the tailgate creaked and fell open, and he was prodded down.

There were no lights, only a faint glow over a black wall of trees from a layer of cloud over the City.

Two men led him away from the truck. A small, low building appeared, just a ghostly outline in the dark. They led him around it.

Behind was an open area, in middle of which a single small lantern stood on the ground, its flame a dim, yellow arc. Uniformed men loitered in twos and threes.

His guards walked him to a man standing alone, double bars gleaming on his collar, and they saluted and extended a sheet of paper. The officer returned the salute, took the page, and held it up to catch the light.

"So. You're Max Wyse." The voice was low, but infused with authority.

Knees beginning to shake, Max licked his lips and tried to swallow. "That's right."

"It says here you entered the City looking for James Dornan. With a message, it says."

"That's right."

The officer nodded, still reading.

Then he looked up.

"You have some balls, I'll give you that." To the guards, "Okay, we're ready. Bring him."

They led him toward a deeper darkness, away from the lantern, to a group of four or five nearly indistinguishable in the dark.

"Max Wyse," intoned the officer as they came to a halt, and he felt transported again to this morning in the clearing, the sun in the trees, and in her hair . . .

A stocky figure emerged from the group, dim yellow light gleaming from the smooth outline of his head.

The officer quietly continued: "This is Mr. James Dornan."

"*Shit!*" someone hissed. "Get the cuff off!"

Knees still shaking, Max shook hands with the Corporation's chief executive.

71

"I'd like to hear your plan, Mr. Wyse."

Three men sat around a table in the middle of a dank, windowless room in the low building, the walls of cement block, one bare light overhead.

Max shrugged at the officer. "I don't have one."

"Then why are you here? If you don't mind my asking."

He turned to Dornan. "All of you in the City call us exiles. You think we live in some kind of wilderness. But you really don't know a thing about us. If you need a place to go, my town is safe, safer than here. For you, anyway."

The officer answered.

"We may just know a little more than you give us credit for."

"All right then, tell me this. If he comes with me and we make it out of here, how will you keep Frank Gambrell from tracking him wherever he goes?"

"What do you mean?"

"Don't play dumb with me. I know about the transmitters everyone has. I won't do this if it means my town gets invaded."

"You may be invaded either way."

Dornan's body shifted. "I suppose you mean the personal tags." The voice was deliberate, but relaxed, as though they were meeting to discuss some routine business matter. "Senior executives aren't tagged. Besides, they're passive. A tag is activated when it's in range of a scanner. There are scanners all over the City, but not outside."

"No? Then I'd like to know how Frank tracked me on the North Road."

"You'll have to explain that."

"It's a long story. Let's just say I'm . . . tagged. I'm pretty sure he used that to find me, outside the City."

"I'd like to know how you were tagged."

"He was picked up with Doctor Stevens," the officer explained.

"I see. And yet you got as far you did yesterday without setting off an alarm."

"He has a security code. But no alert."

"What does that mean?" asked Max.

"It means . . ." Dornan mused, "It means that either our friend Frank has something very clever up his sleeve, or else he's over-looked you. What do you think, Captain? It does seem he's been a bit preoccupied lately."

"Maybe so, Jim. But there will be a record of everywhere he's gone. If Gambrell can't find you, but finds out *he* came *here,* then turned around and went home again, it's likely to tip him off. I'm sure Mr. Wyse would like to avoid that very outcome, and I'd personally like to buy us more time."

"Any ideas?"

"I think so. Suppose we take Mr. Wyse up on his offer. And suppose the record were to show that Mr. Wyse came into the City, as it will, but then exited west instead of returning south."

"All right. Go on."

"It shouldn't be too difficult to get the tag out of him. It can be taken by someone else, say as far as Highway 3, well outside any scanners. There it can be destroyed. Anyone who tries to follow will waste valuable time, maybe days, before giving up."

"I like it."

"Wait a minute," Max objected. "If that's the North Road, I don't think it's far enough."

Dornan looked thoughtful. "You probably mean Lakeview Drive. You're right, there are scanners along there. Highway 3 is on the other side of the lake. All right, Captain. Keep going. How do we get it to the highway?"

"Well, we'll want the trace to show speeds consistent with Mr. Wyse's usual mode of transportation. We'll need the horse. I trust we have your permission, Mr. Wyse?"

"Let's hear the rest."

"You and Mr. Dornan will leave by automobile. Neither of you will be tagged. As long as you can evade any patrols along the way, you stand a very good chance of making it out of the City undetected."

"And one of your men here rides the horse, I suppose." Dornan added.

"That's right. We'll remove his tag as well, so the trace will show only Mr. Wyse's tag, moving at his usual speed, until it disappears. Gambrell may even conclude that he took you to Westboro. He might suspect you of planning an insurgency from there."

"I thought Westboro is still infected."

"That's our assumption. But no one's about to go test it, so no one knows for sure. It could keep Gambrell off balance and guessing for a few days. And that may be the best we can hope for."

Dornan rose to his feet, and the officer followed.

"All right, Captain Vick. If we can't pull something together in the next few days, then it's probably all over anyway. Let's do it."

Max stood up and faced Dornan.

"Wait a minute."

"Something on your mind?" Dornan asked.

"Paul Stevens was my friend. Your . . . *executive*, Richard Martin, destroyed him."

"So what are you looking for, Mr. Wyse? Hindsight is always twenty-twenty."

"I'd like to know how it's going to be different. What's *your* plan from here on out?"

"Like you, I'm playing it by ear. Look, I'll admit to making mistakes. But I won't apologize for it. If that's not enough for you, you're free to go."

The face was unmoved, and Max studied it, not sure what he was looking for. Calm eyes gazed back, almost indifferently. It felt like a challenge.

"All right. Let's do it."

Dornan turned on his heel and strode from the room, and Vick held up a hand.

"Please, Mr. Wyse. Wait here."

He followed Dornan out.

A short while later, a half-dozen soldiers entered. One introduced himself as a medic, instructed Max to remove his shirt, and began wiping down the table.

Fumbling with his buttons, Max glanced at the others standing by. "What's with the audience?"

The medic pulled on thin gloves and picked up a scalpel.

"There's no anesthetic."

"Oh . . . *Christ.*"

He lay prone on the table as directed, turning his head away. The medic pulled his arm to straighten it, took a few seconds to prod the flesh below the shoulder, rubbed it with something cold, then pinched the flesh, hard, and Max grunted as the men leaned into his back and arm, then screamed as the knife bit.

In less than two minutes it was done, and he was helped to his feet, chest and belly bathed in sweat, while the medic wiped blood from a small, white capsule, then dropped it into a clear plastic bag.

He held it up, grinning.

"It's going to be sore for a while. There are four sutures in your arm. They can come out in a week. Get someone to snip each one and pull by the knots. They should slide right out. Keep it clean until it heals. I understand you don't have antibiotics. Remember, an infection can be life-threatening."

He peeled off the gloves and extended his hand.

"Good luck."

One of the soldiers escorted him out, while another was entering. Their eyes met, briefly, as they passed.

Outside, in the clearing, he heard a muffled yell from within.

———————

Two hours later, the sky was growing light.

An automobile was parked in front of the cement block building. Dornan and Captain Vick were standing by it, and Max was brought to them as Vick was speaking.

"Fighting was reported overnight, somewhere north of here. Holdouts loyal to Martin, we understand. But apparently it's over. Things are quiet now."

Dornan grimaced. "Let's hope it served as a distraction."

Vick went on. "Corporal Johnson should be out of the City by now. He's to ride north around the lake. It will be at least another hour, maybe two, before he reaches Highway 3."

"Then what?" Dornan asked.

"He's to destroy the tag, wait until nightfall, then ride back to Lakeview, and take Lakeview south to join up with you."

"He knows where to look?"

"He's been briefed, yes, by Mr. Wyse."

Dornan took the keys Vick held out.

Max got into the car with him, and in a moment the engine roared, but the car did not move.

"Balls," muttered Dornan, letting up on the gas. "I haven't done this in a while."

He shifted it into gear, and the car lurched forward.

Max looked back, watching Vick and his small outpost until the car was in the trees and the outpost lost from sight.

"How do we know this guy Johnson actually made it?" he asked.

"We don't."

They followed the same general route west, taking back streets, the buildings now lit by morning sun rising behind.

Then they were out of the City and turning onto Lakeview, and Dornan accelerated.

"Does any of this look familiar?"

"No. But keep going."

They came to the lake, the road skirting its eastern shore, and Max looked through his window for the restaurant where he had met with Robert. But it was on the far side, across miles of open water cloaked in layers of mist blazing white as the sun rose.

Dornan's voice brought him back.

"Well? Is this your North Road?"

"It looks right. Keep going."

The road dove into the trees, a black ribbon leading farther and farther south, curving a little where the trail was that led to where Greg was beaten . . . and he felt himself back in the meadow with Robert . . . then listening to him talk about industry . . . then seeing him slung over his horse.

"There!" he blurted. "You just missed it."

Dornan slowed.

"What? You mean the dirt road back there?"

"Yeah. That's the main road."

"That's the main road?" Dornan slowed to a stop and turned the car around. "Just what is it you're president of?"

"You'll see."

It was a crawl over a mile or more of still-ungraded road until the pub came into view.

Max pointed.

"Stop there."

They came to a halt in front of the sagging structure, bare of paint, Dornan glancing over his shoulder as if wondering whether he should turn back.

"Is this your house?"

"No. But I'm hungry. How about you? I'll buy."

Dornan cut the engine.

Over breakfast, he asked about the chances of taking the City back from Gambrell, and Dornan shrugged.

"It may come down to timing. He'll be at his most vulnerable in the next few days. But if we do nothing and he plays his cards right, things may come together. Security and the army may decide to accept him as legitimate."

"So, if he plays his cards right, why do they need you?"

"Why?" the older man laughed. "Because Frank's no businessman! He doesn't know how to trust people. Especially people who don't think the way he does. He'll stifle good ideas because they threaten his authority. He'll stifle good people for the same reason. Business will fail, and he'll try to fix it with force, and that will fail as well. He'll run the City into the ground. And you with it, by the way."

"Yeah. I know. Believe me."

72

Still not quite believing this was real, Agnes stood with James Dornan in the living room of Barbara's home.

Max had brought him here for dinner. On horseback. She had stood speechless at the spectacle of the Corporation's chief executive climbing down from Robert's horse and walking across the clearing with Max. But she had shown him a generator, her wiring, the dam, explaining how it all worked, and over dinner Dornan had plied her with questions, *technical* questions, not the sort she would have expected from a corporate executive.

Now she stood with him before a bookcase burdened with rows of textbooks, while Max and Barbara were in the kitchen with the dishes.

"Are these yours?" he asked.

"They were Robert's. He brought them from the City."

"And who is Robert?"

"He was the man in my life."

"Was?"

"He's . . . well, he's dead."

"I'm sorry to hear it." He was studying her, making no attempt to hide it. "You know, I don't think most of my engineers are much more than repairmen. They can patch things up when they break, but I doubt whether many of them would be able to connect two wires together if someone hadn't been done it before."

"Robert wanted to learn how to make the wire."

"We need people like him. Like you."

"You don't know who Robert was, do you?"

"Should I?"

"He was Robert Larsen. Your Vice President of Security."

She saw the shock he could not hide. But he answered evenly.

"Well, I'm sorry for you. But he got what he deserved." She said nothing, and he continued a little more gently. "Remember, he was tried and found guilty."

"Of what? Crossing Richard Martin?"

"Of breaking rules and violating policy. He was a danger."

"How can you believe that?"

"It's what the court found. And it's their job to find out."

"Or was it to do what Richard Martin wanted? And if you expect people to obey rules they know to be wrong . . . well, look at you now."

"I don't need a lecture, young lady."

"No, of course not. You'll work it out for yourself. Eventually."

She expected anger. Instead, he laughed, quietly, his eyes frankly taking her in, and frankly appraising.

"I can see what he saw in you."

He pulled down a book and opened it.

"This is where I started. Many, many years ago. Structural Engineering. I was going to design a new kind of bridge."

"What happened?"

"There was more money in management."

"What about your new kind of bridge? What happened to that?"

"The old ones were good enough."

"Said who?"

"The money." He returned the book to its shelf. "So, Mr. Larsen wanted to be an engineer. That doesn't sound like the man I knew."

"You do know what was done to him."

"I know. Don't expect me to apologize."

"I haven't asked for an apology."

"Everyone involved did the job they were trained for. Martin may have pulled a few strings to get rid of a rival, but he couldn't have done it if Larsen hadn't given him a damned good pretext."

"I haven't asked for an apology."

"I'm not . . . I suppose I was, wasn't I?"

"I haven't asked for it. Robert wasn't trying to be an engineer. He wanted to find a sustainable level of industry we could all go back to. To start over. He wasn't successful. It's surprising how complex even rudimentary industry is."

"Believe me, I know."

"Robert said the Corporation depends too much on scavenging. He used to say it was living on borrowed time."

"And you agree?"

"I think you're living on borrowed time, but I don't think scavenging is the main reason."

"No? Then what is?"

"Thousands of human minds doing nothing more."

He nodded slowly.

"Compared to one who is."

"More than one. You haven't met my partner."

"I'd like to meet him. Is he just a business partner?"

"Just?" She laughed, startled at the thought. "We probably spend more time together than lovers!"

"No significant other?"

"Who? Me or Steve? I don't know about Steve, but I'm not looking."

"That's the only real way to find one."

"Not interested."

"Which must make you irresistible to men."

"Not really. They get the hint."

"I said *men*. Not boys."

"So a man is someone who won't take no for an answer? I'd rather be around boys."

"A man knows what he wants and doesn't give up."

"And how is that different?"

"A man doesn't want what he can't have. Or shouldn't have."

It was a moment before she could answer.

"You make that sound simple and easy. I think I know better."

"Simple things–the ones that matter–are rarely easy. Some men understand this . . . Look, I said 'men', but don't take it literally. It's not what I meant. I think you're one of them." He nodded at the books. "Maybe Mr. Larsen was right. But if people like you leave us, what do you expect to happen? Why didn't you work on your ideas in the City?"

"You should be asking yourself that question."

"I'm asking you."

She ran a hand through her hair.

"What can I tell you that you don't already know? I was an employee. I did what I was told. No one in authority would have cared."

"You don't know that."

"Of course I do! Why should they care? What would be in it for them?"

"Recognition. Promotion. Higher pay. The usual things."

"Recognition and promotion matter to people who care about such things. I don't. But if you do care about them, why risk losing them by taking a chance on something completely untried that, if it works, will be appropriated by people above you? And if it doesn't work, will be hung around your neck by people above you? You're a businessman. Would you invest in a risky proposition if the best you could hope for was a pat on the back? And the worst might be to lose everything?"

"There's more to it than that. You can't succeed without taking risks. You've got to have some balls—Excuse me. You have to have some guts, too."

"Did *you* care about recognition? When you were making your fortune? When the world was coming apart? Did *you* care what anyone thought?"

"Of course not. But there aren't many Jim Dornans around."

"Of course not! There's no room for them! They don't fit. You fire them and they starve. Or you put them in cages and turn loose the people who *hate* them!"

She had to look away, to not let him see her face.

He answered quietly, after a long moment.

"I don't buy that. Many people hated me, at one time or another. It didn't matter. I didn't care."

"And why didn't you care?"

"Because they couldn't stop me."

"They had no *power* to stop you."

"No—I suppose that's your point, isn't it?"

"You see? I was right. You worked it out for yourself."

He looked amused. "I can see we're not going to be friends."

"No. We're not going to be friends."

"I don't see what this is going to accomplish." Barbara handed him a dish. Max wiped it dry and put it away. "And it's dangerous just having him in town."

"He could be anywhere, as far as they know. He's not tagged."

"It's still a risk!"

"Well, it's a risk we have to take."

"Is it? I seem to remember the Committee telling you not to deal with the City on your own. What do you think they're going to say about this? Bringing the *Corporation's CEO* here? Over to dinner, for God's sake."

He shrugged, wiping another dish.

She shook her head and picked up a bottle, and he followed her out of the kitchen.

They sat around the coffee table with glasses of wine, and Dornan told stories about the Corporation, about better days, and Agnes grew animated, laughing over things only she and Dornan understood. They spoke like comrades, like refugees from another country, and Max could only listen in silence. It rankled, until the conversation paused, and he changed the subject.

"You know, I don't see how you can afford your army. We have a hard enough time paying for a handful of deputies. Couldn't you put that money to better use? On something important? Like learning how to make gasoline, for instance."

"Well, Mr. Wyse, I wish life were that easy."

"Who said anything about easy? What're you going to do when you run out of gas?"

"There are a hundred things we could run out of, and any one would be a disaster. We have to manage it all. It's a big job, and keeping the City safe is part of it. Yes, the military is expensive. But not having it would be irresponsible. Even you have your deputies."

"Maybe military strength *is* important. But you can't have it without economic strength. And economic strength comes from people who build. Who *create.*"

Dornan settled back in his chair.

"No argument there. We have hundreds of technical people."

"I don't mean just employees. I mean people who come up with their *own* ideas. Things no one else has thought of before. Not something the boss told them to go work on. We don't always know who they are, or what they'll do. *They* don't always know. But that's just the point. No one would have guessed what Agnes could do. But all she needed was a place to work and the freedom to do it."

"That's quite a luxury. I think you can invent something and still be an employee."

"Not if you don't have the freedom to do it."

"So, what do you call freedom? How free are you if you have to spend every waking hour of every day working just to have food on the table?" He glanced at Barbara. "No disrespect intended. But it can't be easy living this way. And Agnes is a very lucky young lady to have you as a friend."

It was late. Max had not slept in a bed since the night before last, and he was exhausted. But the conversation turned to the situation in the City.

Dornan talked about *wire.*

"Frank won't be squeamish about this. We can count on him putting his commandos on it, at least. But he'll have to be careful. It's not easy to make."

Barbara sniffed.

"Well, we do things a little differently around here. If you want our help, the Committee will have to decide."

"What's the Committee?"

"The people elected to govern this town."

"So what do they say about my hiding out here a few days?"

"I think Max is going to have to answer for that."

"Christ!" he blurted. "By the time *they* decide anything, it'll be over."

"Max, you–" Barbara started, but he ignored it.

"Robert was right about one thing. We're *all* living on borrowed time. You're running out of gas, and probably other things as well. The rest of us are just one step away from the stone age. And it's probably not so different in other cities. Maybe we're all going to end up fighting over whatever scraps are left, until there's nothing left at all."

Dornan yawned. "So what's on your mind, Mr. Wyse?"

He snapped back: "I want to know what's on *yours*."

"As I told you before, I don't have a plan yet. It was good enough for you then. It's a little late to change your mind now."

Max stood up, ready to get Dornan back to the pub.

"I haven't changed it . . . I'm going to give you three days."

"Oh? And what then?"

"And then I'm going to make my *own* decision."

Dornan smiled, an insufferable look of amusement in his face.

"Fair enough."

Before they left, Barbara pulled Max aside, away from the others, and whispered, "Max, let him stay here. It's safer. You can't just drive up to my place."

"Who can't?"

"Anyone from the City. Anyone they send looking for him."

"They'll probably send commandos. They'll be on *wire*. I've seen what it does. Jack was using it. You'll be dead before anyone knows they're here."

"But . . . they could do that at the pub! Couldn't they?"

"I have a twenty-four hour guard at the pub. If anyone comes for him, their orders are to turn him over without resistance."

"Good God, Max! He *trusts* you."

"So do other people."

73

Well after sunrise the next morning, Max returned to the pub. Corporal Johnson had arrived during the night, and was talking with Dornan over coffee when Max walked in and unceremoniously sat down at their table.

Dornan nodded curtly.

"What can I do for you?"

He had slept. His head was clear. And the two mile hike from the farmhouse in the cold light of day had finished off any illusions he might have had that James Dornan could pull a few strings and ride back to the City in triumph.

"I was going to ask you the same thing."

"Well, suppose you tell me what your intentions are."

"Meaning what?"

"Corporal Johnson here tells me you have a guard on my car."

"He's right."

"Do you have some other way for us to communicate?"

"What do you have to communicate?"

"Damn it! I can't formulate a plan if I can't communicate with my people!"

"Maybe. But you're not going to just drive back and forth and lead Frank's commandos here."

"So, what do you propose? You knew there would be risks. This is a bad time to lose your nerve."

Johnson looked down, suppressing a laugh, but looked up again when Max addressed him. "Corporal, excuse us a minute."

Johnson looked at Dornan, who nodded, then shrugged and took his coffee to the bar.

Max lowered his voice. *"Fuck* you." Dornan's eyes froze. "You've been sheltered at the top too long. When you and Johnson come up with a plan to use the car that makes sense to me, then I'll authorize it. Until then, it's off goddamn limits."

He got up and walked out.

But his hand was shaking.

Mike brought out his horse, and he mounted, picking up the reins as another rider turned in from the road.

It was Agnes, smiling broadly.

"Hi, Max! What do you think?"

"What do I think about what?"

She held up her reins.

"I think I'm getting the hang of this, don't you?"

"Oh. Yeah. Sure."

"Thought I'd practice my riding and come out here for breakfast."

"Okay, Agnes."

He kicked his horse, trying to dismiss the look of hurt in her face as he passed.

"Don't talk to me about democracy," Dornan was saying. "I can't imagine a bigger cesspool of corruption and ineptitude. If it's not politicians selling the souls they haven't got for campaign money, it's politicians saddling the rest of us with taxes and paperwork for one pet project or noble cause after another. And don't bother trying to whitewash it. I played the game. I know what it's about."

Agnes had joined him for coffee. Johnson had left to get some sleep.

"But I do agree with you on one thing," Dornan went on. "We can't keep using *rope* to keep people in line."

"Well, I suppose that's something. But why? Do you expect me to believe you've developed a conscience?"

"Look, young lady, I don't apologize. For anything."

"Then why?"

"Why not use *rope?* We will, for a while. But I don't want it getting outside the ranks of manual labor. And it's starting to. We can't afford that. You see, I agree with your friend Max on some things. He's not the only one who can see the need for intellectual work."

"I think he'd say *creative* intellectual work. Unfettered."

"There have to be limits to everything. Or there would be no order. And even geniuses need order."

"You know, I think I'd have an easier time believing you if you weren't so . . . so *sardonic,* I think the word is. It's hard to take what you say seriously."

"Well, I'm at an age where I don't like to be too serious."

"So I take it you don't buy Max's theory."

"Your friend doesn't understand organization. Yes, we need a few creative people. But we need a lot more to turn the cranks to make what the geniuses invent. People who are smart, dependable, and *manageable.*"

"So what are you going to do without *rope?*"

"Television."

"Television . . . ?"

"Oh, come on!" He laughed. "Are you *that* young? Look, a television is an electronic appliance. It receives images and sound." He held up his hands about two feet apart. "Like a theater on your table top. All kinds of shows recorded by actors, and live events as well. All in your living room."

"I know what it is. We had one somewhere, when I was a child. But I don't see how it keeps people in line."

"It's *entertainment.* It's funny. It's sad. It's exciting. It takes people out of their real lives, and most of them can't resist that."

"I don't see how a little picture could be that entertaining."

"You'd be surprised. In the old days they couldn't get enough of it. There's an art to producing the shows, but it isn't that hard. And we don't have to invent anything. We just have to get it working again."

"So you think if you entertain people, they'll stop plotting against you."

"In all the history of the world, there has probably never been a revolution in any country with the right entertainment. It's much too effective at keeping people occupied when they have nothing better to do."

"Ah, the catch! Who decides when they have nothing better to do?"

"That's the beauty of it. They'll decide for you. They'll watch that little theater for hours at a time. As long as you keep the shows coming. And we have thousands of recordings."

"And you think this will work."

"I know it will. Remember, I lived in the day. My wife and kids, God rest their souls, practically lived in front of it."

"Because they had nothing better to do."

"They didn't think so."

"And you? You had something better?"

"If I hadn't, we wouldn't be having this conversation."

"You know, I can't quite visualize the Dornan household."

"Well, don't get me wrong. We socialized. We entertained. We traveled. But I have to admit, it wasn't all that hard to stay late at the office, when I needed to."

"Then what was the point?"

He surprised her. His face softened.

"You've been hurt. But time heals. One day you won't have to ask me that."

She could not help smiling.

"You think I'm unhappy?"

"I wouldn't make that mistake. But people fall in love. They get married. They want a home. You will, too. When you let yourself."

"Maybe. But if I'm going to fall in love, it won't be because he makes me feel safe, or because I'm homesick. There has to be a better reason."

"Young lady, what makes you think reason has anything to do with it?"

"Maybe that isn't the right word. But it isn't what I want."

In the afternoon, as Barbara worked in her kitchen, she could see Agnes through a window, sitting at the picnic table between house and barn, her chin cupped in her hands. On the table rested a turbine, but she seemed to have forgotten it.

Barbara dried her hands, left the house, and walked over.

"Hey, you." She sat down.

Agnes smiled.

"Hey, you."

"What're you thinking?"

"Oh . . . trying to decide."

"Decide what?"

"Jim offered me a job. In the City. In a new research department."

"Oh?"

"He said I could write my own ticket."

"Oh."

"It would mean a lot of money. A lot of responsibility."

"Sounds tempting."

"What do you think? Any advice?"

Barbara thought for a moment.

"Will he still be 'Jim' when you're working for him?"

"I don't know. What do you mean?"

"You know what I mean."

"Well . . . I suppose I do."

"Sounds like a hard decision."

"I never thought I'd get a chance like this! I never thought anyone like Jim Dornan would pay the least attention to me." She caught Barbara's look. "As a *professional.* Not a mattress."

"I'm sure you're flattered. What are you going to say to Max?"

"To Max? I don't know. Why?"

"How will you break it to him?"

"What do you mean?"

"Come on, honey. He risked his life for you."

"Oh, I suppose he did. But that's not a reason to stay. He'll just have to accept that."

Barbara said nothing. She got up and walked back to the house.

74

*W*estboro *was still infected.*

Max had heard this during the meeting at Vick's outpost, and later at the pub had quietly asked, "Bill, when I was sick and ended up here, what happened to my clothes?"

"Burned 'em."

"Why?"

"Didn't want anyone else to get it."

"Get . . . what?"

"You know. Cargo Flu."

"Christ, Bill. Weren't you afraid of it? Or are you immune?"

"I already had it."

"Explain that."

"I know where you went. I've been there. Got sick the first time, too, just like you. Now I can go there and it doesn't bother me."

"What makes you think it was Cargo Flu? I was sick in my guts. Nothing wrong in my chest."

"It's what they all died of out there. What else could it be?" Bill cracked a rare smile. "It just ain't what it used to be."

On the third morning after the dinner at Barbara's, Max walked into the dining area of the pub. Dornan and Corporal Johnson were huddled at a table.

He went over to them.

Johnson had made one trip into the City overnight, exchanged news with Captain Vick, then returned well before dawn and reported to Dornan.

Now the two stared at him in silence.

He sat down.

"Time's up. What's the plan?"

Red-eyed and sallow, it was plain that Dornan had not slept.

"We need more time."

"Why?"

"Because we haven't worked it all out!" Dornan snapped. "That's why."

"You don't know what to do, do you."

Neither answered. Once more, the cold weight of reality lodged in his belly. But now it felt right.

He glanced across the room and nodded.

At the sound of footsteps, Johnson turned, tried to stand, but was held down by a meaty hand on his shoulder.

"Not so fast, Corporal."

The table was surrounded, by Bill, Bert, and armed deputies.

At the sight of weapons, Dornan flared.

"What's the meaning of this?"

"I'm sorry," Max told him. "You're going to have to trust me."

The two were blindfolded and their hands bound, Dornan bellowing, "This is your idea of *trust?*"

They were led away, and Max stayed behind, seated at the table by himself, giving his nerves time to settle, very much conscious of what he had just done, and to someone still a force to be reckoned with. And very much conscious of what he was about to do.

Agnes walked in. She glanced around the empty room, saw him, and came over.

"Max, do you have a minute?"

"Yeah, sure. Coffee?"

"No. I want to find Jim, but I have something to say to you, since you're here."

She pulled out a chair and sat across from him.

"What's on your mind?"

"Max, I want you to listen to me."

"I'm listening."

"I want you to understand something." She sat stiffly erect, hands in her lap. "Jim Dornan offered me a job. In the City. And not just any job. A very important one."

"All right. Go on."

"I realize you may have saved my life. And you did so at some risk to your own. I'm not sure I understand your reasons, but I *am* grateful. Still, grateful as I am, that's not a reason to turn him down."

"Listen, no one's—"

"Wait. I'm not finished."

She placed her hands flat on the table.

"Max. I decided I don't want the job. I'm going to turn him down. But for reasons of my own. Reasons that have nothing to do with anyone else . . . Max?"

"It's okay."

"Do you . . . ?"

"I get it. It's okay."

"God, I am *so* glad." She slumped. "I was dreading this . . . You know, Max, you've changed somehow. You're not what you were when we met."

"I suppose not."

"Well, is he around? I want to tell him."

"You missed him. He's going to be busy a while."

"How long a while?"
"Oh, at least a couple of days, I'd say."

———————

That evening, when Agnes was in her room putting her things away, there was a knock at her closed door.

"Come in!"

Barbara walked in, but stopped at the sight of small piles of folded clothing arranged on the bed.

Agnes saw the question in her face, and laughed.

"*Un*-packing. If you must know."

"Well, I am truly glad. But what changed your mind? I thought you were all set to go."

"I decided flattery wasn't a good enough reason, either."

75

Daybreak.

Corporal Johnson stood up and stretched.

Ignoring the deputies nearby and their cradled rifles, he proceeded to relieve himself in the open.

They were camped by some nameless road that cut through grassy fields and wild brushland in the middle of nowhere. On the far side of the road, a hundred, two hundred yards to the north, a wall of trees began. Down the road to the west, a tract of two-story homes, ancient and dilapidated.

Crows cawed in the distance. A horse snorted.

Johnson zipped his trousers and studied the houses.

The yellow light made them stand out, revealed missing shingles and broken windows and thickets of weeds.

He glanced at the deputies, muttering, "I hope these fucking exiles know what they're doing."

Sitting on a log with a blanket around his shoulders, James Dornan said nothing.

An hour later, as the sun was warming, they heard the sound of a car approaching from the east. It appeared to be the car Dornan had taken from the City, but it cruised past and continued down the road, slowing as it approached the nearest of the houses, and turning into a driveway. Two people got out, went up a walkway, and entered the house.

"All right."

Johnson turned.

Bert Morrow and two armed deputies stood there.

"Let's go," said Bert.

"Bullshit." Johnson spat. "We're not going anywhere."

"Now look–"

"We need a meal, sheriff! We haven't eaten since yesterday morning."

"Yeah, sorry about that. You can eat later."

"If you're gonna kill us, fucker, you can do it right here."

"No one's doing any killing, Corporal! Just do as we ask."

"Never mind!" snapped Dornan, lumbering to his feet. "Let's just get this goddamned farce over with."

The deputies trailing a few steps behind, Johnson and Dornan followed the Chief down the road, to the first house. Inside, at a kitchen table, were seated Max Wyse and a large man Johnson recognized from the pub.

He was surprised. The place was clean, the floors swept, with none of the leftover debris one would expect in a home emptied by the old plague.

Wyse spoke.

"So what do you think of this place, Mr. Dornan? Know where you are?"

"Should I?"

"It's Westboro."

Johnson was suddenly ice cold.

"What the fuck. *Westboro?*"

"That's right, Corporal. And there's Flu here."

"You . . . *you fucking bastard!* What the fuck *is* this? Just what do you expect to happen?"

"I expect you to get sick."

"*Fuck!*" he screamed. "Holy *fuck!* You'll fry in hell for this! You bastards–"

"Don't be an idiot, Corporal. If I'm right, you're going to have an unpleasant couple of days. But you'll get over it. And if I'm wrong, well, I suppose Frank Gambrell will have an easier time of it."

Johnson lunged, but someone grabbed his arms and pulled him away. Dornan was yelling, "*So what is this? Some kind of lunatic experiment?*"

"A demonstration. We'll talk again, soon."

76

They were kept in the house and under guard. But Dornan and Johnson were in no condition to escape, and the deputies had little to do. After two days, the fever broke, and that evening they sat down to their first meal since leaving the pub.

An hour after sunset, Max walked in with Bill and found them sitting at the kitchen table, in the light of a small lantern.

The deputies stood back as Max pulled out a chair and sat down.

Dornan was pale, but his fists clenched.

"I hope you–"

"Just keep still. Listen to me."

The corporal said nothing, but his eyes glittered hatred. Bill edged closer to him.

"Both of you are now immune to Cargo Flu. At least whatever is left of it out here. All of us have been through it. Everyone in this camp. So you now have the personal experience to know that the Flu here will put anyone out of action for a couple of days, but they'll recover. You have the means to capture alive anyone Frank Gambrell sends after you. And then we'll see if James Dornan's leadership is all it's cracked up to be."

"And just what the hell do you mean by that?"

He turned to Johnson.

"Corporal, are your men worth a damn?"

"What, the fuck?"

"Is your army worth a damn? Because I'm betting it is. I'm gambling that loyalty and the chain of command *mean* something."

Dornan slowly sat up.

"I'll be goddamned. Why didn't I think of that?"

Johnson looked lost. "I don't get it."

Max nodded at Dornan.

"*He's* their real commander-in-chief. Frank Gambrell's insurrection is illegal. Frank is an outlaw."

"That's not what's being said in the City! They're saying that Gambrell saved the City from Richard Martin."

"I'll bet they are. But the Corporation's chief executive is right here. Forced to choose, which way do you think the army will go?"

The soldier whistled. "That's one hell of a gamble."

"Not if he's right," mused Dornan. "Not if he's right."

Max stood up.

"Okay. I've brought you as far as I can."

"Wait a minute!" Dornan came to his feet. "How do you expect me to do anything out here?"

"You have supplies. You have your car. Bert and his deputies will stay on a while. Tell Bert if you need anything, and we'll do whatever we can. But it's up to you now."

Max stuck out his hand.

"Good luck. We're all counting on you."

Later that night, Corporal Johnson drove into the City with new instructions for Captain Vick.

The words *Cargo Flu* were enough to inspire mutiny among even disciplined troops, who had lived their lives in a world ever vigilant to keep the plague at a distance. The further the better.

But Vick stood Johnson in front of his assembled men.

"The old man went through it!" Johnson shouted. "And he's alive and ready to kick some ass! So am I! Believe me, after *you've* been through it, you'll be ready too!"

Hell, if the old man could do it . . .

It was only late in the evening of the following day, after their tags had been removed and they were on their way out of the City in two dark, rumbling trucks, that uncertainty set in. But by then they were committed, and in a timeless alchemy fear and doubt compounded into a fierce brotherhood and incipient rage against the enemy, whoever he might be. Vick gave his orders, exuding confidence, and the men obeyed, their movements sharp with adrenaline.

Johnson stayed behind at the outpost. He waited two days. Then, under cover of darkness, he drove through the City, twenty-odd capsules wrapped in metal foil on the seat beside him. Reaching Lakeview Drive, he unwrapped the tags, then drove south, toward Westboro, leaving behind a trail of electronic breadcrumbs for Frank Gambrell to ponder.

77

Wisps of smoke rose through dawn air tranquil and cool, drifting blue and gray across piles of debris, the charred remains of the Hutchins house. Small birds chirped and flitted in the trees, untroubled by the figure contorted in the grass below.

A half-mile from the pub, a deputy lay sprawled in the road, the earth beneath him stained black, the fingers of one hand mutilated.

Dozens of miles away, under a brightening sky on the outskirts of Westboro, five camouflaged men waited in a tree line, looking south across acres of empty field, on the other side of which ran an asphalt road, with more fields beyond.

The men had arrived in a truck after midnight near Westboro, armed with information harvested from the exile settlement—and with a captive, a local wanted in the City. Truck and captive secured out of sight, they had worked their way through dark stands trees until they could observe campfires and a detachment of troops near the road, deserters from the City who were presently packing up and slipping away through the night.

Two of the deserters had stayed behind, and before dawn had smothered the campfires. Then they, too, had tried to slip away.

They had not gotten far. Their bodies now dumped in the trees, the commando leader knew the deserters would be back, and when.

He gave his orders. The five commandos spread out inside the tree line. They took *wire*. They waited, and watched.

Late in the morning, an army patrol moved cautiously along the road toward Westboro.

Pinpricks of firelight had been observed overnight, and the patrol walked carefully, approaching a neighborhood of large, dilapidated houses, keeping an eye out for man-made debris. And for bodies. Because this was Flu country.

As they neared the houses, they came upon signs of fires put out near the road, freshly-turned earth and ashes. Also, a scrap of bread and a forgotten can. And the long grass beside the road had been trampled in places, by men and by vehicles.

Reassured by signs of life, they ventured into nearby yards. Behind one house they found a row of slit trenches, field latrines, but recently filled.

Newly promoted, the patrol leader sent two of his men to report back to their unit, Charlie Company, two days out of the City on foot and bivouacked several miles east of here. With his remaining men, he set up a picket a little ways from campsite and houses, to keep the area under surveillance while he awaited orders.

The patrol was not a surprise. The commando leader had been briefed on Charlie Company's mission. And, as the day progressed, more soldiers appeared, teams that fanned out and combed through houses and yards, then joined up at the campsite. By noon, the entire company was arranged along the road. Guards were posted, patrols sent out.

In the evening, the patrols returned. The sun set, and small fires appeared. A final patrol came in, the fires died down, and night fell deep and silent.

None of the commandos slept. There were no rotating watches. They took *wire,* and they waited, observing the campsite from within the tree line.

Sunrise came.

Figures began moving about the campsite. Here and there thin trails of smoke ascended. But before long the distant figures were doubling over. Sounds of shouting drifted across the fields. Knots of gathering men could be seen.

More shouting, now with the unmistakable voice of authority, and the men straggled into lines, an attempted formation. But as the sun climbed higher, the entire company seemed to melt into the earth.

The commando leader turned his head, and threw up.

He wiped his mouth and glanced at the nearest of his men, a dozen yards away, at sunken eyes in a gaunt face.

When the sun was high overhead, a new formation of men crossed the fields south of the road. They moved into the camp and walked among the prostrate company.

These were the deserters, returning as expected.

The leader peered through the trees, searching, but could see only soldiers. No civilians.

Since the mission began, he had not slept more than three or four hours altogether. He could feel every muscle in his body. His legs were like stumps of trees, his knees were on fire. But he did not move from that one spot.

He choked down another wire pill
He thought he had only blinked, but it was night.

Carefully, he reached for his canteen, swallowed what remained, and took another pill.

The night grew black. Branches and leaves shimmered with strange, angelic outlines. Sounds of groaning and farting from the distant camp came to him sharp and close and clear, as though he were walking among them.

Then it was dawn. And it seemed his first day on earth.

Every part of him was shaking, arms, legs, shoulders. But nothing escaped his notice. There were twenty-two captors, sitting, standing, wandering about. They ate a meal, relieved themselves, ate another meal, the sun crawling overhead, then descending toward the houses, long black shadows stretching through the fields like fingers reaching for the camp.

He felt himself weightless. Freed from the earth. From even his body. But there was a presence, too, a dark weight of thought. Something wrong, something missing, and then he remembered, and his body sank back to earth.

James Dornan. Dornan was still not here.

He took a pill, and a deep red fire burned in the west, silhouetting trees and houses. He had never seen such color. He could feel it burn against his skin, but it went out, and a primordial shadow began consuming the world, from the outward edges inward.

A truck rolled into the road.

His shaking stopped.

The truck sat in the road like a smoking ember. Then it turned, and crawled eastward, past the camp and into shadow.

One truck. For one man.

He took a stone from his pocket and threw it at his man nearest.

James Dornan was uncomfortable.

Bracing himself on a rumbling bench in semidarkness, he stared down and tried not to feel claustrophobic. The sun had set, but the heavy canvas covering the back of the truck was like a shroud, the air inside close and oppressive.

Corporal Johnson mopped his face.

Vick had insisted on this arrangement. He could not spare men for a proper escort, not while holding an entire company prisoner, and he wanted Dornan out of sight while in transit on the road.

Dornan raised his wrist. The heavy gold watch was scratched and gouged, but still ran, and it showed a few minutes before eight in the evening.

He was on his way to Vick's camp and what would probably be the final test of his life, after spending three miserable nights sleeping on the ground and hiding out with Johnson, in case something should go wrong, in case Vick's plan backfired. It felt as though events were speeding past him, the world moving on without him, and he had no idea what he would say when the time came, when he must try to persuade Vick's prisoners to follow him.

Maybe I'm just too damned old. Maybe they're better off without me.

He slumped over his knees.

The bench lurched suddenly, and the truck bumped to a halt.

In the sudden quiet, Johnson swore something about a flat tire, and moved to the tailgate.

A staccato of concussions followed, light and sound, and Johnson fell back, stuck or hurt. In a daze, Dornan tried to help, until it penetrated his brain the man had been shot through the face and was stone dead.

Retching, he pushed the body away.

The tailgate dropped. Steely arms reached in, dragged Dornan out.

Captain Vick stood in the middle of the road, peering east into the growing darkness. There was no sign of the truck.

He looked at his watch, and shouted orders for a patrol.

Lying on the ground with night falling, Max Wyse came to his senses dizzy and cramped with hunger, his arm and legs bound.

He had awakened many times like this since being knocked unconscious . . . when? How many nights ago? He had lost track. Sometimes he had been given water. Mostly he had been ignored. Then it seemed he had been abandoned. But they had returned, the silent men with blackened faces.

Now there was something on the ground near him, large and bulky, and still like a corpse, and he stared without breathing at the gray outline of a head, completely smooth.

There was a wheezing gasp from above, and he looked up.

One of the silent men stood by his legs, arm outstretched, a pistol raised to point at the bald figure, the arm shaking badly.

He drew up his knees and kicked, kicked as hard as he could. There was a brilliant flash. Then a weight struck, dead weight on his face. Then muffled sounds, and more gunfire . . . but he couldn't breathe . . . and it was far away.

78

Patches of sunlight raced along the ground under a ragged ceiling of broken clouds sailing low overhead. Long grass bent under gusts of wind. A loose shutter banged from somewhere nearby.

The troops of Charlie Company knelt in the road, hands tied behind them, knelt in long rows facing empty fields, Vick's men pacing slowly among them.

They had been in the road since sunrise, weak but recovering, listening to the wind and forbidden to talk, regarding the wall of trees that began across the fields with a mixture of disdain and dread. The backwoods. Exile country. The end of the line. The wind whipped at them, the shutter banged, and the City seemed a long way off. Because this was Flu country. There would be no rescue sent for them.

Then a new sound, boots on pavement crossing the road.

Captain Vick strode in front of the kneeling men and faced them, feet planted apart, hands clasped behind his back rigid and straight, uniform improbably crisp, looking across the assembled troops with eyes that seemed to weigh each man.

His voice carried easily over the wind.

"Listen up! You men are lawful prisoners! And the charge is insurrection!"

The troops stared back. But one among them snorted contempt.

"Get real."

Vick pointed to him. "You! On your feet."

The man stood up awkwardly, wrists bound behind his back, double silver bars on his collar.

"You are Captain Raddick, Charlie Company commander."

"No shit, Vick."

"What was your mission, Captain?"

The officer smiled, a wicked smile, the smile of a cat watching its prey make a futile attempt at escape.

"To track down a lousy bunch of deserters."

"On whose authority?"

"The authority of the goddamned Corporation, Vick. That's *my* authority. What's yours?"

A rolling gasp swept the kneeling men as James Dornan walked up and stood beside Vick. His head and face were scratched and bruised, but he stood unbowed, gazing over the men in the road.

The troops stared, and Vick shouted, "You recognize this man?"

From out of the murmuring, a young voice blurted, "They told us he was dead!"

"Shut your face, soldier!" snapped Raddick.

Then Dornan spoke: "Captain, you are relieved."

Raddick stared at his commander-in-chief.

"On your knees, Captain!"

Slowly, Raddick complied, the troops watching in stunned silence.

"You were told I was dead!" shouted Dornan. "You were told wrong. But that does not absolve you. You are part of an insurrection. You have aided an enemy."

He paused, scanning the faces before him.

"When the situation returns to normal, there will be an investigation. A full accounting. Each man will be judged according to his actions." He looked pointedly at Raddick. "And the judgment may be harsh."

Dornan now walked along the line of troops, a tough, determined figure against a backdrop of wilderness, his step easy, confident, and youthful.

"You men are fortunate Captain Vick orchestrated a humane capture. Because he would have been within his rights, and he would have done his duty, had his orders been to kill. And believe me, gentlemen, those orders would have been followed. To the letter."

He stopped and faced the men, lowering his voice so they had to strain to hear.

"That is war. And that is why we do not take war lightly."

He walked back along the line.

"I have instructed Captain Vick to give each of you the opportunity to reaffirm your oath of loyalty. The oath you took when you joined. Each man who does so will be allowed to prove himself. The mission will be dangerous. But it is what you trained for. It is what you swore to do."

He halted by Vick and faced the formation.

"If any man here is unable to take that oath, he has my word he will be treated decently. But he will remain prisoner, and he will be judged when this is over."

Dornan paused, watching them, and for a time there was only the wind.

"There are two men who once served our city with distinction. Each was blinded by his own ambition. Each betrayed his fellow citizens. Richard Martin is dead. Frank Gambrell will be brought to justice. And that, gentlemen, will be your mission.

"I misjudged them. I hope I have not misjudged you."

79

Captain Chuck Raddick had been with the Corporation's army just a little over than a year, but it was a role that fit him like a second skin, in a way his previous job of driving delivery trucks for Logistics never could, or the job before that of holding down a security desk, or the one before that working on a farm. None of these jobs had been difficult; each had bored him to within an inch of his sanity.

Not that he had ever complained. Not too much. He did what he had to. But the captain's commission was a gift, and it cemented his loyalty forever.

Vick's desertion was hard to take. It was hard to believe. But Vick was a college boy, had probably never had to really *work* for anything, and just didn't get it. And this was the result.

So when Raddick was escorted into one of the nearby houses, he thought he knew what to expect. The one thing he could not explain was the man who was unquestionably James Dornan sitting with Vick behind a table in a bare room.

"Fuck yourself, Vick."

There was an empty chair, and Raddick pulled it out and sat down.

"Fuck yourself, if you think I'm going to turn against the men I've served with."

"Is that what you think this is? You think we're going to ask you to turn traitor? Chuck, let me ask you something. Who do we serve?"

His laughter was sudden, loud, and genuine.

"Oh, shit! If you have to ask me that, it explains a lot. We serve through a chain of command, Vick. Even when we don't like someone in it. That's what we do."

Dornan pounced.

"Exactly, Captain! But don't confuse the chain of command with a desk and chair."

"I don't know what you're talking about."

"Son, Frank Gambrell may be sitting in my chair, but that doesn't make him CEO."

"*Politics.*" Raddick nearly spat. "Not my business."

"Normally I'd agree with you. But these aren't normal times. And just as we can't allow an officer to pick and choose whose orders to follow, we can't allow one civilian to kill another, or force him out, and take his place. I'm sorry if this puts you in a difficult position, Captain. But you and your men were set up. And you should know that."

"And how should I *know* that?"

"Because, man," Vick broke in, "one of Gambrell's commando units took the fuel depot, on *his* orders."

"How do *you* know that? Why in holy hell should I trust *you*?"

"Think about it. They weren't killed, and they weren't captured. There wasn't any fighting. When Gambrell took over, they just stood down."

Raddick swore under his breath. There was something wrong, he could see that. But it was no damned business for a company commander.

Dornan leaned in. "Captain Raddick! You don't have all the answers you'd like, but you're a line officer with a combat decision to make. Lives are at stake. Our *homes* are at stake. We don't have much time. You're going to have to commit. You're either with us, or against us."

Something was fucked up, he could see that. But this should *not* be his decision. His job was to carry out orders.

Legitimate ones.

What the hell was Dornan doing here?

"Which is it, Captain?"

He drew a long breath.

"Okay . . . okay. I'm with you. They didn't tell me anything about Mr. Dornan. So what he says still goes. God help me."

After a long moment, Vick seemed to relax.

"All right. Let's figure out where we are. You were in radio contact with the City, is that right?"

"That's right."

"Until when?"

"The morning we got sick. I told them I was losing my shit, literally. After that, I don't know. I lost the radio."

"We found it. It's secured."

"What about my roster?"

"Everyone's accounted for."

"So they'll think we're all dead. At least I don't see them sending anyone else out here."

"Neither do I."

Vick got up and began pacing, and Raddick watched, because the man's tension was contagious. It commanded attention, and this commanded a bit of Raddick's grudging respect. Despite the college air.

"What about it, Vick? What're you thinking?"

"I'm thinking it's time we made our move."

Dornan growled, "And just what move is that, Captain?"

On the surface, Dornan seemed angry, but Raddick sensed fear, and he shut his mouth and listened.

"No one knows you're alive," Vick replied.

"And?"

"And it's time we show them."

"Spit it out, Captain!"

Vick stopped pacing.

"We march to the City. With Charlie Company. They're not suspect, as yet, and that gives us cover. Whenever we encounter a checkpoint or patrol, we turn them against Gambrell." He pointed a finger at Dornan. "That is, *you* turn them."

"And just what makes you think I can persuade everyone we meet?"

"This is exactly what Frank is afraid of. Or he wouldn't be going to so much trouble to stop you. You know there had to be more than one of his commandos out here. And they weren't operating on their own authority."

This much he knew, and Raddick interrupted.

"I was briefed there was a team operating in the area. But not on their mission."

"Of course not. But it proves my point. It's time, Jim."

Dornan's voice began rising.

"And have you thought through what happens the first time it goes wrong? If fighting breaks out? The rest of the City will shoot first and ask questions later!"

"Probably. But we're outnumbered, and we're out of time. If Frank finds out Chuck's men aren't dead and haven't been checking in, he'll issue standing orders. If he hasn't done it already. And once that happens, it's all over. For us."

Raddick demanded, "Then let me check in!"

"And report what? That you all got sick, but now you're better? He'll smell something wrong. *I* would, and so would you."

"So I don't get it. How's this play out?"

"We assume you've been written off. We assume the rest of the army has no orders regarding you, one way or the other. When you show up, they should welcome you. Which is exactly what we want. You help us get Jim to the rest of our units, and we turn as many as we can, as fast as we can, before Gambrell gets wind. If we can persuade enough of them, the others will question his authority. And that may be all we need to turn the tables. It's all we're likely to get."

"No shit, Vick. That's a hell of a crap-shoot. What makes you think he isn't ready for something like this? Maybe he doesn't know we're alive." He glanced at Dornan. "But he can't assume this man is dead."

"No, but he can't use rest of the army to bring in James Dornan, dead or alive, either. There'd be mutiny."

Vick sat down again.

"We have to move fast. Gambrell has his commandos. He gives them *wire* and they do what they're told. But I think we're still one step ahead. We need to *stay* a step ahead. So it's time to make our move."

He looked at Dornan.

"We knew it would come down to this, Jim. It was *always* a crap-shoot."

Dornan leaned back, rubbing his face with both hands.

Then he slapped the table.

"I know. I know. Someday someone should study this mess. They might learn something. All right, let's get on with it. Before I lose my nerve."

80

The previous night, Vick's patrol had been led by the sound of a gunshot to where Dornan lay just inside the trees. Near him sprawled a man heavily camouflaged and clearly from a City commando unit. Underneath the commando, they found Max Wyse, suffocating, but alive.

After capture, the commando regained consciousness. He was kept locked up and under guard. He was provided food and water. But he took nothing.

Interrogation was useless. He would sleep suddenly for short periods, fifteen or twenty minutes, then awaken thrashing and shouting gibberish. Then for an hour or so he would stare at anything that moved, before abruptly falling asleep again. Human speech made no impression, not even to elicit eye contact.

He died the following day.

The company medic was called to examine the body, and made his brief report. There were no signs of injury.

Vick ordered the man buried without ceremony. The medic watched grimly, but with full approval. He had examined the remains of Vick's two dead, discovered in the trees. That report had been considerably longer.

———

Max slept half the morning.

Vick and Dornan were busy, so after a canteen bath and cold meal, one of the men drove him back to the pub, the soldier relating as much as he understood of what was being planned.

The soldier dropped him off, and he walked behind the pub.

Near the stable, one of Bill's horses was saddled and tied to a rail. Bill came out of the stable at that moment, and stopped, one hand raised awkwardly in front of him.

"Oh, Max. Oh, Christ."

"What? What's the matter?"

"Max . . . Agnes is okay. She's inside. She wasn't there."

"Wasn't where?"

"With Barbara–Wait! Max, don't go alone!"

There must have been more, but he couldn't recall it later.

What he remembered was the wreckage. He remembered coming through the trees on Bill's panting horse, into the clearing, the wreckage spread out before him, half the walls collapsed, the roof caved in.

He dropped the reins. The horse slowed on its own and came to a stop.

He could see her face, a swollen mask framed in her familiar hair, and he climbed down and started toward her, but his legs failed and he fell to his knees, choking, overwhelmed with the rabid sound of flies, and squeezing his eyes shut at the sight of her body in the grass before him.

———

It was sometime later. He was still on the ground, and pushed himself to his feet, then walked to the remains of the house, where he picked through debris until he found a blanket that had mostly escaped the flames.

He returned to her, struggling with his one arm amidst clouds of flies and tears now blinding to drag the blanket and cover her.

Then he walked away. He saw the picnic table, saw the string of lights pulled down and smashed, and he bent over, his chest rigid, his teeth clenched against an inhuman howl deep in his throat.

———

Quiet sounds came from somewhere behind him.

Horses. Voices.

Then a hand on his shoulder.

"Buddy . . . you okay?"

He was sitting at the picnic table, staring into the trees. He wanted to get up, wanted to leave, but the reasons behind that question were too enormous.

"I can't bury her, Bert."

"Yeah, don't worry, buddy. We'll take care of it."

He wanted Bert to know he understood, and he nodded, but the reasons were still there, like a hanging cloud, and he could not escape.

"It's over, Bert. Isn't it."

Bert took his hand away.

"Well, buddy, we don't know yet. Dornan and Vick–"

"I don't mean Dornan and Vick. I mean *us*. Our town. Our government."

"Oh. Yeah. I think maybe it is. Look, all anybody really cares about right now is survival. You know? And that's what *you* should be thinking about. Maybe the town was a good idea and all, but . . . well, everyone's just got bigger problems. And you'd better lay low awhile. A lot of people are saying you're the reason this happened."

What people were saying . . . wasn't real. The flies were real.

He stared into the trees.

"It's over. We're all going to end up like this."

There was a sound like Bert clearing his throat and a space of silence, before the Chief found the words to answer.

"Oh . . . I don't know. We got along all right before."

But they were just sounds, sounds without meaning.

Because he was alone.

He had been alone when he pulled the blanket over Barbara. He had been alone that starry night on the hill near Westboro. Now he understood how absolute it was. The one, final, absolute.

He stood up.

As Bert stepped back, he searched the homely face for something that was missing. Something he had glimpsed in John Anderson. In Frank Gambrell. Seldom anywhere else.

A kind of totality. A kind of ultimatum.

The Chief watched him warily.

But he shook his head and looked across the wreckage.

"You all right, buddy? What're you going to do?"

He glanced again at Bert, but there was no answer there.

81

Agnes sat at a table in the empty dining room of the pub, her arms folded, the coffee in front of her untouched. She stared at it vacantly.

It was late afternoon. People would be arriving at some point, for dinner. But it didn't matter. There was no reason for her to move. No reason at all.

Earlier, there had been noises outside. A car. Voices. Bill and Max. Whatever they said hadn't registered, but that didn't matter either. Because she knew where Max would go, and what he would find.

She had come to the pub days ago, thinking to meet Dornan on his return and explain her decision. But Dornan hadn't returned, and she had spent the night. In the morning, Bill would not let her leave. Something had happened, and he went himself to check on Barbara.

When he returned, he took her aside and explained, probably as gently as he knew how, what he had found.

She remembered screaming, beating her fists against him, and that he had stood silently and let her. Then he had put his heavy arms around her and she had struggled until her knees buckled while he half-carried her to a room and put her to bed. Later, with her eyes dry and her throat raw, she had gotten up and opened her door–and found him dozing in a chair just outside.

Now her mind was made up. She had to get away from here. She had to get away. As soon as Frank was gone and the City was safe, she would go back where she belonged.

Bill understood. At least he seemed to. He had left her alone.

The front door swung open, and into the room strode Max Wyse.

He stopped by the door, looking at her from across the room. His face was streaked with dirt and ash. His shirt was stained, his hair wild. The eyes held her. They were clear, cold, brilliant.

Something was slung across his shoulder, and he walked to her and dropped it on the table, a heavy canvas bag that hit with a thud, rattling cup and saucer.

"I understand you're leaving."

The words reached her.

"That's right. And I think you know why." She wasn't afraid of him. There was nothing he could do that would make her afraid, ever again.

"You left something of yours."

She knew what it was. She didn't have to see it.

"I won't be needing that."

"That's too bad." It was a whisper, the gray eyes steady on her as she glared up at him, her anger rising.

"What do you want, Max? What are you going to do? Threaten me? Scare me? It won't work."

"I told you once before. We have freedom here. If you want to leave, that's your decision. I can't stop you."

She gasped. It was as if he had struck her, and she jumped to her feet, shaking, her voice was shaking, and she screamed, *"Freedom? Freedom? You talk about freedom? People are dead! Your so-called government has disappeared! There are people in this town who will shoot you on sight! Freedom? Don't make me laugh!"*

For a moment she wasn't sure if she had made actual sounds or just imagined it, because he stood looking at her as if waiting for a reply.

When he spoke, his voice hadn't changed.

"Here's the deal. You find Steve. You put your business back together. Don't worry about the town. I'm going to put *that* back together. You and Steve, and everyone else, will have a civilized place to live, and the freedom to do what you want."

His eyes were on hers, and she knew he wasn't seeing her.

"Max." Watching his face, she thought she understood, that she might reach him. "Max, believe me, I know what you're going through . . . " But the face didn't change, and she stopped, afraid of something in him that might break if she continued. And more afraid it wouldn't break.

"Find Steve."

He strode across the room. The door slammed behind him.

She stood with her hands clasped and raised to her lips. Then, slowly, she reached down, feeling the familiar shape of her generator under the rough fabric.

Then she picked up the cold coffee, and drank it standing up.

82

A loose formation of nearly a hundred men jogged with packs and rifles along the road to the City.

Officers were on horseback, Raddick near the head of the column, Vick in the middle, junior officers alongside their platoons.

A truck followed, the back of it uncovered and carrying a half dozen men seated with rifles in hand. In the cab, in the passenger seat, rode James Dornan, one heavy elbow hanging out his open window.

They had started out the previous morning, the day after the interview with Raddick. Dornan had joked with the driver as they left Westboro and rolled along behind the troops. But he had grown pensive that evening, when they stopped for a cold meal and a few hours' sleep. Now he was silent, intent on the road ahead.

The horses had been provided by the town. A few young men had volunteered as well, Mike among them, jogging with the others.

Bill had stood in stony silence the night Mike announced his decision and stated his reasons.

"Max is right, Dad. If the City is run by somebody like Frank Gambrell, they'll fall apart. They'll come here. They'll take over everything we have. But if Mr. Dornan wins, why should he ever help us, if we don't help him now?"

Mike had waited awkwardly for whatever judgment his father might pronounce. Then, stung by the silence, but unwilling to show it, he had turned to go.

A hoarse whisper stopped him. *"Be careful, Mike."*

He turned back.

"Don't worry–"

But Bill threw both arms about his son's shoulders in a ferocious hug, roughly slapped the young man's back, and let him go.

————————

The column moved steadily north and east, alternately jogging and marching, stopping from time to time for a mouthful of water or a quick meal.

There were no flank patrols. Vick had decided against them. Scouts moving along parallel tracks, working their way through trees and brush, would have slowed the column. The plan was to make contact with as many City units as possible, before they received new orders, because once they received orders they would follow them. So Vick kept only a point team on the road a half mile ahead, and drove the men to cover ground.

He was counting on the fact that Raddick and the men of Charlie were still tagged. Those tags would be identified when they reached the first scanner, still miles ahead. Vick intended to ignore any radio calls, forcing Bravo Company, deployed along the western edge of the City, to send out a detachment to intercept them.

That detachment would take Dornan to Bravo's commander.

At least this was how they had planned it, after Raddick had explained the order of troops around the City. Bravo's commander was the next logical step. Dornan would have to turn him, and do it quickly.

The day was warm, man and horse dark with sweat, and Vick glanced at his watch and called a halt for a half-hour rest.

It was not far now. One more push, and they should hit the first scanner.

————————

Inside the town office, on the main road, Bert Morrow snorted.

"It's over, buddy. Get it through your head. No one wants to hear it."

Max Wyse stood before him like a marble statue, although Bert could not have said just what it was that made him think of marble. And this one had frightening eyes.

"You are Chief of Police. You have a job to do. It's time to do it."

"Okay, buddy. Have it your way. I resign."

"I don't accept your resignation."

Bert laughed, but there was panic in it, and he stopped.

"Buddy, are you off your rocker? Barbara's *dead*. Remember? There's no Committee—hell no *town* left. Most of 'em will shoot anyone who even *mentions* town government. There's nothing we can do! There's nothing *you* can do. You got that?"

"The town's still here. We have to pick up the pieces."

"God *damn* you! Why won't you listen? There's no *point!*"

"They need us—" Max seemed suddenly to choke. Cords stood out in his neck. His arm lifted as though to reach for something, and the

Chief stepped back, wondering if a stroke were about to put a final end to the town's president.

But it broke. The shoulders sagged, and Max exhaled a long, shaky breath.

"Bert . . . maybe they don't know it. Maybe they forgot. But they need us. Old man Anderson was right. Barbara would have understood. We *all* need this."

"Jesus, Max . . ."

"Listen to me, Bert. Just listen. Try to understand. There isn't any choice. Because you're either building a world or else you're imagining it. And you and I can't afford to live in our imaginations."

Bert stared at him and nodded, as though he understood.

Maybe he was beginning to.

The troops stood at ease in dappled patches of sunlight on Lakeview Drive, where the road ran straight under heavy oak and maple branches, dense and tangled overhead.

Vick was quietly sending runners up and down the column with orders for scouts to move out, to protect the flanks, and shortly he watched them move into the trees. He looked front and rear, one arm raised in silent question. Officers on horseback waved all clear.

There was nothing more he could do. Raddick and Dornan were in the truck with a small escort on their way to the point, where a detachment from Bravo had made contact. It was in Dornan's hands now, and Vick could only sit calmly erect in the saddle, keeping his face deliberately impassive, from time to time checking the rear and scanning the trees on either side.

At the head of the column, a lieutenant on horseback beckoned suddenly, frantically, and Vick urged his animal along the edge of the road past the waiting troops, and joined him.

The lieutenant whispered, "A minute ago. Thought I heard something. Sounded like a shot."

Vick bent his head to listen over the small noises drifting around them. The swish of a tail. The creak of leather. A muffled cough.

"*Christ!* Come on!"

He kicked, and his horse bolted, hooves slamming asphalt. The lieutenant caught up, and they flew, crouched low, wind whistling past. There was sunlight ahead, where the road came out of the trees. There was the truck on the shoulder, and men crowded around something in the road.

Vick reined in, leaped down, and pushed his way through.

In the middle of the pavement sprawled James Dornan, face up, his arms flung out, his white shirt stained red.

Vick shoved someone out of his way and crouched down, feeling the neck, desperately feeling for a sign of life.

A lone voice came from behind. "He's dead, man."

Everything went quiet.

The voice continued gently. "There's nothing you can do."

Vick stood up.

"What happened?"

No one answered. No one seemed to hear, and his disbelief exploded. *"What the holy fuck happened?"*

"Snipers!"

"At least two, sir! From different directions!"

"No question who they were after! You okay, sir? Sir?"

He stepped back.

Other men were standing about or moving away, with no direction, no order. They blurred into a smear of green, and he looked down the road, toward the City, toward Frank Gambrell, the man who now held all the cards. Who would do with them as he pleased.

The sun seemed to dim, and the men became strange, anonymous souls drawn with him, irresistibly, toward disaster. This was defeat. Failure. Irredeemable, and final.

He thought stupidly of the day, two years before, when he had accepted his commission. It seemed another lifetime. Someone else's life, someone who had a place in the world–

"Vick!"

Something grabbed his arm, shaking him.

"Vick–you all right? The fuck's the matter? Let's *go!"*

He laughed.

"Go? Go where? Where are we going, Raddick? It's over."

"Jesus, Vick. I thought you were the smart one. Use your head. Gambrell just made a serious mistake."

"Yeah? And what mistake was that?"

"He didn't kill *us."* Raddick spat. "He didn't kill us, Vick, and he left us with *this."* He nodded at the body in the road. "The evidence."

Vick stopped laughing, and Raddick smiled, his wicked smile, the cat watching its prey.

"You get it, Vick? No one would believe *you,* a deserter. But with me and the body . . . What're you staring at? You with me?"

"Yeah. Yeah, I'm with you."

There was someone standing idly nearby, as though awaiting orders, but not in uniform, and Vick barked, *"You* there! What's your name?"

"Mike, sir! Mike Durgin."

"You an exile?"

The young man flushed. Vick saw it.

"Never mind that, son. You're Corporal Durgin for the time being. I need that body in the back of the truck and a driver in it ready to go in five minutes. Can you make that happen?"

"You bet! Sir!"

"All right, soldier. Snap to it."

Mike saluted, and Vick watched long enough to see him grab two men by the arm, talking to them rapidly.

One of the men glanced at Vick, and he nodded, then turned back to Raddick, who was watching with an odd look.

"Better get Bravo's guys formed up here, Chuck. They're witnesses. We're going to need them."

83

Business dropped sharply after the commando raid on the town, but running the pub, serving and cooking, washing and cleaning, was still a job for two strong backs, and Bill managed with the help of the young man Bob Smith, Mike's childhood friend who had worked for them on and off since Mr. Smith passed years before. Bob wasn't much of a cook, a bit scatter-brained around the kitchen, but Bill was thankful for the help.

The afternoons were the hardest, the place empty and silent after the lunch dishes were washed and put up, and Bob puttering in the stable or brushing the horses. It was hard to keep occupied. Once he found himself staring out a back window, wondering if he would have to get used to this–then he swore and went in search of something to clean.

It was Friday, a few days later, when he heard a truck grind to a stop outside. A door slammed, and he stood still, unable to breathe. Then . . . the whine of gears, the truck turning around . . . the roar of the engine as it drove off . . . and he sagged against the bar . . .

Then voices outside, behind the pub.

He stomped to the back door and yanked it open, standing with his fists on his hips.

"Mike! What the *hell!*"

Bob and Mike were leaning against the rail fence, talking.

Mike looked up and laughed.

"Sorry, Dad! I'm back."

"Just when were you planning on letting me know? You could give a man a heart attack!"

But even now he remembered unfinished business.

"Bob! Jump on a horse and find Max Wyse. Probably at the town office. Tell him who's here, and pretty quick. He's going to want to know."

An hour later, they sat around a table in the empty dining room, Max, Bert, Bill, and Mike.

Wearily, Max rubbed his face. It was only a few days since he had found Barbara, and he was not sleeping.

"Glad you're back, Mike. But we need some answers. That okay?"

"Yeah, sure."

"Okay. Tell us what happened. Did it work?"

"You mean the grand plan? Well, Frank Gambrell's out, I know that much. I hear they arrested him. But Mr. Dornan's out, too."

"Dornan's out? Why? What happened?"

"He's six feet under, Max. Shot dead, right in front of us. Ah–sorry. Didn't know you were friends with him."

Max blew his cheeks out.

"It's okay. We weren't friends exactly."

But he fell quiet. It would be difficult to imagine the City without James Dornan.

Bill asked, "So what happened? Did the army take over?"

"I don't think so." Mike frowned. "I don't understand how these people do things, but some vice president was promoted, or selected, or whatever they do. I guess she's in charge now."

"She?" repeated Bill, and Max laughed weakly.

"Elizabeth White, I'd imagine."

Mike nodded. "Yeah, I heard that name a few times."

Max exhaled and leaned back, resting his gaze on the rafters. All seemed well, for the moment. The Corporation was back in control, hopefully getting things organized. The day had always to come when they would have to manage without James Dornan. It had just arrived sooner than anyone expected.

"You done with me?"

"Ah . . . yeah, Mike. Thanks."

Bert cleared his throat after Mike got up and left.

"So, okay. Now what?"

"Now you and I have a Committee meeting to set up. Time to get *ourselves* organized."

He pushed himself to his feet.

"Ready?"

"Jesus, buddy, I don't know. I don't think *they're* ready. And you're still kinda persona non grata, you know?"

"Yeah, I know. We're not here to make friends."

The Chief sucked his teeth. But then he nodded, and stood up with Max.

84

The first one was the hardest.

Dan Walsh stood in the yard in front of his house, feet spread apart, sighting down the barrel of a shotgun planted firmly against his shoulder and aimed squarely at Max Wyse, not ten yards away.

"Wyse, you got thirty seconds to get your sorry ass off my property! You too, Morrow! I got a new policy! Wanna hear it? Shoot first, ask questions later!"

"No one's doing any shooting," soothed the Chief, trying to project confidence despite his hands high over his head. "And anyway you can't kill us both with that thing."

"It's pump-action. I could kill six of you. Twenty seconds!"

"Okay, okay . . . Come on, buddy, let's go. We'll think of something else."

Max tore his eyes from the black hole at the end of the gun, letting them rest on the house behind Walsh, two stories of peeling clapboard and boarded-up windows, a roof missing shingles–and, dangling from one eave, a short length of electrical cable, thick and black and frayed.

"Ten seconds!"

He stared at the wire–and put his hand down.

"Might as well pull the trigger, Dan. I can't say what I came here to say in ten seconds. And I'm not leaving until I say it."

"You god-damned son of a bitch!" The voice rose a half-octave. "You think I'm kidding?"

"C'mon, buddy," Bert hissed.

"Dan, I owe you an apology. And a report."

"I don't want your goddamned report! I want you off my property!"

"There was a coup in the City, Dan. Frank Gambrell took over. He sent commandos for Dornan, but we took Dornan to Westboro and turned the tables on Gambrell."

"I don't want to hear it!"

"You have my apology for not warning everyone. We knew there was a risk. But the good news is that Gambrell is gone. The City has new leadership. Some people paid for that with their lives. And I was nearly one of them."

"You think *I* care? You think I need *your* protection?"

"You saw what a handful of commandos did. What do you think an army could do?"

"They had no reason to come here! Not until you started meddling with them! God *damn* you!"

"Shit," muttered Bert.

"Dan, you remember Frank. Here was out here meddling with Jack while I was still trying to figure out what to do with myself. You know about Richard Martin. He was trying to rope us all into his war plans, and it had nothing to do with me, or you, or with anyone else around here. You forget all that?"

Walsh said nothing. But the shotgun held steady.

"Dan." He spoke evenly, as distinctly as he could. "Dan, if the City fails, if they can't sustain themselves, they'll come here. They'll take every farm, every ranch. You'll grow what they tell you to grow, and you'll turn over what they want. Your property won't be your own. And they won't let you leave, because they need what you know. They've doped their own people to keep them in line, and they'll do the same thing here. We can't ignore this, Dan. It's not over."

"You're crazy! You know that? What can *you* do about it? What can anyone?"

"We've already done something. And you know what? We couldn't have done that much without you and everyone else on the Committee."

Walsh sputtered and laughed, an explosion of derision that shook his lean frame and made the end of the shotgun weave crazily in the air.

Bert stepped backward. *"Jesus . . . "*

Walsh shouted, "You were singing a different tune a month ago!"

"I know, Dan. But it's because I wanted you all to do more."

The barrel of the gun lowered to point at the ground between them.

"What do you want?"

"We're meeting tomorrow. We need you. Be there."

After a long moment, Walsh nodded. He looked tired.

"All right."

85

The first day of summer, weeks later. In the town office, the meeting room was packed. And it was hot. Children waved homemade fans by the open windows. It didn't make much difference, but no one complained.

A thin sheaf of paper lay on the meeting table now pushed to one end of the room, an old wooden gavel resting on top. Facing the table, a half-dozen chairs formed a semicircle occupied by Committee Members. Behind them, as witnesses, stood fifteen or twenty townspeople.

Seated at the table, a silver-haired man reached for the gavel and held it up. The murmuring died, leaving only the quiet rustle of fans.

The gavel banged down.

"I call this meeting to order! Members of the Committee, I have here the vote of the Town. Do I hear a motion?"

One Member raised his hand.

"I move we recognize and record the vote."

Another answered. "Second."

The rest nodded.

"Done!" The silver-haired man made a note, then beckoned.

Agnes stepped forward from the crowd.

She walked to the table. He extended the papers to her, and she hesitated, as if the reality of it had not quite reached her until this moment. But she took the pages, turned to face the Members and witnesses, and began to read.

"We the people, to secure our common welfare, hereby make and agree to this Compact."

She read the words evenly, line by line, her voice clear and measured, as though taking vows of marriage.

". . . but the Committee shall make no Law without a written statement of the intended common Benefit, and of how said Benefit justifies the imposition of said Law and its Penalties."

The Members each listened intently, as if hearing it for the first time.

"...each Member shall be charged with a Duty of Care and Loyalty to the Town, and to the people he or she represents."

The children had stopped fanning, and her voice was the only sound.

"...each Officer shall be charged with a Duty of Care and Loyalty to the Town, and to the Committee."

She reached the end, speaking slowly, stressing each word.

"We, the Committee and Officers of the Town henceforth to be known as Andersonville, solemnly swear to uphold this Compact to the best of our abilities."

She handed the papers back.

The man behind the table thanked her. He set the last page down by itself and placed a pen by it, carefully handling the old plastic pen as though it were fragile china. The Members stood up and filed to the table. Each took up the pen in turn and signed.

The last was Dan Walsh.

He accepted the pen, but hesitated. Then he put it down, while the others looked at him, questioning. From a pocket, he withdrew a quill and a small, stoppered bottle.

"Sandy McCane's little girl has a knack for these things. She's figured out how to make ink, and she's been teaching me. Makes me feel like a country lawyer."

He pulled the stopper from the bottle, carefully dipped the point of the quill, and signed his name.

The man behind the table reached for the paper.

Walsh stopped him.

"You have to let it dry first." He winked at the others. "Not as handy as an old ballpoint. But those things won't last forever, and then we'll be on our own."

In the back of the room, Max Wyse stood apart and listened.

He could not see into the coming years. But the old world, familiar and hopeless, was receding from view, fading from memory, and he held this moment for himself, feeling a silent height in it, standing unconsciously straight as he had stood watching Aubrey touch the sky, marking a brief moment that seemed to justify the sweep of time.

There were more formalities, but he stayed in the back and listened.

Agnes made her way to his side, slipped an arm through his.

"They should have named it after *you.*"

He laughed easily.

"No. Andersonville has a much better ring to it."

86

Dawn.

A rider comes to a halt at the brow of a hill. An evenly-packed dirt road leads down the slope, past a trim white farmhouse, shingles dripping in the gray light. The road descends, disappearing into early morning mists that gather in the distance.

He is alone. His hair is black, with strands of silver at the temples, his face with the fine lines of early middle age, but the eyes are clear and untroubled as they survey the fields spread out below.

The sky grows brighter.

A faint line of smoke rises from the farmhouse chimney, rises up cutting across the pink horizon. Nothing else stirs, and the earth seems to pause, holding its breath in the moment before sunrise.

To his left, trees are struck with an orange splash of sunlight. The light brightens and creeps down the hillside, until it glints on strands of electrical wire that stretch from pole to pole, making thin lines of fire, a living trace of human thought that follow the graded road, parallel lines that seem to extend and slowly converge, to the edge of sight, forever.

The rider spurs his horse.

He passes the farmhouse. A man and woman wave from the yard, and he acknowledges with a nod, but his only hand stays sure on the reins, and he continues on his way.

About the Author

D. M. Smith was born in Boston and has lived in New England, California, and Texas. Educated as an engineer, he started two technology companies and has since embarked on a second career in writing, sometimes pursued while driving around the American Southwest.